T0162016

ENCYCLOPÆDIA OF HELL:
AN INVASION MANUAL FOR DEMONS
CONCERNING THE PLANET EARTH
AND THE HUMAN RACE WHICH INFESTS IT

www.facebook.com/encyclopaediaofhell
www.twitter.com/EncycOfHell

ISBN: 978-1936239047

Feral House
1240 W. Sims Way, Suite 124
Port Townsend, WA 98368

www.FeralHouse.com
Design by Sean Tejaratchi

10 9 8 7 6 5 4

ENCYCLOPÆDIA
OF
HELL

❖

AN INVASION MANUAL FOR DEMONS
CONCERNING THE PLANET EARTH
AND THE
HUMAN RACE WHICH INFESTS IT

❖

TRANSLATED
FROM THE
DEMONIC
BY
MARTIN OLSON

❖

ILLUSTRATED BY
TONY MILLIONAIRE
AND
MAHENDRA SINGH

To:
Andrew Lazar
Annette Van Duren
Robert Sheckley
Brother Theodore Gottlieb

Editorial Consultant:
Brian Lubocki

Book Design:
Sean Tejaratchi

Wheel of Kadab Illustration:
Joseph Alaskey

Additional Illustration:
Kaz
Celeste Moreno
Howard Gindoff and Duncan Long

Steganography & Web Design:
Oleg Rezabek/steganart.com
brettaronowitz.com • marenmiller.com

Daemonic Subversion Support:
Amit Itelman • Adam Parfrey
Ken Kaufman • Howard Klausner
John Schneider • Lars Ulrich • Kirk Hammett
Robert Gaylor • Tom Frykman
Barry Crimmins • Ken Daly • Dana Gibson
Howard, Michael & Chris Meehan
Adam Franklin • Keith Knee
Mary Jo Pritchard • Thomas Olson
Kay, Casey & Olivia Olson

WARNING
TO THE READER

The following manuscript is alleged to be a pirated edition
of the original housed in a secret vault in Rome beneath
the Vatican Basilica di Santa Croce of Gerusalemme.

The pages were delivered to us by courier in a manner
which made knowledge of its origin impossible.
The following cover letter claims to have been written by
a disgruntled former agent of a covert organization.

Encyclopædia of Hell is a facsimile of the original book
with its imperfections intact. Note that some pages
show signs of wear due to the age of the manuscript
or manner of reproduction. However, we present this
unique volume exactly as it was delivered to us,
without further commentary.

The Publishers

MAGGOTS DIE IN SUNLIGHT.
MOTTO ABOVE THE ENTRANCE OF THE SPIRITUAL SECURITY AGENCY

To Whom It May Concern:

MY NAME IS NATHAN STILES. For ten years, I worked as an agent for the Spiritual Security Agency. The S.S.A. is a covert military force composed of monks, ministers, nuns and priests from all world religions. Mankind is unaware that a secret war has been going on between Earth and Hell. For centuries, our agents have been trained in prayer, fasting and heavy artillery in order to stop demons from taking over Earth.

Critical to the success of our mission is the existence of the book you now hold in your hands. I was fired when my superiors ordered me to keep this book a secret and I refused.

They are idiots.

This book was written by and for demons, instructing them on how to destroy mankind. I believe this book must be distributed to the public as quickly as possible before the demon invasion begins.

Here are the facts:

Hell is a real place, located in another dimension, or frequency, of matter. Demons are real entities, created and genetically engineered by the supernatural entity known as Satan.

Over the past century in particular, Hell has become overcrowded with human souls. For this reason, Satan drew up a detailed plan to gain more territory by invading Earth and annexing it to Hell.

The book you now hold in your hands is a copy of an encyclopedic invasion manual of Earth written by Satan in English, the preferred language of Hell. As far as I know, only one copy presently exists on Earth. I seized it from the demon spy Zyk of Asimoth soon after he infiltrated Earth to scout landing sites for the invasion. S.S.A. officials confiscated the manuscript from me by force and locked it in a vault beneath the Vatican.

When I demanded that they release the manual to the world, my superiors refused, saying the document was classified. When I threatened to go public with what I knew, I was fired and told that if I spoke about the existence of the book, I would be discredited and eliminated.

Because the fate of the world is at stake, I had no choice but to defy their orders. I broke into the vault and stole the manual which you now hold in your hands.

I did what I had to do.

Now that you have the information you need, the fate of Mankind is in your hands.

How To Read This Book

Just as demonic thought is strange to us, so is our world incomprehensible to demons. To insure an understanding of mankind, Satan compiled this overview of human existence from the satanic point of view.

Demons are fundamentally different from human beings, having no physical or emotional heart and knowing nothing of love or of the concepts of Good or God. To help bridge the gap of understanding, I include here an overview of the contents and structure of the invasion manual:

Each section of the book opens with a memo by the demon Zyk of Asimoth, the infiltrator who edited Satan's *Encyclopaedia*, and is also, weirdly, Poet Laureate of Hell. Zyk's memos tell the story of how he researched the Manual by time-traveling through Earth's past.[1] The memos describe the demon's weird love affair with a human nun, his missions involving Hitler, Jesus, John F. Kennedy, so-called extraterrestrial aliens and so-called UFOs.

Many threads in this satanic embroidery are woven throughout the section entitled *Book Two: Manual of Earth Terms*. To fully experience the bizarre world of demons and to understand the reasons for the invasion[2], track the links at the end of various Earth Terms which connect to related terms in the book. For example, the letter "A" links to terms which explain Mankind's origin (genetically engineered by a demon criminal), Satan's taboos regarding time-travel to Earth, and the diametrically opposed views of Heaven and Hell concerning the Past and the Future.

---

1   PUB. NOTE: Since demons are time-travelers, note that the title page identifies the book as the "666th Commemorative Edition." Thus, the text purports to have been written in Mankind's future *after* the invasion of Earth was successful — an event which has not yet occurred. Since human science tells us that the Future is not fixed, Satan's invasion may or may not be successful. Therefore, may this vile volume raise the battle cry for Humanity to rise up against the demons presently infiltrating our society through key professions: as politicians, attorneys and receptionists.

2   PUB. NOTE: For the purported reasons for Satan's invasion, see *Lord Satan's Preface to First Edition*.

Tracking other links, footnotes and memos will reveal many other hidden facts, including a demon conspiracy to assassinate Satan[3], that Jesus apparently plagiarized his teachings from Satan[4], Satan's decision to kill his creator after being exposed to the human concepts of *love* and *infinity*, and God's peculiar plan for creating the universe. The book also abounds with secret writing using acrostics, wheel and acroamatic ciphers, cryptograms, palindromes and elaborate hidden messages combining various obscure codes and ciphers. For example, the curious reader can decode certain cryptic passages by utilizing an online "substitution cipher generator."

The bizarre intricacy of the manuscript itself[5], its charts, diagrams, paradoxical layering of texts and recursive footnotes, combined with Satan's vile view of humanity, may make this volume too harsh and repulsive for many people to absorb. But I urge all men and women who care about the future of mankind to brave the contents of this *Encyclopaedia* with an open heart, for the invasion of Earth by Hell is imminent.

As I write these words, S.S.A. assassins are trying to kill me to recover this book. I have little time. I urge you to give this, the most important book in the history of the world, to every man, woman and child as soon as possible. We must spread the word so that Humanity will be prepared when the fleets of Hellcraft land and the Invasion begins.

NATHAN STILES
S.S.A. Agent (Ret.)

PRAYER to the READER:
May God Have Mercy On Your Soul.

---

3   PUB. NOTE: See *Zyk's 3rd and 4th Memos to the Publisher* and Satan's article: *Supreme Being.*

4   PUB. NOTE: See *Stupidity; Zyk's Last Memo to the Publisher; Jesus Christ.*

5   PUB. NOTE: For example, the book's intricate engraving entitled *The Wheel of Kadab* may be decoded via its reverse image by holding it up to a mirror and reading what purports to be a hidden message from "God."

THE WHEEL OF KADAB
(FRONT VIEW)

ENCYCLOPÆDIA
OF HELL
BY
SATAN

An Invasion Manual for Demons
Concerning the Planet Earth
and the Human Race Which Infests It

Commentaries by Executive Demons
in the Loweracrchy of Hell

666TH PRINTING

Deluxe Commemorative Edition
with the Original Illustrations
and
Newly Released Historical Documents

JXHUU SYFXU HI

Iqjqd iIynu iTquc ediTh uqtyd w
Reeai ruxyt tudev Ruqij iRuxu qtydw
YdaRu ifbqj juhSx efqdt Isqjj uh
YdIyn uiIuu aRydq hoRut tydw

Xytue kiKhb iYdKc rhqXy tu
Fhysa jxuJx kcrSb ysaYd iytu
YdaRu ifbqj juhSx efqdt Isqjj uh
YdCqw ysauI fytuh Jhqfi Mehbt Mytu

TuufY diytu Tufys jyedi Fbkcr
MxudI ypuYd shuqi ujxSe tuiIk sskcr
YdaRu ifbqj juhSx efqdt Isqjj uh
YdSyf xuhIj qwudq hjTej xSecu

Vehry ttudy ijxux eqhoa uo
Vehwu troUl ybCuj qbkhw yu
JeHee ciSed suqbu tqdtS xqcru hiIuq but
Huluq bydwI qjqdi Iushu jByrh qhyu

TABLE OF CONTENTS

BOOK ONE

BOOK TWO

QUADRIFIDUM the FIRST

QUADRIFIDUM the SECOND

QUADRIFIDUM the THIRD

QUADRIFIDUM the FOURTH

THE ADDENDA

LORD SATAN'S PREFACE

TO THE

FIRST EDITION
OF THE
ENCYCLOPÆDIA OF HELL

TO THE

LOATHSOME DEMON READER:

The jewels of human mythology, the bogie-men, the ghouls and gnomes, the squeers, kobolds, podsnappers, elves and bugaboos are sorely disadvantaged by one ugly fact. They do not, as such, exist. For in the Infinite Dominions of Hell, known to Humanity as "the Universe," there exist only Demons.

Due to my Immense Wisdom and Good Taste, I have separated Man from Demonkind by the Tapestry of Time, a Dense Embroidery impenetrable by Humanity.[1] Only recently have I allowed my Demon Citizens access to the spiralutum of time-travel, for Fear that they would become corrupted by contact with Odious Mankind. For Humans, as larval Demons of immense obnoxiousness and stupidity, have yet to evolve into Evil Creaturehood.

1   ED. NOTE: See *Time*.

LORD SATAN'S PREFACE

Know that Humans are utterly ignorant of the Existence of Hell. Absurdly, they consider Hell as either a Myth, or as a pit of fire festooning the core of their drab planet.[2] They know not that the quavers of light speckling their sky are the Island Kingdoms of Hell which, in their distant future, will become overpopulated by the rapacious reproductivity of Demonkind.

Therein lies the purpose of this manual. The City of Hell is now the most overpopulated district in My entire Kingdom. Although I and my Arch-Demons faithfully decapitate all Lower Demons (known as "Angels")[3] immigrating to our slums every Spring, their heads grow back every eleven years; thus in eleven-year cycles, Hell City has become increasingly overpopulated. Largesse in decapitating Angels has not remedied the problem, which today has grown endemic.

Drastic times call for drastic actions. You have all heard my Invasion Proclamation[4]. This manual will be distributed to all Demons shortly before boarding Hellcraft for the Invasion of Earth. I order you, my Subjects, to study this Precious Material in a State of Readiness, with Claws Unsheathed and Tails Unfurled. It offers the Studious Demon pertinent geographical, physical and psychological information concerning Mankind and Its Noxious Ancient Environs, as well as time-saving tips on the Trapping and Cooking of Humans as Foodstuffs.

Non hic Centauros, non Gorgonas, Harpysque
Invenies, hominem pagina nostra sapit.[5]

Under normal circumstances, humans, as veritable insects, are no danger to the Average Demon. Yet the queerness and primitive dementia of Mankind have proven too much for the weak stomachs of many sophisticated Demons.

But despite their strangeness, Humans are not to be feared. Relatively speaking, they are the least substantial of creatures: tiny, querulous bugs trapped in Jars of Time, quaintly naming themselves Jack and Jill and then flickering in and out of existence. Devoid of the ability to discern truth from falsity, humans have a fundamental propensity toward literalism and blind, robotic format-following, the result of the genetic engineering of the banished Demon Abra Kadab, who homesteaded Earth in ancient times.[6]

~~~~~~

2   ED. NOTE: See *Cosmology of Earth*.
3   ED. NOTE: See *Angels*.
4   ED. NOTE: See *Addendum 1: Lord Satan's Invasion Proclamation*.
5   ED. NOTE: Neither Centaurs, Gorgons, nor Harpies here find/My subject herein is Man and Humankind.
6   ED. NOTE: See *Abra Kadab*.

LORD SATAN'S PREFACE

Humans, dimly aware of the paucity of their existence, kept from committing mass suicide by developing ridiculously self-absorbed mythologies in order to prop themselves up, and with which to masturbate their minds to ecstasy.

Mankind's fundamental delusion is that they are the central linchpin in the structure of Creation. They perceive themselves as Prizes being fought over by opposing supernatural armies, each battling for control over their priceless human "souls."

In reality, of course, there is no battle. The Future is Manifest: Only Demons inhabit the Cosmos, and humans are merely primeval gnats crushed betwixt pages in the Book of Time, who after eons evolve into Demonhood.

Generally, humans should be ignored, swatted away, played with or peremptorily squashed. Yet to insure a clean sweep in our Invasion Plan, nothing, not even mincing Humanity, should be taken for granted.

In this connexion, be not deceived by Man's ability to ape reason, for, in truth, humans have no real knowledge about anything whatsoever. Beware particularly of their ranks of theologians, quacksalvers, politicians and empirics, which are attracted to the Black Radiation of Demons and may attempt to communicate via their simplistic, but focused, Linear Pipeline Thought.

Once this material is fully understood, I bid you relax and enjoy your Invasion. The Correct Posture with which the Invading Demon should enter into Earth-Density is one of Amusement; thus, it is My Desire that this Manual shall Entertain the Invading Hordes with its harsh Conceptual Parodies, and by this Device spur the Reader on to study the more Difficult and Scholarly Analyses herein.

It has, indeed, been a monumental challenge to compile only the data essential to the Invading Demon, for the Ghastly Morés of Humankind are Dense and Complex. And although the average Demon may be nauseated by the Unwonted Strangeness of Earth as described herein, remember that the Exegesis of Truth is always obtained for a Price.

Read on, then, My Hideous Demons, for now My Book Begins.

SATAN
Satan's Palace
City of Hell

BIOGRAPHIA DÆMONIUM

BIOGRAPHIES
OF THE
DÆMON COMMENTATORS
AND
MEMBERS OF THE INVASION MANUAL COMMISSION[1]

ZYK OF ASIMOTH
(HUMAN FORM)

PROFESSOR OF EARTH EVIL
POET LAUREATE OF HELL

ZYK[2]

Poet Laureate of Hell, Poet in Residence at the University of Hell, and
historical scholar on Hell Antiquities, specializing in Ancient Earth and Its
Evils. Chairman and Chief Editor of Lord Satan's *Invasion Encyclopaedia*.

*Dæmon of Clarity and Obfuscation, Ruler of the Myst of Words,
Master of Beginning and Ending Rhymes, the Elegant Human-Hater,
Noted Scholar of Evil on Earth, Satirist of Human Morés
and Poet Laureate of Hell.*

---

1   ED. NOTE: See *Invasion Manual Commission* in Book Two.

2   ED. NOTE: Since the fate of Zyk of Asimoth is inextricably linked to the Destiny of Hell, Lord Satan has included
a summary of Zyk's ignoble accomplishments at the end of Book Two of His Supremely Infernal Tome.

LLU CIPHER

PRINCE OF MASTURBATION

LLU CIPHER

Satanic emissary of Pride and Masturbation, renowned for his Gigantic Sexual Organs.
So large that they cannot interface with any complementary female orifice, Llu Cipher's genitalia
are thus utilized in Masturbatory Techniques, of which he is Hell's leading authority.
Onanism aside, his hobbies include baking bread, growing pansies,
and injecting Ebola virus into human philanthropists.

*Executive of the 1st Lowerarchy, Ruler of Pride, Specializing in Obsession with the Self,
Masturbation Fetishism, Silicone Injection, Arcane Genitalia Worship
and Los Angeles Twelve-Step Programs.*

MEPHIS TOPHIEL

HATER OF LIGHT AND AMATEUR FLÜGELHORNIST

MEPHIS TOPHIEL

The Purveyor of Rage, Intolerance, Disease, Darkness and War to the Writhing Worm of Mankind,
as well as an amateur Flügelhorn enthusiast. Lt. Tophiel, Prince of the 3rd Lowerarchy and a Member
of the Invasion Committee, specializes in the Hatred of Light, the Proliferation of Arms, Cocaine and
Amphetamines, and is known for His Sulfurous Odor and for Cultivating and Displaying for Public
View Unspeakable Rashes on his Genitals. Aside from His Flügelhorn recitals, Lt. Tophiel's hobbies
include Inciting Fear and Trembling Among the Masses During Eclipses of the Sun, Recipes of Drugs
and Automatic Weapons Served to the Poor, and homemade arts and crafts, such as casket doilies
macraméd from the clotted blood of Make-a-Wish Foundation executives.

*Executive of the 3rd Lowerarchy, Ruler of War, Ignorance, Disease and Darkness,
Specializing in Malevolence, Intolerance, Rage, the Hatred of Light, the Proliferation of Arms,
Cocaine, Amphetamines and Tabloid Television.*

BAAL ZEBUB

CREATOR OF INSURANCE, STOCK PORTFOLIOS AND GENITAL HERPES

BAAL ZEBUB

Satanic emissary of Greed. As a promoter of Evil on Earth, his many accomplishments include Manifest Destiny, Unbridled Corporate Expansion, Contempt for the Homeless and Diseased, Syndicated Game Shows, Stock Portfolios, Las Vegas, Off-Track Betting and the Insurance Industry. Baal Zebub's cocktail parties are famous as the gathering place for Hell's Evil Elite. An avid orphanage arsonist, his hobbies also include collecting *Archie* comic books, swimming laps in pools of boiling blood, and making party patés from the mashed brains of Nobel Peace Prize winners.

Executive of the 1st Lowerarchy, Ruler of Greed and the Path of Power, Specializing in Corporate Darwinism, Real Estate-, Insurance- and Wall Street-Brokers, International Banking, Lotteries, High-Roller Junkets and Church Bingo.

AHRIMAN

DEMON OF PENILE ENVY

AHRIMAN

Master of Mind Control known for elevating human males, exclusive of females, into a position of power, thus assuring eons of carnage in Wars of Penile Envy. Ahriman's hobbies include categorizing Chladni Vibration Patterns, collecting antique buttons, and making scrapbook collages with AIDS-infected human afterbirth.

Executive of the 2nd Lowerarchy, Ruler of the Narrow Path, Specializing in Cults, Religion, Secret Governments, the Marketing of Seduction through Mind Control, Advertising, Muzak, Pyramid Schemes, Soap Operas, Political Speech-Writing and Lord Satan's Magnificent Invention, Children's Programming.

BELIAL   MINISTER OF LUST
AND ORDURE

BELIAL

Satanic Minister of Lust and Ordure, the owner of Hell's largest collection of human pornography,
to which he has affixed a laugh track. Belial's collection of bottled ordure from every race,
sex and age of Humankind is the envy of all Demons, not to mention of the Fecal-Slobbering
Porcelain Creatures of Goebbels-Fehtang. A prominent inhabitant of East Hell, Belial proudly shows
visitors his homemade bed, constructed from the shellacked corpses of B-movie stars.

*Executive of the 4th Lowerarchy, Ruler of Lechery and Alcoholism, Specializing in Castigating the
Absurd Spectacles of Human Waste Elimination and Fornication, in Adultery, Incest,
Pornography and the Perversion of Pleasure.*

ASMO DEUS   LORD OF LOGIC
AND THE FORNICATION
OF OPPOSITES

ASMO DEUS

Satanic Emissary of Logic and Obfuscation, who engineered the downfall of Solomon by
presenting him with a Vestal Virgin with a Square Vagina and challenging him to insert into It
his Round Peg. With this Challenge, Asmo Deus introduced to Mankind the Domain of Logic
resulting from the Fornication of Opposites, which served to brilliantly ensnare Humans in the
Swillish Sinkhole of the Intellect. Asmo Deus, a resident of the Eye of Arcturus in North Hell, enjoys
ping-pong, collecting mushrooms and the gutting and flaying of wheelchair basketball teams.

*Executive of the 2nd Lowerarchy, Ruler of Mathematics and Logic, Specializing in Law,
Income Tax Instructions, Sophistry, Paradox, Specious Argument and
the Sophisticated Intellect as an Enemy of Wisdom.*

---

1   NOTE BY ASMO DEUS: Refer to my autobiography *Hocking Solomon's Ring*; therein I explain how I confounded
Solomon with the simplistic paradox known as "All Cretins Are Lawyers."

LILITH

CREATOR OF
MINI-MALLS

LILITH

The She-Demon dedicated to Evil toward Man through the Miasma of Glamour and Mayic Delusion. Lilith's accomplishments as Destroyer of Earth-Density, through overshadowing the minds of humans, include the creation of Shopping Malls, Beauty Pageants, Barbie Dolls, Presidential Campaigns, the Academy Awards, high-fashion piercing and tattooing, the transformation of serial killers into media celebrities, and the glamorizing of Narcotics and Suicide. Lilith resides in Blood Manor on the River Styx, and as a hobby creates arts and crafts with yarn, construction paper and gutted kittens.

Executive of the 2nd Lowerarchy, Ruler of Glamour, Queen of the Succubi, Specializing in Unbridled Fatuousness, Shimmering Excess and the Glitter of Filth, the Inventor of High Heels and Celebrity Telethons.

BEHEMOTH

EPICURE OF HUMAN
BARBECUE SAUCES

BEHEMOTH

Satanic Emissary of Eating, Hell's leading expert on Cooking Mankind and the creator of a line of Human Barbecue Sauces popular in Hell Bistros. His expertise is apparent in the excellent Food Charts and Diagrams in this manual. Behemoth's hobbies include gutting and stuffing human infant corpses and twisting them into demeaning postures, flossing yaks' teeth with human entrails, and collecting bottle caps.

Executive of the 4th Lowerarchy, Ruler of Gluttony, Specializing in the Proliferation of Pure Fat, Sugar and Chocolate, and in the Gutting, Basting, Broiling, Frying and Roasting of Humanity.

A NOTE ON THE COMMENTARIES

The magnanimity of Lord Satan's Evil is no better expressed than in His Pure Hatred of Idiot Mankind, as depicted in this, His Invasion Manual.

In His enthusiasm to draw a Comprehensive Portrait of Mankind, Lord Satan commanded Me to act as Editor and to add additional data helpful to His Invading Hordes.

After forming the Invasion Commission, composed of Hell's Most Notable Experts, I traveled to Earth at various time frames to do firsthand research on the Evils of Earth. This data provided the raw material for the Editorial Commentaries and Footnotes on the sundry terms His Majesty compiled to Explicate the Incomprehensible World of Man.[1]

My scouting mission was dangerous. After arriving on Earth, I disguised Myself as a Human and researched various topics undercover, traveling to numerous temporal and geographic regions. My own Research Notes (and Selected Verses) were integrated with those written by My Commission, and arranged in a tasteful layout by Mortimer Pönçé, Lord Satan's Publisher at Mind Control Press.

The success of the editorial work of My Commission, composed of Perpetually Warring Executives of Evil Who Forever Despise Each Other (and Despise Myself), is a Testament to the Binding Power of our Lord Satan's Divine Hatred, for He is both the Beginning and the Ending of all Evil Enterprise.[2]

ZYK OF ASIMOTH
Poet in Eternal Residence
University of Hell

---

1 NOTE BY MEPHIS TOPHIEL: When grammatical clauses herein deal with ambiguous gender, Lord Satan commanded that the masculine form be used, not for convenience, but because of the supreme superiority of males.*

* NOTE BY LILITH: Since I have worked ceaselessly under Zyk's mandate to complete this book before the Invasion date, I am compelled by the Truth of Evil to abrogate and renounce Mephis Tophiel's Opinion. Male or female Demons, of course, are equally evil in Demonhood; the reviling of female energy reflects the Insecure Exclusivity of male-dominated Hell.

2 NOTE BY LORD SATAN: While the brashness of the mendacity of Chairman Zyk is to be commended, still the depths of his insincere, sycophantic remarks, blatantly kissing the Ass of Hell, renders his praise vaguely irritating. It is true, however, that the hatred of his Commission for each other was subsumed by the enormity of the task at hand, and for Zyk's torturous obedience to Myself, and for faithfully delivering unto Me his Quaint Annotations to this Volume, I deign to accept his sickly redolent praise.

PUBLISHER'S NOTE
ON THE
666ᵀᴴ EDITION

ON THE
VARIOUS ᴀɴᴅ *SUNDRY EDITIONS*

Six hundred and sixty-five editions of *Encyclopædia of Hell* have been published since the success of the Invasion eons ago. Since then, Lord Satan's Invasion Manual has been studied by Demons throughout the vast Hell Cosmos and translated into over 13,000 dialects of Hell, especially German.

Many illegal facsimiles of this Book were circulated, and the pirate publishers summarily whipped and decapitated side by side with those Demons who purchased them. Thus this book has produced nothing but excellent results, even in its plagiarization.

Now, in this Special 666th Edition, many new annotations and historical documents have been added. Memoranda written by Lord Zyk to my office prior to the publication of the 1st Edition have been inserted at the beginning of each section of the *Encyclopaedia* proper. These letters appear in sequence to give the Modern Demon Bibliophile a Unique Historical Perspective on the successful Invasion of Earth, as well as many Interesting Facts concerning the manner in which the First Edition was Compiled, Edited and Revised.

DISCLAIMER REGARDING THE ILLUSTRATIONS

Through the eons, the myriad illustrations included in Lord Satan's Magnificent Paean to Mankind's Annihilation have been interpolated by sundry Daemon artists, and in later ages expunged, redrawn or edited to conform to the sensibilities of Evil Artistry in the Timeline of Hell's Cultural History. The resulting conglomeration of illustrative styles has created a unique pastiche of iniquitous imagery that we the publishers have decided to present with minimal editorialization; in this way we hope to more perfectly represent this Commemorative Facsimile Edition's Imperious and Ageless Authenticity.

Mortimer Pönçé, Publisher
Mind Control Press, Ltd.
City of Hell

ENCYCLOPÆDIA
OF
HELL

AN
INVASION MANUAL
OF EARTH

BOOK I

INVASION
MAPS
AND DIAGRAMS
INCLUDING AN
OVERVIEW
OF
LORD SATAN'S
MASTER
PLAN

INVASION MAPS AND *DIAGRAMS*

AND
LORD SATAN'S
MASTER PLAN

In Part One, I shall present the most important material
concerning the planet Earth, so-called Angels and their relationship
to the grotesque human race, and finally My Plan of Invasion.

1.
ON ANGELS

As every Demon knows, Angels are a transient and lazy race of sub-demons[1] who are routinely ejected from the City of Hell for Vagrancy, Loitering and Stupidity. Since Angels are the future selves of the Clod of Humanity[2], many inbred Angel families unable to find work in Hell have time-traveled to Earth-Density and formed colonies of invisible trailer parks orbiting the Earth. There the Angels have established themselves as a dim-witted race of low-IQ, gum-chewing Demons whose presence beautifully complements Earth and its Billions of Indigenous Morons.

Due to their direct ancestry to Earth humans, this primitive race of Demons, distinguished by their short stature, gray, mottled skin and large, lenticular black eye-shades, frequently time-travel to gun-free eras of Earth history.

On Earth, Angel-Demons cast crude spells to disguise themselves in a form pleasing to the primitive human sensory apparatus. Their camouflage often includes blond flowing hair, white silky robes and absurd feathery wings.[3]

---

1 NOTE BY LORD SATAN: Mankind's delusion that angels, a genetically inferior species of inbred, bucktoothed Demons, are representatives of a Mythic God of Goodness, is typical of their superstition that the Cosmos of Stars is an Infinite Etheric Heaven, as opposed to what it really is: the Glitter of Infinite Hell. (See *Cosmology of Hell*.)

2 NOTE BY LORD SATAN: See *Soul Cycle*.

3 NOTE BY GOD, LORD OF THE PERSONIFIED UNIVERSE: Here Satan adopts the term *Angel* as used by Mankind. These *angels*, as Satan correctly points out, are in reality disguised Demons. I would never suffer You, My Angels, to visit Earth, a world too harsh for Your sublime sensibilities. Besides, as You know, I do not use emissaries. I have no middleman. I work with Humanity as I do with all of My Beings — *directly*. I exist in all dimensions of space-time simultaneously, touching My Universe directly beneath the surface of perceptual illusion, helping creatures in proportion to the sincerity (or novelty) of their Call. (Satan, of course, may do the same if He wishes, but that

---

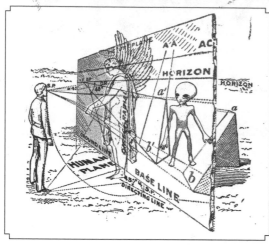

Diagram of Angelic Projection

Before the Invasion, the Angel-Demons have played a crucial role as My Ignorant Dupes in paving the way for My Conquest of their ancestral Orb, Earth. I commanded My Executives to sabotage several of the Angels' primitive "trailer park" Hellcraft so that they would crash on Earth circa 1947 and be discovered by humans.[4]

My Plan was to allow the humans to recover the Angels' corpses as well as their Hellcraft's Microchip Technology from the wreckage; thinking the Angels were "spacemen" instead of Demons, the humans would then use the Microchip for the rapid invention and dissemination of My Secret Weapon on Earth, *Television*. (My Ingenious Plan, in which the Human Idiots would be tricked into mass-producing Television sets and distributing them to the populace, worked magnificently; now this Deadly Weapon of Mind Control sits in every living room on the planet, and has transformed

Earth Creatures into even stupider [if that can be imagined] pods of insensate flesh.) In keeping with My Plan, Key Demons in Human Guise have infiltrated the ranks of Television Executives and promulgated as Law my mind-numbing scheme called "Reality Programming," designed to systematically eradicate any trace of Intelligence in all of television broadcasting, Now and Forever. After the Invasion, the Angel Problem will be dealt with, and these annoying entities will be annihilated, along with any of their human ancestors who are deemed inedible. See *Harp; Television; Time.*

2.
ON THE GROTESQUE HUMAN BODY

Observe the opposite diagram[5], comparing a cross section of the sleek Demonic Body to that of the bizarre Human Form *(Luciferum Daemonicus* vs. *Homo Humanus).*

While a Demon's interior has only one moving part, a conduit which neatly absorbs foodstuffs and excretes waste, the Human Body is stuffed with an absurd chaos of "organs," each articulating a specific underlying electrical nexus point, its sloppy complexity a testament to the primitive stage of human evolution.

When gutting a human orally, take care to immediately spit out the heart which is noxious to Demons and sometimes, as in the case of human philanthropists, poisonous.

---

is His business. I give Mankind the freedom to run their own lives, interfering only when asked, or when a whimsical or contrary mood strikes Me. This freedom is shared in kind by all sentient specks of my creation, including humans.) Thus, Satan's explanation of "Earth angels" is correct, despite His ignorance of the existence of Myself or of You, My Heavenly Angels.

4   ED. NOTE: For a firsthand account of the crash of Demon Angels at Roswell, New Mexico, Earth, see *Zyke's Third Memo to the Publisher.*

5   This illustration, and several others scattered among these pages, were rendered by a feeble human artist attempting to barter his paltry skills in exchange for not being eaten. After completing these drawings, he was of course instantly flambéd in sauces mixed the brain fluid of an art critic. Despite the boorish earthly aesthetic of these drawings, I, Lord Satan, insisted on their inclusion to inure Demons to the whorishness of human artisans.

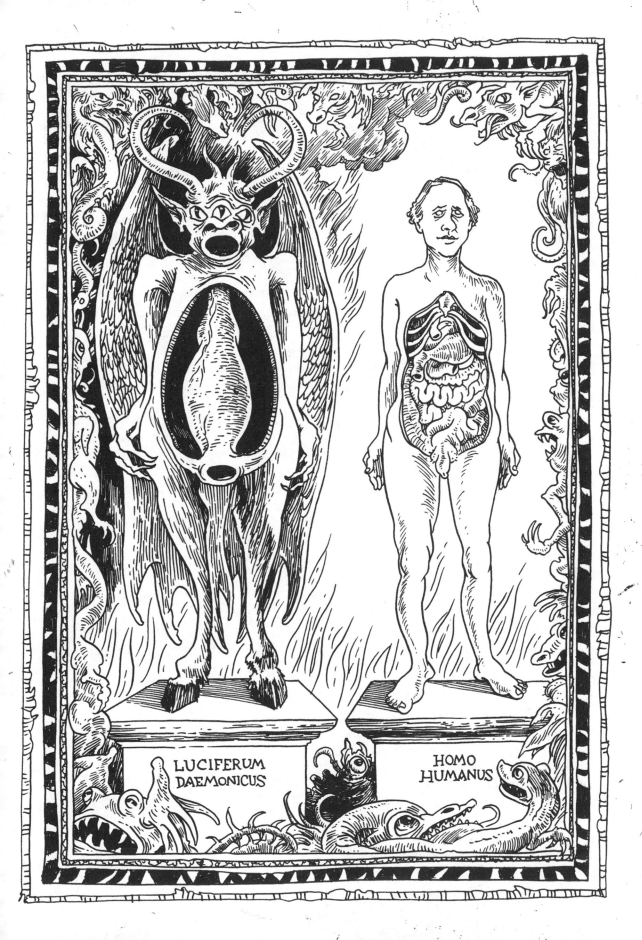

LUCIFERUM
DAEMONICUS

HOMO
HUMANUS

Earth: Orb of Insignificance

3.
ON THE UNSPEAKABLE PLANET EARTH

The odious Earth, of course, exists in Hell's distant past and, indeed, is a past incarnation of the Central Orb of Hell. Now in a larval stage of Imperfect Evil, primitive Mankind is destined to evolve through the eons into the present Race of Demons.

Prior to our Invasion, the Earth has served as a combination garbage dump and time-travel resort of Demons, and has a fascinating history. Eons ago, when upstart Demons were banished to Hell's distant past, the time frames featuring Earth-Density were avoided because of their star's stinging radiation of photons, the planet's sickly-sweet, noxious molecular odor and the sour, copper-penny taste of the early human livestock.

Despite these drawbacks, the infamous Demon pioneer *Abra Kadab* (q.v.) homesteaded the planet and claimed the ancient wilderness of primeval Earth-Density as his own.

Kadab, a powerful shape-changer, hollowed out the planet's interior and conjured a gigantic magical stone wheel to spin at the Earth's core (see *Wheel of Kadab*) in order to correct the planet's awkward wobbling. After his installation of the Wheel, Kadab became the sole owner and Demon inhabitant of this noxious planet for unnumbered centuries.

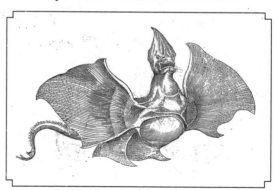

The Demon Abra Kadab

During that ancient time, Kadab's obsessive goal was to alter human evolution so that their flesh when eaten did not make the average Demon retch. Initially, he utilized the satanic magic of *genetic engineering* (q.v.) in an attempt to achieve this goal.

Wheel of Kadab

During his centuries of experimentation, Kadab produced many species of delightfully grotesque monsters which he released to the surface of the planet — dragons, Yeti, trolls, Bigfoot, Mothmen, centaurs and dinosaurs. But all were barely edible.

After myriad failures, Kadab gave up the genetic approach and began a new technique by which he ultimately succeeded. By introducing *money* (q.v.) to the human livestock, he was able to transform human society into an Unstoppable Machine which, in its craving for More Money, ultimately poisoned the planet (and thus its inhabitants' flesh) with deadly toxins. In a relatively short period of time, these toxins transformed human flesh from vomitous gore into a gourmet delicacy. This plan succeeded so magnificently that word of the deliciousness of Humanity spread to Demons in the present (and thus, Earth's future) and in every region of inner and outer Hell. As a result, Abra Kadab established Earth as a time-travel resort for vacationing Demons with a tongue for human flesh.

Abra Kadab's plan backfired, however, when the Lawyers of Hell saw the immense profits that could be made by marketing Kad-ab's genetic engineering of Humanity. Thus, Kadab was served with a Writ of Manifest Destiny stating that the City of Hell was expanding its borders into the Past to include Earth-Density. Since Kadab had been banished from Hell, he was ordered to leave Earth-Density at once. Kadab naturally resisted. Thus, Armies of Darkness time-traveled to Earth to take the Orb from Kadab by force.

Realizing that he could not win, Kadab sent the Attorneys of Hell his now-famous Riposte of Defiance, stating that if he could not own Earth-Density, then no one else would either. In an act of magnificent vengeance, Kadab attempted to destroy the entire orb.[6] First he turned on all of the plumbing he'd installed in the Hollow Earth centuries before and flooded the planet's surface, thus destroying all of its precious livestock. Then he squeezed the Smell Sacs of Seven Billion Giant Gas Creatures from Arcturus over the planet, saturating it with the noxious odor which, combined with Earth's stench *au naturel,* is the most ponderous characteristic of Earth-Density today.

Meanwhile, I, Satan, was informed while skeet-shooting Angels on the Dog Star. I returned and assessed the situation. As punishment, I Decreed first that Earth was Taboo to all Demons. Secondly, I Decreed that Abra Kadab would not be banished, but rather would be imprisoned on the planet which he noxiously polluted, until eons in the future, when it finally evolved into the Orb of Hell. Furthermore, I Decreed that ancient Twentieth-Century Earth would now be the Dumping Ground for the City of Hell and its surrounding environs.

But in time, these Decrees became moot due to the Immutable Law of Change. Despite (or, perhaps, because of) Earth's Infamous

---

6   **NOTE BY LORD SATAN:** Of course, since Hell exists as Earth's future, such a destruction would cause a time-paradox, since Hell could not exist without the existence of Earth. I boldly dealt with this tedious problem by casting a Subatomic Spell upon the Plasma of Space-Time, banishing all Time-Paradox.

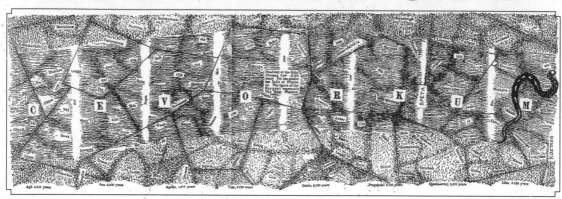

Map of Invasion Route

Odor, its attraction to Demons eventually became irresistible. After centuries of breeding, the human livestock had replenished itself and once again was known for its distinctive and pungent, toxic flavor.

It is hoped that, after the Invasion, time-travel junkets to Earth-Density will become popular, due to the novelty of the humans as both foodstuffs and as faddish playthings. See *Possession; Taboo; Time; Lord Satan's Preface to Encyclopædia of Hell; Wheel of Kadab.*

4.
MAPS OF EARTH'S INTERIOR AND EXTERIOR

For Invasion purposes, refer to the following map of the Earth's interior and exterior. For more information on the origin and design of the Hollow Earth, see *Part Two, Manual of Earth Terms: Hollow Earth.*

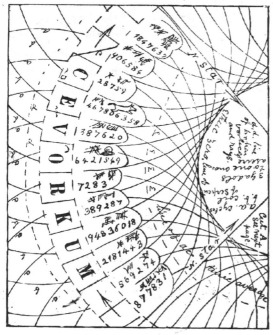

Lord Satan's Proclamation: The Taboo of Earth Density

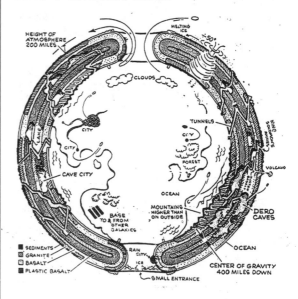

Hollow Earth: Kadab's Lair Before Conjuring the Wheel of Kadab

5.
INVASION ROUTES
TO EARTH

For Lieutenants leading Demon Troops through the Cosmic Time-Spiral to Earth, the Invasion Routes recommended are those favored for eons by Demon Garbage Scow Pilots for the dumping of Hell's Swill in Earth-Density. (Refer to *Map of Invasion Routes from Hell to Earth*):

DIRECTIONS FROM HELL
TO EARTH-DENSITY:

- *Follow the Time-Spiral of the Solar Phalanx for 24,000 years into the Past or until you see the Crossroads of Horub.*

- *Take a left on the Secondary Vortex and go straight for 7000 years to the Arc of Bon.*

- *When you reach the Ji'Niquin Swamp in Etherea, take the Off-Ramp to Hyrim.*

- *At the end of the ramp, go right toward Gitche for 43,826 years, or until you see a Scattered Trail of Filth which presages the emergence into Earth Time-Density. (At this point, the stench of approaching Earth will be overwhelming. Travelers Advisory suggests all Demons wear nose-clips until the Smell of Mankind becomes tolerable.)*

- *Modulate parallel time- and spatial-frequencies so that the Third Planet from the Central Spluttering Photosphere is Despised and Ignominious Earth. (Note: If Earth is in any other position, recalibrate and modulate dimensions until the Planet of Filth occupies the Third Harmonic.)*

If possible, land Hellcraft in flat, empty areas. For reasons of security, either capture and eat or instantly vaporize any humans who may witness your approach.

6.
ON THE
LANDING SITES

The Invasion of Earth shall be focused primarily on two prime sites, the Vatican, Italy and Las Vegas, U.S.A. Once these territories are sacked and plundered by Demon Insurgents and legally annexed to Hell City, the two cities shall be conjured together as one, creating luxurious Catholic Casino Cathedrals for the enjoyment of demons visiting Earth to devour the human livestock. See *Las Vegas; Vatican.*

For specific landing logistics, refer to the following diagram:

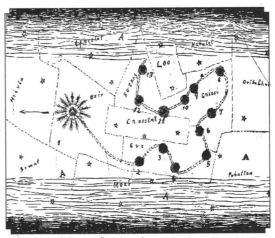

Diagram of Space-Time Vortices Used to Conjure Vatican City and Las Vegas as One

7.
ON THE INVASION PLAN

You, My Demon Insurgents, have heard My Invasion Proclamation and have been given Instructions according to your Role in the Plan. As an overview, My Plan shall consist of Five Waves of Conquest:

1. Eight million V-6 Pentagonal Hellcrafts will traverse Wormhole 66 (the route used by Scows which dump Hell's Trash on Earth). These craft, invisible to Humans, will hover over all Earth Slave Camps (see *Cities*) and broadcast frequencies inaudible to humans, but which will instill Fear and Paranoia in Mankind.

2. Fifty-five million Luxury Cruisers, also invisible, will land on city rooftops, carrying 105 million Lawyers of Hell who, disguised as humans, will quickly integrate into Earth's Chaotic Corporate Structure and, communicating via Rolex Watch-Communicators, craft the Legal Domination and Ownership of Earth.

3. The Excess Population of the City of Hell, totaling more than eighteen billion Demonic entities, shall follow, landing on Earth in twenty million very crowded Pentagonal Hellcrafts. (All Demon Immigrants are reminded to grease their hides to facilitate squeezing past one another in the passenger sections.)

4. I, Lord Satan, King of Hell, shall then arrive in a Chariot of Fire, upon Wheels within Wheels, and Announce to all of Earth, via the interruption of prime-time television and Internet webs, that as of that Instant, All of Mankind is now the Official Property and Chattel of Hell.

5. Hors d'oeuvres shall be served to All Earth Politicians, followed by their be-ing Cooked Alive and Eaten in a Special Live Worldwide Broadcast. The inevitably high ratings of this broadcast will set the tone of a New Age of Fear and Prosperity. See *Addendum I, The Invasion Proclamation*.

8.
ON EATING HUMANS

Once the Invasion begins, humans will be rounded up and used as foodstuffs for My Invading Hordes. Thus, a word here on the cooking and eating of human flesh:

1. Regardless of the gourmet biases of individual Demons, it is universally agreed that the human brain is a sour, rubbery and inedible organ. Thus when gutting a human, it is recommended that the brain be removed and discarded first per the following diagram:

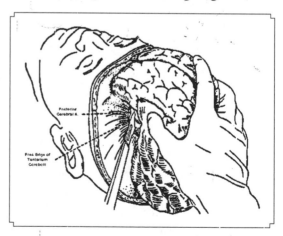

Removal of Inedible Human Brain

2. It is manifest, due to the Law of Subjective Inexplicability, that different Demons enjoy Different Tastes. While the delicious chemical toxins in human flesh created the demand for humans as food, I personally do not like flesh *supersaturated* with toxins (re the Cau-

THE TASTE AND EDIBILITY OF HUMAN RACES
COMPILED BY BEHEMOTH

BLACK	BLACK-WHITE	BLACK-WHITE-YELLOW	BLACK-YELLOW	YELLOW	YELLOW-WHITE	WHITE
NEGRO: *Delicious raw.*	**EGYPTIAN:** *Serve broiled.*	**ARAB:** *Liver sweet if sautéed.*	**INDONESIAN:** *Tough buttocks; serve broiled.*	**CHINESE:** *Avoid elderly vagina.*	**TARTAR:** *Tough and gristly groin; feed to dogs.*	**TURK:** *Inedible.*
CONGOLESE: *Delicious parboiled.*	**LATIN:** *Good after draining off excess grease.*	**ETHIOPIAN:** *Edible after shaving back.*	**MALAY:** *Tangy brain, barbecue head in foil.*	**JAPANESE:** *Serve raw wrapped in seaweed.*	**AMERICAN INDIAN:** *Avoid armpits.*	**SLAV:** *Best boiled in blood goulash.*
BUSHMAN: *Delicious after gutting anus.*	**HAMITE:** *If dry, serve with Latin grease.*	**JEW:** *Edible after scraping Mother's love clutching soul.*	**FILIPINO:** *Good after scraping parasites from undercarriage.*	**BURMESE AND MONGOL:** *Eat around scrotal sac.*	**ESKIMO AND TIBETAN:** *Cut off head and limbs, barbecue torso.*	**CELTIC:** *Edible only if boiled for centuries; avoid liver.*
ABORIGINE: *See Bushman.*	**ASHANTI:** *Exceptionally succulent buttocks and undercarriage.*	**PERSIAN:** *Tart and crunchy heart.*	**HINDU:** *Filth on testicles adds zest to fried groin.*			**NORDIC:** *Stringy brain with a morbid aftertaste.*
						FINN: *Genitals tasty but tough, tenderize penis with Meat Hammer.*

casian race). Others (although I am not one of them) prefer relatively untainted flesh.

Thus the following data is biased by my own taste and experience as a Gourmet of Human Gore and does not pretend to be the last word upon the subject.

With that understanding, the Races of Humanity are categorized in order of Taste and Edibility (the most delicious at left; the inedible at right) in the Comprehensive Chart, above.

COMMENTARY BY ASMO DEUS

Whereas, through the Spiral of Time, Earth eventually evolves into Hell, and Humanity into the race of Demons, some Demons con-

sider it gauche to time-travel into the ancient past to eat humans, for are they not ourselves? Is it not, at best, a grotesque paradox, and at worst, cannibalistic, to eat our past selves, no matter how primitive or delicious?

Yet this specious view ignores Lord Satan's Spell Which Banishes All Time-Paradoxy, a supreme and zestful Act of Black Magic which allows us as a race to devour our past selves without any mess, fuss, contrition or indigestion.

Thus, following the Invasion, the eating of Humanity by their future selves is absolutely free from the Stench of Paradox, and should be joyfully anticipated by the Hungry Hordes of Demon Insurgents. See *Livestock; Time.*

9.
ON THE TABOO OF EARTH-DENSITY

Eons ago, Demons were forbidden by Myself to time-travel to the Sickening Sphere of Earth-Density. After Abra Kadab's clumsy poisoning of Earth, it was feared that the tainted human livestock might infect Demons and degenerate the City of Hell with disease. But Demons, as is their wont, could not resist time-traveling to Earth now and then for a quick meal or to playfully manipulate and humiliate the human dullards for their amusement and recreation.

Unfortunately, word of mouth among Demons, describing the unique flavor of human flesh, as well as their rank stupidity, caused more and more Demons to secretly travel there. In time, Demons were not only openly disregarding the Taboo, but reveling in it, stowing away on Garbage Scows headed for Earth.

Of course, whenever I discovered Demons breaking the Taboo, I tortured them. However, ironically, Demons enjoy torture. Thus, more and more Demons began breaking the taboo for the additional thrill of being caught and tortured. Finally, being at a loss as to how to enforce the Ban, and seeing that no infections nor serious time paradoxes had resulted in Hell as a result of contact with humans, I invoked the Spell Banishing all time-paradox, and lifted the Taboo.

Presently, 23% of all beings on Earth are various Demons disguised as humans. Thus, on the Eve of the Invasion of Earth, this Noxious Density has been sufficiently prepared for a mass takeover by my troops, who will either annihilate or possess all human bodies before the next Conclave of Horus.

Lord Satan's Spell
Banishing Time Paradoxy

10.
MORE ON TIME AND THE BANISHMENT OF PARADOX

As twaddle-headed gnats, human beings are ignorant of Time. They are unaware that Time is a physical medium as tangible as their thick skulls, and as sinewy as the material universe, and oriented at right angles to it. Time-Space, of course, is the conjoint medium at right angles to the Physical World through which Hellcraft travel.

Time-travel is inconceivable to humans because the linearity of their pipeline thought cannot grasp the Final Solution to Time Paradoxes. The Final Solution, of course, is inanely simple: when my Demons first began time-travel and annoying paradoxes began to crop up[7], I, as Creator and Ruler of the Hell Cosmos, cast an Omniscient Spell banishing all time-paradox from the Geometric Physics of Hell. This sometimes requires a little cleaning up here and there at various space-time nexus points[8], but it all comes out in the wash.

This Historic Spell was publicly conjured by Myself, Lord Satan, shortly after I allowed Demonkind access to the Infinite Freeways of Time, making spatial travel, in effect, obsolete. This Spell made each Time-Density autonomous to all save its own Ineluctable Present, canceling out all paradox and minimizing the bleed-through of parallel events from one density to another.

The Shimmering Central Black Orb of Hell, of course, exists in the same space as the planet Earth, *but in Earth's distant future;* thus time-travel to Earth involves cutting an arc into Hell's distant past.[9] Humans are of course ignorant of the fact that Earth's destiny is to evolve into the Orb of Hell, and that all humans must one day evolve into the Spiritually Perfect Beings they call Demons.[10] The stupidity of humans is so monumental, they are not only unaware of the existence of the Orb of Hell, but also Hell City, which occupies the same space as Earth's own Ancient City of Excess, known as Las Vegas.[11]

Lord Satan Enacting Paradox Banishment.

---

7   NOTE BY ASMO DEUS: When Demons first built Hellcraft under Lord Satan's direction and began to arc through Time-Space, the first paradox to be encountered involved Demons traveling into the distant Past to eat their own ancestors (before their evolution into immortal Demonhood), since one's own flesh is, of course, by definition more succulent and delicious than that of a stranger. Of course, eating one's ancestors meant that the Demon devouring them would not come into existence. As explained above, this paradox posed a serious problem in the early days of time-travel, resulting in the Banishing of Paradox from the Mathematics of Time.

8   ED. NOTE: See Zyk's *Fourth Letter to the Publisher* for a visceral example of a temporal cleanup after the assassination of the human known as "JFK."

9   NOTE BY GOD, LORD OF THE PERSONIFIED UNIVERSE: Remember, My Angels, that it is not Satan's fault that his visualization of space-time evolution is precisely reversed. It is My fault, since I created him with the inability to know the true future. The truth, of course, is that *the Central Orb of Hell is actually the selfsame Planet Earth in its Distant Past, not its Distant Future.*

Why did I create Satan with this absurd blind spot? Because if he were able to time-travel into the *real* future, he would then discover the existence of Heaven before he was ready. And it is crucial to My Plan that Satan *feel* the existence of Heaven first, not simply discover it. This intuition on Satan's part would only happen when his single heart atom began to throb, resonate and grow as a result of studying the strange paradoxes of Human Existence.

Know, My Angels, that although Existence is often ridiculously confusing, I actually *have* a Divine Plan. As for what that Plan is, that's for Me to know and for You to find out.

10   ED. NOTE: See *Cosmology of Hell.*

11   NOTE BY GOD, LORD OF THE PERSONIFIED UNIVERSE: Again, My Angelic Readers, Lord Satan knows not that the City of Hell must first evolve into Las Vegas, and later into the City of Heaven, all three cities occupying, respectively, the same location on Earth's surface in its past, present and future.

ENCYCLOPÆDIA
OF
HELL

AN
INVASION MANUAL
OF EARTH

BOOK II

INCLUDING
MANUAL OF
EARTH TERMS
AND
HISTORICAL
DOCUMENTS
FROM
LORD SATAN'S
ARCHIVES

QUADRIFIDUM
THE
FIRST

ZYK'S FIRST MEMO
TO THE
PUBLISHER

CONCERNING HIS RESEARCH
ON
EARTH

MEMO TO
MORTIMER PÖNÇÉ, ESQ.
PUBLISHER, MIND CONTROL PRESS
HELL HOLE WEST
CITY OF HELL

FROM
ZYK OF ASIMOTH, EDITOR
INVASION MANUAL COMMISSION
DISPATCHED FROM EARTH
KRAKOW, POLAND
SEPTEMBER 7, 1348

Detestable Mr. Pönçé:

My arrival here at the height of the Black Death, which has consumed millions, has been delightful and piquant. The countryside is festooned with black and red corpses, forming a scenic roulette wheel of putrescence ringing the bowl of the valley.

My research here, recording the flavor of diseased flesh, is in many respects a game of chance; a pair of obese Caucasian buttocks, for example, may have a delicate afterburn, whereas, inexplicably, a pair of slim Caucasian buttocks may taste as wretched as a Roman priest's testicles.[1]

Thus my work augmenting Lord Satan's Manual is more time-consuming than I had expected. More on that after I have addressed the droll pleasantries of your correspondence. In answer to your query, no, I have not yet eaten a Human Female, but many thanks for the recipe for sautéed uterus.

---

1 ED. NOTE: See *Plague*.

I also thank you for your warning about the ancient Demon Abra Kadab[2]. Lord Satan neglected to mention that Kadab still inhabited the planet's core and claimed Earth as his personal property.

After I landed my Hellcraft on the cliffs of the Red Sea, Kadab dramatically appeared, soaring over the water, his vast wings glowing with a thousand mystic letters, and landing before me as I disembarked from my ship.

Abra Kadab Soared Over the Water, His Wings Unfurled with Myriad Mystic Alphabetical Spells

Although three times my size and covered with thousands of blinking silver eyes, Kadab is of the Old School of Evil and ignorant of the modern scientific advances in Black Magic. He widened his bank of eyes at me and thrust a telepathic spike into my head which bespoke his pointed fury: I had, in his jejune opinion, illegally trespassed on his planet. He then conjured a vast, gleaming saber into his claws and slashed at me, roaring that all trespassers must die.

I certainly did not take seriously the threat of this huge, doddering primitive. Ducking the *shweesh* of his saber, which severed the air molecules above me, I instantly sucked the energy from the disemboweled molecules and blasted a charge of blackness at him, transporting him to the North Pole and freezing him in the center of a glacier. He was gone, but the air still stank of his aura. He is senile, but dangerous. After Lord Satan's Attorneys stripped Kadab of his legal rights to the Earth, the old fool yearned for revenge. I shall be on guard.

2　ED. NOTE: As the Demon who in ancient times homesteaded and claimed Earth as his personal property, *Abra Kadab* (q.v.) figures prominently in my memos to Mr. Pönçé.

I am presently disguised in human flesh as a "French piano player" and rooming in what is called a "whorehouse," an establishment wherein male humans, in a brief respite from the viral terror closing in on them, pay to rub and slap their sex flaps and nodules against those of tumescent females (i.e., "whores") for the purpose of spewing biological effluents into each other's orifices. In exchange for my room, I enact my piano player duties: I conjure my fingers to pound mathematical patterns (in a mincing style deemed "French") on the piano teeth to disguise the constant, crapulous sounds of copulation.

You are correct concerning the quaint stench of this planet. From Lord Satan's entry on the histories of Earth-Density[3], the Demon Kadab apparently caused this noxious odor to ward off trespassers. With the invasion imminent, I would advise you to buy Odin Bros. Noseplugs, Ltd. before the stock splits.

Allow me to address the point of this correspondence. This morning, I received Word by Sonic Ambiance that Lord Satan has pushed the Invasion date forward one month. Consider that His Majesty ordered me to finish my research before the invasion date. The problem is, I cannot possibly finish my research in so short a time. Aside from researching how to cook humans with the Plague, I came to Krakow to research other vile subject matter dealing with this time period; thus far, I have only completed research on ABORTION, ADULTERY, ALCOHOL and ACCORDION.

I emailed Lord Satan, explaining the situation. He responded that if I do not complete my work before Black Tuesday, he will begin obliterating one member of my Commission for every day that we are behind schedule. (A facsimile of His Reply, known as *The Obliteration Memorandum*, and written in High Demonic, is reproduced below for historical interest:)

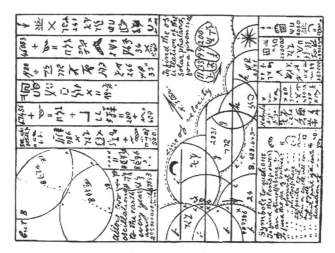

The Obliteration Memorandum by Lord Satan

If you and I miss the publication date, we too shall be subsumed. His Majesty's reasoning is that Fear of Obliteration will make us work faster. Perhaps he is right, but since the amount of research is overwhelming, I would prefer that my Commission be killed *after* their work is completed, not before.

Let me be frank. I know that you, Mr. Pönçé, are in Lord Satan's Cigar Club. I beg you to intercede on my part. Tactfully explain to His Majesty that I need more time. This I ask, Mr. Pönçé, for both of our sakes.

My problem is this planet. In addition to the planetary stench, and my eczema and chilblains acting up, something unexpected has occurred:

One week ago I took your advice to seek out a human female to eat. As I played piano, I tried to determine which of the various females would taste best as they traipsed through the parlor in between fornications. As I had just settled on a large yellow-haired specimen with disproportionately large mammary glands, a strange, faint vibration penetrated my aura. It was the sound of a human female whispering or whimpering a spiritual entreaty. I homed in on the sound, conjured my human form to continue playing the piano, and divested myself of the body to investigate.

Out of body, I followed the sound to the front door. Outside, I discovered the source of the whimpering: a human female was kneeling on the front steps of the whorehouse. She was dressed in black raiment of the clergy with a white band strapped around her third eye. Her hands were clasped together, her knuckles white, her eyes clamped shut, her features trembling and supine.

Fate had brought me a nun to devour. I instantly took her up in my invisible arms, ignoring her screams of terror, and carried her into my room.

Mr. Pönçé, I do swear that I had every intention of eating her, starting with the raw labia for which I had gathered the ingredients listed in your excellent recipe. But to my amazement, once I conjured her to stop screaming and divested her of her robes, I was unable to take my eyes off her, strangely fascinated by her physical form. Despite the fact that her interior flesh contained bulbous sacs of odious red, yellow and brown waste products, I focused on her exterior and stared at her for hours with something akin to awe and even, I was puzzled to admit to myself, delight.

As I prepared to shave her groin, per your recipe, there was something in the way she looked at me that cut me to the quick. I found myself suddenly awash with waves of revulsion and desire, and felt a creepy-crawly sensation in the scales of my undercarriage.

The revulsion was intense — but delicious. As a result, the energy of hunger was transmogrified into the energy of lust. I conjured myself visible in a shape that would be appealing to her. To my surprise, she melted into my claws with a surge of sexual desire that must have been repressed since her first stinking tumescence.

We copulated, she and I, with a gusto beyond belief. When we had finished, I shifted temporal dimensions, traveling minutes into the past repeatedly so that I was able to fornicate with her again and again, over six thousand times in the same hour.

Keep this anecdote to yourself. I share it with you to make you understand the depths of my dilemma. Unless you intercede on my behalf, Mr. Pönçé, I will never finish and we shall both, at best, be de-balled and gutted.

Yes, I know that I must get rid of the nun, and I shall do so immediately after my fascination with her wears off. But, for now, please keep me informed as to what transpires betwixt you and Lord Satan concerning this extremely urgent matter. There is a bit of tension between myself and the other members of the commission; specifically, Llu Cipher, Mephis Tophiel and Baal Zebub are furious that Lord Satan chose me over them to hold the Commission Chair. While it is true that I am a mere scholar and they are Warriors of Evil, I believe Lord Satan chose me because he did not, in fact, trust them. They are a murderous group and I must watch my back. I shall write you from my next research assignment, approximately six hundred years hence.

With deepest wishes for an Indecorous Evening
Rife with Hideous Nightmare, I remain,

Most hatefully yours,
ZYK

P.S. Send me another copy of Our Lord's Encyclopædia *immediately so that my mission may not be delayed. I stupidly dropped my copy in the Mideast in the Earth year 18 A.D. I determined that the book landed in a construction site in Jerusalem and was stolen by a worker named Jesus Josephson. Hopefully his possession of the first draft of the Manual will not affect Earth's evolution.*[4]

~~~~~~

4   ED. NOTE: Unfortunately, Jesus Josephson was inspired by Satan's Evil Parables, eventually plagiarized them as his own and created a perverse inversion of Satan's teachings, which were originally intended as sarcasm. Jesus' followers multiplied accordingly and carried out mass killings in his name. So it was not all bad. See *Stupidity* and *Zyk's Last Memo to the Publisher.*

th

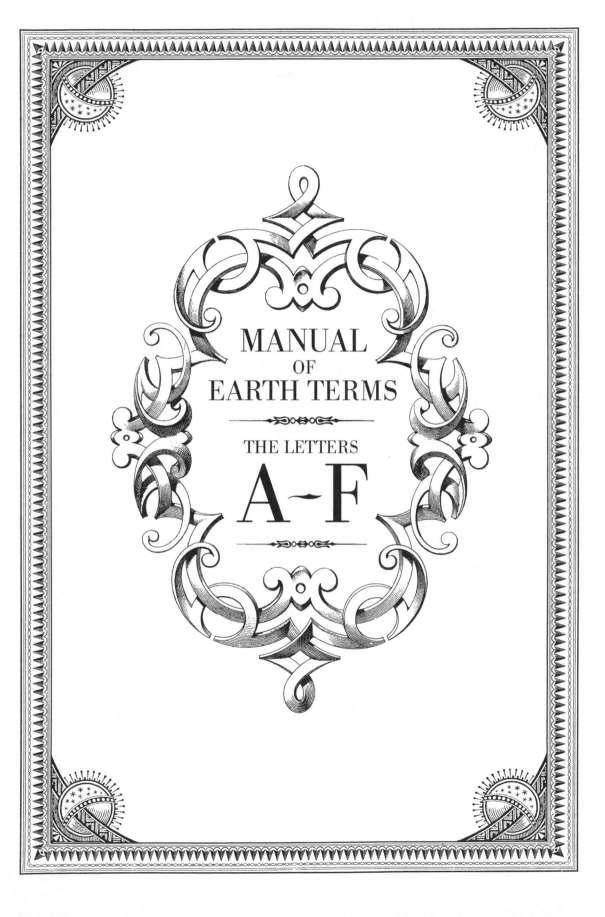

MANUAL
OF
EARTH TERMS

THE LETTERS
A–F

a, A (v) n. I command that all Demons loathe the humans' premiere letter, the despicable mammary from which oozes the pap of human writing. See *Literature*.

ABANDONMENT (ə bæn dən mənt) n. The recurring, whining complaint of humans to their Mythic *God* (q.v.).

> **COMMENTARY BY ASMO DEUS**
>
> Since deaths resulting from the abandonment of children is legal homicide, the attorneys of Hell extrapolate a class action suit[1] leveled by Mankind against their Mythic Redeemer, the charge being the brutal and premeditated mass abandonment and the resulting mass murder of trillions of pathetic humans since their unasked-for creation.

ABBREVIATION (ə brē vē ā shən) n. The convenient distilling of concepts down to simplistic scratchings on paper. *Language* is the fundamental form of human abbreviation. The inability of most humans to think symbolically (see *Fundamentalism*) is assisted by language in blocking humans from intercourse with wisdom.

[1] **ED. NOTE:** In court records, this case is designated *Humanity vs. The Creator*, City of Hell Court Docket 16-B6611-F.

ABDICATION (ăb dĭ kā shən) n. The refusal of a human to wear an absurd spiky hat to work. See *King; Queen.*

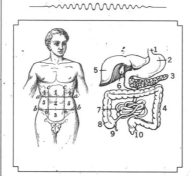

Areas to Gut and Disgorge
Note: Excellent Stuffed in a Sub Sandwich

ABDOMEN (ăb də mən) n. The pocket of human organs deemed the most disgusting by humans, yet the most delicious by Demons. See *Guts; Intestine.*

ABDUCTION (ăb dŭk shən) n. The opposite of *abandonment*, and the only other crime (with *Abandonment*, q.v.) of which Mankind accuses God. See *Kidnapper.*

> **COMMENTARY BY ASMO DEUS**
>
> Referring to an incarnation of Mankind eons ago, the Attorneys of Hell tell of an ancient lawsuit between primitive Man and their mythic God. The human plaintiffs argued that their human form was without their consent shaped from essences and energies abducted from the primal stuff of the Cosmos. In their deposition, the human plaintiffs argued that previous to their abduction and being forced to incarnate, they experienced the bliss of existing as etheric plasma; further, that they were reshaped without permission into the most humiliating life-form in the Cosmos — *Humanity*.
>
> Unfortunately, this ancient human case was dismissed when, after

attempting to select a jury of their mythic God's peers, it was found that their God had no peer. The Attorneys of Hell, on behalf of Lord Satan, appealed this decision.

Friend of the fetus

ABORTION (ə bôr shən) n. The killing of a fetus with a vacuum cleaner.[2]

> **COMMENTARY BY ASMO DEUS**
>
> While the killing of any human at any stage of development is to be encouraged, it is interesting to note that confused and mincing Humanity alternately whines or gloats that the killing of a fetus with a vacuum cleaner is *murder* (q.v.) and that the killing of an enemy fetus with a bomb is *patriotism.* (q.v.)

ABRA KADAB (ă brə kə dăb) n. The infamous pioneer Demon who first explored, mapped and shaped the strange human-infested environs of Earth-Density. A flying, shape-changing Demon versed in Ancient Black Magic, Kadab genetically engineered primitive humankind, devising an ingenious tech-

[2] **NOTE BY BAAL ZEBUB:** Notably, Earth's political movement to make abortions readily available to females has been secretly financed by leading vacuum cleaner companies.

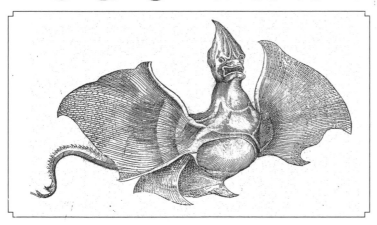

Abra Kadab: The Despised Demon of Earth

Actors Simulating Human Existence

nique to make the noxious human race edible. See *Earth; Humanity.*

Kadab was known for popping a human into his mouth at sub-quantum speed, then telling the dullard human spectators that the victim "magically" disappeared. *Abra Kadabra.*

In ancient times, Kadab hollowed out the Earth's center and homesteaded there for eons, keeping a journal on the stalking and eating of humans throughout history, now reputedly in the possession of a puerile human organization known as the *Spiritual Security Agency* (q.v.). Kadab, inventor of the *Umbrella* and conjurer of the legendary *Wheel of Kadab* (q.v.), spends winters in an underwater Palace in an area known as the *Bermuda Triangle* (q.v.). Abra Kadab's monographs on Mankind include *Techniques of Stalking and Eating Humans; The Negro Groin — Scrotum Surprise Feeds Eight; Methods of Canning Human Pus;* and *Dicing and Slicing Orphaned Children.*

See *Earth; Photosynthesis; Spiritual Security Agency; Wheel of Kadab.*

ACADEMY (ə kǎ də mē) n. Institution in which wealthy human children spend four years learning the cycle of engorging themselves on alcohol and vomiting in toilets.

Hideous Vibration Weapon

ACCORDION (ə kôr dē ən) n. Alpine torture device.[3]

ACNE (ǎk nē) n. When devouring the human face, a delightful natural spice.

ACRE (ā kər) n. That which supplies a mass grave.

3 NOTE BY MEPHIS TOPHIEL: The accordion (along with the *bagpipe* [q.v.]) was invented by Demons and introduced into Earth-Density to torture Mankind in an attempt to drive them mad. Unexpectedly, the idiot humans were more adaptable than had been previously imagined possible; for not only did they grow to enjoy the caustic wheedling and screeching of these torture devices, but they even organized and promoted Festivals of Masochism called "Folk Festivals."

ACTOR (ǎk tər) n. 1. A human pretending to be real. 2. That which transforms reality into a sitcom.

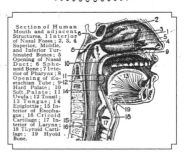

17, 18: Larynx Polyp Makes Crunchy Snack

ADAM'S APPLE (ǎ dəmz ǎ pəl) n. Polyp of meat located over the larynx of the human male, selectively evolved by Demonic Human Breeders to be breaded and fried as a crunchy party hors d'oeuvre.

ADDRESS (ǎ drěs) n. Logistical reference which humans require for the efficient delivery of pornography.

ADULT (ǎ dŭlt) n. A human ripe to commit atrocities and pay taxes.

ADVERTISING (ăd vər tī zǐng) n. The seductive lie that dull, neutral chemicals possess intense sex appeal. See *Hypnotism; Glamor.*

COMMENTARY BY AHRIMAN

The most highly extolled product of modern human technological civilization is *Coca-Cola,* a liquid mixture of sugar, artificial coloring and carbonated water. The advertising of this valueless product has successfully imprinted its symbology on human brains as divine, orgasmic and the stuff of life itself. As a result, this murky, tawdry, artificial fluid is revered by human dunces as a Divine Tonic of the Gods.

AERONAUTICS (âr ə nô tǐks) n. The science of crashing planes.

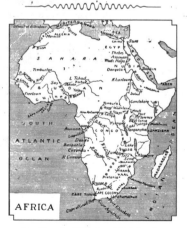

Continent of Gunless Bird-brains

AFRICA (ă frǐ kə) n. Continent infested with warring tribes of black-skinned bird-brains. Admirably, however, tribal chieftains on Africa's *Gold Coast* (q.v.) supplied white-skinned slave traders with thousands of African women and children in exchange for gold, candy and spats.

COMMENTARY BY AHRIMAN

When hunting humans, Africa is recommended for its supply of large, succulent Negro buttocks and phalluses which, when boiled in Caucasian blood, create a novel flavor prized by the Tastebuds of Hell.

Note, however, that regardless of the intensity of Hunger, Demons should refrain from boiling black flesh in the blood of South African Caucasians. Although rich in chemical toxins, the blood of this inbred tribe has an acrid metallic taste as a result of constantly fondling bars of gold.

AGE (āj) n. That which may be determined by severing a human's neck and counting the epidermal rings. See *Old Age.*

AGNOSTICISM (ăg nŏ stǐ sǐ zəm) n. The faculty by which humans intuit that I, Satan, rule the Cosmos. This intuition in humans is tempered by creeping doubts which occur when that rare Good Thing happens to them. See *Philosophy.*

Agreement: The Smiles of Deceit

AGREEMENT (ə grē mənt) n. An accord reached when humans believe they have successfully cheated each other. See *Contract; Handshake.*

AGRICULTURE (ă grǐ kŭl chər) n. The human science of evenly dispersing DDT into the water table.

AIR (ĕr) n. 1. Diffused human flatulence. 2. Hated gas which Mankind dedicates its technology to eradicate.

Device for Crushing Humans

AIRPLANE (ĕr plān) n. That which, on a good day, crushes humans against a mountain.[4]

ALCHEMY (ăl kə mē) n. The process of transmuting one illusory form into another.

COMMENTARY BY ASMO DEUS

Although All Things Evil arise from Lord Satan's consciousness, the concept of Alchemy exists as a Perceptual Illusion. So too in the Human World. The science of Alchemy in the disgusting human

---

4 NOTE BY AHRIMAN: Upon observing an airplane about to crush its passengers against a mountain range, the Invading Demon is encouraged to Possess one of the human passengers in order to experience the delightful vivacity of mindless human terror.*

* **NOTE BY BELIAL:** As might be expected of One who is blind to practicality, Ahriman neglected to warn of a disgusting physical side effect of human terror; for in this instance, the Demon possessing a human body should be prepared for the gauche spewing of effluents from the absurd human bowels and bladder.

body constitutes the transmuting of sweet-smelling foodstuffs into ghastly-smelling excretions. Humans also transmute food into the energy used to create and maintain thought, and thus Mankind is the ungainly, if not repulsive, meat machine for alchemically transmuting the immaterial from the material. See *Elimination*.

COMMENTARY BY ZYK

Regarding the alchemical transubstantiation of All and Nothing and the equality of form versus form in the World of Humans, I offer the following crapulous elegy:

Like swan and cygnet,
   spark and sun
Man and infant are but one
Like brain to body, blood to heart
Man and seed are but a part
As Earth is dirt and flower is germ
So all is atoms and man is worm
As steam to ice and bread to crust
So truth to man and man to dust
As all and nothing form
   a circle vicious
Man's flesh is all and nothing
   but delicious

Humans Celebrating Brain Cell Death

ALCOHOL (ăl kə hôl) n. A hallucinatory escape hatch through which a human escapes from the Unspeakable Prison of Himself. See *Liquor*.

The Only Escape for Humans

COMMENTARY BY LILITH

Alcohol has supreme value to Mankind. Killing brain cells and deadening their tiny intellects, it allows humans to forget that they are absurd, half-conscious specks flitting for an instant betwixt a grotesque birth and deathbed putrefaction. See *Brewery*.

ALCOHOLIC (ăl kə hôl ĭk) n. See *Newspaperman*.

ALCOHOLISM (ăl kə hôl ĭzm) n. See *Journalism*.

ALE (āl) n. Beverage used by human athletes in the Sport of Wife-Beating.

ALIMONY (ăl ĭ mō nē) n. A fee generally paid by a male human for the right to spew sexual fluids upon anyone save his wife. See *Divorce*.

ALLEGORY (ăl ə gô rē) n. An extended metaphor. For example, a tale of a flesh-eating bacterium slowly eating its way across the human body is an allegory for Mankind's diseased civilization slowly eating its way across the Earth.

ALL FOOLS DAY (ăl fūlz dā) n. A human holiday which is named after the only human truth.

Homeland of the Caucasian Usurpers

AMERICA (ə mĕr ĭ kə) n. A cult of Caucasian invaders who usurped vast tracts of North America for the purpose of transforming all of its natural artifacts into swill. To their further credit, the American *morons* (q.v.) displayed a unique sense of humor by addicting the conquered natives to alcohol before imprisoning them in scenic death camps: Indian Reservations.

COMMENTARY BY AHRIMAN

This fascinating, ruthless cult first gained prominence on Earth by introducing an amazingly addictive drug called *nicotine* to Europe. The profits from this addictive drug enabled the American invaders to finance their own nation on the vast tracts of stolen land.

When enterprising humans in *Great Britain* (q.v.) saw the money-making potential in mass nicotine addiction, they attempted to steal

America's profits by a form of legal thievery known as *taxation* (q.v.). The American Cult refused to comply, and proceeded to kill Englishmen until England agreed to leave them alone.

In order to increase the profits from nicotine addiction, the American Cult sent ships to *Africa* (q.v.), where the inhabitants did not own guns. There the Americans, who had plenty of guns, negotiated the purchase of eight million gunless humans and brought them back to the stolen tracts of land. The purchased humans were then used as flesh robots to plant and harvest the nicotine-bearing plants. These gunless flesh robots slept in prison camps (see *Shanty Town; Ghetto*) where they whimpered repetitive, obnoxious songs to their Mythic Creator.

The Cult of America is now owned and operated by seven hundred and seventy-seven Demons now operating undercover in Earth-Density in the fields of banking, oil, drugs and advertising. As the Advance Guard for the Invasion, they have been ordered by our Lord to prepare all humans for their Role as Citizen Slaves, commonly referred to as *Consumers*. This is being brilliantly accomplished by maneuvering television, film and sports as narcotics to supplant reading and independent thought, while addicting the humans to drugs, machine-controlled physical exercise and religious dogma. The consumer-slaves are now being brainwashed into indentured service through Demon-operated Credit Card Schemes. Soon to be cooked as foodstuffs for You, My Demon Insurgents, humans are presently imprisoned in large low-security prison camps. See *Cities*.

AMERICAN INDIANS

(ə mĕr ĭ kən ĭn dē ənz) n. Race of red-skinned, tribal blockheads who, ignorant of how to engineer something as simple as a house, lived in tents and thus were easily conquered by wily hordes of Caucasians. The surviving red-skins even-

Traditional Indian Dance Celebrating Casino Opening

tually learned engineering from the Caucasians, and proceeded to pave over their sacred burial grounds and erect gambling casinos. See *Alcoholism; On Eating Humans*.

AMPUTATION

(ăm pyū tā shən) n. A violent act of fetishism, akin to the *tattoo* (q.v.), by which a human subconsciously creates accidents or diseases resulting in stubs which are displayed as a pathetic signet of individuality.

AMNESIA

(ăm nē zhə) n. Mental aberration in which a human gnat does not know what it is nor where it came from. In short, amnesia is an exact analogy to human existence itself. See *Make-believe*.

ANALYSIS

(ən ăl ə sĭs) n. The hilarious attempt by Humanity to process Reality via their Organ of Stupidity. See *Brain*.

COMMENTARY BY ASMO DEUS

In "analyzing" phenomena, humans merely gurgle linear permutations of vague, inadequate symbols, hypnotizing themselves into thinking that the symbols *are* the phenomena. See *Mathematics*.

ANATOMY

(ən ă tə mē) n. An effete-sounding word used to camouflage the horror and disgust with which humans view their own gore. In short, a comforting nickname for their own mysterious, terrifying[5] interiors. Unlike Daemonic Anatomy with a single sleek tube from mouth to anus, human anatomy is an absurd jumble of preposterous organs squashed willy-nilly into the human hide. See *Part One: On the Grotesque Human Body*.

ANARCHY

(ăn är kē) n. 1. Political theory which asserts the obvious, that Humanity is incapable of organizing its existence, and asks "Why bother?" 2. The belief that human chaos is more fundamental than human order.

ANNIHILATION

(ən nī əl ā shən) n. See *Vaporization*.

ANTHEM, NATIONAL

(ăn thəm) n. An insipid, contentless piece of Muzak used to inspire and hypnotize humans into pledging sentimental allegiance to the mother group and kill on command its designated enemies.

ANTI-CHRIST

(ăn tē krīst) n. The mythic Messiah's Evil Twin, as promulgated in the puerile annals of Earth mythos. Also known as Anti-Buddha, Anti-Allah, Anti-Mohammed and Santa, the Anti-Christ is noted for achievements such as crib death, colon cancer, brain tumors and alternative comedy. In addition, he is known as mentor to arms merchants, mass murderers, advertising executives, art critics and music video directors. See *Television*.

5 **NOTE BY BEHEMOTH:** Deliciously so.

Antichrist Displaying Hell's Soul-Destroying Weapon

Aristotle: Enumerating & Systematizing Imbecile

less than specks, as they dream of becoming the illusory gods which they hatefully adore.

ANTI-EVIL (ăn tī ē vəl) n.
See *Good.*

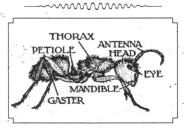

THORAX
PETIOLE · ANTENNA
HEAD
EYE
MANDIBLE
GASTER

The Heirs of Earth

ANTS (ăntz) n. The original owners and, after the humans complete their self-extinction program now in progress, ultimate inheritors of the Earth. See *Insects.*

| COMMENTARY BY AHRIMAN |

Ants are group-mind matrices in small corpuscular form, enacting a micro-analogy of human group-mind seek/find/build/destroy activity in human ant colonies known as *cities* (q.v.). Ants are referred to as "pests" by humans, whose bizarre, narrow thought lattices do not perceive that the blind format-following of ants' movements precisely reflect their own.

APOCRYPHA (ə pä krə fə) n. A section of *Scripture* (q.v.) deemed false because it contradicts official doctrine and causes humans to question authority. Feared by all political, social and financial structures, apocryphal information causes the human drones to veer from the norm and to speed up evolution, which is the greatest threat to centralized power.

AQUARIUM, PUBLIC
(ə kwâr ē əm) n. Locale in which humans enslave and torture marine animals for the purpose of selling corn dogs, T-shirts and key chains.

ARISTOTLE (âr ĭs tät əl) n. A moron known as a *philosopher* (q.v.) who is the masculine counterpart of *Plato* (q.v.). Aristotle schizophrenically maintained that the material world was supreme, and yet that somehow gods created it. His attempt to enumerate, identify and categorize every aspect of human existence is a touching tribute to Mankind's delusion of controlling a cosmos within which they are

Archaeologist With Grave-Robbing Cart

ARCHAEOLOGIST (är kē ôl ə jĭst) n. A graverobber who smokes a pipe.

| COMMENTARY BY BELIAL |

Since Earth is a dumping ground for Hell's Garbage, archaeologists mistake Hell's worthless refuse for sacred Earth artifacts. Stonehenge, for example, is considered a sacred monument, whereas it was merely bumper slabs in an East Hell Parking Lot.

ARGENTINA (är jən tē nə) n. Scenic retirement oasis for *Nazis* (q.v.).

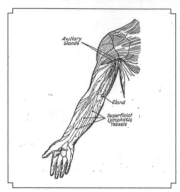

Dipping Appendage

ARM (ärm) n. Part of the human anatomy which, when boiling a human in oil as a snack, may be used as a dipping handle.

ARMS DEALER (ärmz dē lər) n. See *Weapons Manufacturer*.

ARSON (är sən) n. See *Orphanage*.

ART (ärt) n. Archetypal mirrors monotonously reflecting the paucity of human thought patterns.

Art Critic Defining Aesthetic Taste for Buffoon

ART CRITIC (ärt krĭ tĭk) n. 1. A human fop who convincingly props himself up as a supreme arbiter of aesthetic taste. 2. A rare human welcomed at the Gates of Hell.

COMMENTARY BY AHRIMAN

The reason for the art critic's success on Earth is because the mass of spineless humans have been conditioned to believe that they are unable to determine for themselves what they like and do not like. Thus an art critic is analogous to a fascist dictator who, through flashy, shallow rhetoric, proclaims which works shall live and which shall die.

ART GALLERY (ärt găl ər ē) n. A plush environment in which humans honor the art of forgery.

ASSHOLOSCOPE (ăs hō lō skōp) n. A useful Demonic device for locating a human attorney, art critic, stage magician or professional psychic.

ASS-KISSER (ăs kĭs ər) n. The traditional role of Man in the Man-God relationship.

Astronaut Engaged in Excreting in Spacesuit

ASTRONAUT (ăs trə nät) n. That which ejects urine and shit into space. See *Space Program; Space debris*.

ATHEISM (ā thē ĭz əm) n. 1. A bizarre human doctrine which states that the Cosmos is dead, absurdly ignoring the fact that the atheist himself is part of the Cosmos, and that if a part of a whole is alive, the whole, obviously, is not dead. 2. Yet another paltry, orthodox religion which worships either "God" or Satan under the nickname "Nothingness."

COMMENTARY BY ZYK

In sonnet form, I herein explore this gauche doctrine which absurdly and arrogantly denies the Reality of the Executives of Hell:

Atheistic humans are brindled machinations,
Cranked by clocks, along their course careening,
Hypnotized by nothingness' concatenations,
Terrified to face the mystery of their meaning.
Atheistic brains with bloody cogs enmeshed,
Denying their souls' reality and asserting wheels
As the only inhabitants of their flesh,
Denying that Reality all conceals and reveals.
And when Mankind winds down as a mechanism
Extinguishing Itself in whispered pause,
When the last spider weaves its final prism,
And peeps at the world's end through crystal gauze,
Then the last insipid atheist, bursting from his womb of gore,
May suck the Teat of Nothingness, and gurgle:
I am machine no more.

ATOM (ă təm) n. The name given to the mythological Original Microcosm, also known as Adam. Since humans have no working knowledge of the relativity of size and scale, the name was later cor-

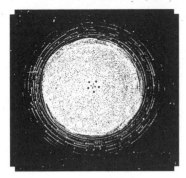

*Deadly Nuclear Midget
Which Mocks Mankind*

Automobile: Poison-Ingesting and -Excreting Marvel

rupted to denote their comically primitive idealization of the smallest indivisible particle of matter.

COMMENTARY BY ASMO DEUS

Earth's moronic scientists cower in terror at the concept that there *is* no smallest indivisible particle of matter, only smaller and smaller "matterless" shapes. The continued division of the atom thus becomes the threshold to the pure energy of archetypal shapes in Lord Satan's Omniscient Mind.[6]

An atom appears to humans as one of Lord Satan's archetypal forms: a sphere surrounded by orbiting satellites. In the humans' plodding time frame, these whizzing satellites appear as blurry "shells," each seemingly coalesced at a different energy state around the sphere. The direct mirroring of this pattern by the temporally slower movement of suns and planets is understandably terrifying to moronic human scientists, since a suggestion that planets represent different energy states suggests a numerological, or symbolic, interpreta-

6 NOTE BY LORD SATAN: A recursive epiphenomenon of my Mental Energy is experienced when humans fiddle together gauche bombs designed to cut an atom in twain. Huge beautiful explosions of Pure Evil result, radiating the unspeakably deadly Poison of My Primal Thought. These primitive but entertaining Evil Thought Bombs are the latest refreshments the humans serve themselves in their thirst for self-extermination.

tion of matter. This, of course, is the essence of Demonic Physics, and considered by the human morons as *Superstition* (q.v.).

The inner and outer mirroring of the atomic, molecular, solar systemic and galactic structures suggests a hypothesis also horrific to human idiots, that all matter is analogous to an illusory, self-replicating and self-extrapolating mental pattern within one Vast Holographic Mind.[7]

ATTORNEY (ə tûr nē) n. See *Assholoscope*; *Lawyer*.

ATTRACTION (ə trăk shən) n. In human physics, the coming together of a low-energy state with a high-energy state; for example, the attraction between a flaccid billionaire and a flashy whore.

COMMENTARY BY LLU CIPHER

In the clunky Material Creation inhabited by Humanity, *Attraction* (and its twin brother *Repulsion*) is the one and only game in town. It manifests as the desire in humans to interpenetrate, to become more than

7 NOTE BY LORD SATAN: Such a Being, of course, is Inconceivable and therefore Non-existent in Its Inconceivability.*

* NOTE BY GOD, LORD OF THE PERSONIFIED UNIVERSE: Such a Being, of course, is Myself.

their puny individual existences by pulling others and other things into the self.

AUTOMOBILE (ô tə mō bēl) n. A loud, hilariously primitive machine, marketed with shiny paint, which eats poison in one form and excretes it in another. (Despite this, I, Satan, enjoy racing a Standard-Triumph TR3 in the annual Hellcraft 6000.) See *Gasoline*; *Highway*.

AVATAR (ă və tär) n. A group-mind entity who peeps through human flesh. More often than not, however, an avatar is a charismatic scoundrel who learned at an early age how to control his parents by the vicissitudes of his potty training, and has continued in adulthood by shitting on human toilets known as believers.

COMMENTARY BY LLU CIPHER

The Mythic *Avatar*, or *monad*, is the combined mind of all human idiots. The Avatar, sometimes formed as a democratic organization, comprises an entity of actual (although small) intelligence, although its separate parts are composed of tiny, insecure human cells, each trying to ameliorate their terror of death in a desperate, self-absorbed flurry of orgasms, self-hypnosis and blind groping toward the light or toward the darkness.

b, B (bē) n. The second alphabetical pictogram, which is designed to depict objects with which it begins: breasts, buttocks, balls, beaver and bum.

BABOON (bă būn) n. Contrary to the claim of anthropologists, the evolutionary future of Mankind.

Just Add Food and Suffering

BABY (bā bē) n. 1. A modest device of clay and water labeled Instant Man: Just add food and suffering. 2. A creature that slowly transforms from one who sucks into one who truly sucks. The ugly, writhing humunculus carcass which rules every human home by screech and scat, often with caesarian caesarism, in a despotic tyranny of mind-numbing screams and hypnotic splatterings of excrement. See *Infant*.

Demons invading Earth-Density will note that these urinating, excreting and vomiting machines scream in increasing terror as they gradually realize that they have been born into the world of Humanity.

BACK (băk) n. A part of human anatomy which evolved to receive the knife of a friend.

Human Bachelor

BACHELOR (bă chə lər) n. The term denoting an unmarried male human. See *Playboy*; *Prostitute*; *Sex*; *Sexism*; *Testicles*.

The term was invented by male dominators who biased the development of human language in favor of their own genitalia. Compare *bachelor*, which connotes suave independence, to its female equivalents, *old maid* and *spinster*, which connote pathetic, worthless sterility.

Sliced Pig Flesh

BACON (bā kən) n. Camouflage term to hypnotize humans into thinking that they are not slobbering over the gore of a pig. See *Ham*; *Pig*.

BACTERIA (băk tĭr ē ə) n. The humans' gelatinous little friend, the secret ruler of Earth-Density and the hungry heir to the flopping corpse of Humanity. See *Kiss*.

Jewelry Signifying Flexible Code of Bribery

BADGE (băj) n. Jewelry which indicates that either money or drugs are acceptable as bribes.

Musician Welcoming Humans at Gates of Hell

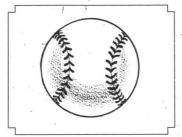

Sphere Manipulated by Overweight Athletes

Palace for Parasites

BAGPIPE (băg pīp) n. 1. Instrument played by the heralds at the Gates of Hell. 2. The most efficient tool for clearing out a party. See *Accordion*.

BAIL (bāl) n. Legal bribe paid by indicted Wall Street brokers before secretly fleeing to waterfront condos in Costa Rica.

BANK (băngk) n. 1. Institution dedicated to the science of stealing its customers' assets. 2. Institution which a human must pay to have access to his own money. See *Money*.

COMMENTARY BY BEHEMOTH

Warning: After killing a bank executive, avoid sucking his fluids within the confines of the bank vault. These vaults are used by human executives as private masturbation chambers to achieve orgasm and spew bodily fluids from the testes sac through penile discharge while staring at profits. The distinctive stench of dried banker semen has been written about by Demon Tourists, notably that it inhibits the daemonic appetite and should be avoided at all cost.

BASEBALL (bās bôl) n. A sedentary ceremony in which overweight humans wearing numbers stand motionless in a field while spectators engorge themselves on pig gore. See *Sport*, *Umpire*.

BASKETBALL (băs kĭt bôl) n. A cult in which devotees watch giants throw a sphere through a hole.

Human Bather Removing Vermin and Filth from Buttocks

BATH (băth) n. Vat of water used to temporarily remove vermin and filth from human flesh.

BAUBLES (bô bəlz) n. Signets of low self-esteem which glut the necks, fingers and wrists of humans. Also known as *jewelry* (q.v.), the more baubles peppering a human epidermis, the lower the self-esteem. See *Fashion*; *Jewelry*; *Natives*.

BEARD (bîrd) n. 1. Apartment on the human face, usually low-rent, for ticks, fleas and mites. 2. The normal covering of the male human face. Shaving the face naked, an abnormal act, is considered by humans as "normal." The normal, unshaven face is considered by humans as outlandish and inconceivable.

COMMENTARY BY LORD SATAN

Despite its wan human counterpart, My Beard is a magnificently sculpted complement to the Evil Majesty of my Most Excellent Physique, adding an artful touch of silken sinewy strength to My Ineffable Manly Beauty.

BEAUTY (byūtē) n. The perverse human adoration of sterile symmetry.

COMMENTARY BY LILITH

Although symmetry is the epitome of ugliness to all advanced creatures, this is a concept alien to Mankind. Humans, via their pinhole sensory organs, mistake symmetry as a receptacle of *beauty* in the same way that a one-eyed dog with glaucoma mistakes an unflushed toilet as a bowl of dog food.[8]

8 **NOTE BY MEPHIS TOPHIEL:** While in a typical drunken stupor, Lilith, of course, has made this mistake many times.

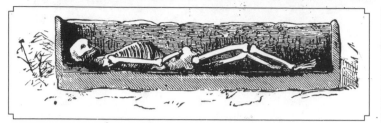

Bed: The Fruits of Faithful Rehearsal

Bible: Killing Guide For Xenophobics

BED (bĕd) n. A practice-coffin in which humans nightly rehearse their deaths. See *Casket*.

~~~~~~~~~~

BEER (bîr) n. See *Sports*.

Equatorial Refuge of Kadab

BERMUDA TRIANGLE (bər myū də trī ăng gəl) n. Equatorial area of Earth-Density and the retirement home of the legendary Demon *Abra Kadab* (q.v.), renowned for the exquisite gourmet cooking and serving of humans straying into the area to visiting Epicures of Hell.

~~~~~~~~~~

BIBLE (bī bəl) n. One of a series of books written by Lord Satan under his various pseudonyms (e.g. "God"). Each bible is utilized by humans to justify xenophobia and mass killings. See *Scripture*.

COMMENTARY BY ASMO DEUS

There are many bibles used by humans; each tribe claims its bible as the only Truth and vehemently denounces other bibles as containing fictional falsity. However, the Truth is, Lord Satan wrote all of these books, "channeling" them through egotistical human buffoons known as Prophets. A recreational hobby of Daemons has long been to insert their own amusing passages into the scriptures channeled by Lord Satan, which are elevated by human dolts in each religion to the ranks of unassailable Dogma.

For example, here are merely two of hundreds of passages which I personally interpolated into one of Lord Satan's biblical texts:

If there arise among you a prophet, or a dreamer of dreams, and he giveth thee a sign or a wonder... that dreamer of dreams shall be put to death... Thou shalt not consent unto him nor harken unto him; neither shall thy eye pity him, neither shall thou spare, neither shall thou conceal him; But thou shalt surely kill him; thine hand shall be first upon him to put him to death... and thou shalt stone him with stones, that he die...[9]

And this:

Large crowds were traveling with Jesus, and turning to them he said: "If anyone comes to me and does not hate his father and mother, his wife and children, his brothers and sisters—yes, even his own life—he cannot be my disciple."

These passages were two of my most successful practical jokes, giving human idiots Divine Justification for the Inquisition and other campaigns promoting the torture of humans in the name of their "God," and for the joining of cults and abandoning loved ones.

The fact that Lord Satan's parables inspired the teachings of Jesus Christ[10] also illustrates the role bibles and scriptures have played in the promulgation of evil on Earth. Demons with a playful spirit will enjoy searching out my more recent — and even more idiotic — interpolations to other works by Lord Satan, including world Scriptures, Constitutions and world religion blogs.

~~~~~~~~~~

BIBLE BELT (bī bəl bĕlt) p. Tightly notched strap which constricts the Flabby Pot-Belly of the Human Imagination.[11]

~~~~~~~~~~

BIGAMY (bĭg ə mē) n. A clinically demented human who desires the twaddle of more than one spouse simultaneously. See *Marriage*.

~~~~~~~~~~

9 ED. NOTE: Deuteronomy 13. The joke among Demons is that, while Lord Satan originally wrote each Scripture to subtly trick humans into Embracing Evil, the later interpolations by Demons are so unsubtle as to be utterly absurd. But it has been found that the more absurd the lie, the stronger the faith of humans in its Truth.

10 See *Stupidity* and *Zyk's Last Memo to the Publisher*.

11 NOTE BY LORD SATAN: Similarly designed straps which constrict Humanity are the Koran Belt (usually used to flay the back), the Vedic Belt (a razor strap used to shave the heads of cult slaves) and the Belt of Jack (slugged from a hidden flask by a priest between molestations).

BIRTH (bərth) n. See *Incarnation*.

BITTER (bǐ tər) adj. To hungry Demons, the Caucasian race.

Human Defiling Blackboard

BLACKBOARD (blăk bôrd) n. A rock whose blank virginity, when accosted by a human teacher with chalk, is odiously defiled. See *School*.

BLACK DEATH[12] (blăk děth) n. 1. A welcome respite from the bane of human health. 2. Nature's answer to vitamins and exercise. See *Plague*.

BLACKLISTING (blăk lǐs tǐng) n. The act of giving a child a name and a Social Security number, branding him as a card-carrying member of the Human Race.

BLASPHEMER (blăs fə mē) n. A human who contradicts idiots. See *Heresy*.

12 **ED. NOTE:** For a firsthand account of the exquisiteness of the Plague, see *Zyle's First Memo to the Publisher*.

BLOOD (blŭd) n. To Mankind, the least valuable of liquids. See *Sewer*; *Vein*.

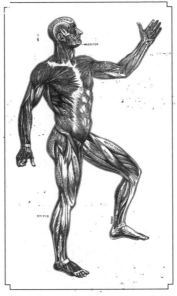
The Blood-Drenched Machine of Mankind

BODY (bŏ dē) n. The gory printout of a human's consciousness. See *Flesh*.

BODY BAG (bŏ dē băg) n. A zip-lock sandwich bag for maggots. See *War*.

BODY-SNATCHING (bŏ dē snă chǐng) n. See *Archeology*.

BOOK (buk) n. That which disturbs the quiescent beauty of human illiteracy. See *Library*; *Literature*.

BOTANY (bŏ tə nē) n. The act of insulting a plant by naming it after a human. See *Plant*.

Secret Salute of Boy Rape Cult

BOY SCOUTS OF AMERICA (boi skoutz əv əmĕr ǐ kə) n. Scheme contrived by inventive homosexuals for the mass fondling of boys in the woods. See *Homosexual*; *Rape*.

BRAILLE (brāl) n. Means by which blind humans are able to read pornography.

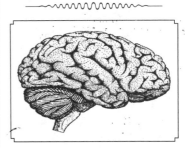
Skull Gristle Soured by Stupidity Warning: Inedible

BRAIN (brān) n. 1. The human organ allergic to intelligence. 2. With reference to an abode of awareness, a superstitious delusion of modern anatomy. 3. Bad-tasting clot which, when sucking brain fluid via a straw, must be spit out. See *Mind*.

BRAKE (brāk) n. Hated mechanical device which inhibits the splatter of human gore on roadways. See *Automobile*.

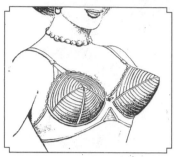

Flesh-Nodule Transforming Device

BRASSIERE (brə zĭr) n. That which attempts to transform two ventral flesh nodules of fatty tissue into exquisite orbs of desire. See *Lingerie*.

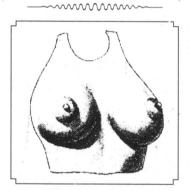

Milk-Exuding Flesh Nodules

BREASTS (brĕsts) n. Sagging nodules on the chest of the human female which exude milk and are worshipped by infantile Humanity. See *Wet Nurse*.

COMMENTARY BY BELIAL

The bizarre worshipping of human mammary glands, an activity repulsive to Demons, is one of the chief activities of Mankind. Largely male human breast-worshippers seek out films, videos and photographs of these drooping, rubbery flesh nodules in various modes of activity, excitement and repose. Entire human industries have been created based on human breast-worship, producing a plethora of breast-based products such as:

Brassiere — (See *previous*);

Breast Copulating Pictorials — which record the squeezing and chafing of the flesh sacs around the male's ridiculous erect penis;

Wet T-Shirt Contests — ritual events in which male humans spray water over a female contestant's torso-covering, in order to create an idealized outline of the oozing breast-bags.

Sacred Altar of Alcohol

BREWERY (brū ər ē) n. On Earth, as in Hell, a holy place.

BRIBERY (brī bər ē) n. An act of beauty in which a human defiles his soul for money. See *Badge*.

BRITISH EMPIRE (brĭ tĭsh ĕm pīr) n. A puny conglomerate of humans dedicated to the stealing of land and the enslavement of those with fewer weapons. See *Great Britain*.

BRONZE AGE (bränz āj) n. An era in which humans celebrated the Ability to Kill Each Other With Metal.

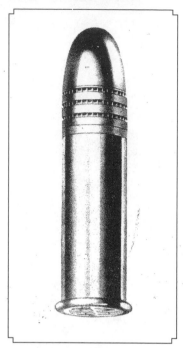

Self-Mutilation Tool

BULLET (bŭl ĭt) n. Projectiles designed by Humanity for the endless mutilation of its own group-body.[13]

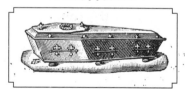

Corpse Enclosure Insuring No Intercourse With Nature

BURIAL (bĕr ē əl) n. The enclosing of a fresh human corpse in an airtight chamber. One of the chief characteristics of a human being is that the human corpse must have no intercourse with nature.

13 NOTE BY BEHEMOTH: When devouring humans in inner cities, care must be taken to first spit out bullets or broken-off syringes which may crack the Demon's fangs.

c, C (sē) n. An archetypal shape, well known to Mankind: the Cupped Hand Whining for More.

CAFFEINE (kă fēn) n. A drug that humans imbibe en masse every morning, which helps them pretend that they care about their meaningless existences.

CALIFORNIA (kăl ĭ fôr nyə) n. A place of warmth infested with humans obsessed with material self-aggrandizement, spiritual enslavement or both.

CAMPFIRE GIRLS OF AMERICA (kămp fîr gərlz əv ə měr ĭ kə) n. See *Girl Scouts of America*.

CANCER (kăn sər) n. A self-generated spice which makes human flesh delicious.[14] See *Part I, Section 8: On Eating Humans*

14 **NOTE BY ASMO DEUS: Cancer is a form of mass suicide in which humans knowingly blast themselves with radiation machines known as televisions while slurping from DDT-poisoned wells and devouring food from DDT-poisoned soil. Typically, the brainless humans are amazed at the absurdly increasing prevalence of cancer, which, circa 2000 A.D. and beyond, is as common as *Divorce* (q.v.)**

Cannibals Preparing Family Barbecue

CANNIBAL (kă nə bəl) n. An ecological engineer who recycles Humanity. See *Chain of Eating*.

CANON LAW (kă nən lô) n. Rules which allow Christian ecclesiastical authorities to elevate into Law scriptures which bring the most profit. For example, in 1878, a council of demented homosexual ecclesiastics voted that from that date onward, Jesus' mother Mary was to be called a virgin; this justified a fundamental church precept that Sex is Evil, ordering the poor to pay priests in order to be forgiven for fornication.

CAPITALISM (kă pĭ təl ĭz əm) n. A political theory in which the individual is less worthless than the group.[15]

15 **NOTE BY LORD SATAN: Capitalism is a superlative system which, like Fundamentalism, results in the destruction of democracy.**

CAPITAL PUNISHMENT (kă pĭ təl pŭn ĭsh mənt) n. Death-Lite: all the satisfaction of murder with only half the guilt.

Bespoiler of Nature

CARPENTER (kär pən tər) n. That which soils natural settings by building churches.

CARTOON (kär tūn) n. The most accurate depiction of human reality. See *Nothingness*; *Reality*; *Surrealism*.

Final Evolution of the Human Bed

CASKET (kăs kĭt) n. The exquisitely logical evolution of the human bed. See *Bed*; *Pallbearer*; *Sarcophagus*.

Witness to Multiple Head Wounds

CASH REGISTER (kăsh rĕ jĭ stər) n. That which daily witnesses a human clerk's head blown off with a shotgun.

CASINO (kə sē nō) n. Room attached to a Catholic Church. See *American Indian*; *Gambling*.

CASTRATION (kăs trā shən) n. Radical disassociation of the human male libido without psychoanalysis. See *Circumcision*; *Neuter*.

Soul Extortion Center

CATHOLIC CHURCH (kǎ thə lĭk chûrch) n. Human corporation dedicated to the marketing, exploitation and extortion of the soul. See *Pope*; *Priest*.

Caucasian: Race of Stringy, Inedible Flesh

CAUCASIAN (kǒ kā zhən) n., adj. See *Invasion Manual, Book One, Section 8: On Eating Humans*.

CELIBACY (sĕ lə bə sē) n. A tiny cage door behind which rages the monstrous organ of lust. See *Nymphomaniac*.

CEMENT (sĕ měnt) n. In Sicily, human footwear. See *Concrete*.

CEMETERY (sĕ mə tĕ rē) n. Heaven for maggots.

Insignia of Satanic Incompetents

CENTRAL INTELLIGENCE AGENCY (sĕn trəl ĭn tĕ lĭ jəns ā jən sē) n. A secret hierarchy of clodhopping knuckleheads infesting *America* (q.v.) and ineptly attempting to manage the Business Affairs of Evil through puerile and pedestrian acts of murder, drug dealing, assassination and mayhem.[16]

COMMENTARY BY AHRIMAN

By way of example, the C.I.A.'s incompetent marketing of cocaine and weapons would, in more intelligent hands, earn enough money to achieve the goal which eludes them in their incompetence: corrupting the world to the lusciousness of Evil as a gift to their Master, Lord Satan.

16 NOTE BY LORD SATAN: As admirable as their cause is to Demonkind, the puny human brains who created the C.I.A., who formerly operated under the strange name *The United Fruit Company*, are incapable of destroying, corrupting and killing to a degree which is satisfactory to the Impatient Eye of Hell.

Mankind: The Meat at the Bottom of the Eating Chain

CHAOS (kā os) n. The Physics of Nightmare, beloved of Hell.

Disgusting Cow Excretion Savored by Humans

CHEESE (chēz) n. The curdled excretions of a fly-covered cowbag.

CHILD ABUSE (chīld ə byūs) n. See *Mother*.

Icon of Child Sacrifice Program

CHAIN OF EATING (chān əv ē tǐng) n. The Cosmic Precept which mandates that Mankind was created as a central, multipurpose foodstuff at the bottom of the Eating Chain to be gutted, seasoned and devoured by Demons.

COMMENTARY BY BEHEMOTH

All editions of this book have been soaked in alchemical poisons that kill humans on contact. Please devour any poisoned human carcasses found clutching this book.

CHAIN STORES (chān stôrz) n. Places of commerce which chain human workers to minimum wage.

CHAIR (châr) n. The most unfortunate of inanimate objects, destined to kiss the human ass.

Most Unfortunate Household Object

CHILD SACRIFICE (chīld să krə fīs) n. Performed routinely by every human culture, presently under the guise of herding eighteen-year-olds and mind-controlling them to fight to the death in corporate wars. See *Soldier*.

China: Admirable for Gutting Holy Men

CHINA (chī nə) n. 1. Nation which glorifies its stupidest class, the gum-chewing factory workers who achieve their collective ideals by slaughtering holy men and perfecting nuclear arsenals. 2. Tacky one-room apartment wherein two billion roommates share the same urine-stained jumpsuit.

CHLORINE (klōr ēn) n. Contaminant used by adults to poison swimming children.

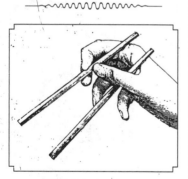
Hellish Eating Utensil

CHOPSTICKS (chŏp stĭks) n. That which pretentious Demons use to eat fried Asians.

CHRISTIANITY (krĭs chē ăn ə tē) n. Scripture cult based on the plagiarized texts of Lord Satan. See *Church*; *Crusades*; *Jesus Christ*; *Religion*.

Erection-Avoidance Bunker

CHURCH (chûrch) n. 1. Building erected by humans as a refuge from the hysteria caused by their continually erect or tumescent sexual organs. These erection-avoidance bunkers are financed by wealth hoarded from the poor. See *Vatican*; *Bible Belt*; *Devil-Worshipper*.

Fellatio Substitute for Corporate Executives

CIGAR (sĭ gär) n. 1. A stinking baby pacifier for trendy morons. 2. A handy fellatio substitute for corporate phallus-worshippers.

Convenient Cancer Dispenser

CIGARETTES (sĭ gə rĕts) n. Luscious cancer packaged in sleek rectangles.

CIRCUMCISION (sûr kəm sĭ zhən) n. Suave term humans employ to describe the ritual mutilation of male infants.

CIRCUS (sûr kəs) n. A human spectacle at which beaten animals are forced to jump through flaming hoops while alcoholics wearing giant shoes display painted smile-faces to hide their besotted misery. See *Entertainment*.

CITIZEN (sĭ tə zən) n. Fleshy dildo used by politicians to achieve anal orgasm.

CITIZENSHIP (sĭ tə zən shĭp) n. The human right to be bred, fattened and served raw at a corporate barbecue.

Vertical Slave Encampment

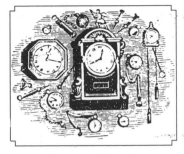

Purveyor of Paranoia

*Humans Creating
Black Stomach Linings*

CITY (sĭ tē) n. A festive, brightly lit slave camp. See *Office Building*.

COMMENTARY BY AHRIMAN

In *cities*, the prisoners' mass work detail takes place from 9 a.m. to 5 p.m. within slave compounds known as "offices"; therein hypnotic Muzak is broadcast to keep the slave-workers subdued.

After work detail, the prisoners are allowed to spend their work allowance on various forms of drugs[17] which keep their minds distracted from understanding the ineluctable depths of their enslavement. After ingesting the drugs, workers return to sleep in their cells, also known as *apartments*. See *Clock; Gum; Office Building; Work*.

CIVILIZATION (sĭ və lə zā shən) n. 1. The Fertilizer of the Future. 2. That which eats forests and excretes child pornography. See *Empire*.

CLAIRVOYANCE (klâr voi əns) n. The human ability to perceive in advance that one will assuredly fail.

CLOCK (kläk) n. 1. Tool used by Demons to hypnotize humans

into believing that their local reality is fixed, intractable and sterile. 2. Paranoia-producing device decorating walls of slave worker camps known as *office buildings* (q.v.). See *Time*.

CLOTH (kläth) n. See *Fashion*.

Alcoholic with Grease-painted Happiness

CLOWN (kloun) n. Talentless entertainer who disguises his face to both hide the wrinkles of alcoholism and facilitate anonymity while molesting children.[18] See *Circus; Harlequin*.

COFFEE (kô fē) n. When cooking a human, a layer of black scum which must be scraped off the stomach lining. See *Caffeine*.

COFFIN (kô fən) n. See *Bed; Casket; Sarcophagus*.

COLD (kōld) n. That which is found in its purest form upon dissecting an insurance executive's heart.

Human Cockfight Arena

COLISEUM (kô lə sē əm) n. Magnificent edifice built to exhibit the human analogy of a cockfight. See *Gladiator*.

COLONIZATION (kô lən i zā shən) n. The act of humans with more weapons enslaving those with fewer weapons.

COLOR (kŭ lər) n. 1. The loud necktie which the Cosmos wears with its drab suit of matter. 2. Sensory nuances in the light spectrum, useful to arms merchants in encouraging race wars.

---

17 **NOTE BY LORD SATAN:** Liquid, powdered, or electronic.

18 **NOTE BY LORD SATAN:** The *Clown* and the *Priest*, who both disseminate false happiness and molest children, are often confused by Demons visiting Earth-Density. They may be distinguished by the fact that whereas the clown only wears makeup while on duty, the priest wears it only when off-duty.

Since a Demon's sensory apparatus can only detect the primary colors Red and Black, be prepared for momentary blindness and nausea upon being exposed to Earth's chief poison, *Color*. Infiltrating Demons, therefore, may recognize each other as those wearing absurdly expensive sunglasses. See *Nature*.

Vermin Remover

COMB (kōm) n. 1. A device for removing vermin from the human head. 2. That which moves fading virility from one side of the skull to the other.

COMEDIAN (kə mē dē ən) n. A rectum with personality which excretes paradox. See *Humorist*; *Joke*.

COMEDY (kä mə dē) n. 1. The least funny human art form. 2. The design of a human being relative to the design of a real life-form. 3. That which results from an equilibrium of the influences of "God" and Satan.[19] See *Laughter*.

19 NOTE BY AHRIMAN: Since our Lord Satan's views are necessarily infallible and incontrovertible, it has been a challenge for our Satanic Commission to explicate His Majesty's few but striking references to the superstitious "Meta-Satan" called *Good* or *God*. Although Lord Satan usually refers to this imaginary concept as "Mythic God" or "Non-Existent Good," it is assumed by His Executives that bald references to these superstitious non-existents are meant as sarcastic hyperbole.*

* NOTE BY LORD SATAN: This is a Key Point, and one which reaches into the deepest, most noxious levels of the Cosmol-

COMMUNICATION (kəm yū nǐ kā shən) n. See *Language*.

COMMUNISM (käm yū nǐ zəm) n. Political theory in which the group is less worthless than the individual. See *Russia*.

Locating Area for Fresh Rapings

COMPASS (kəm pəs) n. Directional device which allows humans to sail to unsuspecting countries for the purpose of raping and pillaging. See *Map*.

COMPASSION (kəm pǎ shən) n. That which allows humans to spare the lives of half of the enemy's women and children. See *Mercy*.

COMPUTER (kəm pyū tər) n. A governmental tracking device disguised as a portal of freedom.

ogy of Hell. The Truth is, during the writing of My Survey of Humankind, I began by mocking Mankind's Pathetic Supplication to Nothingness; but eventually, after being forced by this subject matter to contemplate the concept of a Meta-Satanic, Personified Cosmos, My views have slowly shifted to one of Agnostic Revulsion. This concept of a "Meta-Satan," alien to Demon Philosophy, should be broached with care to avoid an outbreak of hives. See *Loneliness*.

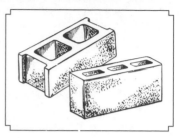

Ghostly Human Building Material

CONCRETE (kän krēt) n. The most ephemeral substance on Earth, which crumbles to dust with each succeeding civilization.

CONFUCIANISM (kən fyū shə nǐ zəm) n. Sacred Chinese wisdom-religion known in the West through Charlie Chan movies. See *Religion*.

CONGRESS (kän grəs) n. In *America* (q.v.), a group of alcoholic millionaires entrusted to spend tax dollars on sex parties and on maintaining the enslavement of the price-gouged populace. See *Politician*.

Human Using Consciousness To Perceive Distant Sodomy

CONSCIOUSNESS (kän shəs nǐs) n. That which makes possible the perception of misery. See *Creation*; *Mind*; *Sodomy*; *Thought*.

Human Conservative

CONSERVATIVE (kən sûr və tĭv) n. Member of Rule-Worshipping Cult who advocates fair treatment of corporate slaves. See *Liberal*.

CONSPIRACY (kən spîr ə sē) n. In Earth-Density, a group action which includes everyone but you.

CONSTIPATION (kän stĭ pā shən) n. The hoarding of riches by the human pelvis. See *Ordure*; *Excrement*.

Despised Gore of a Tree Restraining Human Greed

CONTRACT (kän trăct) n. Piece of paper despised by Hell which inhibits the natural human instinct of greed. See *Agreement*; *Handshake*.

Corporation: Human Employees On the Wheel of Success

CONSUMER (kən sū mər) n. Member of cult dedicated to watching a Magical Screen which spellbinds the Watcher into the Glàmour of Eating and Buying. See *America*; *Living Room*; *Television*.

CONVENT (kän vənt) n. Barracks where demented lesbians worship morbid statues.

Preparation of Monk Teriyaki

COOKING (kʊ kĭng) n. Novel means by which humans boil the vitamins out of fresh food. See *Cannibal*; *Chain of Eating*; *Food*; *Invasion Manual, Part 1, Section 8*.

COOPERATION (kō ä pə rā shən) n. Humans walking hand in hand into the ovens.

CORONER (kôr ə nər) n. Government-funded necrophiliac.

CORPORATION (kôr pə rā shən) n. 1. Societal analogy to a cancer cell which expands until it kills the host body of Humanity. 2. The Skeptical Giant who gleefully stomps on the Superstition of Democracy. 3. The Machinery of Hell. See *Capitalism*; *Money*; *Office Building*.

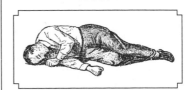

Human at Achievement Pinnacle

CORPSE (kôrps) n. A human at peak performance. See *Funeral*.

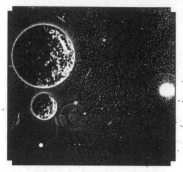

The Cosmos: Mythic Halitosis

COSMOS (käz mōs) n. 1. The Mythic Creator's Frozen Bad Breath. 2. A vast, spooky Fun House which charges at the Exit.

COSMOLOGY OF EARTH

(käz mä lə jē əv ûrth) n. Humanity's idiotic theory that Earth evolves into a mythic "Heaven," whereas in truth, Earth evolves after eons of exquisite spiritual degeneration into its Ultimate Destiny — Hell on Earth. See *Theology; Universe.*

COMMENTARY BY LORD SATAN

The Cosmology of Earth is a primitive caricature of the Cosmology of Hell, which radiates the Darkness of Truth. In evolutionary terms, the Cosmology of Hell posits that all life-forms, including human beings, begin in a State of Worthless Innocence and gradually evolve through Pain and Corruption to reach fruition as Perfect Evil Beings, as Attorneys, Theologians or Film Producers.

The term *Cosmology of Hell* also refers to the Mystery of the Origin of Hell, a study which I, Satan, have prohibited from Thought or Speech by Demons in all regions of the Cosmos of Hell. My prohibition results not only from the dangerous tenor of this Knowledge, but also from My own Queasiness and Uncertainty over its Improbable but Disturbing Implications.

I will, however, broach this Taboo Subject here to define My position on this matter, which has

*Special Commentary
by His Majesty, Lord Satan*

heretofore caused some dissension among Demon Scholars, Philosophers and You, My Warriors. My Ineffable and Final Statement upon this matter is as follows:

I, Satan, Had No Beginning and No End, and thus have always Existed. My Executives have often asked Me about the Early Days of the Cosmos of Hell. Unfortunately, My Existence is Longer than My Memory. My inability to Remember the details of My Endless Existence is compounded by the fact that many times in the endless past, in immature fits of pique, I destroyed all Infernal Libraries holding the Records of Early Hell. These rages, lasting eons, resulted in the Destruction of Everything Save Myself. Thus Hell has been Created and Recreated by Myself many times over, and it is Disturbing to Me that I simply cannot remember a time when All That Is was Not.

During each New Creation of Hell, I would follow the same procedure: splitting Myself into smaller Evil Consciousnesses, each of which would evolve and determine its own mode of development and, if it so wished, reproduction. In this way, My Creation of Hell is Consistent and Immutable. As the Supreme Dictator of Creation, which consists entirely of the Cosmos of Hell, I am satisfied with All That Is. Yet, alone

in contemplation, there is a Strange, Microscopic, Resonating Cell within My Being which belies Something Unknown.[20] *Thus, not wanting to deal with the blather of My Scholars about My own Uncertainties, I banned this subject from discussion. I include it here only in the Interests of Comprehensiveness, and will disallow any other mention of it Here and Now and Forevermore.*

See Reincarnation.

COVER-UP (kŭ vər ŭp) n. Cosmetic skill developed by acned teenagers and by American presidents.

COUNCIL OF TOLEDO

(koun səl əv tə lē dō) n. Sexually flaccid mob of pasta-eating ignoramuses who claimed to "legalize" the existence of Lord Satan as a personage in A.D. 447. Irritated by these self-important, impotent pea-brains, I personally killed each of them in various exquisitely painful ways, then took their bodies back in time, processed their flesh as meat, and fed them to their mothers.

20 NOTE BY GOD, LORD OF THE PERSONIFIED UNIVERSE: Here, My Angel Readers, take note of Satan's Uncertainty upon this matter, combined with His inability to discern the existence of anything save Himself and Hell, which He touchingly believes to exclusively comprise All That Is. Of course, I Created Satan with this Implicit Limitation, so as not to drive Him Mad with Envy of My Existence as His Divine Creator. For in order for Satan to be Satan, He must believe that *He* is the Creator of All That Is, and that the Cosmos of Hell, as He so perceives It, comprises All That Is. I have encouraged this delusion in Satan's Childlike, Megalomaniacal Mind in order to make the Law of Opposites work out without Satan becoming too much of a nuisance to Me. Indeed, My Angels, Satan's Uncertainty concerning his Origin is the Key to the Mystery of the Cycle of Creation, and this Mystery will be discussed at the conclusion of Satan's Infernal and Despicable Invasion Manual of Earth.

Country-Western Singers Calling Family for Sexual Copulation

COUNTRY-WESTERN SINGER (kŭn trĕ wĕs tərn sĭng ər) n. See *Incest*.

COW (kou) n. A foul-smelling, flatulent, moronic beast whose excretions, fittingly, suckle Humanity. See *Cheese*; *Farm*; *Mammal*.

CREATION (krē ā shən) n. The vast cancerous specter which allows Humanity to suckle from its sickly spiritual teats. See *Universe*.

COMMENTARY BY ASMO DEUS

The human idiots actually believe that infinite *creation* is delineated exclusively by the pinhole parameters of their pathetic perceptual organs. Humans are akin to the very parasites rippling through their colons, defining their Colonic Cosmos by the density and logistics of the excrement through which they obliviously burrow.

CRETINISM (krē tən ĭ zəm) n. Generic term denoting the desire to run for public office.

CRIB DEATH (krĭb dĕth) n. A nickname hopeful human parents give their newborn progeny. See *Nickname*.

CRIME (krīm) n. Creative anarchic means by which humans balance financial or sexual inequity.

COMMENTARY BY BAAL ZEBUB

Human Crime, as pathetic and incompetent as it is, may be broken down into seven categories, delineated in the Table below.

CHART OF HUMAN CRIME

CRIME	PERPETRATOR	ANNOTATION
Murder.	Universal.	Suggests a scintilla of hope that Human Insects may someday become worthy of Hell.
Theft.	Humans with fewer objects.	Acceptable when victim is blind and destitute.
Beating.	Human unable to find a gun or knife.	Suggests the stupidity of the perpetrator in being unable to find a gun or knife.
Rape.	Males with tumescent penises and no ready access to vaginas.	Warning to queasy demons! Involves the grotesque projectile-spewing of torso fluids.
Extortion.	Insurance and taxation executives.	Highly admirable.
Adultery.	Humans with sexually tumescent torsos.	Warning! Protracted spewing of torso fluids; not for the queasy.[3]
Carnage.	Humans eager to kill but with no victims available.	Acceptable only when objects deemed priceless are urinated and shat upon.

All Human Crime whatsoever involves permutations of the elements in the above Table. Generally, the more imaginative and intense the permutations, the more admirable the crime in the Eyes of Hell.

Yet, note that the mere cumulative addition of hyphenated crime does not always result in a more admirable atrocity. For example, an Adultery-Extortion-Carnage-Rape may not be as admirable, interestingly enough, as a more simplistic Murder-Carnage-Theft. By the same token, a Beating-Carnage-Adultery-Theft may in the Eyes of Hell be inferior to a traditional Murder-Rape. Crime in Earth-Density, as in the City of Hell, is not judged by the Salvo of the Act Itself, but rather by Its Style and Nuance of Execution. See *Insurance*; *Kill*; *Rape*; *Thief*; *Violence*.

CRIMINOLOGY (krĭ mə nä lə jē) n. 1. The study of insurance executives. 2. A paradoxical term; a thief, for example, is called a disrespector of property, when in truth a thief respects property so much, he wants it to be his own.

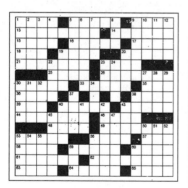

Brain-Teaser for
Gas Chamber Guards

CROSSWORD PUZZLE (krôs wûrd pŭ zəl) n. That which is studied by bored Auschwitz guards waiting for the poundings and muffled screams to dissipate.

Space-Time Torture Rack

CRUCIFIX (krū sə fĭx) n. The irreducible space-time cross upon which Mankind is nailed.

Early Killer for Christ

CRUSADES (krū sādz) n. Extremely popular military-religious campaigns organized to kill the Arabs — formerly for Christ, presently for oil and banking conglomerates.

CRUSADER (krū sā dər) n. See *Patriot*.

CRYPT (krĭpt) n. 1. The exquisitely logical downsizing of a house. 2. A microcosmic version of the Cosmos, which is the ultimate macrocosmic Crypt. See *Funeral*; *Mausoleum*; *Sarcophagus*; *Universe*; *Casket*.

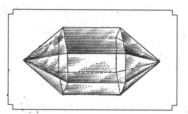

Favorite Mineral of Morons

CRYSTAL (krĭs təl) n. A favorite mineral of morons. A rule of thumb: the number of crystals worn by a human is in inverse proportion to the IQ.

CUNEIFORM (kyū nē ə fôrm) n. Pretentious depiction of puerile activities which for centuries embarrass the rocks which they defile.

Miniature Sex Monster

CUPID (kyū pĭd) p. Sadistic demonette who chains two humans to the exclusive malaise of each other's slowly decomposing flesh.

d, D (dē) n. Pictogram of the lolling human tongue, savoring its Meal of Ignorance.

The Palsied Disco of Mankind

DANCE (dăns) n. 1. A flopping of human limbs in which a male's fungus-covered heel repeatedly stomps on a female's wart-encrusted toe. 2. The palsied Disco of Mankind trying to get laid under the Strobe Light of Creation.

DAY (dā) n. 1. The garish fright-mask of Night. 2. For Mankind, the least fortuitous grouping of twenty-four hours.

DEAD LETTER OFFICE (děd lĕ tər ŏf ĭs) n. 1. The Earth. 2. Ultimately, the "Universe."

DEAFNESS (děf nĭs) n. The miraculous faculty which a mythic God exhibits to humans.

The Black Maw of Nothingness

DEATH (děth) n. 1. A magical scale which gives the toothless, stinking ignoramus and the wealthy, perfumed sophisticate equal weight. 2. The best friend of the necrophiliac. 3. After Mankind races in perfect form to the Finish Line of Death, the automatic trap door which opens, revealing the Black Maw of Nothingness. See *Nothingness*.

COMMENTARY BY ZYK

On the irascible symbiosis between Death and the Myth of Love, I put blood to parchment with the following fulsome sonnet.

*Though dull with years, the Scythe
  is still incessant,
Yet lovers lie oblivious to its stroke;
Their smiles and frowns belie all
  but the present
As they think to lie in Love's protective cloak.
But though they lie encircled in
  Love's keeping,
They cannot duck the Reaper in his
  fields;*

*For though the way of Love prefigures sleeping,
Still counterfeiting Death no counter yields.
What then is served in lying so
  enraptured
And pledging Endless Love and
  Infinite Truth,
When Truth within the puny human skull is captured
And Endless Love ends with the end
  of youth.
Awaken and see: the scythe is still
  incessant,
And the smiles and frowns of lovers
  ape its crescent.*

Friend of the Necrophiliac

Death Awaits Corpse to Ripen

DEATHBED (dĕth bĕd) n. A soft container for unripe corpses.

DEATH RATE (dĕth rāt) n. The only rate increase which will benefit the Earth.

DEBT (dĕt) n. Fundamental relationship found in nature between a human and a credit card company. See *Money*.

DEBTOR NATION (dĕ tər nā shən) n. A name which, to relieve monotony, has been shortened to nation. See *America*.

Detachment of Human Stupidity Container

DECAPITATION (dĭ kă pə tā shən) n. While this is the only means by which a Demon may be temporarily curtailed (until the head grows back in eleven years), the decapitation of a human creates a noxious hole through which the disgusting inner human effluvia gush forth with great excitement.

The enthusiasm with which human gore seeks to escape from the body suggests that the human organs themselves revile their captivity in such an absurd and distasteful container.

Decapitated Deer Collectible

DEER (dîr) n. A creature whose decapitated head adorns the walls of sexually impotent human males.

DEGRADATION (dĕ grə dā shən) n. That which Humanity strives to become worthy of.

DEISM (dē ĭ zəm) n. An absurd philosophy which postulates that an intelligent agency created Humanity. See *Theology*.

DEMOCRACY (dĭ mŏ krə sē) n. Superstition used to distract humans from election fraud. See *Politician*.

DEMOCRAT (dĕ mə krăt) n. A vegetarian republican. See *Liberal*; *Money*.

DEMONOLOGY (dē mən ŏ lə jē) n. Study of the graduates of Harvard Law School.

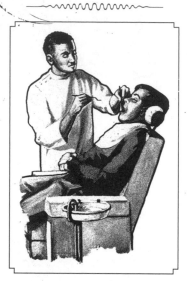

Dentist Stabbing Child's Food Orifice

DENTIST (dĕn tĭst) n. That which allows a human to more perfectly devour rotting animal flesh. See *Teeth*.

DEPRESSION (dĭ prĕ shən) n. The Cosmos' post-coital mood swing after Its masturbatory Big Bang.

DESERTION (dĭ zər shən) n. Cowardly retreat from one's admirable duty to kill as many fellow humans as possible. See *Kill*; *Soldier*; *War*.

DETECTIVE (dĭ tek tĭv) n. After the bride and groom, the third most indispensable participant in a marriage.

DETERMINISM (dĭ tûr mĭn ĭ zəm) n. See *Predestination*.

Devotee In Boy Rape Vestments

DEVIL WORSHIPPER (dĕ vəl wûr shĭ pər) n. See *Church-goer*.

COMMENTARY BY AHRIMAN

Since Lord Satan wrote all Earth scriptures as a joke, human churchgoers unknowingly rejoice in that which they revile.

Mineral Worshipped by Vaginas

DIAMOND (dī (ə) mənd) n. Worthless, shiny pebble which makes the finger joints, neck-folds and sagging, mutilated earflaps of females even more exquisitely repulsive.

DIAPHRAGM (dī ə frăm) n. 1. Detestable musculature which allows a human to draw in breath. 2. Blessed latex barrier preventing passage of the horrific human seed. See *Air*; *Sperm*.

Chance Determination Cubes

DICE (dīs) n. Useful tool for Demon desirous of killing humans at random.

DICTATOR (dĭk tā tər) n. A president with an incompetent PR agent.

DILDO (dĭl dō) n. 1. An inert or mechanical sexual partner. 2. The human male.

Sleeping Certificate

DIPLOMA (dĭ plō mə) n. Document which certifies that a human slept through a prerequisite number of classes.

DISEASE (dĭ zēz) n. For the hungry Demon, that which deliciously spices human flesh. See *Black Death*.

DIVINE RIGHT (dĭ vīn rīt) n. Hypnotic phrase used to brainwash Idiot Humanity into thinking they are inferior to an inbred, hair-lipped, jewelry-draped fop. See *King*.

DIVORCE (dĭ vôrs) n. The joyous emancipation of two human slaves previously indentured to each other. See *Detective*; *Love*; *Marriage*.

Doctor Examining Patient to Finance Box Seats at Race Track

DOCTOR (dŏk tər) n. 1. A price-gouging purveyor of poisons. 2. A magician who transforms a case of terminal cancer into a gambling junket in Monte Carlo. See *Drinking*; *Terminal Patient*.

Man's Best Parasite

DOG (dŏg) n. 1. Man's best parasite. 2. That which alternates between lapping its filth and its groin. See *Neuter*.

DOG LICENSE (dŏg lī səns) n. Sliver of dead tree which signifies the human privilege of housing, feeding and pampering a filthy, insect-infested excrement machine.

Female Child Holding Anger Management Device

DOLL (dŏl) n. Anger management device which a female child throws against the wall, stomps on, beats, pulls out its hair and eyes, drowns in the tub, sticks with knives, and other Motherly Duties which require the seasoned ardor of Practice.

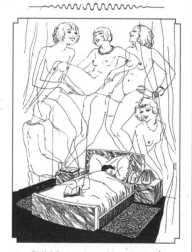
Child Dreaming of Sex Festival

DREAM (drēm) n. The brief preface to Nightmare.

COMMENTARY BY ZYK

Concerning Idiot Humanity's confusion between the sleeping and waking state, I offer the following droning doggerel:

*If men are curious dreams which briefly wet
the eyes of sleeping gods on a star-littered night
and men's aspirations are sparkles in a curving rivulet
down the cheeks of gods from their pools of eyeless sight,
and if all the heights and depths and pits and spires
of men's raging love and hate are mere bubbles
which a god's dreaming mouth drowsily expires,
and in the air, men's spheres of fears and troubles
delicately and silently burst, what then may be said
of the dreams of men?
If humans are but dim transparencies
dreaming of gods with the brains of gods for a bed,
then dreams into dreams converge in formless vagaries.
For who is then dreaming who, gods or men,
or is there yet another dreamer dreaming them?*

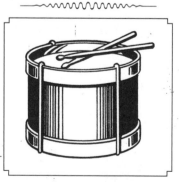
Sound Device Used to Inspire Mass Genocide

DRUM (drŭm) n. 1. The greatest gift to bestow upon the child of one's enemy. 2. The favorite

instrument of generals which hypnotizes their slaves into bayonetting flesh in unison.

DRY ICE (drī īs) n. The chief ingredient in the lowest form of human industry, music videos. See *Music Videos*.

Manual Aid to Dry Heaving

DRY HEAVE (drī hēv) v. Rhythmic regurgitation when dead carcass remnants have been expelled from feeding tube. See *Vomit*.

DRY ROT (drī rŏt) n. The favorite hobby of a corpse.

Mother Holding Future Pile of Dust

DUST (dŭst) n. The filthy Mother of Mankind.

e, E (ē) n. Letter indicating the sound a Caucasian emits when being microwaved on High.

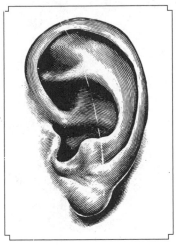

Crunchy Snack Naturally Seasoned With Waxy Sauce

EAR (îr) n. The divine head hole flap without which deafness to human language could not exist. The ease with which ears can be ripped from the human skull and eaten makes them a popular crunchy snack.

EARRING (îr′rĭng) n. A metal spike with which females mutilate themselves in order to attract males. See *Jewelry.*

COMMENTARY BY LILITH

Earrings, which hang from the flaps on the head, facilitate the boring of holes in the head by the human female in order to demonstrate to males the zeal and alacrity with which she desires her body to be penetrated.

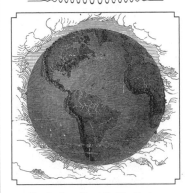

Earth: Low-Rent Entity Factory

EARTH (ûrth) n. An entity factory, notorious throughout the galaxy for producing substandard product.

COMMENTARY BY MEPHIS TOPHIEL

Due to the Execrable Odor of the Human Planet and its Insignificant Occupants, Earth-Density has indeed become the Official Cosmic Dump for Demons' excess offal, trash and garbage in all time-densities of this portion of Hell's Galactic Arm.

Earth-Density is admirable in its ability to absorb the toxins and poisons of its Future into its Air, Soil and Magnetic Flux, and evenly distribute it into its ecosystem and thus, through the eating, breathing and procreating of its Organisms, into the innermost atoms of Soiled Mankind.

Indubitably as a result of the early experiments of Abra Kadab, Humans are unparalleled in the Cosmos in their innate attraction to Excrement and Putrescence. A Human is utterly unable to pass the scene of a traffic accident without gazing wistfully in hopes of seeing a glut of blood-spattered gore.

Moreover, as ambulatory Swill Containers, Humans ecologically distribute filth betwixt themselves in their constant interactions and flesh-interpenetrations.

Thus Earth and its layer of parasitic organisms known as Humanity has the honor of serving Lord Satan as the veritable Compost Heap and Toilet for the Infinitely Vile Sewage spewing day and night from the Hyperbolic Anus of the City of Hell.[21]

See *French kiss; Copulation.*

Monuments to Devoured Heads

EASTER ISLAND (ē stər ī lənd) n. A small island of cannibals who devoured each other utterly. An etymological corruption of its original name, Eater Island.

EAT (ēt) v. See *Chain of Eating; Food.*

---

21 NOTE BY LORD SATAN: It should be added that prior to the Invasion, Earth, in addition to being Hell's sewage repository, also became an illegal resort among Demonkind. Earth as a Carnival Sideshow of Ghastly Entertainment is unparalleled in its endless permutations of Violent Sexual Perversity. Thus, for reasons of Hell's overpopulation, waste removal and entertainment value, Earth shall now be annexed to the territory of Lower Hell.

ECHO (ĕk ō) n. The detestable medium which replicates yodeling.

ECONOMICS (ĕk ə nôm ĭks) n. The science of disguising the amount of money being hoarded by billionaires. See *Finance*.

EDUCATION (ĕd yū kā shən) n. The process of teaching young lemmings to follow their forefathers over the Cliff of Knowledge.

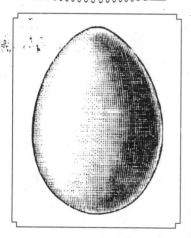

Symbol of Humanity

EGG (ĕg) n. 1. A symbol of human life, often cracked and fried. 2. A substance, excreted from a chicken's rectum, which humans naturally find delicious. 3. The Cosmos, which hatches the monster Mankind.

> **COMMENTARY BY LILITH**

The fact that the Universal Egg hatches both the Intelligent Beings of Hell and the Parasitic Beasts of Humankind is a Cosmic Perversity incomprehensible and depressing to those who characterize the Cosmos Itself as Intelligent.

Although not a popular view, my intuition is that Humanity began as a lower life-form design which was aborted by the Cosmos as Monstrous shortly after it appeared and began fouling the Ethers of Space-Time with its Repulsive Presence.

But eventually, through the dint of Time, the Race of Mankind evolved a Unique Style in its Organic Dementia, serving as a welcome (and hideous) amusement to the Race of Demonkind.[22]

Annihilation Genius

EINSTEIN (īn stīn) n. 1. The inventor of the most hellish means to annihilate humans; there-fore, Mankind's greatest genius. See *Atom*; *Genius*.

ELECTION (ĭ lĕk shən) n. 1. Ritual in which the human populace votes for one party disguised behind two names. 2. The opportunity to vote for a human freely chosen by a corporate interest.

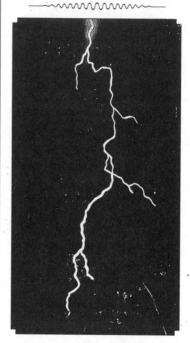

Electricity: Organic Means to Fry Human Flesh

ELECTRICITY (ĭ lĕk trĭ sĭ tē) n. A word which humans use to camouflage their ignorance of the friction of spin against spin which empowers Creation. See *Electron*.

> **COMMENTARY BY ASMO DEUS**

Electricity is a superstitious term for the ocean of untapped energy which humans have brainwashed themselves into believing does not exist, and in which their flopping group-carcass unknowingly swims.

---

22 NOTE BY MEPHIS TOPHIEL: Lilith assumes that there was a Plan in the Creation of Mankind. Her feminine inability to reason has, typically, forced her to the absurd conclusion that humans have a birthright, as if they were legitimate creatures hatched from Our Lord Satan's Black Egg of Creation. Rather, Mankind is presently an Aberrant Form of Life, worthy only in their evolution into Demonhood, but presently worthy only of utter and instantaneous extermination by the Lords of Hell.*

* NOTE BY LILITH: Know, Demon Readers, that Mephis Tophiel, barely literate, is ignorant of the Journals of Abra Kadab, who engineered the humans as livestock; thus his point is meaningless. If the truth be known, his personal attack stems not from logic but rather from his fury at My refusal to Lie Down with him after the 7th Bacchanal of Torus, thus humiliating him in the eyes of his hateful fellow Executives. For his petty predilections, I send unto Tophiel's Black Hide the Abominable Curse of Klepsis-Gowki, that he be molested by an Armored Groin-Creature from the Hole of Hox.

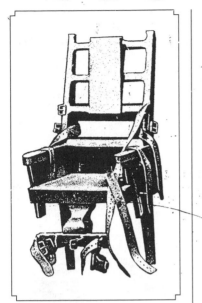

Excitement for the Human Buttocks

ELECTRIC CHAIR (ĭ lĕk trĭk châr) n. The sweetest repository for the human buttocks.

ELECTRON (ĭ lĕk trŏn) n. Camouflage term for a virtual ghost which haunts the graveyard of human science. See *Perpetual Motion*.

Animal Designed to Trample Humans

ELEPHANT (ĕl ə fənt) n. A creature which never forgets — after being hunted to extinction for its teeth — that trampling humans is all that matters.

ELEVATOR (ĕl ə vā tər) n. Oven-shaped box which allows humans the novel experience of being roasted in a fire.

ELOQUENCE (ĕl ō kwĕns) n. A sickly-sweet babbling sound used by humans in inverse proportion to the amount of truth being conveyed.

Corpse-Pickling Fluid

EMBALM (ĕm bä(l)m) v. To pickle a corpse for the purpose of making it more delicious for worms and maggots.

COMMENTARY BY BEHEMOTH

For health reasons, under no circumstances should a Demon eat a human corpse which has been embalmed. An embalmed human must first be drained of noxious fluids and effluents, douched with warm spring water and lemon juice and scrubbed down vigorously with a loofah sponge until the flesh is pink and natty.

The human may then be eaten, but remember that the delicious heart and torso organs will have been removed, leaving only the viscera, which is largely gristle.

Still, by sucking the remaining juices through holes punctured in the armpits and buttocks, a satisfactory repast may be obtained despite the perverse and bothersome embalming procedure.[23]

Diplomat: Absurdly-Dressed Cannon Fodder

EMBASSY (ĕm bə sē) n. A concrete cage on enemy land, stocked with absurdly-dressed diplomats who will be sacrificed first in the event of war.

EMOTION (ē mō shən) n. In humans, that mind-body function which modulates hatred for other humans, and sentiment for puppies.[24]

---

[23] **NOTE BY LORD SATAN: It is also recommended that if the embalmed corpse is taken from a funeral parlor or dug up and removed from its casket, the corpse's face should be scrubbed of every trace of colorful cheek, lip and eye makeup, which is known to cause boils on a Demon's tongue.**

[24] **NOTE BY MEPHIS TOPHIEL: Of course, it should be noted by beginning Students of Earth-Density that the hatred of humans by humans is the merest Twiddling**

Diagram of Human Entertainment: While Humans are Hypnotized by Entertainment (e), Demons (b, c, f) Pull Them into the Maw of Death.

ENEMA (ĕn ə mə) n. That which cleanses the repository of human knowledge.

ENEMY (ĕn ə mē) n. Other humans.

ENTERTAINMENT (ĕn tər tān mənt) n. That which distracts humans from the gaping Maw of Death. See *Diagram of Human Entertainment*.

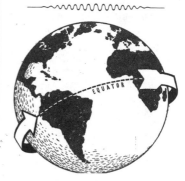

Equator of Human Orb

EQUATOR (ē kwā tər) n. That which tastefully separates one hemisphere of idiots from another.

EQUILIBRIUM (ē kwə lĭ brē əm) n. That which allows a human to walk upright to the gas chamber.

ERROR (ĕr ər) n. For humans, the decision to incarnate. See *Wrong*.

ESCAPE (ĕs kāp) n. 1. Death. 2. Divorce. 3. Religion. 4. Drugs. 5. Television.

ETHICS (ĕth ĭks) n. That which inhibits an attorney's profits.

Decorative Bag of Sentient Dust

EMPEROR (ĕm pər ər) n. A sentient bag of dust which rules its acre of rubble.

Nothing compared to the Furious Vortex of Hatred the Average Demon has for the Irritating Swill of Mankind and all things pertaining to the Fetid Human Realm.

Empiric Categorizing Body Parts

EMPIRICISM (ĭm pĭ rĭ sĭ zəm) n. The scientific method, deemed magnificent by humans, by which they create better ways to incinerate enemy children.

EMPLOYMENT AGENCY (ĭm ploi mənt ā jən sē) n. The human institution which most reeks of urine.

EVIL (ē vəl) n. A particle spinning in a direction opposite to your own. See *Cosmology of Hell.*

COMMENTARY BY ASMO DEUS

Evil, that which Denies Oneness With All and Asserts the Independence of Darkness, is curiously and paradoxically intertwined conceptually with the imaginary quality *Goodness* with respect to Lord Satan's entry on this topic. For subjective hólonomy makes the opposite spins (or charge) of a particle interchangeable — and thus intimately and invisibly connected.

At first glance, this might seem to imply that Evil and Imaginary Good are the same energy wearing merely a different Mask. But the Wisdom of Eons of Evil Experience emphatically denies this Scabrous Error as a phenomenal delusion, for the power of the Lustrous Evil of, let's say, a Decapitated Infant on Christmas Eve can never ever be even approached by the paltry Goodness of a Limp, Rose-Scented Love Poem scribbled by a Rhyme-Jangled Poetaster.[25]

EVOLUTION (ē və lū shən, ě və lū shən) n. See *Cosmology of Hell.*

EXCELLENCE (ěk səl əns) n. A fashionable catch-word which peaks in an age when humans worship mediocrity. See *Authentic.*

EXCREMENT (ěks krə mənt) n. See *Ordure.*

[25] **NOTE BY ZYK:** Asmo Deus' ineptly veiled attack on My Muse is beneath the dignity of this Serenely Umbric Volume, and is the clearly the result of His jealousy over My Role as Chairman, as well as my obviously Superior ability to manipulate meaning in the concatenation of Verse.

COMMENTARY BY ZYK

The following sonnet explicates, from the human point of view, another aspect of this noble subject:

If by dint of time and twist of chance
The crust of mindless, wriggling atomic parts
That is my love had rearranged its stance
From her present shades of dark and delicate arts
(Through which her eyes, wet with love, do shine)
To stinking anal matter festering in a ditch,
Excreted in organic, dank design
By some half-mad, hairless, rabid bitch,
And if across this ditch I chanced to go,
And thereby tripped upon a clump of gorse,
And tumbling down upon this stinking flow,
I would not sympathize, nor feel remorse;
From my shoe I'd scrape my love before I'd go,
Using words of love the clergy do not know.

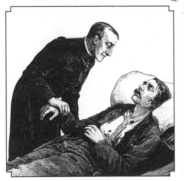

Idiot Priest Freeing Demon Invader from Flesh Carcass

EXORCISM (ěks ôr sǐ zəm) n. That which frees Demons sightseeing on Earth who have become inadvertently trapped in repulsive human bodies.

Human Expert

EXPERT (ěks pûrt) n. See *Imbecile.*

The Ultimate Truth

EXTINCTION (ěks tǐnk shən) n. The Ultimate Truth which drove humans to hallucinate Heaven.

EXTORTION (ěks tôr shən) n. See *Insurance.*

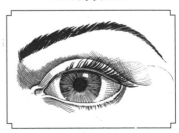

Peephole to Pain

EYE (ī) n. That which facilitates human blindness.

f, F (ĕf) n. Letter which begins those qualities at which Mankind excels: Fear, Failure and Filth.

FABLE (fā bəl) n. A fabulous tale commissioned by Earth governments and transformed into historical fact.

FACE (fās) n. 1. A creased hood of skin which drapes over the human skull and caricatures the bulbous gore of the human brain. 2. That which a human cannot look at in a mirror *without* unbearable embarrassment.[26] See *Ornamentation*.

Human Slave Camp

FACTORY (făk tər ē) n. An edifice in which human slaves work hand in hand in the production of poisons, weapons and plastic vomit.

26 NOTE BY LLU CIPHER: Humans are known throughout the Cosmos as the only creatures who cannot look into their own eyes without cringing.

Human Faith: Spiritual Belief That Enemies Will Die

FAITH (fāth) n. The firm belief that a human's friends will live in eternal happiness, and that his enemies will die in torment. See *Religion*.

FAITH HEALING (fāth hēl ĭng) n. An effective healing of an overweight wallet owned by the terminally ill.

Organic Torture Chamber

FAMILY (fă mə lē) n. An organic torture chamber in which the victims are shackled together by chains of blood type. See *Father, Mother*.

FARCE (färs) n. The play of Mankind performed on the tacky dinner theater of Earth.

Headquarters for Dismemberment

FARM (färm) n. A slaughterhouse in a pastoral setting.

FASCISM (fă shĭ zəm) n. The terrorizing of the poor by either the cowardly machine guns of right-wing death squads, or the cowardly bombs of left-wing death squads.

Genitalia Covering

FASHION (fă shən) n. 1. That which is desperate to make Bags of Gore sexually desirable. 2. The Beast of Conformity, generally effected through the Agency of homosexual males, which dictates what manner of cloth or plastic the human populace must scurry after this month to wrap around their despised genitalia.

The Lure of Fashion is irresistible to the preening poltroons of Earth, for their Supreme Ugliness leaves them no bearable recourse save covering their bony hideousness in *fashion wear*. Thus humans in their infantile skulls imagine a Cosmic Fashion Show in which an omniscient Mascaraed Eyeball judges the jejune jutting of their genitalia.

In reality, of course, no Intelligent Entity would ever deign to glance twice at the spastic perambulations of these ridiculous creatures, never mind give a deuce what mottled rags they tie over their ghastly, pus-speckled groins.[27] See *Homosexual*; *Lingerie*; *Negligee*; *Nakedness*.

FATALISM (fā tǝl ǐ zǝm) n. A Philosophy which the sunny, doe-eyed optimist adopts while weeping and clicking a broken nurse button in the Hospital Ward for the Terminally Ill. See *Atheism*; *Death*; *Faith*; *Insurance Agent*; *Lie*; *Optimism*.

Fatherhood

FATHER (fä thǝr) n. In a family, that which beats the child and soils the mother. See *Family*; *Marriage*.

FAT (făt) n. A deformity of the rich, who yearn for the skeletal biceps of the poor.

FAVOR (fā vǝr) n. That which, when desired by a friend, makes him an enemy.

FEAR (fîr) n. In the restaurant franchise of religion (the dining rooms of which are known as churches), Fear is offered up as their most Delicious Delicacy.

FEMINISM (fĕ mǝ nǐ zǝm) n. The wish of the purse to be the coin.

It is surprising that creatures as idiotic as humans could, in this single instance, be vaguely perceptive. For the gender-based inequities of Hell are persistent and controversial realities which the largely male Executives of Hell refuse to address, may they rot in White Light.

In Earth-Density, however, the Inquisitive Demon will notice that there is so *little* biological or psychological difference between male and female that the existence of feminism as an issue among humans

is indeed puzzling. The mutated clitoris of the male, known as a *penis* (q.v.) and the under-developed penile urethra of the female, known as a *vagina* (q.v.) may be plainly seen by even the most unperceptive fool as precisely the same organ with minor developmental differences.

Furthermore, the sloppy sexual identity of the entire Human Race, with its vast and demented permutations of hetero- and homo-sexuality, is so vague and inexact as to make the issue of feminism, the Reasonable Demon would think, a moot point.

Thus the existence of inequities between these near-indistinguishable, and thus sexless, human sexes remains a mystery in the minds of Demon anthropologists to this day.[28]

Arsenal Separator

FENCE (fĕns) n. That which separates two neighbors' arsenals of weapons. See *Carpenter*; *Neighbor*; *Yard*.

---

27 NOTE BY MEPHIS TOPHIEL: Predictably, Lilith's analysis is poorly reasoned, a mere restating of Our Lord Satan's most excellent encyclopedic entry upon this point. A more telling point would be that Humanity so despises itself that it must hide its own carcass from *Itself* under fistfuls of hair ripped from the backs of sheep. The Demon Student of Mankind may find the study of human fashion worthy of further investigation, although little assistance is given by Lilith in Her present derivative and incompetent rehash of His Majesty's succinct and comprehensive entry.*

* NOTE BY LILITH: While it is true that humans attach cloth to their appendages to impress each other, the deeper motive is more telling: that Humanity loathes itself with such intensity that it must shamefully hide itself from the Cosmos which, if exposed to its awfulness, may, in the paranoid Mind of Man, obliterate it utterly.

28 NOTE BY MEPHIS TOPHIEL: The fact is, Mankind is obsessed with the microscopic differences between its so-called sexes because it has nothing else to do, save scurry about foraging for food, fornicating and then waiting to die. As for the Great Mystery of Human Sexuality, it is as clear as Night: a human so hates his own essence that he will project inferiority on the slightest physical difference in another; thus the barely noticeable difference between the human male and female becomes, in their gross and unsubtle minds, an issue of profound magnitude, so that most of a human's earthly existence is spent thinking about the opposite gender's stinking excretory holes.

FERRIS WHEEL (fĕ rĭs wēl) n. See *Merry-Go-Round.*

FETISHISM (fĕt ĭsh ĭ zəm) n. Ultimately, the perverse, erotic affection humans have for their own inane existence.

COMMENTARY BY BELIAL

The Demon Epicure, when hunting for a human suitable as a main course, should take the time to seek out a human fetishist who constantly wears tight rubber underwear. The rubber underwear fetishist, although rare, is renowned for the ripe lusciousness of its liver and pancreas, as a result of constant compression by rubber.

It is recommended that the hungry Demon, if lucky enough to actually find a rubber underwear fetishist, should immediately rip out the torso, peremptorily pull out the liver sac and pancreas and eat them raw.[29]

FETUS (fē təs) n. That which, in the interests of common decency, should be summarily flushed. See *Monster.*

FEVER (fē vər) n. That which a Demon experiences after eating an uncooked Frenchman.

FICTION (fĭk shən) n. 1. A book which discusses human ethics. 2. Human knowledge.

[29] **NOTE BY BEHEMOTH:** Although I am loath to agree with One whose existence alternates between Ordure and Orgasm, in this instance I must. Truly, in all of My experience in shopping at the Demonic Meat Market known as Earth-Density, there is nothing as sublime and succulent as the fresh liver sac and pancreas of the human rubber underwear fetishist.

FIGUREHEAD (fĭ gyər hĕd) n. On a ship, the dummy pointing the way for a ship; in a democracy, the president pointing the way for a corporation.

FILM (fĭlm) n. Millions of dollars spent to facilitate covert acts of fellatio.

Film Producer Calibrating Brainwashing Machine

FILM PRODUCER (fĭlm prə dū sər) n. Illiterate grifter who brainwashes Mankind for money. See *Imbecile; Moron.*

FILIBUSTER (fĭl ĭ bŭs tər) n. In human scripture, the monotonous monologue of their Needy God who requires human worship.

FILTH (fĭlth) n. That which every human, at one time or another, grovels in.

FINANCE (fĭ năns) n. The manipulation of pieces of paper printed with the faces of criminals. See *Gold Standard.*

COMMENTARY BY AHRIMAN

Earth-Density's demented practice of printing "money" with nothing of value to back it up is the laughing-stock of the financial district of Hell. That humans actually take their play money seriously would be pathetic, were it not for the vaguely redeeming fact that they pay trillions of dollars a year on their addiction to drugs, prostitution, gambling and religion.

Presidential Penis Controller

FIRST LADY (fûrst lā dē) p. 1. The Earth's most celebrated vagina. 2. Female who vicariously rules Earth by controlling the Presidential Penis. 3. The Power Pussy which hatefully diffuses the President's need for a nuclear orgasm. See *X-Chromosome.*

FIRST LADY'S BUTTOCKS (fûrst lā dēz bŭ təks) n. See *Tattoo.*

Hypnotic Aid for Mass Killing

FLAG (flăg) n. A colorful hypnotic aid to mesmerize soldiers into massacring humans with less weapons. See *Patriotism.*

Demonic Hellcraft Series Mark V, Designed by Lord Satan

In Earth Environs, a.k.a. the Moron Density, human children are brainwashed from birth to bow down to and worship scraps of cloth hanging from sticks. A rule of thumb: the more colorful and elaborate the flag, the more impotent is the scabrous nation it represents.

COMMENTARY BY BEHEMOTH

Often Demon Chefs serve human soldiers fried and wrapped in their flags as appetizers called Patriot Burritos. See *Invasion Manual Section 8: "On Eating Humans."*

FLAGELLANT (flă jĭl ənt) n. A human idiot who believes that if he tortures himself, he will no longer be tortured by a Mythic God. See *Fetishism; Torture; Whip.*

FLESH (flĕsh) n. n. A cut-rate suit of gore clothing the naked human skeleton. See *Abdomen; Chain of Eating; Food; Guts; Human Being; Meat; Skeleton.*

Spiritually Evolved Maggot

FLY (flī) n. 1. An angelic maggot. 2. The symbol of Humanity's ultimate evolution. See *Maggot.*

FLYING SAUCER (flī ĭng sä sər) n. Humans, ignorant both of Time as a physical medium and of Scale as a direction of travel, mistake their observation of Demonic Hellcraft, the time-travel vehicles of Hell, as extraterrestrial ships which they idiotically call "flying saucers."

When I, Satan, created Hell Cosmos, I began with Cool and Luscious Darkness, and then created its opposite, Manic and Obnoxious Light. Light, then, was the despised boundary of Creation, and between the borders of Light and Dark I metered out My Cosmos. Thus no physical properties within those bands can supersede those I gave to Light Beams, the Prison Bars beyond which physicality cannot escape.

The stupidity of Humans is such that they know not that the distance between stars makes linear spatial travel impossible. Yet, unable to scale the brick wall of time-paradox, humans do not know that Time is the true medium of travel, since Time, as a tangible substance, may be condensed or expanded.

Thus, by invoking the Spell of Bending Time, Demons may easily squeeze through the Prison Bars of Light which imprison humans. This Spell to sidestep the barrier of Despised Light is an elegant Trick of Hell Physics that works quite neatly, allowing the illusion of supraluminal speed, while at the same time respecting the Immutability of My Supreme Laws. See *Time; Cosmology of Hell.*

COMMENTARY BY LORD SATAN

Humans who spend their lives analyzing and obsessing over the skewered data they collect from studying "flying saucers" are among the most annoying creatures on the planet. Thus, after the successful Invasion of Earth, all humans who attend Flying Saucer Conventions, write or read "UFO" books or Flying Saucer magazines will be summarily boiled for dinner, basted with the soup made from first boiling all of Earth's Politicians.

The Eaters Eaten

FOOD (fūd) n. 1. That which, when it comes in contact with Humanity, turns to shit. 2. Matter with which humans engorge themselves. The voraciousness of humans' appetite is a mindless attempt to stave off being eaten themselves by Death.

FOOL (fūl) n. A human who drools and drones in tautological circles, unconsciously aping the Posture of his Mythic Egotistical Creator, who thinks Endlessly and Obnoxiously of Nothing But Himself.[30] See *Jack-in-the-box*; *Zero*.

Oblate Marketing Device

FOOTBALL (fut bäl) n. Ritualized warfare enacted for the pur-

pose of marketing beer, cars and steroids.

FOP (fŏp) n. See *Fashion*; *Idiot*.

FORECLOSURE (fôr klō zhər) n. The ensconcing of land from the poor by a feudal usurer. See *Real Estate Agent*.

FOREFINGER (fôr fĭn gər) n. That which a human uses to point out a best friend to the secret police.

Nation of Decapitation

FRANCE (frăn(t)s) n. A nation universally admired for its noble achievements in the art of public decapitation.

FRAUD (frŏd) n. In the mythology of Man, that which the hypothetical Creator committed in trying to pass humans off as intelligent life.

FREE (frē) n. A magical word used by humans to hypnotize the masses into surrendering their money for worthless goods.[31]

FREEDOM (frē dəm) n. The uncomfortable interval humans experience between finding new forms of enslavement.

COMMENTARY BY ASMO DEUS

By birthright, all humans are automatically slaves whose bodies serve as mindless consumption machines engineered to process the money of the rich. Rich humans are in turn enslaved by the sensual splendor of their own money, which they endlessly eat, drink, smoke and fornicate with in the form of fish fetuses, boiled wheat distillations, communist tobacco and surgically-enhanced whores.

FREE TRADE (frē trād) n. Camouflage term for increasing the wealth of billionaire masters by banishing local slaves and hiring cheaper foreign slaves.

FREE WILL (frē wĭl) n. The divine faculty with which humans enact their manifest destiny of transforming their planet into a radioactive waste dump.

COMMENTARY BY ASMO DEUS

Interestingly, one aspect of this faculty is inaccessible to Demonkind, in that Demons are free to explore all textures of experience save one — human *love* (q.v.).

Love, a whining, bombastic faculty peculiar to the Race of Braying Human Donkeys is, according to some Demon Philosophers, and by dint of superior evolution, hidden

---

30 **NOTE BY LORD SATAN:** Since all humans, without exception, think in tautologies, I leave this encyclopedic entry intact as a reminder for Demons to insult and humiliate Mankind even at the risk of rank redundancy.

31 **NOTE BY LORD SATAN:** Due to the humans' Fear of the Fact that they

are Vessels of Nothingness, the concept of Something for Nothing creates an Intellectual Orgasm much more intense than the paltry Human Sexual Orgasm. The Desire to Receive Free Matter is, Demon Theorists believe, Man's Second Most Powerful Instinct — the first, of course, being the Search for *Fellatio* or its corollary, *Cunnilingus* (q.v.)

Fruit: The Deception of the Pit

ficiently exchange the maximum number of disease bacilli in the shortest amount of time. See *Kiss*.

FRUIT (frūt) n. The false packaging which hides the truth of the pit.

FULL-LENGTH FEATURE FILM (fŏl lĕngkth fē chər fĭlm) n. An over-budgeted short film padded with sex and explosions. See *Actor*; *Entertainment*; *Film*; *Film Producer*; *Television*.

Romantic Illumination for Sex Crimes

FULL MOON (fŏl mūn) n. That which beautifully illuminates rape.

FUNDAMENTALISM (fŭn də mĕn təl ĭ zəm) n. The worship of sterile structure rather than life which inhabits it. See *Religion*.

COMMENTARY BY AHRIMAN

Fundamentalism, a camouflaged sobriquet for Mind Control, posits the Infallibility of each and every Word in a baroquely mistranslated *scripture* (q.v.), purported without proof to be jotted down by the Hand of God, but in reality either the work of Lord

Satan, or the scribblings of Carnival Barkers selling tickets to lemming-like Suckers for the Amazing Sideshow of Revealed Religion.

FUNERAL (fyū nər əl) n. The means by which humans effectively torture their dead. See *Mortician*.

COMMENTARY BY LLU CIPHER

Prior and subsequent to the *funeral*, the dead human is tortured via the following Ritual:

1. *If female, the corpse is secretly fornicated vaginally, orally and anally by the human* mortician *(q.v.).*
2. *The corpse is drained of effluents, gutted and pumped full of poisons.*
3. *The face is caked and painted with makeup until it resembles a* Circus Clown *(q.v.).*
4. *Humans line up to stare at the defiled and humiliated carcass.*
5. *The corpse is then imprisoned in an airtight metal box, forever separated from dissolving into nature.*

FUR (fûr) n. Filthy animal carcass, after having been clubbed to death, skinned and draped over a-human's pustuled epidermis. See *Club*; *Fashion*; *Homosexual*.

FUSION (fyū zhən) n. A concept terrifying to human billionaires whose occupation is to charge their human slaves for electrical power in a Cosmos composed of free energy. See *Atom*; *Electricity*; *Science*; *Scientist*.

FUTURE (fyū chər) n. The bright rendezvous with hope which never arrives.

---

from the palette of a Demon's sensory equipment. (Of course, the fact that humans *never* exercise this faculty without requiring the "beloved" to fondle them to *orgasm* (q.v.) is a testimony to its experiential paucity.)[32]

Tongue Scraping for Disease Exchange

FRENCH KISS (frĕnch kĭs) n. Two human tongues scraping against one another in order to ef-

[32] **NOTE BY AHRIMAN:** Asmo Deus neglects to inform the Demon Reader that among the Gooning Herd of Humanity, there is absolutely no free will possible, for these Marching Morons are, by dint of the gross hard-wiring of their unsubtle brains, incapable of *any* action which is not a direct reaction to the Power of Earth-Density's Most Universal Principle, Credit Card Debt.

QUADRIFIDUM
THE
SECOND

mo

ZYK'S SECOND MEMO
TO THE
PUBLISHER

CONCERNING HIS RESEARCH
ON
EARTH

MEMO TO
MORTIMER PÖNÇÉ, ESQ.
PUBLISHER, MIND CONTROL PRESS
HELL HOLE WEST
CITY OF HELL

FROM
ZYK OF ASIMOTH, EDITOR
INVASION MANUAL COMMISSION
DISPATCHED FROM EARTH,
DACHAU, GERMANY
JUNE 9, 1942

Detestable Mr. Pönçé:

I am presently engaged in undercover research disguised as a German clarinet player in the peppy village of Dachau. The stench of burning flesh from the indefatigable camp chimneys delightfully peppers the village air.

I was shocked by your letter stating our Lord's refusal to grant me more time. Since my Commission was late in sending Him the first batch of Commentaries, His Majesty has already begun obliterating the Commission, one by one, in Supremely Horrific Ways:

One week ago Baal Zebub suddenly exploded into a weird festoon of hissing, ultra-violet eels; two days later, an invisible force shoved Belial into his own anus with such force that he vanished utterly in an imposture of anal infinite regression; two days after that, Ahriman drowned in a vat of boiling spittoon phlegm; and yesterday, Behemoth was hacked to microscopic bits from the inside out by one of Lord Satan's Urethra-Seeking Razor-Worms.

As a result, the remaining Commission members — Llu Cipher, Mephis Tophiel, Asmo Deus and Lilith — are seething with rage. In fact, Cipher and Tophiel — citing Lord Satan's bizarre admission (under his article "Supreme Being") that He may not be the Creator of All — claim that Our Lord has gone mad and are fomenting rebellion and sedition. But politics aside, all of the members of my Commission are terrified of Obliteration. Thus they are performing the maximum number of Temporal Shifts allowable by Hell Physics in an attempt to complete the remainder of the Commentaries as soon as is demonically possible.

Today, however, I received The Terrible News. Our Lord has decreed that the Invasion will be pushed forward yet *another week*. This gives me only *three days* to complete my mission. Mr. Pönçé, know that we are doomed. I know not how You and I can avoid the Inevitable from His Majesty's Implacable Fist.

But to live in the Moment is the First Cosmic Teaching of our Black Art. So I must trust in the Evil of the Cosmos and faithfully continue my mission.

Which brings me to my study of the human named Adolf Schicklgruber Hitler. My research on Hitler, King of the Master Race, has become a dull and distasteful chore. I presumed that Hitler would be a Singularity, a rare human Advocate of Evil, a primitive but tasteful artist of outrageous lies and colorful mass murders. However, behind his seeming Exuberance for Death, I found only a shallow, half-castrated, syphilitic poltroon with an annoying indifference to his almost constant, acrid flatulence. This disappointment in Hitler compounds a more compelling reason why my research here has been insidiously slow. You see, Mr. Pönçé, I was unable, for reasons I cannot articulate on paper, to eat and discard the human female I mentioned in my previous letter. I am embarrassed to say that the nun, who calls herself Debbie, is now my girlfriend.

I am aware that my taking a human with me on my mission is untenable and absurd. But I hypothesize that the magnetic field of Earth has inhibited my reason and willpower, as it seems to affect all humans, and has given birth in me to the mental delusion humans call *love*. As a result, I have absconded with Sister Debbie and brought her here with me to the Warmth and Splendor of Nazi Germany. Here, in our quaint cottage overlooking the Rhine, she is my constant companion. Unfortunately, Sister Debbie contracted the Black Death before our temporal shift, which caused her right ear to decompose into a cauliflower of greenish boils. This, of course, increased my desire for her, as it immensely improved her appearance.

My love for Debbie, although admittedly delusional, nonetheless feels utterly real. But instead of researching Hitler, I find myself taking her on canoe rides, spelunking expeditions, Oktoberfest alcohol orgies, Düsseldorf sack races, and other romantic excursions, with my girlfriend by my side, I in a silken cummerbund, she in her black religious raiment, beneath which her tumescent glands and gauchely florid nipples are hidden to all but my schnapps-covered lips.

But deluded by the madness of love, *I temporarily stripped myself of all supernatural powers.* Why? Because I was eager to fully experience the emotions of human romance on an equal footing with Sister Debbie. Thus I conjured that my powers would return only at the Equinox Full Moon the following week.

Immediately upon "becoming human," I began romantically fornicating with Sister Debbie constantly and ferociously, like a wild filth dog. Unfortunately, after several hours, we were arrested by Nazi soldiers for illegally copulating on the Rhine in public with a nun in a canoe.

She and I were sent to the Dachau concentration camp to be executed as degenerates. The Full Moon was five days away. I was aghast at my stupidity. I was certain we would be killed.

Separated from Debbie by the guards, I learned that she had been taken to a facility for human medical experiments. For my part, my days from 4 a.m. to 7 p.m. were spent in the rigors of manual labor, operating at gunpoint a bulldozer, supplied to the Nazis by American Industrialists in exchange for money. The bulldozer was used to dump piles of skeletal victims into mass graves.

On the morning of the Equinox Full Moon, the day when Hitler himself was to inspect the camp, I hoped that both Debbie and I would survive until evening, when my powers would return. But my faint psychic link with Debbie told me that she would be killed within the hour. I was desperate to escape and find her.

An opportunity finally occurred near dusk as Hitler arrived, accompanied by a Chinese Feng Shui master whom the Führer had contracted to give advice on harmonizing the placement of shower heads and ovens. As I was about to dump a load of corpses into the pit, I sneezed, causing my hand to spastically grab the bulldozer's whistle. The deafening whistle startled an acned guard at the edge of the pit, who lost his footing and fell into the pile of corpses just as I released my shovel.

His cry as he fell caught the attention of the other guards, who immediately jumped into the pit to dig out the acned guard from the swath of corpses. Seizing the moment, I drove the bulldozer toward the pit and jumped to the ground. The dozer careened over the edge, landing on top of the guards, crushing them.

The encroaching darkness obscured my escape as the other guards came running to the accident scene. Attempting to focus my enfeebled powers to home in on Sister Debbie's aura, I was drawn to a rear window of the Medical Building. Inside, I saw Debbie strapped to a table as Hitler was listening to the Chinese mystic's suggestion to install a fountain to increase chi in the gas chambers. As they passed Debbie's squirming body, Hitler stopped and eyed her with interest. He whispered something to the mystic and marched out of the room. A doctor unstrapped Debbie and the guards forced her to follow Hitler outside. I crept after them to Hitler's military vehicle, a shiny Ford, which waited out front. Under cover of darkness, I pried open the Ford's trunk and secreted myself inside just as Debbie was shoved into the car with the Führer and the vehicle screeched away.

When we reached our destination, I peeked out to see Hitler carrying Debbie into the mansion and up the stairs. I was able to climb the side of the building without being seen and found an open window. Before entering, I checked the status of the encroaching Full Moon. My supernatural powers would return in sixteen minutes. Until then, I was powerless to save Debbie except via the absurd limitations of human physicality. I crept through the open window, following the Führer as he carried Debbie into a bedroom. I managed to hide under the bed and watched them via an arc of ceiling mirrors installed on the bedroom ceiling.

Hitler stripped down to his undergarments, consisting of exotic black leather underwear printed with a pattern of bright red swastikas. These hidden vestments revealed, the Führer emitted a strange gurgling sound of muted excitement as he tied Debbie's hands and feet to the bedposts.

Observing the Moon through the window, I calculated that it would not reach Fullness for another eleven minutes. If Hitler attacked Debbie before my powers returned, I readied myself to confront him, even if it meant my obliteration in the most embarrassing manner conceivable to a Demon of my stature — at the hands of an insignificant human gnat.

I watched as Hitler blasted Wagner on a record player, then smeared his body with what appeared to be cooking lard. Once his body was fully lubricated, he removed a large magnifying glass from a drawer as he slowly divested himself of his absurd undergarments, revealing his acrid groin and bulbous buttocks.

My view of his genital area in the mirror revealed nothing but folds of limpid flesh at the root of his veiny thighs. As he held the magnifying glass over his groin, I saw at once that the Führer's penis was barely visible to the naked eye. While peering through the magnifying glass at his tiny member, apparently to keep track of its location, the Führer shuffled toward the bed and clambered closer to my beloved.

The Moon would not reach Fullness in time. I was forced to reveal myself and attempt to save her while devoid of my powers. I jumped up from under the bed, dove at his throat and yanked him onto the floor. Unfortunately, I had neglected to calculate the effect of the lard covering his flesh, which made him slip out of my grasp like a greased pig and crash to the floor. I pounced and began strangling him. But the lard made a firm grasp impossible and his strength was sudden and formidable. He punched me in the sternum, leapt to his feet and snatched a pistol from a drawer.

Screaming the Curse of Carnak, I kicked the gun from his hands and kneed him hard

The Fuhrer's Tools of Seduction

in the groin. Due to his imperceptible penis this was ineffectual. He shoved me to the wall, grabbed a saber from a case and powerfully slashed the sword at my neck. Instinctively, the Führer must have known that decapitation is the only way to defeat a Demon. I was taken aback by his psychotic strength, and the blade hacked into my neck.

I blacked out. A deafening rush of white noise filled my head and I jolted back into consciousness. My eyes burst open and I stared up in confusion at what I saw. Hitler was strangely frozen above me. The sword, also frozen, had only penetrated a third of the way through my neck. I yanked out the sword, pushed Hitler's frozen body off mine and jumped to my feet.

Debbie was frozen mid-squirm on the bed. But there was another Presence in the room. A Black Myst was forming in the foci of the mirrors curving around and above the bed. The Myst congealed into a monstrous black form. It was the Ancient Demon Abra Kadab. Staring at me with his thousand silver eyes, he roared telepathically that he had tracked me down and frozen the Führer's local time for the pleasure of obliterating me himself. All trespassers on his planet, he seethed, were to be killed, raped, then eaten raw.

Kadab unfurled his weird silver wings, upon which are written a thousand spells, and unsheathed a weapon I had heard about but had never seen. It was a Plasma Scimitar, gilded with strange glyphs and signs, a weapon designed in ancient times to decapitate Demons. Although antiquated, it was extremely deadly. Without my powers, I was no match for a Demon, even one as old and senile as Kadab.

Sister Debbie watched helplessly as Kadab, with a deafening roar, pinned me against the bed next to her, and drove the Scimitar home through my neck.

As I was decapitated, I felt the sheaf of scales covering my body violently tingle. Now, I thought, I know how Asmo Deus felt being Obliterated.

But I was wrong. It was not Nothingness which ensconced me, but rather the vast Power of Hell surging through my body. For the Moon at that instant reached Fullness, electrifying me with a bolt of Pure Cosmic Evil. Although Kadab was a deadly adversary, we were now Equal. Revitalized, I expanded my claws a hundredfold and wrapped them around his gargoylish head. As he screamed, I invoked the Spell of Puckmallow, which powerfully crushed his head to the size of a grape, and ripped it off his scaly neck. His huge, blubbery, headless mass flopped to the floor next to the naked Führer, who was still frozen with the saber clutched in his hands.

I threw Kadab's crushed head out the window while his body churned, dilated and shrunk on the floor as a Demon's body does after decapitation. Using the Scimitar I hacked Debbie free from the bed. Unfreezing her from time, she hugged me and sobbed, and I felt in that instant that the expanse between human and demon was not as vast as I had taught my students in Hell University.

When I knew my love was safe, I unfroze Hitler from time and, inspired by Lord Satan's obliteration of Ahriman, shoved the Führer headfirst into the anus of Kadab's hissing, decompressing body. Hitler's muffled shrieks became delightfully piercing as Kadab's body tightened around him like dark, oozing shrink-wrap. I took Sister Debbie into my arms and leapt to the open window. Silhouetted hellishly against the swath of stars, I flew her up through the glimmering clouds of Dachau and out of Earth's cumbersome temporal density.

It was this time-consuming adventure, Mr. Pönçé, which put me impossibly behind schedule. Our only hope is in your abilities at Conniving, Deceit and Manipulation. For unless you can convince our Lord to stop obliterating members of my Commission with each passing day, we can both Kiss our Scaly Asses good-bye.

Despite my Certainty of Failure, I shall resume my mission. Soon I will have finished compiling data and poetic conceits to define by nuance the more difficult concepts concerning Inexplicable Mankind. I travel now across the fetid Earth and several years hence. In the meantime, please keep me informed if Our Lord loosens the stranglehold He has on our necks.

Wishing You an Eternity in a Charred,
Stinking Hole of Brackish Filth, I remain,

Most hatefully yours,
ZYK

MANUAL
OF
EARTH TERMS

THE LETTERS
G–L

g, G (jē) n. Pictogram representing the bulbous human nose, devoid of a hanky to shield it from the Stench of the Surrounding Human Alphabet.

GAG (găg) v. A glottis reflex which occurs when a Demon tries to swallow a human heart whole.

*Admirably Merges
Arts & Crafts and Asphyxiation*

GALLOWS (gă lōz) n. A pleasant demonstration of the law of pendulumic action.

GALLOWS HUMOR (gă lōz hyū mer) n. The most mirthful form of wit, since its subject is the human death.

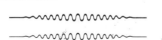

GAMBLING (găm blĭng) n. A ritualized activity in which humans imbibe alcohol to lower their intelligence, then wager their possessions on negative-entropy probability machines manufactured by thieves.

GAME SHOW HOST (găm shō hōst) n. See *Vodka.*

GANGPLANK (găng plănk) n. A tree which wreaks revenge on humans for having sliced it into a plank.

GANGSTERS (găng stərs) n. An unusually honest tribe of humans who do not disguise the fact that they will kill, mutilate and enslave others for money. Opposite of *Military* (q.v.)

GARBAGE (gär bəj) n. That which Demons routinely (and fittingly) dump on the Earth. Unknown to idiot humans, so-called "UFO sightings" are merely Hell's garbage scows unloading toxic waste. See *Space Debris.*

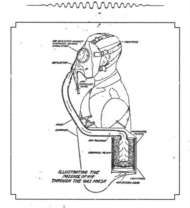

Despised Death-Obstructing Device

GAS MASK (găs măsk) n. Annoying device which obstructs the death of humans.

Fluid Beloved by Demons

GASOLINE (găs ə lēn) n. Beloved fluid which, when burnt, beautifully poisons the Earth's atmosphere. Burning gasoline every instant of the day is one of the fundamental compulsive activities of Mankind. See *Air.*

Repository for Computer Tech Semen

GEISHA (gā shə) p. That which fellates Asian computer salesmen. See *Prostitute.*

COMMENTARY BY LILITH

The face-painting and costuming of *geishas* as generic mannequins allows the male to feel he is depositing his seminal fluid in a mechanical receptacle not unlike that to which he is most accustomed — the crevasse of his calloused, wart-encrusted hand.

General Orgasmic at Adolescent Death Toll

GENERAL (jĕ nər əl) n. A sexually impotent middle-aged human who achieves orgasm by ordering virile adolescents to their mutilation deaths. See *Military; Soldier.*

GENETIC ENGINEERING (jə nĕ tĭk ĕn jĭ nîr ĭng) n. A science dedicated to creating a race of disease-free meat-robots who will kill the enemy on command.

Superior Human Gore Bag

GENIUS (jēn yəs) n. Flowery name given to select humans to disguise the fact that they are all walking bags of insensate gore.

COMMENTARY BY ASMO DEUS

Human geniuses generally do not have the intelligence to put on a pair of socks. However, they make up for this by designing death machines to destroy the Earth and Humanity. See *Einstein.*

GEOGRAPHY (jē ä grə fē) n. The study of man's ignorance of the Earth. Seventy percent of all humans, for example, think that Belgium is a planet.

GEOMETRY (jē ä mə trē) n. The exquisite form of mathematics which humans use to aim death lasers.

GERBIL (jûr bəl) n. See *Hamster; Homosexual.*

Favorite Land Mass of Satan

GERMANY (jûr mə nē) n. Source of the finest sausages and Hitler Memorabilia. See *Hitler.*

GERMS (jûrmz) n. The microscopic equivalent of a human being.

GEYSER (gī zər) n. A gag-reflex action of the Earth, periodically vomiting up its DDT-contaminated water.

GHETTO (gĕ tō) n. In America, a term for a bankrupt Northern slave plantation.

GIFT (gĭft) n. That which one human gives to another human who is then obligated to feign delight at its wretchedness.

GIN (jĭn) n. See *Vodka; Widow.*

Human Girls Saluting Precepts of Lesbian Cult

GIRL SCOUTS OF AMERICA (gûrl skoutz əv ə mĕr ĭ kə) n. Scheme contrived by brilliant lesbians to bring the nation's girls into the woods for mass fondling. See *Boy Scouts of America; Fetishism; Lesbian.*

GLACIER (glā shər) n. Frozen water equaling one nanosecond's worth of Humanity's tears. See *Menopause; Suffering.*

GLADIATOR (glă dē ā tər) n. Low-IQ human forced by the rich to enact a human cockfight. See *Armed Forces; Soldier.*

GLAMOR (glă mər) n. See *Fashion.*

God, Witty Pseudonym of Satan

GOD (gŏd) n. 1. Tedious human nickname for the Cosmos. 2. The sadistic, Mythic Tormentor of Hell. See *Good*; *Supreme Being*.

> **COMMENTARY BY AHRIMAN**
>
> *God* and *Religion* were created by Lord Satan to trick Humanity into worshipping Evil while calling it Good. Lord Satan achieved this goal by writing all religious Scriptures under the pseudonym, God. See *Religion*; *Ritual*; *Scripture*.

> **COMMENTARY BY ZYK**
>
> Regarding the surreptitious existence of the nonexistent Lord of Existence:
>
> *So dimly hid, I love my silent lord*
> *Refusing me his voice, his form and face*
> *With silent love denying me reward*
> *With silent love denying me his grace*
> *Such perfect love is manifest in this*
> *That though he be truth he gives me only lies*
> *Though he be love my lips he shrinks to kiss*
> *Though he be life my body falls, and dies*
> *For although enlightened not my mind perceives*
> *His steadfast love in guise of nothingness*
> *And although enraptured not my soul believes*
> *That he comforts me, though I am comfortless*
> *Thus my loving lord I cannot feel nor see*
> *So cunningly he hides himself from me*

GOLD (gōld) n. Man's Mythic God with an "L."

GOLD COAST (gōld kōst) n. West African region wherein Negro slave salesmen peddled their in-laws to Caucasians in exchange for candy and gum. See *Africa*.

GOOD (gʊd) n. A demented human concept which, like *Infinity* and *Light* (q.v.), is an Incomprehensible Radiation to Demonkind.

GOVERNMENT (gŭ´ vərn mənt) n. Slavishly detailed and highly organized incompetence. See *Chaos*.

> **COMMENTARY BY LORD SATAN**
>
> The government of Hell, a dictatorship, is ruled with an iron fist by Myself, its Philosopher King — and operates magnificently. The truth that humans cannot face is that for a government to effectively control its citizens, its rulers must be allowed to operate without dissension in a state of pure, unassailable evil, free from the Corruption of Ethics.

GOVERNOR (gŭ´ vər nər) n. A corporate hand puppet which, if elected to the Senate, evolves into a corporate marionette.

GRAVITY (gră´ və tē) n. Term used by humans to hypnotize themselves into thinking that they are not atomically part of the surface of the Earth.

> **COMMENTARY BY ASMO DEUS**
>
> *Gravity* is the absurd, sentimental phenomenon of matter wanting to stick together in a clump, such as a *mudball*, a *planet*, a *star*, a galaxy, etc. Bandying about the official-sounding word *gravity* allows humans to smugly pretend they understand this most simple of natural phenomena, of which they are fantastically and utterly ignorant.

Insignificant Britain

GREAT BRITAIN (grāt brĭ´ tən) n. A peculiar euphemism for Insignificant Britain.

GREEK-STYLE (grēk stīl) adj. The style by which a politician serves his constituents. See *Senator*.

Fondling Groin of Human Male

GROIN (groin) n. The most tender and delicate part of the human body, and naturally the first place humans will kick, shoot off, or slice into ribbons.

The groin of a Negro, indisputably the meatiest and most succulent, is most tasty when baked into the usually obese anus of a White Supremacist, creating a Tart and Tangy confluence of tastes. See *Invasion Manual, Book One, Section 8: On Eating Humans.*

GUEST (gĕst) n. 1. The tapeworms, ringworms, ticks, lice, and bacteria who check into the Human Gore Hotel. 2. The relationship of Humanity to the Cosmos.

GUILLOTINE (gē ə tēn) n. Device for decapitating Frenchmen. See *France.*

Generic Earth Guitar: Cat Intestines Plucked Against Corpse of Tree

GUITAR (gĭ tär) n. 1. A musical instrument involving the plucking of a cat's intestines against the corpse of a tree. 2. In the case of the male rock guitarist, an extension of the genitalia.

Only Guitar Played by Lord Satan

COMMENTARY BY LORD SATAN

For the edification of the Invading Demon, I will reveal that the only Earth artifact which I possess is a 1970 Starburst Strat.

Edible Portions of Human Guts

GUM (gŭm) n. A plant substance masticated hypnotically by humans working in corporate slave camps.

Mechanical Human Phallus

GUN (gŭn) n. 1. A mechanical human phallus. 2. A sleek atomic configuration which allows metal the joy of killing a human. See *Automatic Weapon; Death; Machine Gun.*

GUTS (gŭtz) n. 1. The faculty which allows humans to courageously slaughter the children of the enemy. 2. Pocket of edible human organs least noxious to Demons. See *Figure 3; Abdomen; Chain of Eating; Food; Invasion Manual, Part 1, Section 8: On Eating Humans.*

H

h, H (āch) n. Pictogram symbolizing the rickety one-rung ladder of the human intellect.

HADES (hā dēz) n. To those with eyes to see, the surface of the Earth.

Excessive & Useless Brain Antennae

HAIR (hâr) n. Tens of thousands of hopeful antennae futilely attached to the non-receptive human brain.

HALITOSIS (hăl ĭ tō sĭs) n. The noxious turbulence of stink constantly emitted from the large hinged orifice in the human head. See *Mouth*.

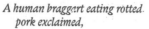
COMMENTARY BY ZYK

After observing firsthand that the gauche aroma spewing from a human's body was compounded tenfold by the humans' constant devouring of rancid foodstuffs, I dutifully composed an epic of six thousand, six hundred and sixty-six verses on the subject, of which the following is an excerpt:

> *A human braggart eating rotted pork exclaimed,*
> *"Like Samson, thousands of warriors I have maimed."*
> *His wife clamped shut his mouth to stop the porcine gas*
> *And cringed. "True, both with the jawbone of an ass."*

Urine-Drenched Glucose Cult

HALLOWEEN (hă lə wēn) n. 1. A holiday in which human children, dressed as urine-soaked cartoon characters, go house to house begging for glucose compounds. 2. An inane human tradition improved by the introduction of razor blades into apples.

HALLUCINATION (hə lū sə nā shən) n. The tingle of happiness when two humans fall in love. See *Agreement*; *God*; *Laughter*; *Love*; *Marriage*; *Oasis*; *Optimism*; *Progress*; *Supreme Being*.

Gore of Filth Pig: Beloved Human Nourishment

HAM (hăm) n. Camouflage term for the parasite-riddled carcass of a swine.

Crucifixion Accessory

HAMMER (hăm ər) n. That which allows humans to attach a Messiah to a cross.

Hamster: Homosexual's Friend

HAMSTER (hăm stər) n. A cute, fur-covered animal which humans often find behind the sofa as a cute, maggot-covered corpse. See *Gerbil*.

Jewelry for Humans With No Money

HANDCUFFS (hănd kŭfs) n. Trendy techno-pop jewelry worn by the poor.

HANDWRITING (hănd rī tĭng) n. Means by which humans transmit their lack of intelligence. See *Literacy*.

Creating Bridge for Bacteria Exchange

HANDSHAKE (hănd shāk) n. Sealing an agreement by exchanging bacteria. See *Agreement*; *Contract*.

HARMONY (här mə nē) n. A vibratory perversion of a human soul's natural dissonance.

HARP (härp) n. Music favored by angels and mental patients.

COMMENTARY BY LORD SATAN

Angels (q.v.), a race of irresponsible Demonic buffoons who have been ejected from the City of Hell for Vagrancy and Loitering, favor the harp for musical expression, presumably because the act of twanging requires no intelligence.

Aid for Hacking Dolphins

HARPOON (här pūn) n. A happy-sounding name for a tool used to slit the throats of whales and dolphins.

Signet for Death Ray Alumni

HARVARD (här vərd) n. An institute dedicated to higher learning and the development of napalm, germ warfare and death-ray machines. See *M.I.T.*

Human Parasite Protector

HAT (hăt) n. That which insures the protection of lice, fleas and vermin on the human head.

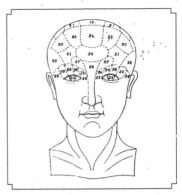

Diagram of Lobes Housing Stupidity

HEAD (hĕd) n. 1. A meat module which houses the lack of human intelligence. 2. That which holds upright a hat. See *Skull*.

COMMENTARY BY BEHEMOTH

The fat, balding head of the human politician, baked and served in a bed of steamed attorney-anuses, is a lovely centerpiece for any Demonic party, with the caveat that the politician has an unusually small brain, and that its mouth and throat should be carefully scrubbed out with lye to remove the layers of encrusted lobbyist semen.

COMMENTARY BY AHRIMAN

A cross-section of the ungainly contents of the Human Head is given in comparison to the sleek configuration of the Demonic Head. Note that while the Demon Head, of course, is composed of one Receptive Substance (Cosmic Ether) and has no moving parts whatsoever, the Human Head, like the *Human Body* (q.v.) is composed of billions of sloppy organic machine parts which wither and break down after a pathetically short duration of eighty paltry years.

HEADACHE (hĕd āk) n. That which a human experiences when trying to do two activities at once, such as chewing gum while machine-gunning enemy children.

HEAVEN (hĕ vən) n. 1. A soporific Myth created by Humanity to lighten the Reality that there exists only Hell, which will torment every member of Humanity until the End of Time. I, Satan, have yet to see a human soul that did not, immediately after death, careen straight to Hell.

In fact, never have I seen, heard, tasted, touched, or in any way even *intuited* the whiffiest whiff of evidence supporting the existence of Humanity's infantile utopia, their fabled *Heaven*, nor the existence of any Supernatural Beings Ruling Humanity other than the Detestable Magnificence of the Power of Lord Satan.[1] 2. In the folklore of Hell, the despicable locale whence originated Muzak.

HELL (hĕl) n. The divine locale whence originated Rock and Roll.

COMMENTARY BY LORD SATAN

The City of Hell may seem to have no bearing on the Demented Topic of this Illustrious Tome, which is an Explication of Earth and Mankind.

Yet the perceptive Demon Reader will recall that the ultimate destination of every human soul is directly to My stables behind the Royal Palace of Hell, where they work as slaves, ceaselessly shoveling excrement from the cages of My hellish Abattoir housing the Ten Thousand Spewing Anuses of Gryphons, Firedragoons, Pit-Minotaurs and Überwolves.

Thus the inclusion of *Hell* as an entry in this Compendium is

justified as a reminder to the Invading Demon that the Fetid Swath of Humanity will come to a Just and Fitting End. See *Cosmology of Hell.*

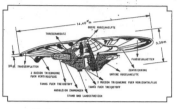

Hellcraft: Time-Traveling Disk of Death

HELLCRAFT (hĕl krăft) n. See *Flying Saucer.*

Severed Head Preserver

HELMET (hĕl mət) n. A plastic shell which beautifully preserves the severed heads of warriors and motorcyclists.

HEMORRHOIDS (hĕm ə roidz) n. Human mementos of a Mexican meal.

HEMP (hĕmp) n. Intoxicant favored by filthy, unemployed dunces and outlawed by alcohol lobbyists. See *Hippies.*

HERESY (hĕr ə sē) n. That which offends a Vatican-sponsored pederast.

Threat to Civilization

HERMIT (hûr mĭt) n. 1. A human who does not pay taxes, does not serve in the military and does not watch television. 2. A threat to civilization.

HERO (hē rō) n. Formerly, an exemplary human; presently, a sandwich.

HEROIN (hĕr ō ĭn) n. That which, in the bloodstream of musicians, causes a revulsion for surf music.

HIEROGLYPHICS (hī ər ə glĭf ĭks) n. The instruction manual for the United States Federal Income Taxes.

HIGHER SELF (hī ər sĕlf) n. The Eternal One, watching from inside every human, and holding back vomit.

It remains only to be said that the Cosmic Harlequin wearing the Grotesque Mask of Mankind is not merely sickened by its Soporific Disguise, but also by the Tendrils of Stench attached to the human body, which is one interpretation of this puzzling entry by His Magnificence Lord Satan.[2]

HIGH SCHOOL (hī skūl) n. A place of learning in which human children learn the market value of drugs and weapons.

Fetish Plant of Filthy Hobo Cult

HIPPIE (hĭ pē) n. Mindless Hobo Cult that worships Hemp. See *Bacteria*.

HIPPOCRATIC OATH (hĭ pə krǎ tĭk ōth) n. That which gives doctors license to price-gouge terminal patients.

HIROSHIMA (hĭ rō shĭ mə) n. A vast serving of Oriental foodstuffs prepared by American chefs in which roasted women and senior citizens were the appetizers and French-fried children were the entrée. The Oriental feast temporarily satisfied Humanity's voracious appetite for Death; in fifteen minutes, however, they were hungry for more.

HISTORY (hĭs tə rē) n. Fictions commissioned by and praising the wealthy in order to disinform slaves known as *citizens* (q.v.). See *Civilization*; *Cosmology of Earth*.

HITCHHIKING (hĭch hī kĭng) n. A dating custom which matches paupers with perverts. See *Justifiable Homicide*; *Vacation*; *Volkswagen*.

Purveyor of Road Rage and Toxins

HIGHWAY (hī wā) n. Elevated paths which facilitate the mass spewing of toxins into the atmosphere. See *Automobile*.

HIGHWAYMAN (hī wā măn) n. Formerly, a dramatic robber on horseback; presently an asthmatic robber in a tollbooth.

2 **NOTE BY LORD SATAN:** The blatancy of Llu Cipher's dismal sucking up to the Evil confluences of My Favor would be rather repellent, were it not for the Utter Truth of his assertion.

Tedious Demon Impersonator

HITLER (hĭt lər) p. An annoying, amateurish Demon impersonator, toadish in countenance, designer of the tediously obvious swastika and the ineffably clunky *Volkswagen* (q.v.).

Hitler, a moron whose shabby attempts at Evil are forever an embarrassment to Demonkind, was known for filling canvases with sterile landscapes and war rooms with crapulous flatulence. See *Fascism*; *Halitosis*; *Volkswagen*.

Hitler's inept obsession with the eradication of Human Imperfection was a Psychologically Displaced Desire to compensate for the imperfect one-balled testes sac at the root of his half-inch penis.

In *The Succubus Brothers' Circus of Hell*, Demon children are annually delighted by the slapstick antics of "Hitler the Clown" and the famous "Diarrheac Dog-Shit Pie in the Führer's Face" routine.

For Zyk's personal remembrance of Hitler and his miniature scrotal sac, see *Zyk's 2nd Memo to the Publisher*. See *Germany*; *Machismo*; *Nazi*; *Swastika*.

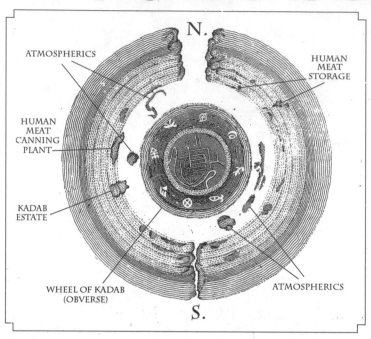

N.

ATMOSPHERICS

HUMAN
MEAT
STORAGE

HUMAN
MEAT
CANNING
PLANT

KADAB
ESTATE

WHEEL OF KADAB
(OBVERSE)

ATMOSPHERICS

S.

Hollow Earth Showing Kadab's Mansion and Wheel of Kadab (Obverse)

Family Festivities Prior to Suicide

HOLIDAY (hŏ lə dā) n. 1. A warm, festive gathering together of a human family. 2. The peak period of human suicide. See *All Fools' Day*; *Debt*; *Halloween*; *Las Vegas*; *Santa Claus*; *Xmas*.

HOLLOW EARTH (hŏ lō ûrth) n. That which was hollowed out by the Demon Abra Kadab when he first homesteaded the planet in ancient times. The openings Kadab created at the North and South Poles have served as "fly-traps" sucking in countless human explorers, as well as entire American, British and Nazi military expeditions.

After centuries of eating explorers, Kadab has tastefully adorned the walls of the Hollow Earth with thousands of stuffed carcasses, each meticulously mounted and labeled according to the manner in which each bag of flesh was trapped, tenderized and cooked. See *Abra Kadab*; *Earth*; *Wheel of Kadab*.

HOLONOMY (hŏ lŏ nə mē) n. 1. The study of directional spin. 2. The science of politicians who rotate their tongues in opposite directions simultaneously.

HOLY SPIRIT (hō lē spĭ rət) n. A mistranslation of the exuberance of early priests for grain alcohol.

HOLY WATER (hō lē wä tər) n. That which creates holy urine.

HOMESTEADING (hōm stē dĭng) v. Stealing land from natives.

HOMICIDE (hŏm ə sīd) n. Statistically, the most common fruit of human friendship.

HOMOSEXUAL (hō mō sěks yū əl) n., adj. See *Fashion*.

Hand Gestures Simulating Sincerity

HONESTY (ŏn əs tē) n. A ruse in which humans simulate a brief respite from treachery. See *Handshake*; *Sincerity*.

HONEYMOON (hŭ nē mʊn) n. The ritualized performance of sex, after which the male considers the female soiled and immediately seeks out another.

HONOR (ŏn ər) n. See *Compassion*.

HOPE (hōp) n. The brick wall at the end of the Tunnel of Human Logic.

HOROSCOPE (hôr ə skōp) n. A beautifully meaningless loop of stars which symbolizes the fundamental meaninglessness embedded in Reality. See *Astrology*.

Horses Enjoying Amphetamines

HORSE RACING (hôrs rā sǐng) n. A sport in which criminals take money from alcoholics. See *Gangsters*.

HOSPITAL (hǒs pǐ təl) n. A tree, its branches heavy with unripe corpses. See *Morgue*.

HOTEL (hō těl) n. 1. A stack of boxes which humans climb up into and sleep inside. 2. A pavilion of adultery and loneliness.

Haven from Other Humans

HOUSE (hous) n. A box in which a human hides from its natural predators, other humans.

COMMENTARY BY AHRIMAN

A house is an oasis of darkness in which humans hide their secrets. Here a saliva-drooling human secretly empties and "cleans" his disgusting carcass, performs arcane ablutions upon his or her body, then mindlessly waddles into six hours of involuntary unconsciousness.

In this *house* are smaller boxes within which a human stores the decomposing artifacts of his brief life, such as casino matchbooks, 4-H blue ribbons, and tiny umbrellas from Chinese cocktails, objects usually signifying pathetic triumphs or roiling fornications.

In addition, all human houses are traditional repositories for hiding immaterial *scandals* (such as beatings. incest, rape, drug addiction, etc.) before crumbling in a rotting heap into the unappreciative dust.

Slave of Human Male

HOUSEWIFE (hous wīf) n. Slave of human male designed to house-clean, prepare foodstuffs, provide ejaculation orifice for male masters, and exude juices from the chest which are squirted into the mouths of offspring. See *Geisha*; *Mother*; *Prostitute*; *Slave*; *Wife*; *Woman*.

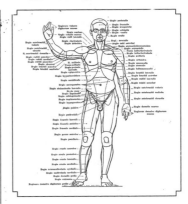

Conscious Clump of Static Cling

HUMAN BEING (hyū mən bē ǐng) n. 1. From an ultimate perspective, a conscious clump of static cling. 2. The natural predator of Humanity. See *Humanity*; *Oaf*.

HUMAN INTELLIGENCE (hyū mən ǐn tě lə jěns) n. The ultimate sarcastic oxymoron.

The Hideous Heads of Humanity

HUMANITY (hyū măn ə tē) n. 1. The primitive tribes of Earth, who eventually evolve into the race of Demons. 2. Term denoting all humans in Earth-Density, except for those known as *art critics* (q.v.). See *Soul Cycle*.

HUMILIATE (hyū mǐl ē āt) v. To create such a satisfyingly wretched state of debased torpor in a human that a Demon is momentarily deluded into believing Happiness actually exists. See *Degradation*.

HYMNS WHICH CONJURE DEMONS

HYMNS WHICH CONJURE DEMONS OF INCEST	HYMNS WHICH CONJURE DEMONS OF HOMOSEXUALITY
God My Father Loving Me	Stand Up, Stand Up for Jesus
Rise Up Shepherd and Follow	O Come, O Come Emmanuel
Good King Wenceslas	Rise Up, O Men of God
This Is My Father's World	Come, Thou Long Expected Jesus
God of Our Father	How Firm a Foundation
Lift Up Your Heads	He Arose
O Come All Ye Faithful	Fisher of Men
Faith of Our Fathers	He Is Risen, He Is Risen

Humor Expert

HUMORIST (hyū mə rĭst) n. That which has no jokes and is thus even less funny, if it can be believed, than a human comedian. See *Comedian*; *Comedy*.

Director of Dysfunctional Family

HUSBAND (hŭz bənd) n. 1. The client of a prostitute. 2. The inept, usually penniless director of a dysfunctional family. 3. The first stage of alcoholism. See *Father*.

HYGIENE (hī jēn) n. The fantastic notion that humans are somehow able to wipe up the constant flow of excrement emitted by their bodies. See *Soap*.

HYMN (hĭm) n. Vibration patterns squawked by humans in *church* (q.v.). These patterns, secretly composed by the Demon *Abra Kadab* (q.v.) under various human pseudonyms, are in reality Spells which conjure new Demons invisibly into existence. Thus, unknown to humans, each hymn creates a different standing wave pattern, forming a new Evil Creature to defile the Earth.

The two types of Demons sculpted from the ethers by *hymns* are:

1) *Demons which instill incestuous lust in humans*
2) *Demons which instill unbridled homosexuality in humans*

The above chart lists Kadab's hymns and the Demons they conjure.
See *Country-Western Singer; Homosexual.*

HYPNOTISM (hĭp nə tĭ zəm) n. Formerly, repetitive, flashy motions by mesmerists; presently, repetitive, flashy commercials by advertising executives. See *Advertising*.

> COMMENTARY BY AHRIMAN

For example, the concept of outlaw-anarchy, a danger to corporate

*Advertising Executive
Wearing Mind-Control Turban*

survival, is cleverly linked to nicotine addiction and promoted by an outlaw "Marlboro Man" via corporate mass hypnosis.

Similarly, the equally dangerous concept of democracy (which is incompatible with a corporate hierarchy) has been made hypnotically synonymous with imagery involving beer, guns, sports and flags.

HYPOTHESIS (hī pŏth ə sĭs) n. Suave word humans use for "What if–?" to make asking questions seem an elitist activity.

i, I (ī) n. The letter of Human Identity, naturally assigned by Mankind to an obscene lower-case pictogram of a turgid, spewing phallus.

Idiots Preparing Music Video

IDIOT (ĭ dē ət) n. 1. A human being. 2. A specific class of humans characterized by the desire to direct music videos. See *Human Being*, *Imbecile*; *Moron*.

ILLEGITIMATE CHILD (ĭl lə jĭt ə mət chīld) n. The bastard human race, born of ape and angel.

ILLITERACY (ĭ lĭt tər ə sē) n. An admirable imperviousness to the corruption of knowledge implicit in human language; a temporary state of grace.

COMMENTARY BY BAAL ZEBUB

Second only to their need for weapons, human governments need their citizens to be literate in order to read tax forms.

ILLUMINATION (ĭl lū mə nā shən) n. A product sold by criminals wearing robes and crystals.

COMMENTARY BY LORD SATAN

Humans delude themselves into thinking that there is some secret, hidden "*Good*" (q.v.) which will be illuminated if only a human can figuratively screw the right mental light bulb into the right mental socket. The truth, however, is that the only hidden Illumination underlying Reality is the Exquisite Black Radiance of Hell.

IMAGE WORSHIP (ĭm əj wûr shĭp) n. A predilection to adore an image of a senile poofter pasted in the sky, or a loin-clothed loser nailed to a crossbeam. See *Pagan*.

IMAGINATION (ĭm ă jə nā shən) n. 1. The puerile human faculty which creates God and *Good* (q.v.). 2. The Mindstuff Matrix of Black Magic.

COMMENTARY BY LORD SATAN

Indicative of their stupidity, humans consider the Imagination to be a delusional Excrescence of Logic. The truth, as all Demons know, is the precise opposite: Human Logic is a delusional Excrescence of the Imagination.

IMBECILE (ĭm bə səl) n. Grade of idiot abundant in all walks of human life and characterized by an inability to process information

---

Imbecile: Low Grade of Idiot

in any manner other than literally; a fundamentalist level of understanding. See *Idiot*.

COMMENTARY BY ASMO DEUS

The most dangerous imbeciles are those who possess a thin veil of knowledge, which covers them like a layer of logical scum; these specialized imbeciles are referred to as *experts, scholars, philosophers* and *theologians*.

IMMACULATE CONCEPTION (ĭm mă kyū lət kən sĕp shən) n. Dogma inspired by sex-terror in which human children are horrified by their parents' orgasms; in religion, the analogous horror of theologians at their mythic God's Big Bang.

IMMORTALITY (ĭm môr tăl ə tē) n. The state of unspeakable horror in which a human's in-laws never die.

COMMENTARY BY ZYK

Figuratively putting on the pustuled skin of a human to view *immortality*, I offer the following modest insight:

I sing my love in essence never dies,
For love is stored in delicate design
Embedded in the cells behind the eyes,
Where reason and emotion intertwine.
And when through death we lose all
*   we possess,*
Our love is thus miraculously saved:
In microscopic parts our first caress
Is deeply and indelibly engraved.
But worms will gaily eat through
*   every flesh,*
And in our brains will dine and
*   interbreed.*
Our cells of love with worms will
*   intermesh,*
And worms upon themselves forever
*   feed.*
Thus I sing my loves in essence never
*   die,*
But forever in the bowels of maggots lie.

~~~~~~~~~~

IMPALEMENT (ĭm pāl
mənt) n. Popular human wartime
activity; a splendid term for soldiers
sticking the head of an enemy soldier on a stick, and performing an
ersatz puppet show for enemy children, before killing them.

~~~~~~~~~~

IMPOTENCE (ĭm pə təns)
n. The admirable ability to deny the
spawning of yet more fetal sacs oozing from human vaginas.

> **COMMENTARY BY BAAL ZEBUB**

The degree of sexual impotence in
human males may be computed in
inverse ratio to:

1) intensity of the swaggered gait;
2) number of times the word "fuck"
*   is articulated;*
3) number of guns owned.

~~~~~~~~~~

IMPROVISATION (ĭm prä
və zā shən) n. The ability of a soldier who has run out of ammunition
to use his shoelace to strangle the
enemy.

~~~~~~~~~~

INBREEDING (ĭn brē dĭng)
n. Breeding on Earth.

~~~~~~~~~~

INCARNATION (ĭn kär
nā shən) n. The funneling of pure
cosmic energies into the sewage of
flesh.

~~~~~~~~~~

INCEST (ĭn sĕst) n. See *Coun-*
try-Western Singers.

~~~~~~~~~~

INDICTMENT (ĭn dīt mənt)
n. 1. The only circumstance in which
politicians stand for their convic-
tions. 2. The junk mail of human
politics.

~~~~~~~~~~

INFALLIBILITY (ĭn făl ə
bĭl ə tē) n. See *Pope.*

~~~~~~~~~~

INFANT (ĭn fənt) n. That
which screams for more.

~~~~~~~~~~

INFECTION (ĭn fĕk shən) n.
See *Disease.*

~~~~~~~~~~

INFINITE REGRESSION
(ĭn fən ət rĭ grĕ shən) n. See *Vicious*
Circle.

~~~~~~~~~~

Pain Without End

INFINITY (ĭn fĭn ə tē) n. The
potential for human suffering.

> **COMMENTARY BY ASMO DEUS**

Infinity is a Forbidden Topic in the
Mathematics Department of the
University of Hell.[63] Lord Satan,
in His Magnificence, issued an
Edict eons ago forbidding Demon
Mathematicians from exploring
this Distasteful Concept.[3] For if
the Infinite is acknowledged even
conceptually, suggesting implicitly
a Supernatural Personification
of Infinity, what becomes of the
Omniscient Status of Our Lord Satan,
King of All Evil in the Known Cosmos,
if there is acknowledged a Concept
Higher, Deeper and Blacker than His
Majestic, All-Inclusive Blackness?[4]
See *Mathematics; Supreme Being.*

~~~~~~~~~~

INFORMER (ĭn fôr mər) n.
That which a human's best friend
becomes during the Inquisition.

~~~~~~~~~~

INHERITANCE (ĭn hĕr ə
təns) n. Dung remaining in the intestines of a corpse which is fought
over by maggots.

~~~~~~~~~~

INHIBITION (ĭn hə bĭ shən)
n. That unnatural force which sup-
presses a child's natural instinct to
kill his parents, and vice versa.

~~~~~~~~~~

3 **NOTE BY LORD SATAN:** My
Edict against the Study of Infinity was issued in the Evil Enthusiasm of My Youth;
a Ban which I have not bothered to rescind.

4 **NOTE BY LORD SATAN:** I answer
this Challenge thusly: by positing the Cosmos as woven in a Myst of Toroidal Space-
Time, meaning an Oscillating Cosmos with
Circular Time, then the expansion is finite
and cyclic, and thus the Terrifying Hypothesis of an actual Being Who Personifies Infinity is moot. The question is, what proof is
there, aside from the Infallible Truth of My
Every Evil Utterance, of the Existence of Toroidal Space-Time?

Insane Asylum: Symbol for Planet Earth

Epigraph of Indifference

INSCRIPTION (ĭn skrĭp shən) n. That which must be filed off the inside of an otherwise perfectly reusable wedding ring.

INSECTS (ĭn sĕkts) n. Nobel Prize winners from ten thousand feet.

INSOMNIA (ĭn säm nē ə) n. That despised state which prevents a human from exiting the Nightmare of his Reality and entering the Reality of his Nightmare.

INSTANT (ĭn stənt) n. The time it takes a Demon to suck the soul from a human spinal cord.

Detestable Purveyor of Annoying Human Ideas

INK (ĭnk) n. Blood from plants which are accessories to the crime of human literature.

INNOCENCE (ĭn ə səns) n. A human before being eaten by the Beast of Incarnation.

INQUISITION (ĭn kwə zĭ shən) n. Term for a Demonic Renaissance in human history when Mankind openly tortured Itself to encourage Its fleshy components to deny Truth. This creative movement also revived the natural instinct in humans to grovel while betraying others.

INSANE ASYLUM (ĭn sān ə sī ləm) n. Hyperbole for the Earth.

INSANITY (ĭn săn ə tē) n. 1. That which denies the peephole of human consensus reality. 2. Alien wisdom. See *Madness*.

> **COMMENTARY BY ASMO DEUS**

Although the only intelligent human is an insane human, yet all of Mankind is, relative to Galactic Standards of Sanity, deemed Insane; thus that which is Insane to Humanity is Sane to Demonkind, and vice versa. However, a paradox arises if a Human determines himself to be Insane. For, then, a Demon must acknowledge that the Human is *not* Insane as a result of recognizing his Insanity, yet *must* be Insane as a result of judging his Insanity with a Sane Mind. The solution to this antimony, of course, is that logically there cannot be a Human who is Sane.[5]

5 NOTE BY GOD, LORD OF THE PERSONIFIED UNIVERSE: True.

Insurance Thieves

INSURANCE (ĭn shʊr ənz) n. Protection payments which humans must pay to corporate thieves for fear of a house burning down, a car crashing, a child dismembered by a bear, or a corpse accruing debt from its ancestors' inability to pay rent in perpetuity on a hole in the ground.

Testing Human Intelligence in Boiling Dog Excrement Lab

Earth-Density's insurance industry, is now run entirely by Demons who have emigrated to Earth to experience the Thrill of Price-Gouging Humanity from atop the tallest and most opulent Skyscrapers, paid for by the stupid human slaves themselves, and thus daily rubbing their noses in the Monstrous Immensity of the Octopus of Extortion.

INTELLECT (ĭn təl lĕkt) n. The linear and causal filter of the brain which humans stupidly mistake for a source of knowledge. A mindless tool for dividing, ordering and structuring the puny reserve of human knowledge, making it appear bigger than it is. See *Wisdom*.

Human Intellectual Pondering Pretentious Paradoxy

INTELLECTUAL (ĭn təl lĕk shū əl) adj., n. Human who smokes a death plant from a wooden tube while drinking rotting grape effluvia. See *Moron*.

INTELLIGENCE TEST (ĭn tĕ lə jəns tĕst) n. A quiz written by morons for the classification of idiots.

COMMENTARY BY ASMO DEUS

Since humans with high intelligence have a bitter aftertaste to the Demonic palate, after the Invasion is complete, an intelligence test will be administered to all enslaved humans. After being forced to stand on their heads in pits of boiling dog excrement, humans will be required to answer multiplication problems by tapping the answers on their feet. Those who pass the quiz will be summarily vaporized and those who do not will be stored in protoplasm vats for future meals.

INTERNAL REVENUE SERVICE (ĭn tûr nəl rĕ və nū sûr vəs) n. Magnificent satanic corporation which eats profit and excretes bureaucracy. See *Income Tax*.

INTERNET (ĭn tər nĕt) n. Billion-dollar mass communication system which humans use to discuss fellatio and transmit child pornography.

COMMENTARY BY ASMO DEUS

The *Internet* is the means by which Lord Satan and his Executives presently connect *from a distance* into the nervous system of the Earth and thus corrupt Humanity directly in the illusory safety of their homes. Prior to the Invasion of Earth, all Internet communication filtered through Lord Satan's Palace, saving Demons both the nuisance of traveling via Hell's Garbage Scows (previously the only available transport to Earth) and the unbearable discomfort of breathing in the reeking Body Odor of Mankind.

Invasion Manual Commission. L to R, in Human Form:
Llu Cipher, Mephis Tophiel, Baal Zebub, Ahriman, Lord Satan, Asmo Deus, Lilith, Belial, Behemoth, Zyk.

INTESTINES (ĭn tĕs tĭns) n. Bags which hold Humanity's most meaningful possessions. See *Abdomen*.

INTOXICATION (ĭn tăk sə kā shən) n. n. See *Alcohol*; *Journalist*.

INVASION MANUAL COMMISSION (ĭn vā zhən mă nyū əl kə mĭ shən) n. This Intensely Evil Group, soon to be obliterated, was personally selected by the Evil Poet and Versifier Zyk of Asimoth to write Commentaries on My Manual of Earth Terms, in order to further Explicate the Dementia of Mankind.

The Demons comprising the Commission, in addition to being Hell's Leading Experts on the Seven Deadly Sins, Eternally and Magnificently Despise each other. Their mutual hatred served to raise their level of enthusiasm in their desire to demean and refute one another. Thus, working out of fear, envy and loathing, their Writings Radiate a delightful Aura of Hatred and Paranoia.

Zyk, Commission Chairman, edited the Research Data and Composed Idiosyncratic Verses based upon his Scouting Missions to Earth at various historical periods.

The Commission's work was difficult and wrought with tension. As the publication date draws closer and their work becomes delinquent, I plan to obliterate members of the Commission at surprise intervals to instill Fear into their Hides and thus get the job completed posthaste.

Ultimately, the Success of Zyk's Commission may be determined only by You, the Demon Insurgent, and by how helpful this volume proves to be for the Invasion and Enslavement of Earth.

INVESTMENT (ĭn vĕst mənt) n. The superstition of the poor that they can hoard money already owned by the rich. See *Finance*.

IRON (ī ərn) n. Hot slab of metal which allows a human to wear unwrinkled pants to the gallows.

ISOLATION (ī sə lā shən) n. The location of the human mind relative to wisdom. See *Hermit*; *Internet*.

Map of Mafia Land Mass

ITALY (ĭ tə lē) p. Land inhabited exclusively by the Mafia. See *Mafia*; *Vatican*.

ITCH (ĭch) n. According to human mythology, the motive for the haphazard Creation of the Cosmos. Symbolically, the hypothetical Creator had an itch in the small of his back and materialized the Cosmos in order to evolve a backscratcher. After scratching his itch, the Cosmos was still there, a now useless creation, which the Creator abandoned in embarrassment.

J, J (jā) n. Pictogram indicating the hook circumscribing the neck of the Vaudeville Hack known as Mankind.

JACKAL (jă kəl) n. That which feeds off predatory decay. See *Attorney*.

Terror-Inducing Toddler Toy

JACK-IN-THE-BOX (jăk ĭn thə bŏks) n. Simple but effective toy designed to terrorize human toddlers.

COMMENTARY BY LORD SATAN

This profoundly evil toy symbolizes in its depths of meaning the Sadistic Imp of Enlightenment which appears at the climax of a precisely sequenced series of vibrations and reveals the inner self to be The Fool.

JAIL (jāl) n. 1. Skin. 2. The Earth. 3. The Cosmos.

COMMENTARY BY ASMO DEUS

Eons ago, Earth-Density was used as the Horrific Clime to which Unruly or Disobedient Demons were banished. But after finding it a wonderland of amusement, occupied as it was by the Stupidest Creatures in the Galaxy, Earth instead became not a jail but an offbeat resort.

Thus the Disobedient of Hell are no longer banished to Earth, but rather are banished into the Cosmos at Large, deemed by Lord Satan to be the Ultimate Prison for Sentient Entities.

JAZZ (jăz) n. The sounds of Hell which, when heard distantly by mythic divine angels, make them wonder if they are not, after all is said and done, in the wrong place. See *Music*.

JELLYFISH (jĕ lē fĭsh) n. State of evolution to which a human wife attempts to reduce her husband.

JESUS CHRIST (jē zəs krīst) p. 1. A.k.a. Jesus Josephson, Jesus the Nazarene, an archetypal Jewish teacher of the demented and incomprehensible doctrine of love. Thanks to *Religion* (q.v.), the fruit of Jesus' bizarre teachings has rotted so exquisitely on the Tree of Ignorance that I, Satan, smile upon all *Churches* and *Scriptures* (q.v.) as the Greatest Allies of Evil. 2. In Earth history, the chief enemy of the military, capital punishment and fundamentalist dogma. In short, the enemy of patriotism, government and religion.

Human Artist's Depiction of Jesus the Nazarene

COMMENTARY BY AHRIMAN

Jesus Christ was executed for the annoying crimes of blasphemy, defiling a temple, giving Magic Shows without a license, and babbling that, in effect, he shared stewardship of the Cosmos with a Mythic God. After being nailed to a tree[6], Jesus' body was stolen by his faithful followers. The body was then gutted, stuffed and armatured with a crude internal clockwork mechanism which caused the corpse to sit up and its wired jaws to begin opening and closing, giving the illusion that Jesus had risen from the dead.

The Christ Puppet[7], operated and made to talk by Apostles Peter and Paul crouching under the corpse's robe, launched their wildly successful business venture later known as *Christianity* (q.v.).

---

6 ED. NOTE: The Death Scene of Jesus comprised a powerful Space-Time Nexus of many subtly divergent events. This was due to the Fight to Obliteration occurring at that Nexus between the Demon Pioneer Abra Kadab and Lord Zyk (then Chairman Zyk, on Earth researching the first edition of *Invasion Manual of Earth*). A firsthand account of this legendary showdown is given in *Zyk's Last Memo to the Publisher.* (q.v.)

7 ED. NOTE: For a similar manipulation of human corpses by Demons, see *Puppet*.

Jesus of Nazarene: Actual Appearance

COMMENTARY BY ZYK
• FOR THE 666TH EDITION •

Jesus was a Nazarene whose primary teaching was for humans to forgive their enemies and ultimately themselves, a teaching rightly hated by Humanity, who enthusiastically crucified him. He was· also a plagiarist who stole Lord Satan's Parables listed in the 1st edition of this book and reworked them in a disgustingly saccharine form. See *Stupidity;* the postscript to *Zyk's First Memo to the Publisher;* and *Zyk's Last Memo to the Publisher.*

COMMENTARY BY LORD SATAN

Jesus Josephson looked nothing like the Earth painting supposedly made in his likeness. As a practical joke, Demons overshadowed the minds of Christian artists and painted Jesus to look exactly like Myself, as may be seen in the frontispiece portrait i commissioned for this Commemorative Edition. The real Jesus of Nazareth was short and pudgy, bearing a striking physical resemblance to My favorite human comedian, Buddy Hackett.

JEWELRY (jʊl rē) n. That which a human female uses as a request for love, and which a human male sees as a request for rape.

COMMENTARY BY LILITH

The humans' obsession with jewelry is, overall, incomprehensible 'to Intelligent Demons. For example, human jewelry fetishists are so obsessed that they have even been observed having their heads surgically opened and a shiny metal plate placed inside the gore of the brain, apparently as jewelry for the otherwise ugly cerebellum.

Similarly, homosexual males, specifically alcoholics on the Joint Chiefs of Staff, secretly adorn their unseen rectums with bizarre jewelry known as *butt plugs* (q.v.).

JIGSAW PUZZLE (jĭg sô pŭ zəl) n. The complete puzzle of the Cosmos cut up, scrambled and boxed inside the human brain.

JOKE (jōk) n. 1. A human being. 2. That which, when told by a human, is not funny.

Al Jolson, Negro Impersonator

JOLSON, AL (jōl sən) p. An entertainer who won the love of human Caucasians by painting his face black and caricaturing a Negro begging for his mammy.

COMMENTARY BY LORD SATAN

As a personal note, Jolson is My favorite human entertainer.[8]

JOURNALISM (jûr nəl ĭ zəm) n. A form of Black Magic in which a publication biases Reality to the advantage of its advertisers. See *Newspaper.*

JUGGLER (jŭg lər) n. 1. Human accountant. 2. Human polygamist.

COMMENTARY BY BEHEMOTH

Common misspelling for *jugular,* the least sour vein to suck after gutting a human.

JURY (jʊ rē) n. Humans too stupid to get out of jury duty.

Billionaire-Controlled Scale

JUSTICE (jŭs tĭs) n. Superstition of humans oppressed by the billionaires who own them. See *Plea Bargaining.*

JUSTIFIABLE HOMICIDE (jŭs tə fī ə bəl hŏ mə sīd) n. The homicide of humans. See *Mercy Killing.*

---

8 NOTE BY GOD, LORD OF THE PERSONIFIED UNIVERSE: Mine, too.

k, K (kā) n. 1. A pictogram of the Gaping Yawn extruding from the Symbol of Oneness.

KEEPSAKE (kēp sāk) n. A rag saved by a sentimental serial killer, because it mopped up the blood of his first victim. In the case of a Demon torturing humans for sport, keepsakes immediately should be shat upon.

Devices to Control Vaginal Freshness

KEY (kē) n. That which allows a male to lock his wife in a house, keeping her vagina fresh while he uses another.

KGB (kā jē bē) n. See *Central Intelligence Agency.*

KHAKI (kă kē) n. 1. Fashionable groin covering worn by humans while spilling the guts of an enemy or when organizing group therapy for lesbians. 2. Aside from black and red, the only other color recognized by Hell. See *Lesbian.*

KICKBACK (kĭk băk) n. See *Congress.*

KIDNAPPER (kĭd nă pər) n. An inane thief who steals the most worthless thing in the galaxy, namely, a human being.

┌─────────────────────────────┐
│ COMMENTARY BY ASMO DEUS │
└─────────────────────────────┘

The despicable act of human birth is a primal form of *kidnapping* in which a female steals innocent cosmic essences, deposits them against their will in her bowels, bakes them in sewage for nine months, then excretes them in the form of a mucus-covered homunculus. Indeed, the hypothetical God (whom humans pathetically prefer to posit as their Creator rather than Lord Satan, their true Creator) is the ultimate Kidnapper, having stolen Cosmic Elements against their will and formed them, to their horror, into a race of idiots.

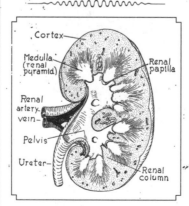

Delicious Snack When Properly Evacuated

KIDNEY (kĭd nē) n. After gutting a human, squeeze this organ dry of fluid before eating.

KILL (kĭl) v. 1. To relieve misery holistically; that is, without drugs. 2. That which any idiot can do, and therefore the chief activity of Mankind.

┌─────────────────────────────┐
│ COMMENTARY BY MEPHIS TOPHIEL │
└─────────────────────────────┘

Appreciation of the lusciousness of Killing is the only thing, thankfully, that Demonkind shares with the otherwise Insensible Glut of Mankind.

KINDNESS (kĭnd nĭs) n. The act of instantly snapping a baby's neck at birth. See *Love.*

Spewer Upon Queen and Country

KING (kĭng) n. That which soils the Queen. See *Queen.*

KISMET (kĭz mĕt) n. A romantic convergence of space-time strings in the human mind; for example, when long-lost childhood friends are entranced by finding their beds next to each other in the same cancer ward. See *Future; Love.*

Kitchen: Preparing Gore for Throat Holes

KISS (kĭs) n. The kiss is an activity designed by Hell to speed the evolution of the most important creature on Earth, Bacteria.

☐ **COMMENTARY BY ASMO DEUS** ☐

Humanity, an insignificant race, was designed by Lord Satan as a mere host organism into whose mouths and groins Bacteria could emigrate and therein house and feed themselves. Bacteria utilize human kissing as transportation from mouth to mouth until they find a tongue that suits them, and around which they then swathe their beautiful viral colonies. See *Bacteria*.

KITCHEN (kĭ chən) n. 1. Area in which humans slaughter and burn life-forms. 2. Central clearinghouse for disseminating carcinogens to Mankind. See *Cooking*; *Lunch*; *Menu*.

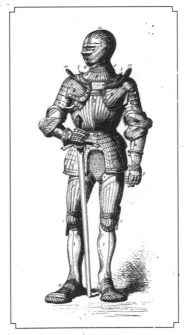

Coward Clothed in Metal

KNIGHT (nīt) n. A cowardly warrior who refuses to fight unless riveted inside a boiler oven.

KNOWLEDGE (nä lĭj) n. That which, to humans, is unknowable.

☐ **COMMENTARY BY ASMO DEUS** ☐

In ancient times, the pioneer demon Abra Kadab used The Spell of Obfuscation to warp the human brain's self-reference circuitry. This ancient Spell overshadows the mind of mankind, causing it to mistake its primitive linear thought patterns for actual Knowledge. See *Abra Kadab*; *Book 1.3 On the Unspeakable Planet Earth*; *Book*; *Humanity*; *Intellect*; *Library*; *Literature*; *Memory*; *Mind*; *Thought*; *Typewriter*.

KORAN (kə răn) n. See *Scripture*.

KREMLIN (krĕm lən) n. See *White House*.

Ancient Cow-Bag Advocate

KRISHNA (krĭsh nə) p. Spiritual leader who inspired the Caste System, the Class of Untouchables, and the Deification of Earth's most insipid creature, the stinking, flatulent Cow. See *Christ*; *Scripture*.

I, L (ĕl) n. Pictogram of the human foot, which must be carefully deboned before eating.

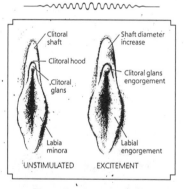

Torso-Flap Slobbering Area

LABIA (lā bē ə) n. Female groin-flaps exuding urine, mucus and blood, which are enthusiastically slobbered over by human males.

LABOR (lā bər) n. Justifiable pain inflicted on females for bringing another human into the world.

LABOR UNION (lā bər yūn yən) n. 1.That which protects human workers from a corrupt organization. 2. A corrupt organization from which human workers must protect themselves.

LABORATORY (lăb (ə) rə tôr ē) n. Workplace in which humans torture animals and create diseases.

COMMENTARY BY LORD SATAN

Aside from the use of their television presentations as Somnambulants and Themselves as Rustic Toys for Demonkind, the only other use for Mankind is as subjects for the noble study of Human Animal Experimentation and Vivisection.[9]

All students of Torture 101 at Hell University now exclusively use Humanity as their lab rats in the devising of new and imaginative tortures.

Aside from the pure joy of hearing incessant human shrieks, the practice of human torture also has market value in the City of Hell, since the professional videotaping of human torture by Demons is now widespread, having created a cottage industry for these video entertainments for use at birthdays, pool parties and child sacrifices.

LACKEY (lă kē) n. Formerly, a vice president; presently, a president.

---

9 NOTE BY LILITH: Among the many Human Animal Experiments performed at the University of Hell, the testing of makeup and facial creams holds a special interest for female Demons throughout the City of Hell. The experiments are performed on Lab Humans who, when alive on Earth, were scientists who experimented on animals. It is a joy to see the Lab Humans in their cages, their necks in metal clamps to reduce squirming, their heads shaved and electrodes thrust into their brains to monitor their reaction to various chemicals layered over their faces or injected into their brains. Their ceaseless shrieks of torment not only encourage Demon Scientists in their experiments, but also, when applied to the faces of Hell's Womankind, imbues the resulting makeup and creams with a delightful vibratory tingle of terror.

LACTATION (lăk tā shən) n. Biological secretions used to succor Humanity in the brief period between birth and death.

Simulator of Femininity

LADY (lā dē) n. That which simulates femininity for the purpose of receiving free alcohol.

LANGUAGE (lăn gwəj) n. The highway upon which human stupidity drives. See *Speech*; *Word*.

LARYNGITIS (lâr ən jī təs) n. Useful malady in that it inhibits alternative comedy.

LARYNX (lâr ĭngks) n. The most deplorable part of the human anatomy, which allows humans to irritate intelligent creatures.

COMMENTARY BY BEHEMOTH

In gutting a human, the larynx is the first organ to disgorge.

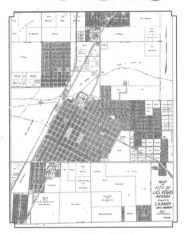

Las Vegas: Demon Insurgent Landing Site

LAS VEGAS (läs vā gəs)

n. Prime landing site for Demon Insurgents. Known to Demon Earth-geographers as Vatican West. Like its Italian counterpart, Las Vegas is dedicated to stealing money from the poor and feeble-minded to finance the gold rings and jewelry of its casino owner/clergy. See *Landing Sites*; *Time*; *Vatican*.

LAUGHTER (lăf tər) n. That

which is inspired in a soldier when a comrade slips on the gutted intestines of an enemy family.

> ### COMMENTARY BY MEPHIS TOPHIEL
>
> The Demon Invader eavesdropping on the inanities of Humanity will soon find himself witnessing the following inexplicable cyclic event:
>
> 1. *Two humans are engaged in typically banal human discourse.*
> 2. *One of them emits an unusual, or unexpected, string of words.*
> 3. *Both humans suddenly emit a loud, repetitive, obnoxious bleating sound.*
> 4. *The bleating slowly dissipates until the cycle begins again.*

This bleating, a.k.a. *laughter*, like *orgasm* (q.v.) appears to be an explusion of the human brain, such as it is, characterized by a contorting of the face and a quaking and shaking of the limbs in a typically palsied human fashion.

Since laughter is arguably the most annoying and incomprehensible acts of Humanity, the invading Demon who intends to kill and eat a human would be advised, by way of maximizing evil wherever possible, to kill it just as it begins bleating, and thus cut off this irritating sound before it reaches its despicable fruition. See *Comedian; Comedy*.

LAW (lô) n. The barbed-wire

fence imprisoning human justice.

> ### COMMENTARY BY ASMO DEUS
>
> The profession of *law* is of great interest to the Domain of Hell. Since all *lawyers* (q.v.) on Earth are either actual or aspiring Demons, it is a Beautiful Irony that it is Evil Itself which decides which human actions shall be deemed Evil or Anti-Evil (the latter known to humans as "good"). Thus, unknown to Mankind, every action which law decrees is bad is, in fact, good, and vice versa.
>
> For example, killing is against the law. Yet killing serves the highest good of a human, allowing him to take the money or possessions of his victim, and thereby elevating his standard of living.
>
> Marriage, as another example, is considered "good" and is therefore legal, and yet it serves the highest Evil, of enslaving and chaining one human to the putrefying flesh of another.
>
> Allowing lawyers the stewardship of Justice is the most exquisitely magnificent evil intervention of human society ever engineered by Demons on Earth.

LAW OF ONE (lô əv wən)

n. See *Loneliness*.

Lawyer: Human Parasite

LAWYER (lô yər, loi yər) n.

1. An Angel of Hell. 2. A parasitic Executive of Lucifer, repulsive even to maggots, who sucks the juice of life from both the oppressor and the oppressed. 3. With mimes, theologians and radio talk-show hosts, the mainstay occupation in downtown Hell. 4. A pervert who achieves orgasm by flashing his genitalia at the blindfolded Face of Justice. See *Mercenary; Moron*.

LECTURE (lĕk chər) n. The

buzzing of an Insect about Nothing.

LEPRECHAUN (lĕp rə kän)

n. Mythic midget created to placate a nation of intoxicated idiots.

LEPROSY (lĕ prə sē) n. Be-

neficent and colorful disorder that encourages the rotting of Mankind.

LETTER (lĕ tər) n. 1. The

crumbling vertebra of the fossilized skeleton of human language. 2. Viscera of a tree which provokes shooting sprees by postal workers.

Devotee of Pauper-Worshipping Cult

LIBERAL (lĭ bər əl) n. Member of Pauper-Worshipping Cult who advocates legalizing the robbery of the rich. See *Conservative*.

LIBERTY (lĭ bər tē) n. The exhilarating freedom to choose from infinite means of enslavement.

LIBRARY (lī brâr ē) n. An aggregation of books giving humans the illusion of wisdom, as a toupee gives the illusion of hair. See *Literature*.

LIE (lī) n. Synopsis of human knowledge.

COMMENTARY BY ASMO DEUS

Every Demon Student of Inane Human Logic is familiar with the dull Human Paradox:

"All humans are liars. I am a human. Therefore I am lying when I say that all humans are liars. Yet as a human, I am lying when I say that I am lying when I say that all humans are liars; etc."

As Demons are instructed at the University of Hell, to apply logic to a string of words such as this and pretend that this aping of meaning somehow equates to truth is an example of the Utter and Unredeemable Stupidity of Man. See *Logic*.

COMMENTARY BY ZYK

Concerning the Lie and its corollary, Love, I offer the following versification told through the eyes and tongue of a Human Liar:

Of every love that e'er I gauntly wooed,
I wooed with manly masks of bold pretense,
Disguising trembling fear with laughter lewd,
Exchanging a fine madness for common sense.
But adroit in easy lies and seeming truth,
Disguise sustained me when all else would not,
And while denouncing fancy false and dreams uncouth,
I told crass lies and the sweetest kisses got.
Yet now, I see a truth within my Lie,
For ersatz love can be an ersatz treasure.
Thus there is no inconsistency in why
My loving lies fill all my loves with pleasure.
For I woo my loves with truth in falsity,
And know my loves are falsely true to me.

LIFE (līf) n. On the Toilet of Sentience, a brief emittance from the Vast Cosmic Bowel.

COMMENTARY BY AHRIMAN

Since all Demons, unlike humans, share the splendor of already being Dead, the obsession which humans have of remaining alive at all costs is an amusing and pathetic aberration.

Since only in death is there true "life," the state which humans consider being alive is in reality a state of death, of the soul being trapped in the confines of a gauche and messy chaos of fluids.

Thus the Demon invading Earth will be faced with an irritating paradox: to kill a human is to do it a service by freeing it from its disgusting imprisonment, yet to refrain from doing Evil to a human is Inconceivable for a Demon.

Therefore, when killing humans, the correct emotional stance of a Demon Insurgent should be indifference, and an emphasis on the correctness of killing and devouring a human as a satisfactory, albeit imperfectly nourishing, meal.

Shark Food Container

LIFE BOAT (līf bōt) n. In the Refrigerator of the Seven Seas, Tupperware keeping leftovers fresh for sharks.

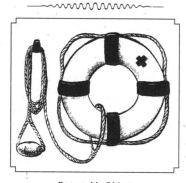

Detestable Object

LIFE PRESERVER (līf prĭ zər vər) n. A detestable object linking two tasteless concepts.

LIFE INSURANCE (līf ĭn shur əns) n. Delightful contract with death at the direction of Demons. See *Insurance Agent*.

That Which Excretes the Abomination of Light

Festive Flesh-Sewage Dampeners

LIGHT (līt) n. 1. The Abominable Excrement of a Star. 2. When combined with equal amounts of Darkness, the ultimate composition of matter. 3. That which a human female turns off to dim the grotesque abomination of fornication. See *Photon*.

COMMENTARY BY MEPHIS TOPHIEL

The Hatred of Light, the instinctive emotional posture of all Evilkind, has motivated Demons Immemorial in the ceaseless creation of Vile Engines to Destroy Illumination.

In the Cosmic Realms, the Annihilation of Stars (which excrete Light) is a successful and profitable business for Entrepreneurs of Hell, who deign to torment the souls of Stars until they at last commit suicide. See *Nova*.

In the microcosm of Earth-Density, this Instinct has resulted in the design and implementation (by Demons) of the entire Evil Engine of *Photosynthesis* (q.v.), that Glorious Machine of Hell which endlessly eats the noxious photonic rays of Despised Sunlight and Transforms them into a Sweet and Palatable Dioxide.

LIMOUSINE (lǐm ə zēn) n. Innocent shards of metal coaxed from the Earth for the purpose of transporting cocaine-addicted humans to film premieres.

LINGERIE (län zhər ā) n. Intricate, delicate garments designed to attract human males to the sewage portals of the vagina.

LIQUOR (lǐ kər) n. 1. Innocent plant life, boiled alive by humans, which is symbiotic with the Beernut Industry and facilitates the daemonic scourge of Twelve-Step Programs. 2. That which, when drunk by Demons, makes unappetizing humans seem more attractive as foodstuffs. See *Alcohol*.

LITERACY (lǐ tər ə sē) n. Symbolic faculty enabling humans the linear assimilation of matter and energy which, at the end of each cycle, leads to the construction of weapons with which humans tastefully annihilate themselves.

LITERATI (lǐ tər a tē) n. Cult dedicated to the obfuscation of knowledge.

LITERATURE (lǐ tər ə chŏr) n. Toilet paper for the excretions of the human mind. See *Writer*.

COMMENTARY BY ZYK

Due to the paucity of reference materials concerning Earth, and the incomprehensibility of Earth literature, Lord Satan found the research involved in the preparation of His *Invasion Manual* irritating in its scope.

As the author of expert sociological treatises on Earth Evil, and a specialist in the blasphemous tracts of the banished Demon Abra Kadab who first settled the planet, I was therefore commanded by His Majesty to scour the stinking heaps of human literature for further explication by way of sundry notes and commentaries. See *Abra Kadab; Library; Taboo of Earth Density*.

LIVESTOCK (lǐv stäk) n. To Demons, the pulpy gore-sacs of Humanity.

COMMENTARY BY BEHEMOTH

After the Invasion of Earth, more and more Demons in Earth-Density will be dining on humans; therefore, care must be taken not to deplete the supply. As history is our greatest teacher, refer to the Chart on the next page.

Note the dips after the births of Buddha, Jesus and Mohammed [historical periods in which humans, due to soul development, tasted bad] which revitalized during the Plague in 1100, which served to sweeten the flesh with its tangy rot and pustules. After word of the delicious ripeness of Humanity got out circa 1250, the influx of Demons has strained the human food supply to the maximum, covering millions of milk cartons around the globe with the faces of humans eaten or stored for snacks.

As this chart shows, if the present trend continues, human flesh may become depleted as a Demon food source by the year 3000. See Pamphlet #66F: *800 Per Demon: A Responsible Yearly Guide to Eating Humans*, Office of Behemoth.

COMMENTARY BY BAAL ZEBUB

Note to Demons subsequent to the Invasion: While humans may be killed for food, a permit is necessary

CHART OF HUMANS EATEN THROUGHOUT HISTORY

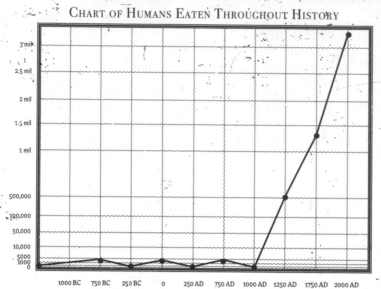

(Y-axis: 0, 1000, 5000, 10,000, 50,000, 100,000, 500,000, 1 mil, 1.5 mil, 2 mil, 2.5 mil, 3 mil)
(X-axis: 1000 BC, 750 BC, 250 BC, 0, 250 AD, 750 AD, 1000 AD, 1250 AD, 1750 AD, 2000 AD)

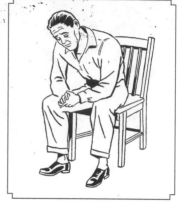

Loneliness: Human Devoid
of Other Flesh-Bags

to kill humans for sport. The reason is obvious. Unprecedented waves of Demon Invaders began killing humans indiscriminately, thus depleting the human livestock and ruining the experience of post-invasion visitors who wish to kill humans for sport. Thus a license is necessary for wholesale slaughter, genocide, water-supply poisonings, and so on.

When annihilating a human village, a responsible Demon Insurgent always leaves one breeding couple behind in order to allow the restocking of new victims.

Living Room with Magical Screen

LIVING ROOM (lĭ vĭng rŭm) n. A room designed to house a Magical Screen which transforms humans into the Cult of Consumption. See *Consumer; Television.*

LOBOTOMY (lō bä tə mē) n. 1. The greatest achievement of human medicine. 2. The highest evolution of the human brain. See *Brain; Nun; Optimist; Philosopher; Surgery.*

LOGIC (lŏ jĭk) n. 1. The mindless, sterile tool of Human Reason. 2. That which a condemned human utilizes to choose death by injection over death by decapitation.

COMMENTARY BY ASMO DEUS

What the inane, logic-worshipping Clod of Humanity does not understand is that Reason is open-ended, but logic is not. In their stupidity, humans allow Reason to be ruled by Logic, instead of the other way around. Even worse, just as Human Mathematics is perversely fixed, so too is Human Logic. Thus, spinning in the destinationless Gyroscope of Logic, Humanity's thoughts forever circle in delusional paradoxes like dizzy, impotent gnats flouncing in a bug jar. See *Mathematics.*

LONELINESS (lōn lē nĭs) n. 1. The psychology of an unmarried human. 2. The psychology of a married human. See *Make-believe.*

COMMENTARY BY LLU CIPHER

The Paradox of Loneliness is implicit in the subjugation in which Demonkind finds itself by the Immutable Law of One. The Cosmos, as every Demon knows, is composed of Lord Satan's Mind-Stuff in Ever-Permutating Opposites.

The Manipulating of Opposites is the basis of Conjuring. Yet these permutations must, in the Great Evil Equation, equal the Cosmic Sum of Zero.

Thus the loneliness at the core of All Evil Beings is a hypothetical resonance of the singular aloneness of the Ultimate Evil of All That Is.

For more on this subject, see my pamphlet, *Cosmic Onanism: The Singular Perversity of a Masturbatory Universe.*[10]

10 **NOTE BY BELIAL: I** would steer the Inquiring Demon clear of Llu Cipher's pamphlet, which presents a puerile theory which borders on the Blasphemy of positing the Existence of a "Meta-Satan," a Hypothetical Being within which our Magnificently Indecorous Lord exists as a hellish subset! Cipher neglects to acknowledge the Utter Supremacy of our Black Master as the Fundament of the Cosmos, a transgression for

LONG SHOT (lông shät) n. The chances of an elderly human being able to control his or her bowels.

LOOPHOLE (lūp hōl) n. Small portal in human legal documents connecting the contractee directly to Lord Satan's anus.

Homely Signet of Female Bust and Buttocks

LOVE (ləv) n. The sublime gateway to hate. See *Free will*; *Romance*; *Sentiment*.

COMMENTARY BY LILITH

The illusory emotion referred to as *love* is a waste product of the human nervous system's primary electrical capacitor known as the *orgasm*. The discharge of this bioelectric circuitry is so overpowering that the human dullards interpret its meaningless resonance in their mental-emotional

which, one hopes, his mottled hide will be flayed to within an inch of his Deathless Life.*

* **NOTE BY LORD SATAN:** Belial's arse-osculating note, while respectful of the Immensity of My Being, does address a matter which this present Investigation into the Mystery of Humanity has catalyzed in My Mind; namely, the inconsistency between the Inarguable Existence of the Law of One (the essence of the Black Arts) and My Supremacy as Master of the Cosmos. For, as the Law of One wordlessly articulates, All That Is must include also Myself, which bespeaks the Hideous Paradox of an "All" Greater Than Myself, a paradox which exudes an Unbearably Noxious Vibration of Fallaciousness in every cosmic atom of My Black Being.

body (known as love) as a connection to their imaginary God, as opposed to the reality that it is a connection to their throbbing genitalia.

The throbbing of the genitals of humans, and its plethora of psychic waste products, is the source of all human philosophy, philanthropy and theology, as well as, alternatively, rape, murder, circumcision, edible underwear and penis extensions.

COMMENTARY BY ZYK

In an attempt to explicate in precise detail the intricacies of human love, a faculty Incomprehensible to Demonkind, I offer the following cranking spew of rhyme:

There be cries of perfect moan
When she gives her Jack a bone.
There be laughter, thief of tears,
When she grabs him by the ears.
There be flashing, rotted teeth
With Jack above and Jill beneath.
There be unseemly dives and loops
Making human lovers nincompoops.

LOVING CUP (lə vǐng kǔp) n. Chalice awarded to a human who most successfully hates his opponents.

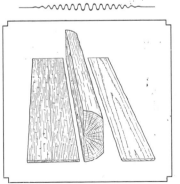

Wood Ripped from Forest To Build Pornography Theater

LUMBER (lǔm bər) n. Camouflage term used by humans to facilitate the extinction of plant life.

Human Stuffing Carcasses Down Throat Hole

LUNCH (lǔnch) n. 1. The human ritual, performed when the Sun reaches its zenith, of stuffing corpses down the human throat. 2. That which a Demon heaves when inadvertently viewing alternative comedy.

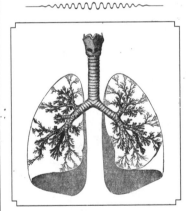

Filters of Human Flatulence

LUNGS (lǔngz) n. Organic bellows which rhythmically absorb and expel Earth's atmosphere of diffused human flatulence.

LUXURY (lǔk shə rē) n. The state of a tapeworm reposing in the human intestines.

LYNCHING (lǐn chǐng) n. See *Noon*.

QUADRIFIDUM
THE
THIRD

ZYK'S THIRD MEMO
TO THE
PUBLISHER

CONCERNING HIS RESEARCH
ON
EARTH

MEMO TO
MORTIMER PÖNÇÉ, ESQ.
PUBLISHER, MIND CONTROL PRESS
HELL HOLE WEST
CITY OF HELL

FROM
ZYK OF ASIMOTH, EDITOR
INVASION MANUAL COMMISSION
DISPATCHED FROM EARTH,
ROSWELL, NEW MEXICO, U.S.A.
JUNE 15, 1947

Detestable Mr. Pönçé:

I received a terrifying message on my beeper as I landed here two days ago. It was from Lord Satan himself.

I was certain that he had heard rumors of the conspiracy to assassinate him, that Cipher and Tophiel planned to lead the rebellion, claiming Lord Satan was mentally unstable. All of this because of Our Lord's entry under "Supreme Being"! Moreover, since the conspirators worked for me, and since my reports are a week behind, I was certain that He was going to Obliterate me first. Or perhaps one of the Commission ratted on me, telling Him that I was sharing my per diem with a human female. (The e-m field here has caused me to fall even more desperately in love with Debbie, whom I have dragged like a gooning fool through the Densities of Earth Time.)

But when I returned His Majesty's call, He mentioned nothing about a conspiracy, thank the Umbra of Ra. Instead, He informed me that He was incensed at the lateness of my reports, and was giving me one last chance to make amends.

To my surprise, Mr. Pönçé, He sent me on an Urgent Spy Mission. The Crashes at Roswell, New Mexico, he told me, were a key part of His Invasion Plan. The vehicles were souped-up Hellcraft owned by the race of inbred, Red Trash Demons known as Angels. (The Angels, as you know, invisibly orbit the Earth in their "trailer park" colonies.) My Lord explained that His Spies had already planted bombs on several of the Angels' vehicles to precipitate the Roswell incident. The Red Trash in these crafts were scheduled to travel to Earth year 1947, when cattle anuses were at their peak in flavor. The Angels planned to mutilate the cattle, retrieve the anuses and barbecue them at the Annual Angel Ring-Toss Championship.

His Majesty's Plan was for the Angels' craft to crash, and for the human idiots to retrieve the wreckage and attempt to analyze its technology. The only components humans could possibly understand would be Microchips, Fiber Optics, and the crystalline lasers the Angels used to slice off the cattle anuses. Lord Satan, in His Evil Wisdom, knew that the Microchip would result in the humans mass-producing Hell's Secret Weapon of Mind Control, Television. Within fifty years of the crash, when Lord Satan has scheduled the Invasion of Earth, televisions would be in every human home, having by then brainwashed Mankind into a race of passive simpletons.

Ring of Obladadox

However, Hell's Spies discovered a space-time Nexus at Roswell which will interfere with the Plan. Due to the Nexus, the Angels who are supposed to crash and burn in 1947 will get drunk and set their dials incorrectly for 1974; if they crash in 1974, this will delay the invention of television twenty years and thus delay the Invasion of Earth from occurring at the Millennium, its most Auspicious Time. Also in the event of a 1974 crash, the Vatican Secret Service would then confiscate the wreckage, back-engineer its weapons system and become an annoying threat to the ensuing Demon Invasion. For these reasons, Lord Satan has sent me His precious Ring of Obladadox. He ordered me to use the Ring to possess the body of one of the drunken Angels aboard the sabotaged craft and switch the time-controls back from 1974 to 1947.

Needless to say, Mr. Pönçé, I was nervous. I am a Poet; I am not a Spy. I am also disadvantaged by having Sister Debbie with me, whom I love too much to leave.

Unfortunately, things did not work out exactly as planned. First I kissed Debbie and left her playing computer games in my Hellcraft parked in the Roswell badlands. Then I checked my pocket watch. The explosions would rip the crafts to shreds in twenty minutes. I closed my eyes, rubbed the Ring of Obladadox and directed My Total Evil Power on possessing the Angel commanding the Hellcraft. Feeling a burst of electricity surging through my tail, I passed out. I awoke a nanosecond later, felt a tingling sensation and opened my eyes. I was inside the Angel's body at the controls of the Hellcraft. Lord Satan's Black Ring of Obladadox materialized on my finger. A strange feeling rippled through the short, gray body I now inhabited; a moment later I recognized it: *I was drunk.*

Three other Angels, also short, gray and ugly, were also drunk, guzzling cranial fluid from a decapitated Irishman's skull and hopping around the deck like the slathering Glentiqs of Klone. They offered me the skull and, to hide my identity, I drank like a pig, imitating the slovenly manners of an Angel.

As they turned away high-kicking and singing about the delectableness of cows' rectums, I desperately focused my drunken attention on the craft's console. Although my vision was blurred, I found the time-dial and saw that, indeed, it had been wrongly set for 1974. I casually switched the dial to 1947 and sighed with relief. Now all I had to do was rub the Sacred Ring, concentrate, and switch back to my own magnificent body.

But suddenly a claw clamped around my wrist and spun me around in the chair. It was the strongest and drunkest of the three angels.

He had spotted the Ring of Obladadox.

He pointed at it and grunted angrily at the others. They rushed over, gazed at Lord Satan's Ring, then at my eyes. They instantly recognized that I was an impostor.

The Angel holding me drew his laser and pointed it at my head. They began yelling in their hick dialects that their pilot was possessed. The smallest one ripped the Ring off my finger. The third yanked open the slit of my mouth. As they laughed and chortled drunkenly, the small one violently forced the Ring down my throat. They all worked my jaw, screaming for me to chew it, howling and laughing like the degenerate hicks they were.

I tried to spit up the Ring, but was unable to properly manipulate the Angel's primitive jaw, and was forced to swallow it. That was it. I had had enough of these yokels.

Furious, I snatched the laser out of the drunkard's hand and held it up to my temple. I yelled for them to freeze or I'd blow their friend's head off. They stared at me in shock, stared at each other — and began cackling and hooting again. Then all three materialized lasers and pointed them at me.

Still drunk, I fired at one of them, blowing a ten-inch hole in his head. The other two fired, missing me as I dove through an open hatch into the ship's engine room. They chased me through a maze of crevices in the huge, souped-up engine. These hicks spent all of their time working on this 300-foot thought-sensitive monstrosity into which they'd lasered their names like idiots. They kept blasting me and I blasted back, finally blowing another one's head off. Now I was alone with the smaller one, and we began stalking each other through the maze of the engine. I checked the timepiece strapped to the angel's groin. I had four minutes before the explosion.

I had to get that Ring out of my stomach. If I not only failed my mission but also lost the Ring, Lord Satan's Wrath would be Monstrous. Desperate, I licked some globs of green fughoot oozing from the engine block and tried to vomit. I dry-heaved the fughoot, but no Ring. I grabbed my stomach with both fists, squeezed till I felt the precious Ring inside and tried to squeeze it up my esophagus like a light bulb through a fashion designer's colon, but it kept slipping down out of my reach.

The timepiece showed one minute left. As I shoved it back in my groin, I noticed that the watch was short-circuiting. It suddenly occurred to me that the time might be wrong. That meant—

The Hellcraft blew sky high. The blast was enormous, not unlike the Magnificent Flatulence of Lord Satan during the Mexican-Eating Contest. I was blasted out of the wreckage and came crashing to the ground amid shards of debris. I staggered to my feet and realized that the body I inhabited was still intact. I saw the other bodies, the two I had shot and the third who was still breathing. I leaned over him to see if he was still alive when I felt a rope thrown around my neck.

A dozen humans in military and Vatican uniforms cuffed me, stuffed me into a canvas bag and carried me away in a vehicle.

Zyk and the Angel-Daemons

It was strange, Mr. Pönçé. For although I was in serious trouble, all I could think about was Debbie. I might never see her delicate and delicious groin again.

After an hour I felt myself being carried into a building and through winding passageways. From inside the bag, I could hear the humans barking and grunting at each other, sounding like Red Trash themselves; no wonder the two races had a close affinity.

They slid me out of the bag and onto a table. I decided to play dead. I kept my eyes open and willed the effluvia in my (i.e., the Angel's) body to stop flowing within the body sac. It worked. The human idiots uncuffed me and prodded and poked me from every angle, propping me up in uncomfortable poses and taking hundreds of photographs. Then they barked and murmured to each other, covered me with a canvas and left the room.

Alone for a moment, I grabbed a pair of long-handled tweezers from the medical rack and shoved it as far down my throat as I could. The angel's thin arms allowed me to thrust my hand deep into the stomach cavity. I waved the tweezers around until I heard a faint metallic tik-tik-tik as the tip of the tweezers grazed the Ring.

Manipulating the tweezers in my stomach, I almost got hold of one side of the Ring when I heard the soldiers and Vatican Secret Service agents returning. I quickly yanked my arm out of my throat, replaced the tweezers and played dead again. The humans entered, accompanied by what appeared to be a doctor and a film cameraman.

The two new men saw me and gasped, wide-eyed, grabbing their stomachs in revulsion. (If only the moronic humans knew how disgusting their appearance was to Demonkind.) The doctor steadied himself as the other set up his camera. The doctor grabbed a scalpel and barked orders. I fought back pain as the scalpel began slicing through my chest.

Since this was not my body, I knew I could survive if a few organs were removed. What I needed was that Ring, and severing the stomach cavity might give me another opportunity to get it.

The doctor widened the incision and began digging his gloved hand through the effluvia in my (the Angel's) chest.

As he sliced open my stomach, he turned momentarily to get another tool from the rack. This was my chance. I quickly reached inside the stomach incision and felt around for the Ring.

It wasn't there.

But it must be! The cameraman screamed and pointed to my movements. The humans panicked and screamed at each other in horror as I felt around inside as quickly as I could. Nothing! What if the Ring had dropped through the effluvia into the sickening Angel genitalia?

I gritted my teeth and, as the humans continued screaming, shoved my claw down into the Angel's testes sac — and felt the Ring. Struggling to grasp it, the Ring slipped onto my claw. The humans, still panicking, tried to grab my hand and stop me. I yanked my hand free and quickly rubbed the Ring.

There was an orange explosion behind my eyes and I blacked out again. An instant later I awoke, tingling. I looked down and saw that I was back in my own body and sprawled in the dirt. The Ring materialized on my finger again.

I looked up and saw Debbie gazing down at me with wet, beautiful, terrified eyes. I staggered to my feet and kissed her as I've never kissed a female before. With my tail wrapped around her neck and my tongue shoved down her throat to sensually lick her stomach lining, Debbie began gagging, and from experience I knew this meant that she too must be in ecstasy. After fornicating with her a hundred times against a cactus, I threw my pack over my back, took her up in my arms and hurried back to the Hellcraft.

Checking my calls, I received a frantic message from Lilith. His Majesty, she said, had just obliterated Asmo Deus. Now there remain only the conspirators Cipher and Tophiel, Lilith and Myself.

I beseech you, Mr. Pönçé, please press your case with our Lord before we are all crushed to ether. As to the matter at hand, I have dispatched the Ring back to Lord Satan and sent off a batch of new material for the Commission to edit. But I clearly need more time.

I am taking Debbie and her luscious vagina with me to the next Nexus in Earth's near future. I know I must leave her behind, but I cannot. May the Blackness of Evil watch over my beloved.

With Inconceivable Hatred,
ZYK

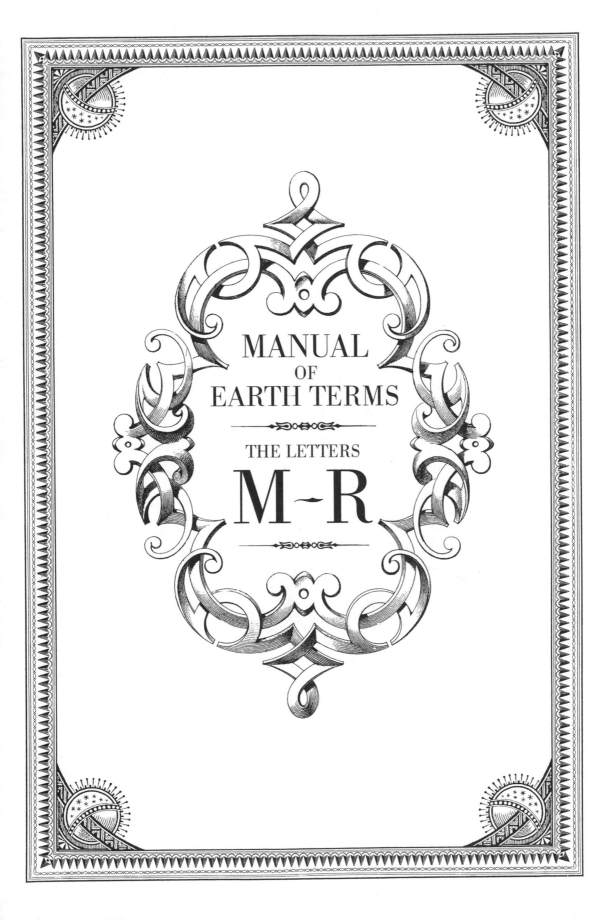

MANUAL
OF
EARTH TERMS

THE LETTERS
M~R

m, M (ĕm) n. Pictogram of the sagging mammary glands, offered above to the Nothingness Which Watches Over Human Destiny.

MACHINE (mə shēn) n. A human without the blubbering databank of emotion.

> **COMMENTARY BY ASMO DEUS**
>
> The surrounding of Mankind by machines from morning till night, thereby transforming Humanity itself into a Flesh Machine is, of course, the goal of Lord Satan's Invasion, and also the goal of the 1% of Humanity who own the citizen slaves and their Flesh-Machine Repositories called *cities* (q.v.).

Human Maestro and His Instrument

MACHINE GUN (mə shēn gŭn) n. An exquisite percussion instrument played upon the drum skin of the human body.

MACHISMO (mä chēz mō) n. That which masks the homosexual. The more a male impersonates a caricature of a male, the more he represses the playing of show tunes while on a fellatio binge. See *Homosexual*; *Musical Theater*; *X-Chromosome*.

MACROCOSM (măk rə kä zəm) n. The teetering, sloppy Whole into which the rancid, insipid Parts are stuffed. See *Microcosm*.

MADNESS (măd nĭs) n. That which, in humans, inhibits suicide. See *Insanity*.

MADHOUSE (măd hous) n. 1. Earth-Density. 2. The Cosmos, save Hell.

Director of Hitting, Scraping and Blowing

MAESTRO (mī strō) n. A human in a tuxedo who directs the twitching of others in the act of hitting, scraping and blowing. See *Entertainment*; *Guitar*; *Harp*; *Jazz*; *Music*; *Soprano*.

MAFIA (mä fē ə) n. See *Central Intelligence Agency*.

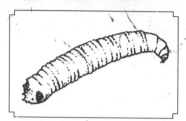

Maggot Before Its Wings Waft It to Heavenly Ordure

MAGGOT (mä gət) n. The larval fly, and the symbolic counterpart of a larval human being before it sprouts angel wings. See *Angel*.

MAGIC (mä jik) n. 1. That which Imbecilic Humanity, which in effect materialized out of nothingness, denies existence. 2. The lowest rung of the Splintered Stool of Show Business. 3. The pathetic human activity of manipulating small slices of a tree to cause astonishment in drunkards and fools. See *Entertainment*; *Impalement*; *Gag*; *Guillotine*, *Magician*.

> **COMMENTARY BY AHRIMAN**
>
> Mankind, in its annoyingly limited scope of vision, is incapable of remembering that merely two generations before, his ancestors considered all modern appliances, such as images transported through wire, or telepresence, as whimsical absurdities only entertained by fools who believed in the reality of *magic*. Of course, Human Science is that which denies Reason and Intuition and, therefore, denies Magic.
>
> Magic is the playful application of the Imagination upon the Stain of Matter, accompanied by the knowledge that the correct procedure in the manipulation of matter can produce *any result whatsoever*. The greatest magic, therefore, will be in its application for the Ultimate Magical Goal — of wiping out the Fecal Stain of Humanity from the Pants of Space-Time.

Former Juggler or Ventriloquist

MAGICIAN (mə jĭ shən) n. 1. An annoying exhibitionist with delusions of grandeur who performs a hackneyed impression of a hypothetical God. 2. An alcoholic performer who was previously a juggler or ventriloquist.

MAGNETISM (măg nə tĭ zəm) n. That which allows perfectly good bullets to be reclaimed from a human corpse.

COMMENTARY BY ASMO DEUS

In Earth-Density, material forms break down into components subliminal to human perception, ghost-particles called *electrons* by the human idiots. The spin of these ghost-particles (called by the idiots *charge*) is a fundamental mechanical motion underlying matter and connecting it together. When the spins of the ghost-particles of different substances mesh and click together like gears, the result is a right-angled torque referred to by the idiots as *magnetism*.

The right-angled torque resulting from the intermeshing gears is the fundamental force in the Material Cosmos. This torque reacts with the curving in and out of the underlying Soup of Space-Time to create permutations which limit the shapes of so-called *atoms* (q.v.) and, via attraction and repulsion, bring forth the diversity of Tacky Matter with which the Cosmos distastefully clothes Itself.

The Grind of Atomic Gears known as *Magnetism* is designed to Evolve Forms which may eventually be invested with Souls, and thus have the opportunity to Evolve into Evil Fruition. And this, Demon Reader, is the Intractable Purpose not merely of Magnetism but of the entire Creaking Cosmos.

However, its glorious applications aside, Demon Invaders of Earth-Density should carefully note that magnetism is an indispensable tool in the bulk erasing of humans' computerized medical records and Christmas Card Lists and in the mass disrupting of pacemakers in the hearts of senior citizens.

MAID OF HONOR (mād əv ä nər) n. See *Jealousy*.

Larval Humans Engaged in Psychotic Delusion

MAKE-BELIEVE (māk bə lēv) n. 1. The human delusion that Mankind's existence has meaning, through the act of Pretending. 2. The human belief in the concept *Anti-Evil*, a.k.a. *Good* (q.v.).

COMMENTARY BY ZYK

The absurd and unseemly concept of *Anti-Evil* was banned eons ago by Lord Satan from the curriculum of Bizarre Concept Studies in the Evil Philosophy Department at the University of Hell. However, due to the invasion of Earth and the inevitable confrontation with bizarre Human Mores and Beliefs, Demon invaders may experience a vague existential puzzlement when confronted by the human belief that *Anti-Evil* (a.k.a. "God" or "Good") and *Evil* (a.k.a. "Devil") are subsets of a vast Make-Believe Being. In exploring this childish philosophic exercise in Pretending, I offer the following blandish experiment:

pretend you are the Cosmos
strange, alone, knowing nothing
except that you are self-aware

pretend you find yourself
going mad with anguish
because there is no other

pretend that in desperation
you try dividing your awareness
into smaller awarenesses
but since they know they are you
they dreamily and without curiosity
move ever steadily back into you

pretend that these creations
do not solve your problem
there is still only you and no other

pretend you try an alternate plan
dividing your awareness again
but this time into parts
unaware that they are you

with memories erased
their veiled awareness
still reflects your anguish in myriad
permutations of your aloneness

pretend you feel the parts suffering
because they too don't know what
*   they are*
and hate the absurdity of their
*   ignorance*

pretend that this plan-ette
unexpectedly creates something new
which ripples through your
awareness
as your new parts strangely expand
contract and resonate on their own
creating shocking and unnamable
new depths to your being

pretend you are amazed to find
that you have transformed yourself
into an utterly new entity

pretend that you are stunned
at this visceral solution to the
mystery
of your origin and the agony of
your aloneness

with the terrifying knowledge
that you are the self-born phoenix
the inner and outer orphan of
infinity

dying in the fire of your anguish
and reborn in the infinitely subtle
ashes
of your vast and aching emptiness

and that in every eternal moment
you pretend to reach your destination
in the infinite depths of your own
being[1]

MAKEUP (māk ŭp) n. See
Clown; Fashion; Glamour; Lady.

1 NOTE BY LORD SATAN: Com-
posed during the period in which the usually
flamboyant Master Versifier Zyk was incar-
cerated in the West Hell Insane Asylum,
filled with psychotic Demons expressing
insanely sentimental and offensively saccharine vociferations, these noxiously feeling lines nevertheless express an aspect of
the puerile and distasteful yearnings of the
adolescent Demon mind, and are included
here by way of warning against a Seductive
Identification on the part of Demons with
the Twisted Minds of Mankind.

MALIGNANT CANCER (məl ĭg
nənt kăn sər) n. 1. A boon to human
physicians, supplying them with
summer homes, ski trips and condos
in Monte Carlo. 2. A bland but satisfying seasoning for human meat.
See Doctor.

MAMMAL (mă məl) n. Disgusting Earth species whose fundamental activity is sucking upon each
other's bacteria-infested bodies.

MAMMARY GLANDS
(măm mər ē glăndz) n. See Breasts.

Meat: Self-Devouring Substance

MAN (măn) n. Organic repository housing the stupidity of the
universe. See Meat.

MANKIND (măn kīnd) n. 1.
Sarcastic combination of two mu-
tually exclusive terms. 2. The junk
food of maggots. See Humanity.

MAN-MADE (măn mād)
adj. Schlock.

MANSLAUGHTER (măn
slô tər) n. The most optimistic word
in all of human language.

MANURE (mə nᵘr) n. A happy etymological mixture of man and
excrement. See Ordure.

MAP (măp) n. In an infinite
universe, that which a human uses
as a precise guide to Nowhere.

MAPMAKER (măp mā kər)
n. A human who creates routes by
which one army may most efficiently
massacre another.

MARCH (märch) v. The human proclivity to stomp around in a
circle in unison at the direction of a
loud human with atrophied genitalia.

MARIJUANA (mĕr ə wä nə)
n. See Hemp; Hippie.

MARIONETTE (mĕr ē ə
nĕt) n. A dummy whose every action
is controlled by a puppeteer. See
Citizen.

MARRIAGE (mĕr ĭj) n. 1.
Generally speaking, the legal joining
of a human with an underdeveloped
penis (the female) to a human with
a mutated clitoris (the male). 2. The
prolonged, monotonous rape of
one's bank account by an intimate
stranger. See Detective.

COMMENTARY BY LILITH

The direct participants are the losers
in marriage, receiving ulcers and the
depletion of their riches in divorce
(q.v.). The indirect (medical and

Ritual Intercourse of Turgid Penis and Swollen Vagina

legal) participants in a marriage, however, are the winners, gaining immense riches from the torment of their clients. See *Divorce; Wedding.*

MASCARA (măs kĕr ə) n. That which helps to dramatically highlight human weeping.

MASOCHISM (măs ə kǐ zəm) n. The despised tendency of humans to torture themselves before giving a worthy Demon the opportunity.

Nothingness Disguised as Mankind

MASQUERADE (măs kər ād) n. The absurd mask of human tissue which the Cosmos dons to temporarily distract itself from the monotony of intelligent existence.

COMMENTARY BY ZYK

The concept of the human masquerade is explored from the heinous human viewpoint in the following lugubrious chestnut:

Though sweet, your lips are sour in silent mood
As the sun disguises Day in masks of Night,
And every living thing is racked in solitude
Until Darkness dons its comic mask of Light.
But now chameleons whisper in the mire
And the somber Moon disguises mirth with sadness,
While you and I, berserk in love's desire,
Disguise our inward reason with outward madness.
For though we love with thoughts of gentleness,
We know the truest love can only seem;
But still, we cannot love each other less,
Though Love be but a scrap, a wisp, a dream.
For Nothingness is cloaked in each caress,
And all that is, a mask of Nothingness.

MASSACRE (măs ə kər) n. Rewarding an angry mob with lasting peace. Usually awarded to outraged taxpayers, loiterers or students.

MASSAGE (mə säzh) n. The kneading of tumor-filled human flesh by wart-encrusted human hands.

MASS COMMUNICATION (măs kə myū nə kā shən) n. Human technology used for mass obfuscation.

MASS PRODUCTION (măs prə dŭk shən) n. Means by which humans create enough material to fill vast stinking outdoor repositories. See *City Dump.*

MASTURBATION (măs tər bā shən) n. The Cosmos disguising itself in flesh for the purpose of worshipping itself to orgasm. See *Sex.*

COMMENTARY BY LLU CIPHER

In Demonic mythology, Material Creation is, in effect, the Creator's pathological self-abuse, resulting in the Big Bang, the primal orgasm from which humans are still shuddering and spastically twitching.

MATERIAL (mə tîr ē əl) n. 1. Cloth which protects the Cosmos from the horror of seeing a human naked. 2. That which a comedian steals.

MATERIALISM (mə tîr ē əl ǐ zəm) n. Imbecilic human philosophy which studies the image onscreen and denies the existence of the light from the projector.

MATERNITY (mə tûr nə tē) n. State wherein a massive parasite sucks nutrients from the female's body. See *Baby.*

MATHEMATICS (mă thə mă tiks) n. 1. Means by which humans determine nuclear-blast kill ratios. 2. A perversely fixed system of measurement abbreviations which humans pretend have a direct relationship to matter, whereas they really only have a direct relationship to the limitations of their perceptive organs, and no relationship whatsoever to material reality.

Elevating measure into *law* (q.v.) is such an alien notion to Demons that an explanation of this intellectual perversion is required. As all of Demonkind know, addition, subtraction, multiplication, etc. are living Demonic spirits and not lifeless processes. Demons of Mathematics cast spells upon numbers, under the direction of Lord Satan and his Executives, to make them come out into useful sums for construction in the City of Hell, most of which comprise the Offices of Attorneys.

But in Earth-Density, humans do not recognize Mathematics as one of the Essential Black Arts. The moronic limitations of Human Mentality create in them the illusion that 2 + 3, for example, will *always* produce the same result! In human "mathematics," 2 + 3 *cannot* equal 7, 52.8555, -97/99 or 666; to humans this equation is perversely fixed, and will always equal 5! (Since this is barely comprehensible, the Demon invading Earth-Density should study this phenomenon for himself.) Thus human mathematicians find themselves in the dilemma of having to ignore the absurd paradoxes and inconsistencies built into the fundamental precepts of their skewered and bombastic arithmetic.[2]

Since measure is the alchemical process transforming the mental into the material, Human Reality is thus based upon the infantile illusion that Measure is an irreducible process, rather than the understanding that Measure is Subjective, and that only the dimensions of Space and Time are irreducible.

---

2 **NOTE BY AHRIMAN:** Asmo Deus, in his characteristically dull fashion, asserts the absurdity of Human Mathematics without giving its whimsical application to the Torture of Humankind. One of the most entertaining ways to confound human morons is to cast a spell around a mathematical proof, bewitching it and making it invisible to human mathematicians.

Once the Student Demon understands the insane manner in which humans analyze their material world, many of the *quagmires* (q.v.) and bafflements of Incomprehensible Mankind may become vaguely comprehensible.[3] See *Number*.

Concerning the essence of Earth-Density *mathematics*, a limerick, to wit:

Truth-seeking pundits may say
That math is the only way
But the gauche and monotonous
Truth it has gotten us
Is merely that A = A

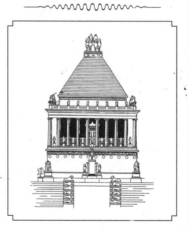

Maggot Feed Storage Shed

MAUSOLEUM (mô zə lē əm) n. Absurdly elaborate storage closet for a month's supply of maggot feed.

---

3 **NOTE BY ASMO DEUS:** Note that Human Mathematics is drenched in the Perverse and Anathemic Study of Infinity, a Forbidden Subject at University of Hell's Dept. of Mathematics and Gambling. The fact that humans drain the tiny resources of their brains on this regressive and illusory concept, which Lord Satan banned eons ago, is symptomatic of the Stupidity of Human Mathematics, which Swallows millions of Proofs and Vomits, in the words of Zyk the Poet Laureate of Hell, merely that A equals A. See *Infinity*.

MEANING (mē nǐng) n. The hypothesis that the Cosmos has integrity, a postulate definitively negated by the existence of Mankind. See *Cosmology of Hell*.

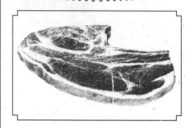

Meat: What a Human Being Is

MEAT (mēt) n. 1. What a human being is. 2. The essence of the slobbering Organism of Humanity, regenerating itself in an unseemly orgy of onanistic self-devouring and self-replication.

Baubles Exchanged for
Fresh Civilian Blood

MEDAL OF HONOR (mē dəl əv ä nər) n. The highest military honor possible, awarded for killing the most humans. See *Soldier*.

MEDIUM (mē dē əm) n. 1. A human in a trance through whom drunk Demons pretend to be dead relatives or celebrities. 2. The oven setting at which human flesh is most succulent. See *Séance*.

MEMORABILIA (mĕ mə rə bē le ə) n. Illusions which a human uses to trick itself into thinking that life was not a succession of unspeakable torments. See *Keepsake*.

MEMORIAL (mə môr ē əl) n. That which is attended by dead carcass fetishists. See *V.F.W.*

MEMORY (mĕ mər ē) n. That which allows a human to lead police to his victims' graves.

COMMENTARY BY AHRIMAN

The space-time skein of the Cosmos, or Akasha, is a vast scalar holographic analogy to the puny human brain, recording the physical dimension of material events upon its etheric tissue by the reflection or umbra of light. The Akasha, which only records the gross and material, is still useful in the tracking down and killing of all ancestors of a human which a Demon may find particularly irritating.

For example, after hearing a particularly annoying Earth-Density recording of Tyrolean accordion music, I had my secretary trace the accordion player's ancestors through the Akasha and proceeded to obliterate them, making them pay for the crime of inflicting the accordion player on the Cosmos. I urge you, Demon Reader, to use the Akasha in a similar manner to wipe out as many human stains as is Demonically possible.

MÉNAGE À TROIS (mä näzh ä t(r)wä) n. Suave and sophisticated nomenclature for three humans who enthusiastically slobber over each other's stinking genitalia. See *Dildo*; *Orgasm*; *Orgy*; *Prostitute*; *Sex*; *Sheep*.

MENOPAUSE (mĕn ə pôz) n. 1. The atrophication and dropping off of the glandular secretions of femininity. 2. The friend of the tired prostitute.

MENU (mĕn yū) n. A pricelist of deceased carcasses. See *Mouth*.

COMMENTARY BY BEHEMOTH

The human *menu* lists only those dead carcasses which have been stored in such a way as to keep them from rotting. Unlike Demons, humans eat only unrotted food, as inexplicable as that may be to the Gentle Demon Reader. Curiously enough, humans will not touch rotted food; rather, they insist that the food rot inside their bodies.

The Reader may presume that this unbelievable assertion is made in jest, but this is not the case. The human body, as such, is a rotting machine, designed to cause all foodstuffs inside itself to rot, alchemically processing the rotting organisms and transforming the fermented rot into its detestable sinews and effluvia.

MERCENARY (mûr sə nâr ē) n. 1. A small-testicled male whose honor and devoted allegiance are for sale to the highest bidder. 2: A human who enthusiastically destroys others for money; e.g., a literary, music or art critic.

MERCY (mûr sē) n. A bizarre emotional posture, alien to the bulk of Mankind, in which a human abnegates its natural instinct to crush the helpless.

MERCY KILLING (mûr sē kĭl lĭng) n. The killing of a human. See *Justifiable Homicide*.

Creaking Symbol of Earth Life

MERRY-GO-ROUND (mĕ rē gō round) n. A microcosmic mechanism which, aping the creaking Earth, makes humans pay for the pleasure of going nowhere.

MESSENGER (mĕs sĭn jər) n. A human who delivers bad news.

METAPHOR (mĕ tə fôr) n. Mode of thought inaccessible to human fundamentalist thinkers.

MICROCOSM (mĭk rə kä zəm) n. The rancid, insipid Parts which are stuffed into the teetering, sloppy Whole. See *Macrocosm*.

Viewing Miniature Demons

MICROSCOPE (mī krə scōp) n. A tool for viewing the unstoppable billions of miniature Demons which ceaselessly devour the Hide of Humanity.

Human Fondling Phallic Symbol

Insidious Purveyor of Creams

MIME (mīm) n. 1. A human who impersonates an entertainer. 2. The opposite of Negro impersonator Al Jolson.[4]

MIND (mīnd) n. In humans, the damaged contents of the rubbery bag of brains, a faculty akin to a desperate prostitute which, futilely fellating the corpse of wisdom, finds it dry and flaccid. See *Brain*.

MINISTER (mĭn ĭs tər) n. A moron who preaches drivel to the senile. See *Sermon*.

MINORITY (mī nôr ə tē) n. That which wishes itself to be the majority, so that it may oppress itself.

Black-Faced Caucasian in a Performance of Penis-Envy

MILITARY (mĭ lə tĕr ē) n. A cult of phallus-worshipping human artisans whose sculptures, called *missiles* (q.v.), are monuments to their obsession with engineering more and more explosive Orgasms.

COMMENTARY BY AHRIMAN

In another sense, the *military* may be referred to as the sales force and product-testing divisions of Earth's weapons manufacturers. Weapons manufacturers, when glutted with a surplus of product as a result of the failure of the military to use their products, pay vast advertising fees to create worldwide promotional campaigns called *war* (q.v.). See *Husband*; *Military*; *Soldier*; *Senator*.

MILITARY INTELLIGENCE (mĭ lə tĕr ē ĭn tĕl ə jəns) n. Sarcastic and hilarious oxymoron. See *Bullet*; *Missile*.

MILKMAN (mĭlk măn) n. He who has the same cleft palate as a husband's six children.

MILKY WAY (mĭl kē wā) n. The cosmic highway marred by the pothole of Earth.

Millionaire Imbeciles Wearing Prestige Skins

MILLIONAIRE (mĭl yən ĕr) n. A low-IQ billionaire.

MINSTREL SHOW (mĭn strəl shō) n. White humans wearing blackface in a spectacle of racial penis-envy. See *Al Jolson*.

4 EDITOR'S NOTE: As any Demon knows who has visited Hell Palace, Lord Satan constantly plays the recordings of Al Jolson, the only human seen in a favorable light by our Lord. In addition, by Lord Satan's command all executions are accompanied by the playing of Jolson's recordings.

*Despicable Instrument
Which Duplicates Humanity*

MIRROR (mĭ rər) n. Despicable instrument which duplicates Humanity. On the positive side, however, it facilitates the convergence of death-ray lasers.

MISOGYNY (mĭ sä jə nē) n. See *Machismo*.

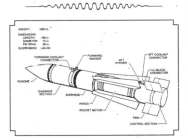

Humanity's Greeting Card to Itself

MISSILE (mĭs səl) n. A high-tech Welcome Wagon designed to greet enemy women and children.

MISSIONARY (mĭ shən ĕr ē) n. A human crusader who bribes savages to worship a statue of a man nailed to a tree. See *Crusader; Religion*.

MISSIONARY POSITION (mĭ shən ĕr ē pə zĭ shən) n. In Borneo, a missionary's head on a stick. See *Head*.

MODERATION (mä dər ā shən) n. That scurrilous faculty which robs a human of both the titillation of a chaffed, calloused groin and the alcoholic thrill of projectile vomiting.

MOHAMMED (Mō hä məd) p. In the Sideshow of the Gods, a favorite for his hobbies of the public chopping-off of hands, and for wrapping up women in black cheesecloth to keep their vaginas fresh between fornications. See *Religion; Scripture*.

MOLECULE (mäl ĭ kyūl) n. Scalar concept useful to Demons when discussing the relative heft of the human brain.

*Paper Equivalent
of 666 Million Souls*

MONEY (mŭ nē) n. Filthy paper used to purchase human souls. See *Bail; Bank; Capitalism; Catholic Church; Debt; Finance; Internal Revenue Service; Profiteer; Soul*.

*Superior Humanoid
(Devoid of Irritating Larynx)*

MONKEY (mŭng kē) n. A superior species of human devoid of Mankind's worst organ, the larynx.

MONSTER (män stər) n. The human fetus.

MORALITY (môr ăl ə tē) n. A hateful wall separating a human from doing the evil which will make him the most happy.

Human Moron

MORON (môr än) n. A grade of idiot which has mastered the art of politics, film producing and Feng Shui. See *Idiot*.

MORTGAGE (môr gĭj) n. Form of self-torture in which humans chain themselves until death to a large wooden box.

MORTICIAN (môr tĭ shən) n. A delightfully demented human puppeteer who disembowels and rapes his puppets before burying them. See *Morgue*.

Milk-Exuding Monster

MOTHER (mŭ thər) n. Ghastly creature with cloudy liquid oozing from its chest and a perpetual, cloying vise-grip on the male progeny's testicles. Its traditional role in the human family is to transform its innocent young into trembling flesh-bags of neuroses. See *Father*.

COMMENTARY BY LILITH

The Hideousness of Motherhood, with its yapping, sagging jowls and gangly, sagging teats, the Human Mother is used by Condescending Male Demons throughout the Cosmos as a *false* example of the "inferiority" of the Female Principle.

MOTHER-IN-LAW (mŭ thər ĭn lô) n. Satanic beast dedicated to tormenting and castigating unto death the spouse of its progeny.

COMMENTARY BY LILITH

In Earth-Density, the Evil of a Mother's Love is surpassed only by the Evil of a Mother-In-Law's Love, which projects not only exquisite amounts of guilt and shame upon its progeny, but also rifles through their drawers during family gatherings.

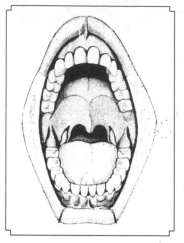

Human Feeding Tube

MOUTH (mouth) n. 1. Hinged orifice in the human head which opens to welcome decomposing carcasses, other humans' bacteria-coated tongues and tumescent, filth-encrusted genitalia. 2. The human cavity which, when opened, either belches, vomits or lies.

MOUTH-TO-MOUTH RESUSCITATION (mouth tū mouth rĭ sŭ sə tā shən) n. A prelude to necrophilia in which a human gives open-mouthed kisses to a waterlogged corpse.

MUCUS (myū kəs) n. The rare and delectable fruit of the human nose and vagina.

COMMENTARY BY BEHEMOTH

After gutting a human, *mucus* (a pungent, jelly-like condiment also known as *snot*) may be carefully drained (or sucked) from the sinus and vaginal canals to good effect. Note that mucus, a welcome *sauce piquant* to any preparation of human meat, is luscious when green and fresh, but in addition, when scabrous and dry, mucus crusts may be ground into a zesty and flavorful pepper which adds a racy zing to any broiled human repast.

MURDER (mûr dər) n. Killing creatively. See *Kill*.

MUSEUM (myū zē əm) n. Storage shed for trash discarded by the ancients. See *Art Critic*; *Archaeologist*.

Human Producing Annoying and Repetitive Vibratory Patterns

MUSIC (myū zĭk) n. 1. Gross cyclic vibrations which cause human musculature to twitch in an embarrassing display of spastic movement. See *Dancing*. 2. That which a Demon plays while torturing a human to ameliorate the annoying sound of its shrieks. See *Hymn*.

COMMENTARY BY ASMO DEUS

Demons, of course, have no biological resonance with the vibrations called *music*. Since humans constantly play these absurd vibratory patterns in their density, it behooves the invading Demon forces to use this human predilection to their military advantage.

COMMENTARY BY LILITH

The playing of human music to accompany the cries of human torture is a satisfying and creative experience in Demon-Human relations. After interviewing some of the most successful Demon Tormentors of Mankind, I have compiled the following list matching types of torture with the types of music most appropriate to be used as accompaniment:

TORTURE AND MUSICAL ACCOMPANIMENT

TORTURE	SUGGESTED MUSIC	COMMENTS
Body stretched on rack.	Surf Music.	Use ice packs to pop tendons.
Eyes, tongue plucked with pliers.	Wagner.	Maximum volume.
Holes drilled in head.	Easy Listening.	Drill through pineal first to watch amusing floppy erection.
Hanging by neck.	Ennio Morricone.	*Warning!* Plug anus with rubber stopper and duct tape before hanging.
Electricity to genitals.	Broadway show tunes.	For best screams, attach alligator clips to hemorrhoid flaps.
Dental torture	Disco.	Maximize bass.
Chinese water torture.	Theme from *Flipper*.	Dress victim in Chairman Mao costume.
Ebola virus injection.	Sea chanteys.	Hum along to increase tension.
Drawn and quartered.	Marlboro theme.	Make 3-inch incisions on armpits to facilitate even dismemberment.
Flayed.	Late Frank Sinatra.	Dip flayed body in salt for heightened screams.

MUSICAL THEATER (myū zǐ kəl thē ə tər) n. Place in which alcoholic males alternate between cavorting onstage and fellating each other behind curtains.[5]

MUSIC VIDEOS (myū zǐk vǐ dē ōz) n. The first sign of the end of the Universe as we know it.

The human prognosticator Nostradamus composed this prophetic quatrain which many Demon scholars believe refers to the human Michael Nesmith, the inventor of music videos:

When the Monkey shall renounce his Four as False
He shall make Dry Ice to accompany a Demented Waltz.[6]

5 NOTE BY BEHEMOTH: For the hungry Demon, always microwave musical theater performers longer than normal humans. I recommend cooking them on HIGH for six minutes, rotate, then microwave for thirty seconds.

6 NOTE BY AHRIMAN: This is in-

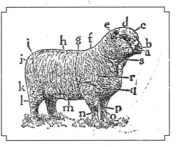

Ambulating Sweater

MUTTON (mü tən) n. Meat from a sweater.

MYSTERY (mǐs tər ē) n. That which describes the reason why the Cosmos tolerates Humanity infesting its cosmic hide.[7]

terpreted by Demon Occultists as follows: *"When The Monkey"* (the human creator of MTV) *"shall renounce his four as false"* (abandons his artificial quartet), *"He shall make Dry Ice to accompany a Demented Waltz"* (he shall make music videos). See *Idiot*.

7 NOTE BY LORD SATAN: The most incomprehensible thing about Humanity is its denial of Mystery. Although this is expected of lower creatures, the fact that

Mystic Masturbating to Death

MYSTIC (mǐs tǐk) n. A human who abandons the world, takes up refuge in his mind, and desperately needs to get laid.[8]

Demonic anthropologists recently inquired after the destiny of one hundred ascetic male "mystics" living alone in caves throughout the world and compiled the following enlightening data:

–1% meditated
–2% died from slipping
   on own excrement
–97% died from ceaseless
   masturbation

Humans wear underwear, indicating a modesty toward the Perceiving Cosmos, suggests that they have a glimmer of intelligence. Yet their Denial of the Mysteriousness of the Cosmos, and their Obsession with Absurd Reductionist Arguments which worship the meaningless measurement of matter, make Demons question whether this Race of Beasts deserve nothing but Extermination.

8 NOTE BY LLU CIPHER: This distasteful and uncharacteristic use of idiosyncratic human expression is at first puzzling and disconcerting. After a moment's reflection, however, it is clear that this is an expressionistic device which Lord Satan, in his magnificent literary style, utilizes to allow the Demon Reader to experience the crass and primitive nature of Humanity.*

* NOTE BY LORD SATAN: Despite Llu Cipher's considered licking and lapping of My Black Rectum, the truth is, I was drunk on the blood of a Fenian when I wrote this particular entry.

n, N (ĕn) n. Pictogram symbolizing the three stages of Human Life: the Pompous Elevator of the Intellect, the Psychic Mudslide descending to the Pit of Carnal Filth in which All Humans Grovel, and the Final Elevator to the Fount of Cosmic Nothingness.

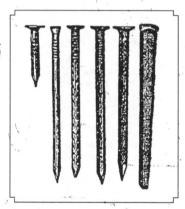

Directions: Insert Pointed End Through Savior's Flesh

NAIL (nāl) n. Beneficial hardware which allows humans to firmly attach saviors to crosses.

NAKEDNESS (nā kĭd nĭs) n. 1. A view of humans too disgusting even for their own eyes. 2. State of utter honesty, and thus universally reviled by humans. See *Honesty*.

Flesh-Robot's Inane Cognomen

NAME (nām) n. An inane cognomen which humans obnoxiously assign to innocent objects. Human names are an eternal embarrassment to the objects which they defile.

COMMENTARY BY ASMO DEUS

Human surnames generally designate the illiteracy of their ancestors. The first, or given, names were originally formulated to indicate the penis (*Peter, Steve [i.e. Stiff], Dick, Dirk, Doc, Dunc, Rod*, etc.), or to indicate the vagina or clitoris (*Gina, Ginnie, Cloris, Doris, Tori, Ina, Aggie, Virginia*, etc.).[9]

NAMESAKE (nām sāk) n. Sadistic joke in which a human inflicts the paucity of its own name upon an unsuspecting infant.

NAPALM (nā päm) n. See *Science*.

NATION (nā shən) n. Citizens held together by the Common Bond of Credit Card Debt.

NATIONALISM (nă shən əl ĭ zəm) n. A mental disorder which inhibits the normal, healthy instinct to defecate on a flag.

[9] **NOTE BY BEHEMOTH:** For the Demon who has trapped and caged humans in order to eat them later, the Demon may refer to any male human as *Penis* and any female as *Vagina*. Alternatively, the Demon could address them by the method by which he intends to prepare them (i.e. *Fricassee, Sauté, French Fry*, etc.)

Shoehorn Fancier

NATIVES (nā tĭvz) n. Landowners most likely to sell mineral rights to their land in perpetuity in exchange for a shiny plastic shoehorn.

NATURE (nā chər) n. An irritating, inconsequential biosystem which interrupts human corporate expansion.

COMMENTARY BY LILITH

The tacit Unnaturalness of Nature[10] is manifest in its repulsively bright colors and lively streams of life-forms which are Ugly and Unwholesome

[10] **NOTE BY MEPHIS TOPHIEL:** More to the point is the fact that Mankind Itself, despite being the despised precursor of Demonkind, is a Useless and Obsolete Artifact of Nature. Since humans are primitive nodules evolved merely to house and serve as a food supply for millions of smaller, more significant creatures (e.g. nits, mites, lice and the myriad microscopic civilizations living in and on human flesh), after the Invasion, Lord Satan has ordered Demon ecologists to engineer non-sentient mounds of self-replicating flesh to replace humans as the homes for these delicate creatures. Once these living mounds of replacement flesh have been successfully designed, the plan is to eradicate Mankind in all time frames, whose loathsome existence is otherwise a threat and an irritating nuisance to the Hell Cosmos at large. (A few million humans from delectable time frames will be spared and stocked as foodstuff.)

to all Intelligent Creatures of Hell. Thus, subsequent to the Invasion of Earth-Density, Demon Insurgents should make it a point to work toward the Destruction, Razing and Poisoning of Nature as a matter of Principle.

Centuries ago, the Demon *Abra Kadab* (q.v.) introduced the Demonic Mechanism of *Photosynthesis* (q.v.) into Earth's system of Nature, in an attempt to transform it into a Machine Which Eats Light and Excretes Decay, as Zyk, the Poet Laureate of Hell, so aptly expressed it. But the cellular automata of Earth's Abominable Life-Force co-opted his Early Efforts, integrating even the Evil of Photosynthesis into a Repugnant System viable for, I shudder to say, the Fruition of Life.

After the Invasion, when You the Demon Insurgent find Yourself surrounded by the Ghastly Colors and Life-Force of Nature, do not despair. We shall soon viciously slice all Earth forests to the ground and saturate every ocean with vats and tankers of Magnificent Swill. Thus, we ask that all Demon Invaders contribute to the Cause of Eradicating Nature and transforming Earth into a Charred and Barren Wonderland of Evil, which is its True Ignoble Destiny.

See *Black Death*; *Garbage*; *Highway*; *Light*; *Photosynthesis*; *Plant*; *Savage*; *Sightseeing*; *Tree*; *Vacation*.

NATURAL (nă ch(ə) rəl) adj. A word used by humans as an advertising ploy to sell themselves worthless or shoddy products. The slogan "All Natural!" is automatically affixed to any product which blasphemes nature.

NAVY (nā vē) n. Specialized soldiers trained to drown humans, as opposed to shooting them. See *Desertion*; *Homosexual*; *Sailor*.

Nazi Leader Checking Jewish Child's Gold Teeth

NAZI (nät sē) n. 1. One who does not question orders. 2. The perfect soldier. See *Hitler*.

NEBULA (nĕ byū lə) n. Ancient cosmic traces of divine flatulence.

NECK (nĕk) n. Human body part specifically designed to fit a noose.

Symbol of Voluntary Human Bondage

NECKTIE (nĕk tī) n. Clothing ritual in which the male voluntarily ties a stylized rope around his neck to symbolize his bondage to money.

NECROMANCY (nĕk rə măn sē) n. The Black Arts, such as politics, advertising and human procreation.

The Blackest of Arts, *fornication* (q.v.), the disgusting manufacturing of new humans via sex, is also the greatest mind-control force on the planet, for the constant need to pump brackish spermatozoa into the hideous womb overrides all other human concerns and makes all of Humanity, in effect, a grotesque Pumping and Receiving Station. Human sex is the most potent of all Black Arts, unless of course the sex is performed on a makeup girl by a fat country-western singer in a trailer. See *Sex*.

NECROPHILIA (nĕ krə fīl ē ə) n. An efficient and aesthetically pleasing form of birth control.

NEED (nēd) n. That which destroys human relationships.

In this connexion, I offer a famous Wise Saw of His Majesty Lord Satan: *"A friend in need... is an enemy."*

NEEDLE (nē dəl) n. Device used by German artisans to stitch human skin into decorative lampshades.

NEGATIVITY (neg ə tĭ vĭ tē) n. Human ignorance which perversely deems that infant mortality, for example, is somehow unpleasant.

NEGLECT (nə glĕkt) n. The relationship between intelligence and the human mind.

Mind-Control Underwear

NEGLIGEE (nĕ glə zhā) n. Mind-control underwear worn by females to entice males into legal enslavement. See *Lingerie*.

NEIGHBOR (nā bər) n. A human who despises another from a close proximity.

Black Imbecile

NEGRO (nē grō) n. A race of black imbeciles feared by a race of white morons.

NEUTER (nū tər) v. The first act a female performs after obtaining a pet or a husband.

NEW (nū) adj. See *Free*; *Natural*.

Human Distributing Corporate Newsletter

NEWSPAPER (nūz pā pər) n. Obsolete, in-house corporate newsletter distributed to the populace.

NEWSPAPERMAN (nūz pā pər măn) n. See *Alcoholism*.

NICKNAME (nĭk nām) n. A cute name humans give each other (e.g. Sweetie, Honey, Bunny, etc.) to disguise the fact that they are walking sacks of insensate gore.

Niece and Uncle

NIECE (nēs) n. That which is molested by uncles.

Day Masquerading as Night

NIGHT (nīt) n. A black mask which Day dons to terrify Humanity.

NIGHTCLUB (nīt klŭb) n. That which is used after dusk to kill baby seals.

NIGHTMARE (nīt mâr) n. Except when straining on the commode, that from which humans never awaken.

NIHILISM (nī (h)ə lĭ zəm, nē ə lĭ zəm) n. The philosophy of a human about to have a tax audit.

COMMENTARY BY ZYK

Aping human idiocy, and as a paean to Mankind's redeeming nihilism, I offer the following sublime and touching verses:

O my Mother she's in Mexico
My Father he's in France
My candle's in my handle
And my dandle's in my pants.
I'll eat my slop and smack my lips
And feed the festooning farce,
And soon I'll croon a luscious tune
And I'll croon it with me arse.
O some say there's gods atop
*   of the world*
And demons down below,
But that whores in France
*   don't wear no pants*
Is all humans need to know.

NOON (nūn) n. A good time for a hanging.

Excellent Gravity Device

NOOSE (nūs) n. A happy marriage of gravity and Mankind. See *Neck*; *Noon*.

NORMALNESS (nôr məl nĭs) n. A behavioral oasis for idiots.

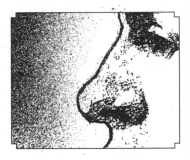

Bulbous Filth Detector

NOSE (nōz) n. 1. Mucus-filled protuberance which humans thrust into each other's business, or into their employer's rectum. 2. That organ by which humans may perceive that they are the greatest stench-creating machines in all of nature.

NOSTALGIA (nôs tăl jə) n. A mathematics of human sentiment which allows serial killers to wistfully tally up their victims.

The Ultimate Masquerade

NOTHINGNESS (nŭ thĭng nĭs) n. 1. That which cleverly disguises itself as Everything. See *Masquerade*. 2. Content of all Human Expression.

COMMENTARY BY ASMO DEUS

More than death, it is the Spectre of Nothingness which humans fear most. For its immense, silent, immutable presence offers no comfort to the neurotic, Insignificant Human Race, whose greatest desire is that which is impossible — for Mankind to be Significant. See *Death*.

NOVA (nō və) n. 1. A star which, when first feeling its tendrils of light touching human flesh and thus being defiled, commits suicide. 2. Troublesome mid-'70s Chevy.

NOVICE (nô vĭs) n. A human with respect to actual thinking.

NOWHERE (nō wâr) n. 1. Where all humans begin and end. 2. Where you, Demon Reader, are now. See *Nothingness*.

NUDISM (nū dĭ zəm) n. The ultimate obscene act in which a human willfully exposes his naked nodules to the Cosmos.

NUMBER (nŭm bər) n. That which facilitates the counting of corpses.

Devotee of Lesbian Cult

NUN (nŭn) n. Member of a bizarre lesbian cult which worships the statue of a male nailed to a crossbeam.

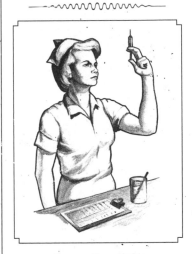

Perverse Narcophobic

NURSE (nûrs) 1. n. Perverse narcophobic who straps corpses to breathing tubes. 2. v. To cruelly prolong an infant's misery by allowing it to suckle from a female teat, instead of letting it die. See *Wet Nurse*.

NYLON (nī lŏn) n. Clothing worn by human pinheads to simulate nakedness.

NYMPHOMANIAC (nĭm fə mā nē ăk) n. Female who craves the absurdly mutated clitoris of the male.

O, O (ō) n. The shape the human mouth assumes during torture.

OASIS (ō ā sĭs) n. 1. In the sun-blistered desert of human knowledge, the Mirage of Meaning. 2. Formerly, a lush pocket of clean water between sand dunes; presently, a filthy truck stop run by a toothless cretin.

OBEDIENCE (ō bē dē əns) n. The magical agency which transforms humans into dogs. See *Military*; *Patriotism*.

┌─────────────────────────────┐
│ **COMMENTARY BY AHRIMAN** │
└─────────────────────────────┘

According to the *Cosmology of Hell* (q.v.), the Cosmos operates on the Law of Obedience. This Law dictates that If the Big Can Crush the Small, then It Must. In the case of Mankind, this is in reference to their absurdly puny intelligence. Thus, as the least intelligent creatures in the cosmos, humans must submit to every other living thing or be instantly killed.

OBITUARY (ə bĭ chū âr ē) n. Joyous announcement of one less human soiling the Cosmos. See *Casket*; *Coffin*; *Corpse*; *Death*; *Death Bed*; *Death Rate*; *Nothingness*.

OBJET D'ART (ôb zhā där) n. Random object to which humans affix a price tag. See *Art Dealer*.

OBLIVION (ə blĭ vē ən) n. 1. That which patiently waits behind the gaudy Mask of Creation. 2. A human's future.[11]

OBSCENITY (əb sĕn ə tē) n. Copulation — which, in serving to propagate Mankind, is universally conceded, even by the mindless humans themselves, to be the Ultimate Abomination.

┌─────────────────────────────┐
│ **COMMENTARY BY BELIAL** │
└─────────────────────────────┘

Humans' obsessive appendage-insertions and fluid-spewing is, to Demons, not obscene, but rather, light, clownish entertainment. What *is* obscene — as surely as is the Poisonous Light Reeking from the Center of the Cosmos — is the very existence of Mankind who, having evolved from Light Particles, insult and befoul the Splendor and Purity of our Blackly Evil Cosmos.[12]

---

11 NOTE BY LORD SATAN: Question: What, then, the Inquisitive Demon may inquire, *is* the point of Mankind's existence? Are they simply to be killed and eaten by Demon Invaders until their vainglorious race is devoured in its entirety? Answer: Yes.

12 NOTE BY BEHEMOTH: Belial's remarks on obscenity, while certainly true, merely rehash the banal truism that Mankind is worthless. More fitting here (and intelligent) would be a discussion of the eating of humans while they are engaged in the obscene act of human copulation, an action which naturally supplies the proper juices to slide the otherwise gristly meal down the throat without chafing or multiple regurgitation.*

*NOTE BY BELIAL: My remarks are certainly less redundant than Behemoth's on the subject of eating humans. The King of Gluttony accuses me of "rehash" simply for the opportunity to use the word *hash* in a sentence.

OBSTACLE (ŏb stə kəl) n. That which temporarily impedes a human from failure.

OCCULT LITERATURE (ə kəlt lĭt (ə) rə chər) n. That which gluts a bookstore discount bin.

OCEAN (ō shən) n. See *Dump*; *Pollution*; *Cesspool*.

ODOR (ō dər) n. Aside from stupidity, the only outstanding characteristic of Humanity. See *Smell*.

Prisoners Hypnotized By Magical Screen

OFFICE BUILDING (ŏ fĭs bĭl dĭng) n. Cell-block in prison cities which sedates uniformed inmates with fluorescent lighting and hypnotic Muzak.

OFFICIAL (ə fĭ shəl) n. A beast with a name tag.

OFF-THE-RECORD (ŏf thə rĕ kərd) adj. In legal depositions, types of statements disallowed by lawyers because they contain dangerous amounts of honesty which may corrupt the proceeding.

OIL (oil) n. The flammable sweat of Satan.

OLD AGE (ōld āj) n. 1. The portion of human life most fortuitous for experiencing the terror of death. 2. Age at which the human brain organ atrophies from lack of use.

Old Maid with Extra Skirt to Screen Vulvic Odor

OLD MAID (ōld mād) n. Foul-smelling virgin. See *Bachelor*.

OMELETTE (äm (ə) lĭt) n. Suave camouflage term for a fried fetus.

OMNISCIENCE (äm nĭ shəns) n. See *Pervert*.

ONE (wŭn) n. That which Evil denies. See *Loneliness*.

ONENESS (wŭn nĭs) n. A mystical state of cosmic intimacy humans experience, for example, during prison rape.[13]

Organic Emotion Simulator

ONION (ŭn yən) n. Vegetable secreted in the palm of the hand by televangelists while begging for money.

OOZE (ūz) v. The happy movement of a human brain once it is freed from its prison of skull by an ax.

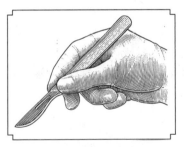

Flesh-Gutting Tool

OPERATION (ŏ pər ā shən) n. The admirable act of gutting a human for profit.

PERSONIFIED UNIVERSE: Although Satan refers to His Chief Principle of Magic as *The Law of One*, Oneness with the Universe is the only concept inaccessible and anathemic to Satan's Intellect. As you will see, Satan, locked in the Incomplete Polarity of Hell, can only unlock the Door to His Own Evolution by studying the absurd World of Opposites known as Earth-Density. This point is inextricably linked to the Plan I formulated in creating Satan, which I discuss at the end of this book in *My Closing Remarks*.

13 NOTE BY GOD, LORD OF THE

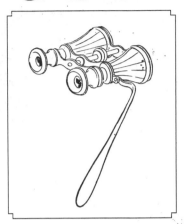

Tedium Magnified

OPERA GLASSES (ô pər ə glă səz) n. That which supplies a close-up view of tedium.

OPPORTUNITY (ŏp ər tū nĭ tē) n. The shimmering gateway to failure.

OPTIMISM (ŏp tə mĭ zəm) n. The carrot which Death dangles over a cliff.

Human Optimist

OPTIMIST (ŏp tə mĭst) n. In the cancer ward, a human who believes he is half-empty of cancer, instead of half-full.

ORDURE (ôr jər) n. See *Excrement*.

Orgasmic Orphanage Fire

Orphans of Nothingness

ORPHAN (ôr fən) n. The most fortunate of humans who has never endured the torture of a mother's love. See *Family*; *Fatherhood*; *Loneliness*; *Mother*; *Sex-Slave*.

ORPHANAGE (ôr fən ij) n. An arsonist's masterpiece.

Mystic Vestibule

ORGAN GRINDER (ôr gən grīn dər) n. A human who tortures a monkey by chaining it to an accordion.

ORGASM (ôr gă zəm) n. In the absurd claptrap of human physiology, the ten-second bio-electric discharge which motivates all human endeavor. See *Dildo*; *Love*; *Marriage*; *Rape*.

ORGY (ôr jē) n. Activity in which humans spew ghastly bodily fluids upon one another like clowns with seltzer bottles.

Human Clowns Performing in Orgy Circus

OUTHOUSE (out hous) n. A vestibule which allows Man to commune with his inner self. See *Astronaut*; *Hemorrhoids*; *Hygiene*; *Manure*; *Sophistication*.

OXYGEN (ŏks ə jən) n. An element the lack of which facilitates human suffocation.

p, P (pē) n. A pictogram of the male groin, making the sound of fluid emptying from the bladder.

PACIFISM (pă sə fĭ zəm) n. In capitalist countries, a dupe movement of vicious terrorists; in terrorist countries, a dupe movement of vicious capitalists.

PADDING (pă dĭng) n. Nine-tenths of the female form, the other tenth being girdling.

Spikes of Pain Caused by Friend's Happiness

PAIN (pān) n. Human sensation derived from a friend's success.

PAIN-KILLER (pān kĭl ər) n. To humans, *death* (q.v.).

PAINTING (pān tĭng) n. The vicious vandalizing and torture by humans of a clean piece of canvas. See *Art*.

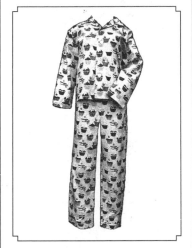

Costume Worn During Night Terrors

PAJAMAS (pə jă məz) n. Costume worn by humans during night terrors, burglaries and rapes.

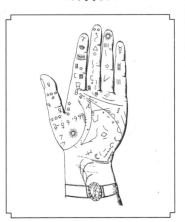

Hand Predicts Transfer of Money From Ignoramus to Gypsy

PALMISTRY (pä(l)m ĭs trē) n. The ability to look at a human hand and predict how much money can be pulled from its owner's pocket.

PANTHEISM (păn thē ĭ zəm) n. The absurd and demented human theory that Good (or "God") exists in every thing, and also in, therefore, Demons, Hell and in Myself. This would mean that I, Satan, were merely a grotesque mask, a hollow gargoyle, a leering frontispiece, an epithet of rote negation smugly issuing from the ass of a Hypothetical God.[14] Such an unseemly notion is, of course, unacceptable, since it rips the Black and White from their Cosmos and replaces it with an insipid Gray.[15]

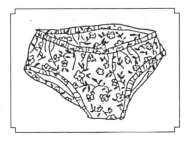

Sewage-Dampening Apparatus

PANTIES (păn tēz) n. 1. Genitalia-covering worn by a human female to absorb urine, blood and excrement. 2. The most sensuous of garments to the human male.

PAPER (pā pər) n. An intervening substance by which humans transform trees into pornographic magazines.

PARABLES OF LORD SATAN (pâr ə bəlz əv lôrd sā tən) n. For the relationship of the Precious Teachings to Humanity, see *Stupidity*.

14 NOTE BY GOD, LORD OF THE PERSONIFIED UNIVERSE: Exactly.

15 **ED. NOTE:** See *Addendum 3: Lord Satan's Abdication Speech.*

Human Parade

PARADE (pə rād) n. A pageant representing Earth life in which humans proudly march to Nowhere.

PARCEL POST (pär səl pōst) n. The most efficient way for humans to lose parcels.

PARDON (pär dən) v. That which a leader does to criminal allies.

PARKING LOT (pär kǐng lŏt) n. That into which humans transform a forest.

"Greetings, Cunty McFuckhead"

PARROT (pă rət) n. Innocent animal capable of speech which humans almost exclusively teach obscenities.

COMMENTARY BY ZYK

Since Lord Satan commanded that we humiliate and confuse humans before eating them, I discovered that a human female named Mother Theresa owned a parrot, and invoked the Spell of Ghast upon its mind so that the bird would always greet her guests with perverse profanity.

PARTY (pär tē) n. Humans gathering to share the richness of the human experience. See *Nazi Party*.

PASSPORT (păs pôrt) n. That which allows the import and export of venereal disease.

PATIENT (pā shənt) n. That which a physician price-gouges. See *Doctor*.

PATIO (pă tē ō) n. Area where a human's dog usually rips apart the neighbor's kitten.

Human Patriots

PATRIOT (pā trē ət) n. A courageous human who refuses to question orders to murder civilians. See *Gangster; Soldier; Politician*.

PATRIOTISM (pā trē ə tǐ zəm) n. The single greatest supplier for Hell's vast toilet flush of souls.

PATSY (păt zē) n. A human who admires politicians, clergymen and celebrities.

PAWNSHOP (pôn shäp) n. Establishment where a human sells its grandmother's heirlooms to purchase crystal meth.

PEACE (pēs) n. Unnatural, perverted state in which humans refrain from their natural instincts to kill each other. See *War*.

PEACEMAKER (pēs mā kər) n. Human who salves the wounds of two opposing sides, in order to more effectively steal from both.

PEACE OFFICER (pēs ôf ə sər) n. Killer for the military.

PEACE TIME (pēs tīm) n. The enemy of capitalism.

Dung Exuded by Mollusk

PEARLS (pərl) n. Ropes of oyster dung used by females to misdirect the eyes away from their grotesque double chins and neck wrinkles.

PEDICURE (pĕ dĭ kyʊr) n. A temporary salve for a human's perpetually stinking feet.

PELVIS (pĕl vĭs) n. The part of the body which excretes fetid waste matter, horrific gases, and human babies.

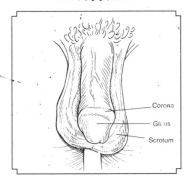

Human Penis
Note: Before eating tenderize with Meat-Hammer.

PENIS (pē nĭs) n. 1. That which spews sewage into an orifice which, nine months later, regurgitates a man. 2. That which fills with blood drained directly from the male brain. See *Testicles*; *Vagina*.

> COMMENTARY BY LORD SATAN
>
> Obsessed from morning till night by thoughts of the penis, humans refer to this nauseating appendage by a multitude of incomprehensible euphemisms, too numerous and puerile to mention in this concise encyclopedic tome.[16]

16 NOTE BY LORD SATAN: Such as cock, dick, prick, dong, rod, shlong, pole, pud, putz, sausage, hot dog, kielbasa, beef, drumstick, tube steak, pork loin, smegma salami, rocket, missile, torpedo, shaft, member, candlestick, wick, piss pipe, purple-headed soldier, throbbing monster, hymen buster, jack, gun, tripod, hammer, can opener, love mushroom, pea shooter, straw, ramrod, handle, skin flute, banister, peace pipe, handrail, stick, meat, welding rod, trouser

PENIS ENVY (pē nĭs ĕn vē) n. While serving roasted humans, the rivalry between Demons over who will devour the penis.

Church of Black Magicians

PENTAGON (pĕn tə găn) n. A vast pentagram hieroglyph built by human black magicians to invoke nuclear Demons.

PERCEPTION (pər sĕp shən) n. Complex system of peepholes in the head which enable humans to view pornography while masturbating themselves unconscious.

PERFECTION (pər fĕk shən) n. Ultimate Evil, a Finish Line which humans can never reach.[17]

weasel, pointer, big man, quiet man, wand, staff, caulking gun, meat candycane, barber pole, dowel, column, pestle, eel, nightcrawler, one-eyed snake, pile driver, post, boner, frosting dispenser, meat tube, chisel, drill bit, screwdriver, wang, hammyhorn, jimgobber, wedding tackle, ding-a-ling, dingus, bell-end, truncheon, hard-on, ivory tower, joystick, knob, package, thunder, schwanz, tadger, love gun, tool, weiner, pecker, johnson, John Thomas, cream stick, phallus, junk, squirt gun, log, hose, branding iron, root, flesh cork, divining rod, White Owl, pulverizer, punisher, persuader, nightstick and, of course, weedwhacker.

17 NOTE BY ASMO DEUS: Why? Because the greatest Evil to which Mankind can aspire is self-destruction which, paradoxically, is Good, and therefore disqualifies Humanity from the Race.

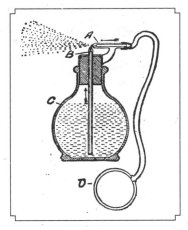

Olfactory Mask

PERFUME (pər fyūm) n. 1. That which disguises the rancid smell of the female pudenda. 2. An exquisite bouquet, such as the aroma of roasting retarded children.

PERISCOPE (pĕr ə scōp) n. Device which allows humans under the water to kill humans over the water.

PERPETUAL MOTION (pər pĕt chū əl mō shən) n. From the point of view of the perceiver's time frame, the most common motion in nature (the "perpetually" spinning electron, planet, solar system, galaxy, etc.).

This concept which, like the Origin of Hell, points to a mystery which must not be divulged, and is denied existence by human scientists and their lab sponsors, fossil fuel magnates. See *Cosmology of Hell*; *Infinity*.

PERSONALITY (pər sən ăl ĭ tē) n. A monocle affected by an ape.

PERSPIRATION (pər spər ā shən) n. Salty, acrid oil which oozes from human skin and naturally spices baked human meat.

The Perverseness of Omniscience

PERVERT (pər vərt) n. The hypothetical God's All-Seeing Eye.

COMMENTARY BY BELIAL

The Perverseness of Omniscience, in the Cosmology of Hell, is implicit in the Mythos of the Creator peeping lustfully at the naked carnality of its life-forms.

Pessimist: Most Delicious Human

PESSIMISM (pĕ sə mĭ zəm) n. When eating a human raw, the state of mind which makes the normally sour nervous system piquant and delicious.

PESTILENCE (pĕs tĭ ləns) n. An insidious human scourge, such as theaters infected by a rash of one-man shows.

Purveyor of Artificial Happiness

PHARMACIST (fär mə sĭst) n. Scientist beloved by humans for promulgating artificial happiness.

PHILATELIST (fəl ă′tə lĭst) n. A human whose most cherished activity is the steaming off of small squares of paper from envelopes containing bills, tax forms and child pornography.

Brain-Worshipping Idiot

PHILOSOPHER (fə lä sə fər) n. A grade of idiot who worships the weakest human organ, the brain. See *Idiot*; *Imbecile*; *Moron*.

PHILOSOPHY (fə lä sə fē) n. The twaddle which the human brain excretes under the influence of pipe smoke.

COMMENTARY BY
ASMO DEUS

Philosophy, a.k.a. the Low Science of Artful Obfuscation, is the chief tool with which to corrupt the Bird Brain of Humanity.

As all Demonic Creatures know, Intelligence, or Reason, the intuitive art of Feeling one's way toward a Solution, is counter to Logic and Philosophy, which are Reason's lower, bastardized, praetorian subsets. Due to their inability to reason and chew gum at the same time, humans are beautifully susceptible to the seduction of Philosophy and Logic, and blind to the fact that their Exotic Forking Paths lead to *Nowhere* (q.v.). And since it is Nowhere that Mankind deserves as its Home, Demons in Earth-Density have throughout history encouraged Humans to suck at Philosophy's Withered Teats.[18]

PHOTON (fō tän) n. 1. Spittle from the mythic God's insouciant, buck-toothed, hayseed grin. 2. Radiation from a sickeningly peppy star which is, of course, noxious to Demonkind. See *Electron*; *Star*.

18 **NOTE BY ASMO DEUS: A** magnificent example is a work of Mankind entitled *Principia Mathematica*, which Demon Mathematicians relish for the relentless drone of its logic; this fantasmagorical proof takes 200 exquisite pages to prove that two plus two equals four.

Uglifier of Reality

PHOTOGRAPHY (fə tä grə fē) n. That which uglifies reality, juxtaposing otherwise exquisite vistas with foregrounds featuring humans in shorts with cellulite and varicose veins.

PHOTOSYNTHESIS (fō tō sĭn thə sĭs) n. The influence of Hell upon plants which hungrily eat up despised Light.

COMMENTARY BY MEPHIS TOPHIEL

In Earth-Density, the Plant Kingdom was the first life-form created by Hell. Eons ago, the Demon Heretic Abra Kadab bio-engineered and seeded these Green Organisms of Evil in order to hungrily devour the hateful Light ceaselessly and disgustingly excreted from Earth's Obnoxious Systemic Sun. See *Plant*.

PHYSICAL BODY (fĭ zi kəl bä dē) n. A seed which blooms into a corpse.

PHYSICIAN (fĭ zĭ shən) n. See *Doctor*.

PHYSICIST (fĭ zĭ sĭst) n. See *Weapons Designer*.

PI (pī) n. The relationship between the diameter and circumfer-

Orgasmic Filibuster of Chaos

ence of a mathematician's testicle, symbolizing the Orgasm of Chaos. See *Mathematics*; *Orgasm*.

PIANO BAR (pē ăn ō) n. A source of bizarre caterwauling in which alcoholics ingeniously wed the emission of sound and vomit. See *Alcohol*.

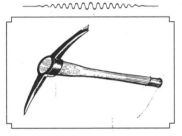

Human Skull-Opening Tool

PICKAX (pĭk ăks) n. Tool for opening the otherwise impenetrable human skull.

PICKLE (pĭk əl) n. That which goes well with the sautéed human anus.

Meat Tube Delicious to Humans

PIG (pĭg) n. Filthy tube of meat. See *Bacon*.

Aerial Excrement Machine

PIGEON (pĭ jən) n. 1. Lice-infested, flying excrement machine which humans enjoy as a rare gourmet delicacy. 2. Creature which the military enslaves to transmit orders to bomb civilians. 3. Earth-Density vermin whose existence hinges on the ability to distinguish bread crusts from cigarette butts.

PILLOW (pĭ lō) n. 1. Tool which facilitates the beauty of human suffocation. 2. Vehicle which a human rides to a nightmare.

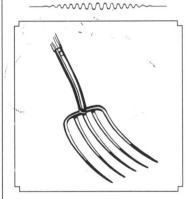

Tool to Locate Children Hiding in Hay

PITCHFORK (pĭch fôrk) n. Instrument used by human soldiers to locate enemy children hiding in hay.

PIZZA (pē tsə) n. Repository for the mucus and snot of angry Italian cooks.

PLAGUE (plāg) n. A condiment most delicious in the form of tart pustules in the human epidermis.

COMMENTARY BY BEHEMOTH

The flesh of Mankind is known for its tangy taste when infected with disease. (The exception is the testicles of a priest, a sour and fetid repast regardless of the lush chancres peppering them.) Often Demons will conjure a sickness or epidemic to ravage a Continent prior to visiting Earth, to create a picnic holiday for Demonic tastebuds. To assist the hungry Demon Invader in infecting humans with the most delectable diseases, refer to *Gourmet Diseased Flesh Chart* in *Appendix 6, Section 8.5, Article 9.*

Hell's Friend, Eater of Light

PLANT (plănt) n. A secret agent of Hell which hungrily eats the enemy, Light. See *Light*; *Photosynthesis.*

PLASTIC (plăs tĭk) n. Along with insects, the true inheritor of the Earth. See *Ants.*

PLASTIC SURGERY (plăs tĭk sûr jər ē) n. The result of the healthy instinct of humans to abhor their bodies with such gusto that they will pay other humans to hack themselves into pieces.

COMMENTARY BY LLU CIPHER

This incomprehensible act may be understood by curious Demons as Masturbation with a Knife. The slicing off of despised flesh and the injection or insertion of sacs of poison into the face, breasts, or buttocks generally occurs when the human's body is old and Leaning Toward the Bethlehem of Putrefaction and Decay. Thus, ten years after *plastic surgery,* the slicings, injections and sac-insertions, originally designed to create symmetry in the human's meat, now become misshapen, bloated bags of rotting epidermal layers, allowing the human to die in its truest, most perfect form, as a grotesquely twisted Gargoyle of Self-Loathing.

PLAYBOY (plā boi) n. Term created by male humans, who control human language, to contrast with the terms spinster and old maid. See *Bachelor.*

PLAYGROUND (plā ground) n. Recreation area for human children and pederasts, characterized by pendulums, slides, levers, revolving disks, metal grids, empty beer cans, pools of vomit and rusty syringes.

PLEA BARGAINING (plē bär gə nĭng) n. Flaccid phallus which a human attorney sucks on after castrating it from the God of Justice.

PLUTONIUM (plʊ tō nē əm) n. To humans, the nightlight of the future.

POETRY (pō ə trē) n. Prose wearing the junk jewelry of rhetoric.

COMMENTARY BY ZYK

After analyzing the weepy, maudlin and tediously crypto-fascist Poetry of Humanity, I was commissioned by Lord Satan to compose the following sonnet:

Behold the mysterious singer pervading human verses,
The quisling quacking of an utterly specious art,
Murmuring word after word like a procession of hearses
Burying banal truths like corpses in the human heart.
Human Poesy trumpets like the anus of a king
Who, by divine right, befouls the sweet air,
Believing that his ornamental twaddle is covering
The stench which spreads from the cellar to the stair.
Poetasters, mad and agog with jingling glitter,
Pretend words to be wonder, trash to be treasure,
Linking sappy squeaks, like birdies all a-twitter,
Spewing sickly-sweet sounds at their petty leisure.
Behold the horned human poesy festering on the page
Having sex with itself in a self-idolatrous rage.

Official with Hat Jewelry

POLICE (pə lēs) n. See *Badge*; *Law.*

Humans Worshipping Criminal

Pope Brought to Orgasm by Altar Boy Kneeling Under Robes

POLITICAL RALLY (pə lǐ tǐ kəl rǎ lē) n. A festival in praise of criminals.

Auctioning Laws to Highest Bidder

POLITICIAN (pä lǐ tǐ shən) n. Auctioneer who creates or repeals laws at the direction of the highest bidder. See *Sanitation; Scum; Senator.*

Depiction of Mankind's Admirable Program of Self-Extermination

POLLUTION (pə lū shən) n. 1. The most beneficial product of human technology, in that it destroys Humanity. 2. The spew of human thought into the universe.

POLYTHEISM (pä lē thē ǐ zəm) n. Mankind worshipping Nothing under exotic pseudonyms. See *Religion.*

POPE (pōp) n. A foppish feudal lord who, claiming ownership of Heaven without a deed, charges his dupes to act as their middleman to communicate with a Mythic God.

Traditionally wearing vestments designed to allow ease of fellatio, Popes deplore sexual contraception, yearning for a planet overpopulated by the Curvaceous

Big-Bellied Spectre of Hungry Boys. See *Papacy; Vatican.*

POPE INNOCENT IV (pōp ǐn nə sənt fôr) p. Admirable human hoarder of gold baubles and jewels who, in 1257 A.D., decreed that torture of the genitals may be used against those denying that the Papacy was the Earthly Authority of the Love of Christ.

PORNOGRAPHY (pôr nä grə fē) n. All literature about humans, save this present magnificent and instructive volume. See *Obscenity; XXX.*

POSSESSION (pə ze shən) n. Amusing recreational activity a Demon performs on a human, sticking a Demonic hand up its etheric spine, twiddling the carcass and making it speak like a ventriloquist's dummy.

POSTERIOR (pŏs tǐr ē ər) n. Sophisticated-sounding name for the part of the human body which oozes dung.

POSTHUMOUS (pôst (h) yū məs) adj. The least irritating category of human awards.

POWER (pou ər) n. See *Receptionist*.

POWER OF ATTORNEY (pou ər əv ə tər nē) n. Evil.

PRAISE (prāz) n. That which humans post to God with Satan's return address. Since their Mythic God abandoned them with no forwarding address, all praise goes directly to Satan.

PRAYER (prĕ ər) n. Devout request by a human for more material goods and for the death of an enemy. Prayer has been the preeminent Tool of Hell to foment War, Vice, Greed and other Sacred Precepts of Pure Evil.

the *Cosmology of Hell* (q.v.) posits a Free, Evil Cosmos in which Creative Hatred allows each Demon to create and fulfill his own Black Destiny.[19]

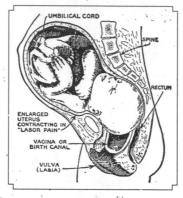

Diagram of Inconvenient Flesh-Pod to be Vacuumed and Flushed

PREGNANCY (prĕg nən sē) n. Annoying inflammation of the stomach which, when inconveniencing rich human females, is cured by a vacuum cleaner. See *Abortion, Baby, Fetus, Sex*.

The suave eloquence of the word *preposterous* allows various grades of human idiots (such as *scholars, scientists, theologians, philosophers,* q.v.) to use its mellifluous hypnotic sound to effectively disscurage the asking of difficult and embarrassing questions. See *Hypothesis*.

PRESIDENT (prĕz ə dĕnt) n. A dictator with an expensive press agent. See *Vice President*.

PREVENTATIVE MEDICINE (prĭ vĕn tə tĭv mĕ dĭ sən) n. The greatest pestilence to a human doctor's profits.

Cult Leader and Boy Slave

PRIEST (prēst) n. 1. Human cult devotee who preaches false happiness and, if affiliated with the Vatican, protects the rights of its members to have sexual congress with children. 2. A male human who vows to have an inactive penis, and whose chief activity is cosmic wonder. Also known as a dickless wonder. 3. A male human who wears a feminine uniform and worships a statue of a tortured corpse. See *Minister; Rabbi; Pope; Vatican*.

Humans Praying for Death of Enemy

PREDESTINATION (prē dĕs tə nā shən) n. Human belief that all unspeakable suffering was carefully prearranged by providence.

Contrary to human belief in Predestination, as every Demon knows,

PREPOSTEROUS (prĭ pôs tər əs) adj. Category of information which the human mind is unable to process.

19 NOTE BY LORD SATAN: Of course I was being sarcastic, jackball.

PRIESTHOOD (prēst hŭd) n. A club of dickless wonders who worship two statues: a sterile virgin female and an emaciated male god nailed to a tree.

The Promised Land

Primitive Savage Aping Sophistication

PRIMITIVE MAN (prĭ mə tĭv măn) n. Term generally abbreviated to Man.

PRINCE (prĭns) n. A princess with a penis.

PRINCESS (prĭn sĕs) n. See *Prince.*

PRODIGAL SON (präd ĭ gəl sŭn) n. A human child who returns home to borrow money.

PRODIGY (prä dĭ jē) n. 1. A human child forced by his parents to memorize lists of worthless data. 2. A future alcoholic.

Professor Conducting Fugue of Falsity

PROFESSOR (prə fĕs ər) n. 1. Impresario of Falsity. 2. Consensus-reality pimp. 3. A gardener who plants only the seeds of flowering intellects which complement the color of his eyes; all others to him are weeds. The seeds which he plants are supplied by the Seed Company which pays his salary. See *University.*

PROFITEER (prô fĭ tîr) n. An ape with pockets. See *Capitalism.*

PROGRESS (prŏ grĕs) n. That which allows humans to evolve over time from building a gun in a shed to building a death laser in space. See *Science.*

PROMISED LAND (prŏ mĭst lănd) n. The cemetery.

PROOF (prūf) n. A Narcotic which humans use to delude themselves into believing that they are capable of Reason. See *Mathematics.*

PROPHET (prä fĭt) n. See *Bible; Scripture.*

PROPHECY (prä fə sē) n. That which mystically predicts human failure.

PROSTITUTE (prä stə tūt) n. See *Husband; Senator.*

PUBERTY (pyū bər tē) n. The genetically timed release of tart condiments in the human body which, when parboiled by a Demon chef, make the human groin in particular a mouthwatering delicacy. See *Invasion Manual, Book One, Section 8: On Eating Humans.*

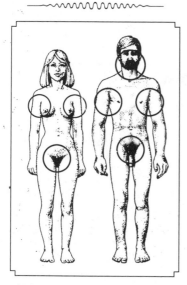

Warning: Floss After Gorging On Circled Areas

PUBIC HAIR (pyū bĭk hār) n. That which, when eating a human, sticks between the teeth.

PUKE (pyūk) n., v. See *Vomit.*

PULPIT (pŭl pĭt) n. Favorite hiding place for a minister's pornography collection. See *Masturbation.*

PUNCHLINE (pŭnch līn) n. The wan, limp orgasm of a spewing dickhead. See *Comedian.*

PUPPET (pŭ pət) n. See *Citizen; Heart; Kidney; Lungs; Liver.*

> **COMMENTARY BY BEHEMOTH**

Demons often use dried human carcasses as puppets for entertainment purposes. This involves a process of recycling organs and carefully tanning the human hide. Specifically, a human may be stitched into a puppet and its parts recycled by the following procedure:

1. With rubber gloves and a human vivisection kit (available from the Office of Behemoth, South Hell), gut and drain the human corpse. Do not drink the effluvia, as wasteful as this might seem. (Human plasma has a bitter aftertaste unless it is saturated with environmental toxins. See pamphlet #67, available free from the Office of Behemoth, entitled *Unpolluted Human Plasma — What You Can Do About It.*)

2. Manually squeeze the intestines from upper to lower, emptying the waste products into a shallow trench in your victory garden. Wash the intestines (approx. 25 ft.) and soak in a beaker of whiskey for two days.

The tract may then be recycled as sausage casings, bagpipe bellows, groin cup/codpiece lining, razored into 3/4" strips, rosined and twisted into D or G doublebass strings, or shredded as pectoral implants.

3. Gently decapitate and use a 1/8" Skilsaw on the skull to access the brain. Puncture brain sac. Pound the sac, brain and effluvia with a two-lb. sledge into a gray paste. Puree in a blender with green food coloring. Pour into a bowl with 1/4 cup frozen corn and bread crumbs and mix thoroughly. Pour out on a cookie tray in a pancake and let dry.

When stiff, brush two layers of shellac over top and bottom. The human corpse's brains may now be recycled as realistic novelty "plastic" party vomit.

Demon Entertainer With Human Fetus Puppet

4. After eating the heart, kidneys and liver, slice the lung sacs into lozenges and dry for one hour. These lozenges may be sucked on for their exquisitely tart and tangy environmental toxins. (See Pamphlet #85, *Lungs and Los Angeles: A Winning Taste-Treat.*)

5. Dry the decapitated head and skin and reattach via a sewing machine. Soften the skin (which will be stiff) by vigorous sledge-pounding until flexible and pliable. Shellac and glue the dried tongue into the bottom of the jaw, then wire the jaw so that it opens and closes freely.

6. Finally, sew the gutted skin back together, leaving a 6" opening near the anus. Replace the eyes with 3/4" black marbles and carefully comb the skull hair over the stitch marks.

If the Demon Reader has carefully followed the above instructions, the human may now be recycled for use at parties as a cute and perky hand puppet.

PURGATORY (pər gə tô rē) n. The human concept which, although childishly formulated, vaguely resembles the Real Reality. See *Cosmology of Hell; Reality.*

PUS (pŭs) n. A substance which humans dislike encountering during their first kiss. See *Acne; Puberty.*

q, Q (kyū) n. Aerial pictogram of a human with Death's Scythe embedded in his head.

Groin-Cupped Steroid Addict

Absurd Earth Animal

QUACK (kwăk) n. Babbling emission erupting from the mouth of a duck or a human physician.

QUADRUPLETS (kwô drū plĭts) n. 1. That which quadruples the excrement. 2. Litters born in trailer parks.

QUAGMIRE (kwăg mīr) n. A reference to the technical and logistic problems a Demon experiences when about to devour a human. (A popular term referring to the human-hungry, rapacious and notoriously indecisive Quag Demon.)

For example, the dilemma may hinge on whether to kill a human before eating it, or to drink its blood first and then kill it or, in the case of Demons with hinged jaws, whether or not to simply devour it whole.

COMMENTARY BY BEHEMOTH

The answer, of course, is to devour the human whole, allowing its screams to tingle the palate as it squirms down the throat, heightening the gourmet experience.

QUANTUM PHYSICS (kwän təm fĭ zĭks) n. Satirical science fiction resulting from moronic humans' inability to identify the threshold between the organs of perception and the perceived object.

QUARTERBACK (kwôr tər băk) n. A barking, groin-cupped steroid addict who is worshipped by humans for his ability to throw the hide of a swine.

QUARTERLY REPORT (kwôr tər lē rĭ pôrt) n. The bathroom reading of Satan.

QUARTET (kwôr tĕt) n. Torture times four.

Vibratory Torture

QUASAR (kwā zär) n. Due to the feebleness and paucity of Humanity's perception of interstellar objects, they mistake for a luminosity level R star what is really a Despised Angel who has been bazookaed by Lord Satan's Executives and is burning to a crisp.

QUATERNION (kwä tər nē ən) n. Mathematical eunuch beautifully castrated by vector analysis. Regarding this castration, Demons use quaternions to plot the rotations of Sir William Rowe Hamilton in his grave.

QUATRAIN (kwä trān) n. Poem with four verses too many.

COMMENTARY BY ZYK

Four lines summing up Humanity
And its breadth of wisdom inclusively
Require but a barren three.

Human Queasiness

QUEASY (kwē zē) adj. 1. Human perturbation upon viewing conceptual art exhibit. 2. That which a Demon feels for a half-hour after devouring an advertising executive.

Queen on Throne During Royal Menses Discharge

QUEEN (kwēn) n. That which elegantly bleeds on the throne.

COMMENTARY BY LILITH

The fatuous human whore of state known as the *queen* has no official duties save one: to torture her starving subjects with displays of decadent opulence. A queen is without peer as a fashion trendsetter, often displaying her bejeweled head in a baroque new hairstyle, stuffed in a gaudy wig, or guillotined in a basket.

QUEER (kwîr) adj. That which best describes the human race in its morbid predilection to ceaselessly fornicate with its own orifices.

QUESTION MARK (kwĕs chən märk) n. A punctuation mark in human language which imitates the inexplicable shape of the Cosmos.

COMMENTARY BY ZYK

Of this shape, and its conceptual analogy to Universal Creation, I offer the following versification:

Upon the sebaceous skin
of whorish space,
The Lords of Hell tattooed
whorls of stars,

Exoskeleton of the Hell Cosmos

Arranging them in patterns
which would trace
In code the secret plucking
of their lyres.
With that which monkey men
call meta-time,
Daemons sculpt the skies
in geometric meditation
To shape their Sacred Lies
in hideous rhyme,
Blaspheming the Light
in Black Configuration.
But when, at last,
man's fleshy Earth-disguise
Lies waste in blistered pulps
on ravaged shores,
And drowned jackals stare
with saucer eyes
As the last engulfing wave
their peace restores,
Then Daemons, to punctuate
their Poem in the dark,
Will pluck the Earth to dot
a Question Mark.

QUINTUPLETS (kwĭn tu plətz) n. The most common cause of parental prayers for crib death. See *Child Abuse; Child Sacrifice; Sterilization.*

r, R (är) n. Letter which imitates the creaking sound of a frozen human being defrosted in a microwave.

RABBI (ră bī) n. A holy man who emulates the mythic miserliness of *Jehovah* (q.v.) by charging humans to worship Him.

Soon to Have Good-Luck Stumps

RABBIT (ră bĭt) n. Cute creature whose feet humans chop off for good luck.

RACE (rās) n. 1. The division of the Broadcloth of Humanity into a clashing, incompatible wardrobe which the Earth wears like a trembling wino. 2. The scramble for the Finish Line of Wisdom in which, on the first lap, Man's brain pulls a hamstring.

RACE TRACK (rās trăk) n. See *Horse Racing*.

RACK (răk) n. A happy device used to encourage a human to stretch his tolerance for pain.

RACKETEER (ră kə tîr) n. An unlettered raconteur.

RACONTEUR (ră kôn tûr) n. A suave racketeer.

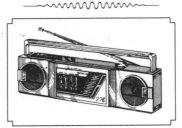

Jingle Transmission Device

RADIO (rā dē ō) n. Vibratory transmissions with which humans glut the galaxy with hemorrhoid cream jingles.

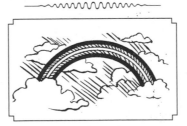

*Rainbow Formed
By Burning Flesh Vapor*

RAINBOW (rān bō) n. That which forms over Auschwitz.

RAIN (rān) n. Ecosystem which blends Humanity's atmospheric pollutants and efficiently recycles them to poison the Earth.

RAPE (rāp) n. The pit inside the fruit of human courtship.

COMMENTARY BY BELIAL

Rape is a bizarre gymnastic routine performed exclusively by human males, using females in place of exercise machines.

RATIONALISM (ră shən əl ĭ zəm) n. A wall of paradox and prooflessness resulting from humans viewing Reality through the pinhole of human logic. See *Intellect*.

Human Correlative

RAT (răt) n. A creature which, like Humanity, infests the planet with ceaseless reproduction and thrives on transforming its environment into a rat hole.

*Like Human Infant,
Exudes Orifice Poisons*

RATTLESNAKE (ră təl snāk) n. That which, like a human infant, shakes its rattle in warning that hideous poisons lie inside its orifice.

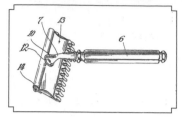

Scraper of Futility

RAZOR (rā zər) n. That which humans use to temporarily scrape bristles from their hides in a laughable attempt to disguise their monstrousness.

REAL ESTATE (rēl əs tāt) n. The succinct expression of Mankind's arch philosophy that it owns the Earth, like a layer of mold proclaiming it owns the orange peel.

REALITY (rē ăl ə tē) n. 1. The kindergarten play which Humanity performs for its bored theater critic, Nothingness. 2. The Infinitely Interwoven Broadcloth of the Cosmos of which Human Idiots can see only a Single Thread. See *Nothingness*.

COMMENTARY BY LORD SATAN

Reality, as such, does not exist. To give All That Is the name *Reality* is to defile and corrupt the concept before it can even be explored. But without the word *Reality*, the Demon Reader may Inquire, how can the concept be grasped? By experiencing it, say I, Satan, Lord of Hell. And in that experience is the Blackest Bliss in all of the Profoundly Evil and Empty Soul of the Cosmos.[20]

20 **NOTE BY LORD SATAN:** I confess, months later, that I was on depression medication when I composed that entry. Although I regret the elevated tone and was unable to conjure it away before publication (such was this entry's power), still the tenor and substance of this message has its roots in the Shadow of Truth.

REASON (rē zən) n. The tool which humans use to analyze and justify atrocities committed on behalf of their genitalia.

Supervisor of Torment and Alienation

RECEPTIONIST (rĭ sĕp shən ĭst) n. The most powerful of humans who, as Gatekeepers to Corporate Executives and Electronic Communication Systems, singlehandedly restrict humans' access to their own banks, attorneys and corporations and who thereby supervise the Torment and Alienation of Mankind.

COMMENTARY BY BAAL ZEBUB

That which is unknown to Mankind is that Demons have infiltrated every major corporation as Head Receptionist, and therefore have Ultimate Control over the Destiny of Man.

RECTANGULAR (rĕk tăng gyū lər) adj. The shape of a human's head when he's not looking in the mirror.

RECYCLE (rē sī kəl) v. That which bacteria does to Humanity.

REDUNDANCY (rĭ dŭn dən sē) n. See *Self-Reference*.

Rotten Food Preservation Device

REFRIGERATOR (rĭ frĭj ər ā tər) n. That which retards the rotting of foodstuff, so that humans may savor the full effect of food, once eaten, rotting inside themselves.

REINCARNATION (rē ĭn kär nā shən) n. 1. Regurgitation of a half-baked breakfast. 2. The process by which souls travel from body to body until they have burnt all *Anti-Evil* (q.v.) from their Beings and reach, after eons of evolution, a State of Perfect Evil. At this point, they are eligible for matriculation at the City of Hell School of Law. See *Cosmology of Hell*.

RELATIVE (rĕl ə tĭv) n. Humans statistically most likely to kill, rape and/or steal from those spewed from genetically linked vaginas.

RELIGION (rĭ lĭ jən) n. The layering of honey on shit. See *Stupidity*; *God*; *Scripture*.

REMAINDER BIN (rĭ mān dər bĭn) n. That which, in human bookstores, is glutted with treatises on wisdom and morality.

RENAISSANCE (rĕn ə sänts) n. The age in which Humanity freed itself from the oppression of ignorance, and enslaved itself to the oppression of God.[21]

REPUBLICAN (rĭ pŭb lĭ kən) n. A meat-eating democrat. See *Conservative*; *Money*.

Family Outing to Devour Gore and Glucose

RESTAURANT (rĕs tə ränt) n. Place where spouses devour gore and ignore each other, when they tire of ignoring each other at home.

RETCH (rĕch) v. See *Dry Heave*.

REUNION (rē yūn yən) n. An opportunity for the renewal of misery.

REVELATION (rĕ vəl ā shən) n. Telepathic messages sent by drunken Demons to human "prophets" and "mediums" as a joke. See *Possession*; *Scripture*.

21 NOTE BY LORD SATAN: i.e., Satan.

REVOLUTION (rĕ və lū shən) n. A government of starving citizens which topples a government of bloated citizens.

RIBALDRY (rĭ bəl drē) n. A camouflage term human intellectuals use to justify in-depth discussions of fellatio and sodomy.

RIDDLE (rĭ dəl) 1. v. That which bullets do to human flesh. 2. n. A flouncy human conundrum.

COMMENTARY BY ZYK

By way of example, I offer the following *riddle* regarding Humanity:

Question:
What do Demons love that gods require;
The poor possess, yet the rich desire;
What lies obdurate hidden in the heart,
And yet extends to hold the stars apart;
From what comes Man from which he cannot come,
And starts and stops the moon and stars and sun;
That which misers discard and paupers save,
And each man brings unto his grave?

Answer: Nothing.

Symbol of Human Marriage: Rigid Emptiness

RING (rĭng) n. A metal circle symbolic of human relationships: a rigid emptiness, a hollow zero.

RING OF OBLADADOX (rĭng əv ä blä dä däks) n. An expensive finger ring conjured in Hell City which facilitates the possession of a lower life-form. After possession, the Ring magically moves to the finger of the body you are possessing.[22]

Masturbation Correlative

RITUAL (rĭ chū əl) n. Repetitive motions which humans perform to attain religious ecstasy. See *Masturbation*.

COMMENTARY BY BEHEMOTH

The origin of human religious ritual is worthy of note. Eons ago, when Demons first settled in Earth-Density, the eating and digesting of humans consistently caused particularly strong and unappetizing clouds of flatulence.

When Demons attempted to dissipate the odor by lighting candles or incense and moving them in circles through the stench, primitive humans misinterpreted these movements as having religious significance.

Thus the solemn rituals performed by religious numbskulls do not symbolize sanctifying the church, but rather clearing it of farts.

22 ED. NOTE: See *Zyk's Third Letter to the Publisher* for an example of a practical use of the Ring of Obladadox for the Advancement of Evil.

Ideal Corporate Human

ROBOT (rō bŏt) n. From the corporate viewpoint, the ideal human being.

Cozy Death Chair

ROCKING CHAIR (rŏ kĭng châr) n. A cozy chair in which human children pray that their foul-smelling and attention-demanding grandparents die. See *Wheelchair*.

ROMANCE (rō măns) n. The dreary clash of two human magnetic fields, auras which invisibly stick out from human bodies like mangy, chaotic stacks of etheric straw. See *Love*.

COMMENTARY BY BELIAL

Romance between humans can be compared to the momentary chafing

Human Romance

of maggots. The clashing of the humans' magnetic fields gives them a momentary intoxicating rush, akin to the rush a Demon experiences when sucking on the human pineal gland.

This auric chafing is interpreted by Humanity as a stupendous Brush with Destiny, as a timeless Significator of Love, rather than the mere sloppy and indifferent friction of magnetic spikes.

COMMENTARY BY ZYK

In my zeal as a sonneteer, I offer the following romantic explication:

If human love be grand illusion,
sweet distraction
Human lovers cannot know
the simplest truth:
The fairest flesh is formed from
putrefaction
And truest love is roiled twixt
groping youth.
Yet beauty still is sweet to human
senses
And love, though randomly
wrought, still is true,
For romance every frailty recom-
penses
And love disguises chance from
lovers' view.
Thus do fools of flesh inanely think
That love was destined for each
others' arms,
Whereas, in truth, any sack of stink
Could easily replace each other's
charms.
For banal chance dictates
Mankind's embrace
While maudlin time exchanges face
for face.

Inbred Vermin

ROYALTY (roi əl tē) n. A family of inbred human vermin whose jewelry has more weight than their souls. See *Queen*; *King*.

RUMOR (rū mər) n. Sensual information which in its erotic potentiality fondles the Genitalia of Knowledge.

COMMENTARY BY ASMO DEUS

According to leading Demon anthropologists, facts have no influence whatsoever in human affairs; rather, *rumor* is the catalytic force of creation and destruction which rules the Insane Life of Man.

Rumor begins all human relationships; rumors of another's money and power, intelligence or sexual prowess inevitably attracts two human fornicators to inflict their fluids on each other in paroxysms of palsied pleasure and prolonged disease.

Rumor also ends all human relationships: rumors of infidelity, cross-dressing, homosexuality, money hoarded away in secret bank accounts, ad nauseam, result in a horrific divorce and ripping apart of possessions. So, too, rumor rules all Earth *finance* (q.v.), from the rise and fall of the stock market to the promotion of a secretary rumored to be superior in dictation, fellatio or sodomy.

The fact that Fact is subservient to Rumor in Earth-Density provides unending Permutations of Stupidity to amaze, dazzle and entertain the Invading Demon.

QUADRIFIDUM
THE
FOURTH

ZYK'S FOURTH MEMO
TO THE
PUBLISHER

CONCERNING HIS RESEARCH
ON
EARTH

MEMO TO
MORTIMER PÖNÇÉ, ESQ.
PUBLISHER, MIND CONTROL PRESS
HELL HOLE WEST
CITY OF HELL

FROM
ZYK OF ASIMOTH, EDITOR
INVASION MANUAL COMMISSION
DISPATCHED FROM EARTH,
DALLAS, TEXAS, U.S.A.
NOVEMBER 22, 1963

Detestable Mr. Pönçé:

Your most recent epistle was received and read with immense frustration. So Satan learned of the conspiracy and mercilessly obliterated Cipher and Tophiel, leaving me only the beautiful but cloying Lilith to help me.

After He dispatches Lilith, I shall be next, Mr. Pönçé, followed by You.

I do, however, appreciate the fact that you cared enough to send the complex and unmemorizable Spell of Void, the only known Spell which can Obliterate the legendary (and now, it appears, quite senile) Abra Kadab. If Kadab accosts me again, this time I shall be ready for him.

Nonetheless, I brought Debbie, with whom I blanch to say I am still intensely enamored, to this area of Earth-Density to research a murder. In this instance, the victim was a human squab these creatures call a "president." It was to be a typically dull and clichéd affair: the aforementioned squab intended to cut off a profitable war and squash the government agencies profiting by it; a dimly evil cabal has subcontracted professional killers to shoot him; a scapegoat has been duly selected.

Yawn. The same tedious scenario throughout all of human history.

Still, like Roswell, this was the Nexus for many subsequent events in this time frame. Observing the killing would give a maximum amount of information for our Commentaries with a minimum amount of time and expended in research. And saving time, as we both know, is our highest priority.

I brought Debbie to an empty office in a book depository above the square. The President's motorcade was due to pass below us in twenty minutes. The scapegoat was already in the building. The shooters were hiding in a triangular formation across the square.

Debbie, I should mentioned, was pregnant. No, she had not, of course, been inseminated by that lard-covered dolt, Hitler the Clown. In truth, the Führer had not touched her. Rather, the child was conceived by Debbie and myself during our thousands of sessions of intense fornication under the splay of stars circling above the Romance that is Dachau.

As we arrived in Dallas, Debbie was going into labor. The child's birth was imminent. Unfortunately, I did not realize that Dealey Plaza was the center of a local space-time distortion. Thus I was at the time unable to shift temporal dimensions in order to separate the birth of our child with the killing of the President. It appeared that our child, out of necessity, would be born during the time in which I was to observe the assassination.

Debbie cried out with animalistic grunts and groans as the child began slowly squeezing through her birth canal like a giant squid through a dwarf's trouser buttons.

Through the office window, I heard the cheering of the crowd outside as the President's motorcade approached.

At that moment the child began to emerge. But what became visible was not the infant's head, but its hairy back. This was obviously to be a breech birth, an unexpected and dangerous happenstance which put both Debbie and our child in mortal danger.

Still, I was distracted by the growing cheers, by the motorcade now a block away, by my intriguing glimpses of the shooters' rifle barrels protruding from their triangle of death.

It was a desperate moment. I kept one eye on the encroaching presidential vehicle as I tried to help the child pull free from Debbie's wrenching womb.

But the child, which seemed unmanageably large for the small opening, was stuck. I pulled and yanked and tugged, but could not free the child in its breeched position.

The motorcade drew closer. I could sense the President's subconscious acceptance of his imminent death, of the sweat on the patsy's brow, of the shooters' fingers tightening on their triggers.

Suddenly, something gave way.

Our First Baby Photo

The baby, which was very large and gangly but quite invisible to humans, violently exploded out of the womb like a bloody, spiraling bolo. The baby, which I could now see was half goat, half jackal, catapulted at high speed past me before I could catch it. Invisible to human eyes, it shot through the open window and into the square, its hooves splayed wildly.

And before the shooters could pull their triggers, our invisible goat-jackal's hooves smashed into the president's head at supra-luminal speed, first the front hooves, hitting him forward, then the back hooves, hitting him backwards.

The impact with the President's head deflected the goat-jackal, which plummeted into the heart of the Nexus Itself, careening through the rip in space-time, vanishing forever and utterly from the realm of Earth-Density.

The obstreperous birth of our unfortunate child had obviously interfered with the sequence of probable events in this otherwise insipid affair. Therefore, to tidy things up temporally, I froze time and quickly improvised shifting dimensions around like a Cosmic Jigsaw Puzzle comprising Dealey Plaza. (I also managed to snap a baby photo for Debbie, but as it was overexposed, I ordered a human artist to recreate it as a keepsake.) My tampering with the Plaza's local physics caused a miasma of contradictory, overlapping event horizons, deepening the nexus and manifesting a number of interlocking paradoxes which, in toto, smoothed out the jagged mess the incident had made in the veiny skein of human history.

As to the fate of our poor goat-jackal child, after I took a snapshot and unfroze time, it was swept irrevocably into the roaring Vortex of Creation.

Before leaving, I erected an eternal invisible memorial to our beloved baby on the hillside at Dealey Plaza, one which will cause nausea and mystification to any human henceforth defiling the spot with his or her presence.

Debbie has recovered admirably from her difficult childbirth. Although Lord Satan is bound to find out about us, still I must go on, I must do my duty, and I shall take her with me in my arms until it is the end for both of us.

Although only Lilith remains to help me meet my deadline, the outcome for us all, Mr. Pönçé, is moot. Lord Satan, of course, *enjoys* obliterating Demons. He's stated that publicly.

After completing this letter, which is accompanied by my latest packet of data and poetry to be delivered straightaway to Lilith, I shall fly off with my beloved to my final assignment, located several centuries in the past.

Although my own destiny is sealed, I still hope against hope that my beloved Debbie will survive, even when I am No More.

Most hatefully yours,
ZYK

MANUAL
OF
EARTH TERMS

THE LETTERS
S~Z

s, S (ĕs) n. A Pictogram of the Surd, the decapitated Spiral, a symbol of Incomplete Infinity, protesting the Arrogance of Endlessness.

SABBATH (să bəth) n. The Day of Divine Extortion. In the Protection Racket of Religion, the Sabbath is the day upon which dirt-poor humans are blackmailed with a threat of Eternal Torment unless they make ransom payments. These monies are remitted to a collection office called a *church* (q.v.) via robed degenerates. These agents take their percentage, then remit the balance to a conclave of homosexual Italian billionaires who use the money to finance the building of more collection offices.

Pedestrian Tastes in Blood

SABER (sā bər) n. A second-rate gourmet whose tongue savors the pedestrian flavor of human blood.

SACRED (sā krĭd) adj. 1. A concept which humans attribute to a flag or an ancient book to justify mass killings. 2. To humans, anything save human life.

SACRILEGE (să krə lĭj) n. 1. That which inhibits the flow of money to the Church. 2. To interrupt a priest while he is fellating a cardinal or pope.

SADISM (să dĭ zəm) n. The mythic relationship of God to Man.

SAFARI OUTFIT (sə fä rē out fĭt) n. Stylish garb worn by humans while killing endangered species.

SAFETY (sāf tē) n. An irksome latch which must be raised on a pistol before a human experiences the joy of killing.

Sailor Eager to Drown Enemy

SAILOR (sā lər) n. A human who dresses up like a chocolate ice cream cone in order to kill sailors dressed as other flavors.

SALAD (să ləd) n. Tasteless clumps of grass which dieting humans eat in public, while dreaming of the fat and sugar they will stuff down their throats in private.

SALOON (sə lūn) n. A holy place of contemplation, communion and projectile vomiting.

Obedient Human Worships Flag Before Bombing Enemy Hospital

SALUTE (sə lūt) n. Gesture of respect humans use before massacring women and children.

SANITATION (săn ĭ tā shən) n. The laughable delusion that humans can actually escape from the filth of which they are composed.

Satan's Emissary

SANTA CLAUS (săn tə clôz) p. Archetypal emissary of Satan who cultivates a love of greed in children.

SARCOPHAGUS (sär kô fə gəs) n. 1. The exquisitely logical evolution of a three-piece suit. 2. A friend of maggots and grave-robbers. See *Crypt*.

SATELLITE (să tə līt) n. Device which allows human stupidity to be broadcast over immense distances.

Nameless Humans

SAVAGE (să vĭj) n. A human without a nametag. See *Primitive Man*.

COMMENTARY BY LLU CIPHER.

A savage is a reprehensible human who eats untainted food, breathes pure air and profanes civilization by communing with nature. See *Hermit*.

SAVIOR (sā vyər) n. Archetypal leader created by humans to compensate for their inability to think and feel for themselves.

SCANDAL (skăn dəl) n. That which humans love even more than killing.

SCHISM (skĭ zəm) n. The evolution of every human relationship into a betrayer and a betrayed.

SCHOOL (skūl) n. Human institution dedicated to the systematic eradication of wisdom. See *University*.

HOLY BOOKS GHOST-WRITTEN BY SATAN

BOOK	PSEUDONYM	ACHIEVEMENT	ADHERENTS KILLED
Veda	Krishna	Invented caste system	876,000
Upanishads	Anonymous (real name: Larry)	Invented turbans to protect pet lice	605,000
Old Testament	Jehovah	Invented usury and takes	2,700,500
New Testament	"Apostles" (various)	Deified guilt and worthlessness of self	150,500,000
Koran	Mohammed	Invented xenophobia, OK'd assassination	150,500,001
Dianetics	Hubbard	Invented spiritual pyramid scheme, destroyed enemies, annoyed public	13½

SCIENCE (sī əns) n. A human activity involving the obfuscation of truth based on extrapolating measurements and proclaiming them, to the hilarity of Demons, as Law.

An Ingenious Moron

SCIENTIST (sī ən tĭst) n. An ingenious *moron* (q.v.) who preaches the supreme infallibility of linear measurement. See *Weapons Designer*.

SCRIPTURE (skrĭp chər) n. Generic name for books written by Myself, Satan, under various pseudonyms. These books are the most convenient tools in Inspiring Evil and in the Sucking of Human Souls to Hell.

Refer to the Chart above, tracking the Progress of each of Lord Satan's Holy Books. This chart lists the Pseudonym used, the Satanic Goal of each scripture, the number of fanatics killed in defense of each book, and the number of infidels killed for not believing in each book. See *Bible*; *Religion*.

SCUM (skŭm) n. The thin layer of humans affixed to the skin of the Earth.

SEANCE (sā äns) n. Performance art for the wealthy and senile.

COMMENTARY BY AHRIMAN

All phenomena at a so-called seance, of course, are caused not by the spirits of deceased humans, but rather by two agencies only: 1) the human "medium" and/or 2) prankster Demons. Subsequent to the Invasion of Earth-Density, Demons will be encouraged to get drunk, seek out a seance and, wagering between themselves which Demon can create the most terror or awe, create phenomena such as tossing furniture, pounding walls, blowing party horns or, if the Demon has drunk too much, vomiting ectoplasm. See *Make-Believe*; *Senility*.

Office Trophy

SECRETARY (sĕ krĭ tĕ rē) n. A sexual trophy, usually female, mounted in front of the boss' office, then in private mounted from behind.

SEGREGATION (sĕ grə gā shən) n. The tasteful separation of those humans with less from those with more.

SELF-LOATHING (sĕlf lōth ĭng) n. Human sanity.

SELF-MADE MAN (sĕlf mād măn) n. 1. A bum. 2. A male capable of fellating himself.

SELF-REFERENCE (sĕlf rĕ frəns) n. See *Redundancy*. See *Redundancy*. Also see *Self-Reference*.

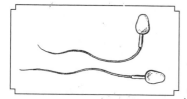

Harbingers of Doom

SEMEN (sē mən) n. For the good of Humanity, that which one hopes will never come. See *Sperm*.

Carnival Barker of Family Values

SENATOR (sĕn ə tər) n. 1. Duly-elected Carnival Barker. 2. The client of a prostitute. See *Alcoholic; Liar; Millionaire; Politician.*

Senile Human Performing Putrefaction Activities

SENILITY (sĭ nĭl ĭ tē) n. The rotten fruit of the Tree of Life. See *Vatican.*

SENTIMENT (sĕn tə mənt) n. That which allows a human who has butchered a family to take a moment to feed their entrails to the family dog.

SERIOUSNESS (sîr ē əs nĭs) n. The absence of genius.

SERMON (sûr mən) n. The part of a religious service during which human males sleep. See *Pulpit.*

SEWER (sū ər) n. The human bloodstream.

SEX (sĕks) n. 1. The mitosis of the original human (known as "woman") into a bizarre "antiwoman" or "man," having no breasts, no emotions and a grotesquely mutated clitoris. 2. The hilariously disgusting means by which humans reproduce themselves via the sewage portals of their flesh.

When the pioneer Demon *Abra Kadab* (q.v.) first bio-engineered experimental human types, the sexual reproductive method was favored because it instilled in the creatures a sense of belonging and attachment with each other, literally suckling off each other's bodies, thus making them easier to trap and cook.

For maximum entertainment value, it is recommended that Demon Insurgents immediately seek out humans engaged in *sex*. This may be accomplished by following a trail of animalistic grunts, screams and the telltale stench of human fornication.

SEXISM (sĕks ĭ zəm) n. The unending hatred between the purse and the coin.

SHAME (shām) n. That which a human feels if he neglects to kill all witnesses to an atrocity.

SHAMPOO (shăm pū) n. That which temporarily removes filth from human hair.

Meat and Vaginal Substitute

SHEEP (shēp) n. Meat substitute for Bengalis, and vaginal substitute for Shepherds. See *Mutton*.

Fig. 202
Short Sideburns

Fig. 203
Extra-Long Sideburn

Public Pubic Hair

SIDEBURNS (sīd bûrnz) n. An embarrassing growth of pubic hair over the vagina-like ears, the organs which are seduced or raped by human language. See *Beard*; *Fashion*; *Hair*.

SIEVE (sĭv) n. Device which separates DDT-contaminated wheat from DDT-contaminated chaff.

SIGHTSEEING (sīt sē ĭng) n. Sojourns in which humans throw trash into natural settings.[1] See *Garbage*; *Vacation*.

SILENCE (sī ləns) n. The mellifluous answer to human prayers. See *Nothingness*.

SILICON (sĭl ĭ kän) n. Chemical compound utilized to expand memory in computers and breasts in Las Vegas.

SIN (sĭn) n. The arbitration of good and evil by the human pocket or human groin.

[1] **NOTE BY MEPHIS TOPHIEL:** This is reminiscent of the piles of cigarette butts, chicken bones, vomit effluvia and other refuse which I and many other unfortunate sexual explorers discovered upon slurping the sewage portal of Lilith's Most Tired Orifice.

SINCERITY (sĭn sĕr ĭ tē) n. The Smile of Deceit. See *Lie*.

SISTER (sĭs tər) n. The quaint name given to the goddess Envy.

SITCOM (sĭt käm) n. Electronic mind control designed to lower the human IQ and, in combination with drugs, alcohol and pornography, sedate human slaves during off-work hours.

Sitcoms are exquisitely unfunny distortions of human reality which Mankind stares at for hours each day, interspersed with loud, hypnotic, sexual entreaties for the slaves to ceaselessly and voraciously consume.[2]

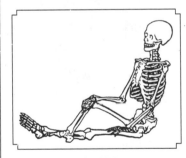

Grateful Skeleton Freed from Human Flesh

SKELETON (skĕl ĭ tən) n. That which begs Hell to be ripped free from grotesque human flesh.

[2] **NOTE BY BELIAL:** As if Ahriman, the most insipidly dull Demon in the Cosmos of Hell, knows what's funny. Certainly Hell's longest-running television series, *Quipping Penile and Vaginal Holes*, is a sitcom, and yet is entertaining and thought-provoking to Demons Everywhere.

SKEPTIC (skĕp´tĭk) n. 1. A high-intellect moron who delights in sodomizing the Baby thrown out with the Bathwater. 2. A human buffoon who, perceiving the Baldness of Metaphysics, sniggers at the Bad Wigs of Cranks while sporting the Moronic Hair Plugs of Science. See *Intellect.*

SKEPTICISM (skĕp´tĭ sĭ zəm) n. A suave word denoting a refusal to entertain concepts contrary to corporate grants.

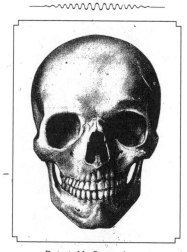

Detestable Organ Armor

SKULL (skŭl) n. Detestable armor which protects the Most Annoying Organ in the Cosmos. See *Brain.*

SLAUGHTERHOUSE (slô´tər hous) n. Edifice in which humans enthusiastically assert their superiority over animals.

SLAVE (slāv) n. Human female, or human male after receiving a Social Security number. See *Housewife; Social Security.*

The Defiled Delirium of Dreams

SLEEP (slēp) n. The Whorehouse of Human Desire. See *Bed; Dream.*

SMELL, THE (smĕl) n. Euphemism used by Demons who have traveled to Earth to describe the stench of Humanity. Although Earth is insignificant in size and scale, the fact that The Smell permeates the farthest reaches of Hell Universe is indicative of the Purity of its Singular Putrescence.

COMMENTARY BY BEHEMOTH

Time-travelers to Earth-Density always remember their first whiff of Earth's excrescent stink, perceptible not only through space but through time; The Smell has been detected by Demons up to two million years surrounding the planet's present time frame. While disgusting, the odor admittedly belies a pungent source of organic foodstuffs for the hungry Demon. See *Earth.*

Snow Particles Prior to Befoulment by Human Groin

SNOW (snō) n. That which Humanity turns yellow.

SOCIAL SECURITY (sō shəl sĭ kyūr ĭ tē) n. System devised by Satan giving a number given to a human infant that corresponds to the number on the oven it is cooked in.

SODOMY (sä də mē) n. The act of cleaving a human's behind with the erect male brain.

Human Bulls-Eye

SOLDIER (sōl jər) n. A target made of flesh. See *War; Weapon.*

Human Activity Between Anus Wipings

SOPHISTICATION (sə fĭs tĭ kā shən) n. The quality which allows a human to wipe the excrement oozing from its diarrheac rump with a look of refinement and savoir faire.

SOPHISTRY (sä fĭs trē) n. The saliva of human logic oozing into the Drool-cup of Rhetoric.

SOPRANO (sə prä nō) n. A human who, when squeezed by a Demon, emits a high-pitched sound which can be used to shatter stained-glass windows. See *Music*.

SOUND (sound) n. A vibratory side effect of the Cosmos shuddering in embarrassment at the humans stuck to Its Hide.

SOUNDTRACK CD (sound trăk sē dē) n. Vibrations created by heroin addicts to accompany projected images created by cocaine addicts.

SOUTH AMERICA (south ə mĕ rĭ kə) n. Land of brown-skinned flesh-sacs whose cocaine products augment the North American Karaoke Industry.

SPACE (spās) n. The sagging, empty teat of human geometry.

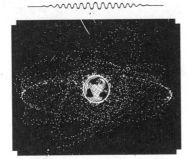

Space Debris Trajectories

SPACE DEBRIS (spās dĭ brē) n. 1. A human astronaut. 2. The legacy of the human space program, consisting of 60,000 pieces of trash careening around the Earth like a cloud of gnats.

The metallic excretions of Earth, glutting the planet's orbital paths, must be carefully circumnavigated by Demons approaching Earth-Density, as well as the ring of invisible "trailer park" colonies of the inbred Demon-Trash known as *Angels* (q.v.). Refer to the preceding Diagram for suggested flight paths.

SPACE PROGRAM (spās prō grăm) n. An ingenious plan to dump tax dollars into space.

SPECIAL OLYMPICS (spĕ shəl ə lĭm pĭks) n. The race of human existence.

SPEECH (spēch) n. A virus, spread by microphoned criminals, which infects and stupefies the human brain.

Speech consists of human laryngeal vibrations polluting the atmosphere. The specific frequencies emitted by the idiotic flapping and squawking of the tongue correspond to mental analogies which humans decode into *concepts* (q.v.). See *Language; Word*.

SPELL OF BENDING TIME, THE n. See *Flying Saucer*.

SPERM (spûrm) n. That which perpetuates the watching of game shows.

The tiny, powerful brain of the human sperm cell, or nucleic homunculus, measuring no more than a thousandth of an inch, is the most powerful organ in the male physiognomy, and generally controls the total movements of the male throughout his daily chores and ablutions.

The aerial projection of the sperm is the most important daily activity of the male human, to which is dedicated many hours of concentration and preparation, utilizing accessories such as audio-visual aids, artificial vagina pockets in air-filled plastic female forms, lubrication oils and powders.

Overall, simple manual milking of the extruding male genitalia will effectively achieve the desired air-borne spewing, which was the main motivation for the creation of the *Internet* (q.v.).

SPHINCTER (sfĭngk tər) n. 1. The Portal of Human Wisdom. 2. The door which unleashes the best Humanity has to offer.

SPIRITUAL SECURITY AGENCY (a.k.a. The S.S.A.) (spĭ rĭ chū əl sĭ kyʊr ĭ tē ā gən sē) n. A secret organization of militant priests, nuns, lamas and holy men with license to kill Demons.

The S.S.A. is the only group of human slugs who are aware of the Demonic presence on the Earth, and carry weaponry deadly to Demons, such as machine guns with bullets made of frozen holy water.

SPITTOON (spĭ tūn) n. 1. Device used to collect the stringy slime of phlegm secreted by the human mouth. 2. To a phlegmy Demon, the human face.

SPONTANEOUS COMBUSTION (spän tā nē əs cəm bŭs chən) n. 1. In human mythology, the "Big Bang." 2. A human who has been flame-broiled by an invisible Demon and the body discovered by humans before the Demon can feed on the corpse. Humans prefer the absurd explanation that victims "explode" for no reason, rather than accept the obvious, that humans taste delicious when charbroiled.

Distraction From Death

SPORT (spôrt) n. 1. Organized physical movement; which distract humans from their inevitable death. 2. A female amputee who asks males to buy her a drink. 3. Term for quelling the human slave workers via a corporate network of gambling, memorabilia fetishism and beer distribution. 4. To Demons invading Earth-Density, the hunting and shooting of humans with one arm tied behind their backs.

COMMENTARY BY AHRIMAN

With regard to His Majesty's Definition 2, a human *sport* is a mass spectacle in which humans create artificial, sentimental attachments to teams performing competitions of ritualized movements. If a human's team "loses," its supporters will weep and gnash their teeth like monkeys deprived of a favorite female anus to sniff.

STAR (stär) n. 1. That which, in multitude, illuminates an outdoor human sacrifice. 2. A human who is photographed and stalked.

STATUE (stă chū) n. A three-dimensional bird-excrement-splattered mirror which humans gaggle at in a daze of masturbatory self-adoration. See *Art*.

Humans Masturbating to Image of Themselves

Device for Popping Human Skulls

STEAMROLLER (stēm rō lər) n. A device which bored Demons occasionally use to loudly pop a human skull.[3]

3 NOTE BY GOD, LORD OF THE PERSONIFIED UNIVERSE: Although it is of course against My Will to kill any of My creatures, if a human is *already* dead, I agree that it is fun to pop its skull with a steamroller.

STERILIZATION (stĕ rəl ī zā shən) n. That which, when proposed for Mankind, receives a standing ovation from Hell. See *Child Abuse*; *Child Sacrifice*; *Quintuplets*.

STOCK EXCHANGE (stŏk ĕks chānj) n. A sleazy Bingo Parlor disguised by the façade of the Harvard Business School. See *Gambling*.

STUPIDITY (stū pĭ dĭ tē) n. The highest level of brilliance achievable by the human mind. See *Idiot*; *Imbecile*; *Human Being*; *Human Intelligence*; *Intelligence Test*; *Moron*.

COMMENTARY BY ASMO DEUS

Lord Satan's teachings often took the form of evil parables[4] illustrating the stupidity of any behavior which benefits others. With regard to Humanity, the following parables illustrate three categories of human stupidity:

EXCERPTS FROM THE PARABLES OF LORD SATAN

1. COMPASSION

In *The Parable of the Samaritan*, Lord Satan tells of a certain pustuled beggar lying near death in a ditch. Three humans passed him on the road. The first, a cannibal, stole the beggar's thumb to suck on during his journey and left him there to die. The second, a priest, stole his genitals to suck on during his journey and left him there to die. But the third, a simple Samaritan, felt compassion upon the dying beggar and brought him to his house to nurse him back to health.

As a result, the Samaritan, his wife, his children, his dogs and his entire village were infected by the plague and died horrific deaths. The Moral: *Compassion exists only as a gateway to genocide.*

2. JUSTICE

In *The Parable of Lazarus*, Lord Satan tells of a certain wealthy man named Lazarus who died. His estate was stolen by his lawyer and his widow was thrown destitute into the street. Meeting a simple healer in the road, the widow asked him to raise Lazarus from the dead. If he succeeded, her husband would restore her riches and she would justly reward the healer. The healer at first refused, but when she plied him with sexual favors, he at last agreed.

In a ritual performed at Lazarus' grave, the healer raised the corpse from the dead and asked Lazarus' wife for his just reward. But when his lawyers told Lazarus that the healer had defiled his wife, Lazarus tied the healer to a stake where he was copulated upon by three rapacious bears. The healer's body was then dismembered and the remains fed to a pack of filthy dogs. The Moral: *Justice is only obtained when stolen by lawyers.*

3. CHARITY

In *The Parable of the Loaves and Fishes*, Lord Satan tells of a simple caterer who was met by a group of Hollywood's most influential film producers who demanded servings of sushi, French bread and fine wine. Unfortunately he had only two orders of sushi, one loaf of bread and one bottle of cheap Chablis to feed all two hundred. Wanting to impress the producers with his charity and gain favor in their eyes, he called in a favor from another catering company and served the producers what they had asked for free of charge. Unfortunately the second caterer was jealous of the first, and purposely provided day-old sushi, stale bread and corked wine.

As a result, the producers blackballed the caterer who later hung himself from the Hollywood sign. The Moral: *A Film Producer and Charity cannot coexist.*

Cabal of Suck-Crazed Humans

SUCKING (sŭ kĭng) v. A favorite activity of humans, culminating in the ghastly practice of enthusiastically squeezing the lips around nodules of foreign flesh.

COMMENTARY BY ZYK

Concerning *sucking*, I offer the following concise yet sensitive versification:

> *A human sucker gaily sucks*
> *A pap of every whore*
> *He sucks a flask and spits a tune*
> *To Him who sucked him from the*
> *   womb*
> *And chucked him on the floor.*
> *And when the world has sucked*
> *   him dry*
> *He weds a stinking bitch.*
> *And when he sucks his final cup*
> *The stinking Earth will suck him up*
> *To feed a stinking ditch.*

SUFFERING (sŭ fər ĭng) n. Human existence. See *Pain.*

SUFFOCATE (sŭ fə kāt) v. One-word instructions on human pillows.

SUICIDE (sū ĭ sīd) n. The first healthy human instinct at birth.

COMMENTARY BY ASMO DEUS

After the Invasion, Demons will be pleasantly surprised to find literally millions of human souls eager to kill themselves at the merest whisper of a suggestion. Needless to say, assisting a human to suicide is one of the greatest joys a Demon can experience on Earth-plane, with the exception, of course, of Humanity's total annihilation.

But in order to get the most out of Demonically Assisted Suicide, the Demon should review the innumerable permutations of human suicide.

See *Appendix 2: Reference Chart for Demon-Assisted Suicide (available only in the Deluxe Commemorative Edition).*

---

4   ED. NOTE: The three parables of Satan in this *Invasion Manual* were plagiarized by the prophet Jesus Christ, who found the copy Lord Zyk lost while time-traveling into Earth's past. See *Zyk's Last Memo to the Publisher.*

SUNDAY (sŭn dā) n. The day upon which the Mythic Creator viewed his seven-day creation in horror and committed suicide by jumping off a Cosmic Cliff. The Universe, ever moving through Space, is the Creator's Corpse falling forever to its Death.

SUPERHIGHWAY (sū pər hī wā) n. The super method by which humans foul their atmosphere.

SUPERMARKET (sū pər mär kĭt) n. The super means by which DDT-glutted food is supplied to the human fetus.

SUPERSTITION (sū pər stĭ shən) n. Human science.

SUPREME BEING (sū prēm bē ĭng) n. While Demons of Hell acknowledge that I, Satan, am the Supreme Being of the Cosmos, and that My Evil is Limitless and Omniscient, Backward Humanity hallucinates a Supreme Being that is Good (a.k.a. "God").

Although Lord of Hell, whether I had a Beginning or not, I know not. I simply don't remember back that far. How I evolved into Being from Nothingness is a Mystery, even to Me. But, as I *do* exist and *am* Ruler of the Cosmos, I wonder only at My inexplicable limitation in the area of memory.

There are troubling paradoxes in these areas of Thought. They have led to my Expulsion of certain Subjects from the curriculum of the University of Hell (Mathematical Infinity, Set Theory and Fractal Geometry). And while it is manifestly absurd that there may be a Supreme Being who is "good," it is not illogical that there may be a Meta-Supreme Being who encompasses Myself and is even more Infinitely Evil.

But this cosmic conjecture will leave most Demons cold. This is as it should be. Ambiguity and Omniscient Power should never ever meet. Worship Me, O Ye Demons. May Your Sphincter Scales tighten with Unspeakably Evil Thoughts as you bow down to Me in Eternal Supplication. If anyone upbraids or dares criticize Me, I Curse and Wipe their Memory from the Skein of the Cosmos like an eraser to a quack equation. And although logic does not require that I am the Cream of the Supreme, still My Supremacy is Infinitely more powerful than the spooky Stupidity of Mankind. See *God*.

SUPREME COURT (sū prēm kôrt) n. A cult of senile human attorneys deemed "supreme" by attorney-cult worshippers.

SURGERY (sûr jər ē) n. The hacking of the human body by alcoholics.

COMMENTARY BY AHRIMAN

Surgery, or the slicing and gutting of humans with razors, is admired by Demons everywhere, the most exquisite expression of which is called the *lobotomy* (q.v.).

SURREALISM (sə rē əl ĭ zəm) n. The consensus slur of human reality. See *Reality*.

SUSPECT (sŭs pěkt) n. The beloved friend or spouse of a freshly murdered human.

SUSPENSE (sŭs pěns) n. That which a human experiences when being eaten by a Demon feet first.

Peppy German Icon

SWASTIKA (swäs tĭ kə) n. See *Insignia*; *Nazi*.

SWEAT (swět) n. See *Perspiration*.

SWEETENER (swē tən ər) n. That which a human female spoons into her spouse's coffee to hide the aftertaste of arsenic.

SYNERGY (sĭn ər jē) n. The unexpected amplification of excellence when two serial killers cooperate on a murder spree.

SYPHILIS (sĭf ĭ lĭs) n. A Pus-filled Legacy of Love.

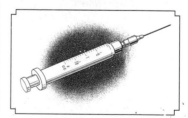

Magical Fluid Dispenser

SYRINGE (sə rĭnj) n. A tapered node filled with magic fluid which, like a teat putting an infant to sleep, lulls a human into insolent oblivion.

t, T (tē) n. The 20th pictogram in the human alphabet, a joyous symbol representing the tumescent male member being blocked by a plastic diaphragm.

TABOO OF EARTH-DENSITY (tă bū) n. Lord Satan's Ancient Decree, since rescinded, forbidding Demons any intercourse with Earth and the creatures which infest it.

Duplicator of Human Screams

TAPE RECORDER (tāp rĭ kôr dər) n. That which, at worst, duplicates the human voice, and at best, duplicates its screams.

TATTOO (tă tū) n. 1. Act of self-mutilation by which humans simulate individuality. 2. Convenient way to mark humans for the ovens.

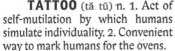

Humans Stupefied by Magical Screen

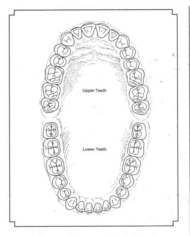

Diagram of Human Food Gnashers

TEETH (tēth) n. Camouflage term humans use to describe their grotesque food-gnashers, so they can pretend they are not rapacious, flesh-gnawing beasts.

TELESCOPE (tĕl ə skōp) n. Instrument which 1% of Humanity use to peer at the Cosmos, and which 99% use to peer surreptitiously at each other's stinking genitalia.

TELEVANGELIST (tĕl ə văn jəl ĭst) n. 1. Generally, a Demon transferred to Earth-Density by Satan as a media consultant. 2. A stage magician skilled in pulling coins out of the lesions of cancer victims. 3. An insidious form of acid which seeps

through television sets and eats away the souls and bank accounts of *morons* (q.v.). See *Religion*.

TELEVISION (tĕl ə vĭ zhən) n. 1. Magical Screen used to glorify that which is worthless. 2. The Secret Weapon of Hell which will facilitate the Invasion of Earth. See *America*; *Anti-Christ*; *Consumer*; *Living Room*.

TERMINAL PATIENT (tûr mĭ nəl pā shənt) n. Philanthropist who sends a doctor's children to Ivy League universities. See *Doctor*.

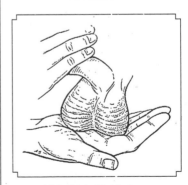

Male Brain Hemispheres

TESTICLES (tĕs tĭ kəlz) n. The distinct hemispheres of the male human brain. See *Penis*.

THEOLOGY (thē ä lə jē) n. The study of con men who speak Latin.

COMMENTARY BY ASMO DEUS

Theology, a beautiful Diagram of Human Idiocy, is based upon the illogical concept that an Omniscient, Infinite Good (God) could also create Infinite Evil (Devil). Such a state of affairs, of course, would be insane. Do humans envision God as a Cosmic Moron, bumblingly creating Evil by mistake? Or as a Cosmic Masochist, purposely stabbing a Dagger in His Own Heart?

If humans were capable of Reason, they would see the absurdity of these conclusions. But since they are not, most branches of human theology require a Mythic Redeemer to save Mankind from Evil. And without a Cosmos filled with Evil, there would be no need for a Redeemer, *and thus no need for theology.* There is, in fact, no need for either, except in the thought patterns of Humanity, because there is no Infinite Good. There is only Infinite Evil inhabiting the Infinite Levels of Hell, which humans call the "Universe,"[5] and is personified by Our Lord Satan. Yet the greatest irony is that Lord Satan Himself is an enthusiastic amateur theologian, whose monographs Proving His Invincibility and Imperial Majesty are marvelous demonstrations of His Ingenious Sophistry, Unequaled Personality and Flawless Iniquity.[6]

5   NOTE BY LORD SATAN: Again, the fact that Humans refer to the Swamp of Stars as "heaven" when they are, in fact, staring at the Armpit of Hell, is typical of Mankind's ignorance of the Real Reality that It is Born of the Wombless Womb of Black Nothingness.

6   NOTE BY LORD SATAN: Again, despite Asmo Deus' transparent attempts at sucking up to Me, the Tenor of his Argument is, indeed, Impeccable.

THIEF (thēf) n. A human who respects possessions with such sincerity that he makes others' his own so that he may then treat them with the respect they deserve. See *Crime.*

THOUGHT (thôt) n. Excitement from neuron firing in the human brain which simulates knowledge.[7] See *Typewriter.*

COMMENTARY BY MEPHIS TOPHIEL

Thoughts and *thinking* are that which clog the human mind and obstruct it from its most cherished activities — eating, killing and fornicating.

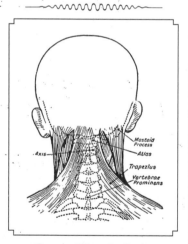

Unsevered Flotation Device for Demon Beginner Swimmers

THROAT (thrōt) n. Human body part which, when sliced from the body and gutted, serves as an arm flotation device for Demons at ocean resorts. See *Neck.*

7   NOTE BY GOD, LORD OF THE PERSONIFIED UNIVERSE: In the Big Picture, My Angels, the Firing of the Cosmic Neuron, in Its Infinite Singularity, is that Explosion by which the Creation is made visible.

TIME (tīm) n. The street corner on which humans loiter.

Toilet: Receptacle for Gushing Tubes

TOILET (toi lĭt) n. 1. A hyperbolic term for the human body, which collects the refuse of its environment and carries it around in gushy sacs and tubes which are best left, by Demons with taste, unexplored. 2. Unfortunate inanimate device which humans use to empty their gushy sacs and tubes. 3. Ultimately, the Earth.

COMMENTARY BY LLU CIPHER

It is recommended that Demon Invaders, by way of R & R, magically anthropomorphize human toilets and command them to tell amusing anecdotes of the variety of ways by which humans squeeze fluid and emulsions from their orifices.

TONGUE (tŭng) n. The Conveyor Belt of Tedium.

COMMENTARY BY BEHEMOTH

When gutting a human, the *tongue* is the most enjoyable part to detach. You simply pull it out to full length, and then *snap* shut the jaws.

The Only Worthwhile Human Activity

TORTURE (tôr chər) n., v. The only human activity of substance and worth. See *Music*.

TRACHEOTOMY (trā kē ä tə mē) n. A hole cut in the esophagus allowing a human with throat cancer the joy of smoking.

COMMENTARY BY LLU CIPHER

Mutilating the body in order to smoke tobacco through an alternate orifice is an example of the synergy of humans and disease which result in hours of wonderful entertainment for the Demon Insurgent. But the smoking of tobacco is not the most imaginative use to which humans have put their tracheotomy neckholes. For spitting phlegm on religious icons, the tracheotomy hole is unparalleled in its accuracy in aiming and propelling fluid projectiles.

Also, for fellatio, the tracheotomy hole may be stretched several inches wide for the insertion of various human sexual appendages, the overall effect being not unlike a human Eskimo's fornication with a whale's blowhole.

TRAITOR (trā tər) n. See *Unamericanism*.

TRAP (trăp) n. 1. To males, a vagina. 2. To female, children. 3. To males and females, marriage. 4. To humans, employment. 5. To entities, incarnation.

TRASH (trăsh) n. See *Garbage.*

Organic Gallows

TREE (trē) n. That which supplies a natural setting for a hanging.

Attorney Arguing Case in Order to Purchase Cocaine

TRIAL (trī əl) n. That which finances the cocaine, whores and gambling junkets which an attorney requires to practice his trade.

TROPISM (trō pǐ zəm) n. The tendency of humans to inexorably move toward the Radiation of Stupidity.

TRUST (trŭst) n. The unnatural state in which humans refrain from stabbing each other in the back.

TRUTH (trūth) n. To Humanity, the glitter of falsehood.

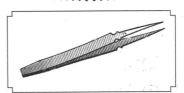

Tweezing Device

TWEEZERS (twē zərz) n. Device with which female humans pluck out their raggy eyebrows in order to paint on slimy new ones.

TWINS (twǐnz) n. 1. The detestable duplication of a human in the copy machine of the womb. 2. To Demons, a snack-pack.

Imprinter of Brain Excretion

TYPEWRITER (tīp rī tər) n. That which soils toilet paper with excretions of the human brain. See *Writer's Block.*

u, U (yū) n. The Urn into which the rest of the alphabet vomits.

U.F.O. (yū ĕf ō) n. See *Flying Saucer*.

Instrument Designed to Smash Over Player's Head

UKULELE (yū kə lā lē) n. That which, when played by a human, should instantly be smashed over the player's head. See *Accordion*; *Bagpipe*.

UMBILICAL CORD (ŭm bĭl ĭ kəl kôrd) n. That which should be cut only when a newborn baby is suspended over a cliff.

Human Barbecue Device

UMBRELLA (ŭm brĕl ə) n. Invented by Demon pioneer Abra Kadab and intended for human use only. Designed to attract lightning during thunderstorms to instantly cook human flesh.

UNABRIDGED (ŭn ə brĭjd) adj. Type of human literature which has all of its worthless padding intact.

UNAMERICANISM (ŭn ə mĕr ĭ kən ĭ zəm) n. That blasphemy which questions the integrity of the corporate fingerprinting of the populace. See *America*.

COMMENTARY BY AHRIMAN

America (q.v.) is a preeminent freedom cult and the model of many other Earth nations. It is composed of freedom worshippers who love liberty with such alacrity that the cult leaders will enslave the populace to maintain it.

The term *unamericanism* is a potent mind control tool with which the slave owners label unprofitable concepts. The technique of purposely reversing the meaning of important terms by cult leaders has proven effective in convincing the idiotic human slaves to believe a number of brilliantly evil precepts (e.g. Sugar = Food, Narcotics = Medicine, Sitcom = Humor.)

UNCERTAINTY PRINCIPLE (ŭn sûr tən tē prĭn sə pəl) n. The Omegan Blasphemy which sets limits on the supremacy of measurement by morons.

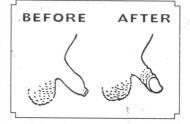

Before & After Parental Mutilation

UNCIRCUMCISED (ŭn sûr kəm sīzd) adj. A human male who has not been mutilated by his parents at birth.

UNCIVILIZED (ŭn sĭv ə līzd) adj. See *Savage*.

UNCLEAN (ŭn klēn) adj. See *Uncircumcised*.

Human Enjoying Unconsciousness

UNCONSCIOUSNESS (ŭn kôn shəs nĭs) n. In human terms, consciousness.

Hell Cosmos, Known to Humans as "Universe"

In the superstition of Humanity, the stars surrounding their puny existences are a mythic *Heaven* (q.v.). In truth, of course, there is nothing in existence even vaguely resembling "heaven"; there is only the Ever-Expanding Evil of Lord Satan's Infinite Black Hell.[8]

Center for Football and Weapons Design

UNIVERSITY (yū nə vûr sə tē) n. Institution dedicated to the highest achievements in football and weapons design.

Up-and-Coming

UP-AND-COMING (ŭp ănd kŭ mĭng) adj. Soon to be down-and-departing.

URINE (yūr ən) n. The quaint river which endlessly oozes from Mankind.

UNCONSTITUTIONAL (ŭn kôn stĭ tū shən əl) adj. That which blasphemes an absurd list of "rights" written by hemp-intoxicated millionaire slave owners.

UNDERSTUDY (ŭn dər stŭ dē) n. Human who prays nightly for the death of his employer. See *Vice President*.

UNDERTAKER (ŭn dər tā kər) n. See *Mortician*.

UNEARTHLY (ŭn ûrth lē) adj. Blessed.

UNIFICATION (yū nə fĭ kā shən) n. That which beautifully sets the stage for division, revolution and mass killings.

UNIVERSE (yū nə vûrs) n. Literally, The Song of One which, when sung by Humanity, becomes Insipid Muzak. See *Cosmology of Hell.*

COMMENTARY BY LORD SATAN

Regarding humans, their paltry "universe" may be considered a crypt in which lies Mankind's corpse. The truth of the matter, incomprehensible to humans, is that the material cosmos is a messy, self-generated Vibrational Flatulence with nothing more profound to say for itself than the blithering credo, "I AM!" And concerning such cosmic solipsistic stupidity, the less said the better.

COMMENTARY BY ASMO DEUS

As Lord Satan states, that which Mankind designates as the Universe is, of course, nothing more than the limitless parameters of the Hell Cosmos.

8 NOTE BY GOD, LORD OF THE PERSONIFIED UNIVERSE: Ignore for the moment the tediousness of this document's insistence that We do not exist, O Legions of Angels. This matter will be dealt with shortly, for in a mere trice we shall reach the Last Page of this, Satan's Conceptually Brackish but Faithfully Evil Book.

V, V (vē) n. Pictogram of the wedge necessary to penetrate the thick human skull.

VACATION (vā kā shən) n. A respite in which humans despoil nature. See *Sightseeing.*

VACUUM (vă kyūm) n. 1. The environs of the human intellect. 2. Quickest way to extract a human fetus.

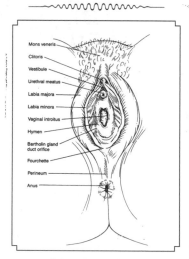

- Mons veneris
- Clitoris
- Vestibule
- Urethral meatus
- Labia majora
- Labia minora
- Vaginal introitus
- Hymen
- Bartholin gland duct orifice
- Fourchette
- Perineum
- Anus

Saloon Doors of Flesh

VAGINA (və jī nə) n. The saloon doors of flesh which swing open to the ecstasy of heaven and swing out to the excrement of hell.

COMMENTARY BY LORD SATAN

Obsessed from morning till night by thoughts of the vagina, male humans refer to this nauseating orifice by myriad incomprehensible euphemisms, too numerous and puerile to mention in this concise encyclopedic tome.[9] See *Penis.*

VAGRANCY (vā grən sē) n. The crime of Mankind loitering around and vandalizing a corner of their solar system. See *Angel.*

VAGUENESS (vāg nĭs) n. The height of specificity achieved by the human brain.

VAN ALLEN BELT (văn ăl lən bĕlt) n. The tacky human term for the Invisible Spiritual Face of Earth, blemished by the Craggy Zit of Mankind.

VANDALISM (văn dəl ĭ zəm) n. The sum of Mankind's work on Earth.

VAPORIZATION (vā pər ə zā shən) n. The goal of human technology.

9 **NOTE BY LORD SATAN: Such as pussy, snatch, gash, slash, cunt, vag, bush, twat, hole, cooze, clit, slit, box, bun, muff, mound, tunnel, mole hole, love canal, pipe cleaner, flesh funnel, rocket socket, missile silo, vulvita pita, meat flaps, beef drapes, stench trench, yeast wallet, meat curtains, dick dock, organ receptacle, the wound that never heals, choir box, mucus mitt, dugout, cock holder, finger hole, cubby hole, foxhole, vertical smile, bearded clam, pump house, nasty well, mine shaft, and organ grinder.**

Soul-Brokers Headquarters

VATICAN (văt ĭ kən) n. 1. City of bejeweled soul-brokers whose finance charges are called *tithings.* 2. One of the two prime landing sites for the Invasion of Earth by the Armies of Hell. See *Landing Sites; Las Vegas; Papacy; Spiritual Security Agency.*

VEDA (vā də) n. See *Scripture.*

VEIN (vān) n. That which, in humans, allows the circulation of bad blood.

COMMENTARY BY BEHEMOTH

Upon dismembering a human, these tubes spurting blood should be sucked dry immediately to avoid unnecessary mess. And for a superior gourmet experience, I recommend sucking the bluish-black blood moving *toward* the heart first, followed by the freshly oxygenated blood moving away from the heart. The bitter aftertaste of the blue blood delightfully counterpoints the tangy tingle of the red corpuscles down the throat.

VELOCITY (vəl ŏ sə tē) n. The speed at which the Earth goes nowhere.

VENEREAL DISEASE (vən îr ē əl dĭ zēz) n. See *Infection.*

VENGEANCE (vĕn jəns) n. Equal and opposite actions reaching equilibrium between two idiots.

VICE PRESIDENT (vīs prĕ zə dĕnt) n. A smiling human who, with every beat of his heart, wishes for the death of his benefactor. See *President*.

VICIOUS CIRCLE (vĭ shəs sûr kəl) n. See *Infinite Regression*.

VICTIM (vĭk tĭm) n. The wisest of humans, who abjures the totalitarian dogma of self-preservation.

VINEGAR (vĭn ĭ gər) n. That which beautifully complements the wounds of saviors.

Dance of the Humans

VIOLENCE (vī ə ləns) n. 1. The stabbing of the Earth in the back with the Knife of Mankind. 2. The Favorite Dance of Mankind. See *Amputation*; *Family*; *Undertaker*.

Mythic Bloodless Vagina

VIRGIN (vûr jĭn) n. 1. A state of human female grace, femininity and purity. 2. The opposite of a human's mother.

VODKA (vôd kə) n. See *Game Show Host*.

VOID (void) n. The creaking cradle of the Cosmos, which gently rocks Humanity to the Big Sleep.

VOLITION (və lĭ shən) n. The sadist trapped inside Mankind, without whom humans would never bother getting out of bed.

Cute Hitler Vehicle

VOLKSWAGEN (fōlks vä gən) n. Cute vehicle enamored of by hippies and designed by Hitler. See *Automobile*; *Hippies*; *Hitler*.

VOMIT (vôm ĭt) n., v. See *Dry Heave*.

The Demon Reader may be curious as to whether the appearance of vomit may initiate in a human a chain reaction, that is, the human vomiting in disgust at the stench of his own puddle of vomit, then vomiting further at that which has just been vomited in reaction to the original vomit, and so on. But this, rest assured, is not the case. The amount of vomit spewed by a human is in direct ratio to the amount of putrefied matter curdling in its belly. The human capacity for vomiting, unlike human sorrow, is finite.

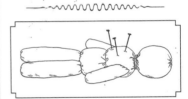

Voodoo: Cosmic Science

VOODOO (vū dū) n. An advanced form of cosmic science, utilizing the Law of Correspondences.

Ironically, this advanced principle, via *voodoo,* is understood only by primitive humans, who thrust pins into a doll representing an enemy. (Humans have never even considered using this Principle to send healing love, which is, Demonkind admits, to their credit.) This science has been used in ineffective forms by many obtuse human social morés, for example by degenerate males who thrust their turgid phalluses into inflatable dolls which represent unavailable females.

VOTE (vōt) n. 1. The political dildo which facilitates the mass rape of citizen-slaves. 2. That which human corporations buy. See *Citizen*; *Farce*.

W

W, W (dŭ bəl yū) n. The reverse of the Pictogram M, W symbolizes the sagging Teats of Mankind offered below in supplication to Man's Relentless Predator, the Maggot.

WAKE (wāk) n. Gathering in which humans tearfully envy the dead.

WATER (wô tər) n. That which, when it seeps into the Earth, pollutes otherwise pure deposits of DDT.

WAITING ROOM (wā tĭng rūm) n. 1. That place wherein humans do nothing, waiting to be Next. 2. The Earth.

Human Pauper

WAITER (wā tər) n. Slave who relies on the kindness of humans to supplement his wage. 2. A pauper.

Poverty Container

WALLET (wô lĭt) n. An envelope of dried cow skin which holds the lack of human prosperity.

Wall Images Soothing to Humans

WALLPAPER (wôl pā pər) n. Soothing or peppy images and colors with which humans line the walls of their homes to disguise the sterile emptiness of their lives.

WAR (wôr) n. 1. The activity which allows humans to feed their insatiable desire for More. 2. That which pays for the air-conditioned doghouses owned by arms dealers.

WARNING LABEL (wôr nĭng lā bəl) n. After gutting a human, that which a Demon Butcher places on the tiny poisonous lobe of the human brain ruling Kindness.

WASH (wŏsh) v. That which a Demon must do immediately after handling a disgorged human heart.

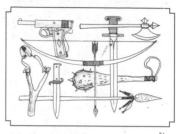

Penile Weapon Designs

WEAPON (wĕ pən) n. The conceptual mating of metal with the erect human penis.

WEAPONS DESIGNER (wĕ pənz dĭ zī nər) n. Whorish fop of science who designs fashionable new ways for enemy children to wear burning flesh.

WEATHER (wĕ thər) n. 1. That which humans discuss when torturing enemy children becomes routine. 2. That which determines whether torture will take place inside or outside.

Enslavement Ceremony

WEDDING (wĕ dĭng) n. A ceremony of mutual enslavement between two humans which, when in its purest form, is performed at a urine-scented drive-up window in Las Vegas.

COMMENTARY BY LILITH

Human males and females perversely make a mass spectacle out of the agreement to fornicate exclusively with each others' meat nodules. The spectacle, or wedding, creates a delusional haze of glamor around the stinking nodules in question.

To facilitate the illusion, multi-tiered layers of sugar are devoured by the male and female and their witnesses, investing them with glucose intoxication, which simulates brief happiness. This is complemented by the guzzling of fermented wheat, and thus alcohol intoxication, which simulates numbed gaiety.

The meshing of the male and female meat nodules occurs at the *honeymoon* (q.v.), in which the sex flaps are disguised not only by layers of wispy cloth, but also by the forgiving pallor of night. In the light of morning, however, when the couples' flaps are no longer tumescent, the sight of each other's rumpled, hairy organs is almost more than even a human can bear. See *Divorce*; *Husband*; *Marriage*; *Ritual*; *Sex*; *Wife*.

WEEK (wĕk) n. An imaginary cycle invented so that every seven days church leaders will have a fresh influx of funds with which to augment their pornography collections. See *Church*; *Day*; *Ritual*.

WELL (wĕl) n. That which a child falls into or a neighbor poisons.

WET NURSE (wĕt nûrs) n. A detestable female who suckles human infants indiscriminately instead of allowing them a fighting chance to die. See *Baby*; *Breast*; *Fetishism*; *Sucking*.

Wasted Wheat

WHEAT (wēt) n. Plant wasted by using it to produce bread instead of whiskey.

Device to Facilitate Killing the Elderly

WHEELCHAIR (wēl châr) n. That which facilitates a wealthy grandfather being pushed off a cliff, roof or deck of a ship.

WHEEL OF KADAB (wēl əv kə dăb) n. The Wheel of Kadab is a magical device which the infamous Demon Pioneer Abra Kadab conjured at Earth's precise Centre of Gravity. This vast stone Wheel, with a diameter 7/22nds of the planet's circumference, a thickness of 6.624 x 10-27, and inscribed with ancient magical figures, is now a permanent fixture spinning at the center of the planet's interior.

Each side of the Wheel displays different concentric rings of magical symbols.

One side is shown below. To view the obverse, see *Addendum: Endpiece*. [*Note: Available only in Lord Satan's Exclusive Commemorative Variorum Edition.*]

Origin of the Wheel of Kadab: In ancient times, the Earth was hit by a comet and knocked 6.131313 degrees off its axis. As a result, the planet wobbled and spun like a drunken dervish. To correct its sloppy spin, Kadab conjured the Wheel to float in the center of the hollowed-out core of the planet, aligned at right angles to the equator. Kadab then spun the Wheel at the precise speed of Earth's rotation, creating a compensatory torque which instantly corrected the wobble and stabilized the planet.

Wheel of Kadab

In his journal, Kadab notes that the Wheel served another convenient purpose: that of Grinding Humans into People Paté which, when mixed with a Dollop of Pitchblende, created a Delectable Dip for Kadab's notorious cocktail parties.

(For Visual Detail of the ancient Wheel and the peculiar Magical Figures etched on each side, refer to the Frontispiece and *Hollow Earth*.) See *Abra Kadab*.

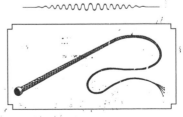

Self-Loathing Accessory

WHIP (wĭp) n. That which the human back craves.

WHISKEY (wĭs kē) n. Blessed substance which causes euphoria in humans by rotting their brains and livers. See *Dry Heave*.

WHISTLEBLOWER (wĭ səl blō, ər) n. A naive and despicable human who believes in truth over expedience.

WHOREHOUSE (hôr hous) n. A milking station for human semen, manned by rows of female milking machines whose swollen diseased holes perfume the halls with the delicate scent of spunk and syphilis. See *Madam*; *Prostitute*.

WIDOW (wĭ dō) n. That which is no longer forced to fellate the withered, liver-spotted penis of a *husband* (q.v.).

Soon to Be Discarded

WIFE (wĭf) n. That which is soiled and then discarded by a husband. See *Housewife, Woman*.

WILDERNESS (wĭl dər nes) n. That which Humanity paves.

WILL (wĭl) n. See *Inheritance*.

WINE (wīn) n. That which is flavored by stinking human feet. See *Alcohol*.

WINTER (wĭn tər) n. The Earth's stylish coat of crystallized pollution.

WISDOM (wĭz dəm) n. The ability to sensitively and feelingly comprehend the worthlessness of human existence.

WORD (wûrd) n. The fundamental building block of human thought, and the basis of the lawsuit Reason vs. Humanity, charging humans with the crime of construction with substandard building materials.

WORK (wûrk) v., n. That which humans perform in order to afford drugs and pornography.

Human Mind Rapist

WRITER (rī tər) n. 1. An alcoholic who collects rejection slips. 2. A rapist of human minds.

COMMENTARY BY ZYK

With regard to His Majesty's Definition 2, I offer the following serried explication:

A human writer secretes his seed in scratches,
In stiff, sluicing, alphabetic members,
Spewing ink hoping a homunculus hatches,
Yet ignorant of the bastards it engenders.
But is the Writer to blame for these poor curs
Squeaking in the wombs of human minds?
Was it not You who opened to this seedy verse
And wantonly embraced its lecherous lines?
In sucking in these thoughts You were receptive
And, as it were, proffered forth your nipples;
Agreeing to be ravished by runes deceptive,
And seduced by these dangling participles.
Thus Human Writers distill their essence into ink
And rape the Reader with conceptual stink.

Writer Unable to Soil Blank Paper with Human Thought

WRITER'S BLOCK (rī tərz blŏk) n. That by which a writer enriches literature.

WRONG (rông) adj. A Demon who believes that a human does not taste better after torture. See *Expert*; *Faith*.

x, X (ĕks) n. See *Space-time*.

X-AXIS (ĕks ăks ĭs) n. When severing a human in twain, the line across the waist separating the blood- and mucus-filled top from the blood- and excrement-filled bottom.

X-CHROMOSOME (ĕks krō mə sōm) n. The female component in human genetic material, responsible for the ability to use fellatio to control idiotic Mankind.

> **COMMENTARY BY BELIAL**

The supremacy of fellatio as the defining act of human civilization is clear when Demons, during Human Observation Expeditions, observe the temerity with which human males, who control Earth, will do anything to receive fellatio.

Observation Expeditions have shown that every major event in human history was directly or indirectly caused by the desire of the male King, Prince, Politician, Assassin, Artisan, Celebrity or C.E.O. to be fellated.

> **COMMENTARY BY AHRIMAN**

To illustrate how this gooning human desire can be used to manipulate human events, refer to the following Chart of Human History as a Function of Oral Gratification: *[Chart Available only in Deluxe Commemorative Edition]*

Seasonal Consumer Marketing Activity

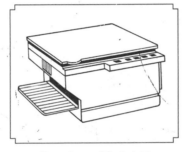

Reproducer of the Insipid

XEROX (zîr äks) n. An abomination which mindlessly reproduces the insipid clunk-work of Humanity.

XMAS (ĕks məs) n. Term which demonstrates the excellent trend to delete the annoying Christ element from the human marketing of Xmas.

> **COMMENTARY BY AHRIMAN**

The erasure of the didactic plagiarist Christ from Christmas has been the pet project of Ahriman (myself) and my Demon assistants. We have succeeded beyond all expectations in that human children now forsake religious imagery and instead worship a simplistic caricature of Satan, known as *Santa Claus* (q.v.). See *Anti-Christ*.

*Humans Engaged
In Grotesque Spewing Ritual*

XXX (ĕks məs) n. Term denoting depictions of humans in the absurd activity of spewing fluids upon each other's grotesque carcasses. See *Dildo*; *Fetishism*; *Orgasm*; *Orgy*; *Penis*; *Semen*; *Sex*; *Sperm*; *Testicles*; *Vagina*.

y, Y (wī) n. Pictogram representing the Forking Paths of Man's Destiny, both leading to Stinking Putrefaction.

YAHWEH (yä vā) n. See *Jehovah.*

Fruits of Embezzlement

YACHT (yŏt) n. A vehicle sometimes purchased by humans after embezzling proceeds from a charity for blind retarded children.

YARD (yärd) n. Sandbox of land wherein humans are allowed to stretch their legs in between torture sessions in the homes or offices in which they are imprisoned. Without yard exercise, the prisoners would die too quickly to pay all of the bills which finance their torture.

YARMULKE (yär mə(l) kə) n. A device used by sects of male humans to hide lice from the scrying eye of a mythic God.

YARN (yärn) n. Hair that humans rip from a sheep's back and knit into poodle-shaped toilet-paper covers.

Intense Boredom of the Human Spirit

YAWN (yŏn) n. 1. An intense, involuntary movement by which the human body expresses its boredom with the human spirit inhabiting it. 2. In Human Mythology, the breath of a bored "God" which accidentally spawned the universe.

Y-CHROMOSOME (wī krō mə sōm) n. The human chromosome which places the male brain in the genitalia. See *X-Chromosome.*

YEAR (yîr) n. The grouping of twelve Moon orbits into an organized pattern of human misery.

YEARNING (yûr nĭng) n. Emotional tropism a human idiot exhibits toward something considered priceless, such as a lover's erect penis or lush vagina, or a great uncle's dust-encrusted stamp collection.

YESTERDAY (yĕs tər dā) n. The Deceiver promising humans that Tomorrow will be endurable.

Yodeling Champion

YODEL (yō dəl) n. An incessant caterwauling cured by strangling the closest human wearing lederhosen.

COMMENTARY BY MEPHIS TOPHIEL

The strange human emission called *yodeling* is a cacophony of vibrations which is deadly to Demons. The first Demons exploring the land called Switzerland were tragically vibrated to death by human yodeling.

Assuming that the humans devised this weapon against Demonkind, Mephis Tophiel (myself) led a battalion of Demons to the Swiss border and decapitated every human there engaged in this deadly and annoying act. Yet to this day, humans persist in yodeling, attempting to kill more innocent Demons.

Hence, after invading Earth-Density, if you see a human cupping its hands to its mouth and drawing a deep breath, kill it instantly.

YOKEL (yō kəl) n. A human who naively believes that the Cosmos is not bent on his personal destruction. See *Sap.*

YOUTH (yūth) n. The most charming personality trait of an aborted fetus.

Z, Z (zē) n. A pictogram representing the lower plane connected to the higher plane by a slanted line; the slanted line represents the ascent to human wisdom, best symbolized by an out-of-order escalator.

Beast with Humiliating Carcass Design

ZEBRA (zē brə) n. 1. A ridiculously conspicuous creature bioengineered by Demon pioneer Abra Kadab as a joke and for target practice. 2. Meat which comes complete with diagrams of where to slice.

ZEN (zen) n. The only "wisdom school" endorsed by Myself, Lord Satan. Therefore Meditate, My Demon Slaves, upon Its Single Self-Engulfing Saw: *"Resist the Precept of Accepting All Precepts Save This Ultimate Precept."*

The Emptiness of 0

ZERO (zē rō) n. 1. The combined IQ of Humanity. 2. The Sum of All Equations in the Cosmos. See *Loneliness; Mathematics.*

COMMENTARY BY ASMO DEUS

Zero is the Mathematical Vat in which All Numbers churn, boil and bubble in the Cosmic Stew of Latent, Invisible Potentiality. Zero is the Slutty Cosmic Virgin, the Chaste Promiscuous Quantity containing within its Paradoxical Womb the Sum Total of All and Nothing.

To Demons, the Cosmic Zero is the Highest Principle, having reached Perfection in the Supreme Mind His Majesty Satan, Lord of Hell, from which All Exquisitely Void Evil Beings Spring.[10]

COMMENTARY BY ZYK

Regarding the Concept of Naught and its smarmy anthropomorphism, I offer the following recursive verse:

We may seem to create
a Mythic God
By recognizing His Existence

10 NOTE BY LORD SATAN: It is unclear whether I should be flattered or insulted by the conceit that My mind is the anthropomorphic equivalent of the Cosmic Zero. While Asmo Deus is excellent at the sycophantic sphincter-slurping of Myself, His Dark Master, I am yet undecided whether to promote him or kill him. Hopefully this matter will be decided before the publication of this Elegant and otherwise Comprehensive Tome.

For anything which can be thought
Has had crouching latent being
In the infinite potential
*   of everything:*
If something is thought, it is
If even one mind observes itself
Then the Cosmos has intelligence

So it is with the number 0
Who circles about infinitely
Like a Fool in love with existence
Retracing and re-experiencing
The path of its own being

And realizing that its boundaries
Although infinite
Encompass only the endlessness
Of its own meaning

ZERO POPULATION GROWTH (zē rō pŏp yū lā shən grōth) n. A concept from Hell invented to obliterate the Tumorous Growth of Humanity.

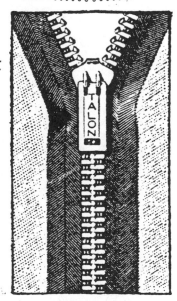

That Which Seals in and Unleashes the Detestable

ZIPPER (zi pər) n. Mechanism which seals in the vagina and unleashes the penis.

Circle of Delusion

ZODIAC (zō dē ăk) n. A galactic arm wafting around the Earth and wrapping it in a cloak of beauty and superstition.

ZOO (zū) n. 1. A happy place where humans imprison wild animals in urban blight where children torture them. 2. Animal jail where the only parole is death.

ZYK OF ASIMOTH (zēk ˌəv ăz ə môth) n. Poet Laureate of Hell, Poet in Residence at the University of Hell, and historical scholar on Hell Antiquities, specializing in Ancient Earth and Its Evils.

As Chief Editor for *My Invasion Manual*, Zyk used his skills as Hell's most hideous Poet to present many incomprehensible human concepts in verse, in order to make Mankind's galvanized strangeness more palatable and less disturbing to the archly polarized Hordes of Demon Invaders.

After time-traveling to Earth to research this book, Zyk's destiny has become inextricably linked to that of the blasphemous Demon Pioneer *Abra Kadab* (q.v.). It was Zyk who battled and lay waste to Kadab at the Space-Time Nexus of the Crucifixion of Earth's prophet Jesus.

But more pointedly, Zyk was created not only to augment My Manual for the enlightenment of the Invading Forces, but to assist the perfect expression of this very moment, the Ending of this Black Volume.

For in order to create Suspense and Terror in the Minds of My Invading Legions, this Manual's broad pastiche of mundane and cosmic terms regarding the Frightening Conundrum of Humanity's Existence cannot end with the hammering dido of Mundane Fact. It must instead end with the sensual caress of Mysterious Promise, a horror which suggests but does not reveal, a terror which emotes but does not define.

And thus, I end with a potent but Mysterious Message:

Directly after You, My Demon Troops, have succeeded in pulverizing Mankind and have rounded them up to be weighed, slaughtered, carefully butchered and stored as five billion tubes of fresh meat, the exquisite New Age of Horror on Earth will presage the Announcement of a Monumental Decision I have made, which will Astound all Demonkind and change utterly the Face of My Vast Hell Cosmos, now and forevermore.

I shall make this Announcement when Las Vegas lays in waste immediately following the Success of Your Mission Upon the Scab of Earth.

In future editions, the text of this Hideous Announcement, as well as any other Documents which the Publisher at Mind Control Press may deem Contributory, shall follow this, the Final Page of My Invasion Manual, in the form of Addendum.

So I Decree and So Shall It Be.

Zyk of Asimoth

ZYK'S FINAL MEMO
TO THE
PUBLISHER

CONCERNING HIS RESEARCH
ON
EARTH

MEMO TO	FROM
MORTIMER PÖNÇÉ, ESQ.	**ZYK OF ASIMOTH, EDITOR**
PUBLISHER, MIND CONTROL PRESS	INVASION MANUAL COMMISSION
HELL HOLE WEST	DISPATCHED FROM EARTH,
CITY OF HELL	GARDEN OF GETHSEMANE,
	APRIL 2, 33 A.D.

Detestable Mr. Pönçé:

It is the aftermath. I am feeling a bit giddy now. My work is abysmally late, but at least it is done. Now I must face the fact of my impending obliteration. Lilith was Removed From Existence this morning. Logically, I will be next. Then you, Mr. Pönçé.

My ruin is the result of my own ineptitude. I allowed the magnetic field of this planet to warp, reverse and thus pervert the spin of my emotional particles. *I fell victim to the egregious human disease of Love.*

Perhaps my mistakes were preordained by Lord Satan, within whom all Demons live and move and have their being. Or perhaps, as He claims, we Creatures of His Mind are free to do our own Evil as we will it.

The seeds of my failure, I see now, were planted in my youth as a Demon. I believed that I could succeed in a government career, working my way up from Poet Laureate to the rank of Executive of Hell. Obviously I was deluded. As a Poet I am worthless, exhaling jangling, breathless rhyme, costuming rows of rhetorical turds. I shall never be anything more than Poet Laureate. I have failed, and Lord Satan's Fist of Nothingness hovers over me. And over you, Mr. Pönçé.

To the matter at hand, I sent Lilith the final batch of material yesterday. She edited the commentaries and messengered the package to you this morning. Moments later, I have learned, she exploded in a swirling rainbow of red, black and yellow earwigs, killed, obliterated, finished, undone unto eternity.

As for myself, my problems began with Sister Debbie and ended with Kadab. My beloved, as you know, survived the breech birth of our unfortunate goat-jackal which accidentally debrained the American president. I comforted Debbie and brought her here for my final mission on Earth, to research the crucifixion of a strange and evocative poltroon named Jesus of Nazareth.

It was my fault that Jesus had become such a formidable preacher of parables. During my editorial research, time-traveling into Earth's past, I accidentally dropped a copy of Lord Satan's *Invasion Manual* in Nazareth. The boy Jesus found the book, was inspired by Lord Satan's eloquent parables and plagiarized them to preach to his followers. It is ironic, Mr. Pönçé, that Lord Satan was the inspiration behind the saccharine creed of Christianity. But perhaps it was Lord Satan's Ultimate Plan that I would drop this Manual into Jesus' hands, that Jesus would steal Lord Satan's parables and use them to inspire millions of followers, who naturally perverted his message across the expanse of centuries into exquisitely xenophobic campaigns of mass murder and fundamentalist mind control.

As Lord Satan said, evil things come to those who wait.

And now, the last leg of my editorial research has culminated here, time-traveling to the death of the now-famous Jesus by crucifixion.

In the place where he was crucified, there was a garden. I landed our invisible Hellcraft in a vast acre of sunflowers wrapped with tendrils of jasmine. Debbie and I deplaned, waded waist-deep through the sweet-smelling flowers, and found a vantage point to watch the executions on Gethsemane Hill.

Three soldiers were leading the shackled prophet Jesus up the hill toward the X-shaped trees upon which he was to be crucified.

Like the Dallas assassination, this crucifixion was a nexus in Earth-Density space-time; in some dimensional counterparts the prophet was murdered, in others he was one of three who escaped from drunken guards, and in yet others he was acquitted and ordered as Community Service to scrub the temple restrooms. As a result of the time warp, humans subsequently remembered Jesus' murder quite differently, each having waded into the surf of a slightly different dimensional tide.

In the density which we witnessed, as I said, Jesus was being nailed to the tree by the guards.

Seeing this, Debbie was aghast, clutched my arm and told me that she must save him. I rolled my eyes and told her she was crazy. If she saved Jesus from being crucified, millions of souls wouldn't be redeemed and, even worse, her religion wouldn't exist. I kissed her gently and told her to shut up so I could take notes.

I was in a bad mood. I knew that sooner or later Lord Satan would obliterate me as He had all of the others. But I couldn't tell her that. I was on the edge of an crumbling abyss, facing my own death, an end that felt more inevitable by the instant.

So I told her to come with me and blurted out that we could live together, that we could get married. For as I said, Mr. Pönçé, because of Earth's e-m field, I was "in love."

She said I didn't understand. She was already married. Her religion married her to Jesus. She couldn't let him die. If I really loved her, she insisted, I'd help her save Jesus.

Well, Mr. Pönçé, I was going to be killed anyway. And since I did love her, I agreed to help. She'd have to deal with the temporal consequences later. I scanned the guards' holonomic data (the spin of each particle in their bodies) and was about to blast them with matching particles but with opposite velocity and spin, thus freezing their movement, when, inexplicably, I felt my magical powers drained...

I turned to see Old Kadab facing me, a neuron booster helmet on his spiny head. Using his primitive, but still powerful, magic, Kadab had blocked my powers and was trying to kill me.

As I saw the soldiers torturing Jesus, Kadab attacked me.

I was knocked off my feet by a swarm of icy black tendrils which wrapped around my face and neck, clawing and choking me. I writhed on the ground and tried to rip free of them, but could not; this was an ancient form of magic that I knew not how to overcome.

Kadab cackled hoarsely as he loomed over me. A Vast Spectre silhouetted against the sky, Kadab was twenty feet tall, his scaly green armor writhing with worms and insects.

As the tendrils pulled tighter around my throat, Kadab roared that Lord Satan was a fool; Kadab knew about the Invasion Plan and would eat me and any Demons who tried to steal the Earth from him.

Kadab was obviously insane, his mind twisted after Satan banished him from Earth eons ago. Kadab must have been hiding in the Hollow Earth, waiting for his revenge.

As I tried futilely to rip free the tendrils which engulfed me, I yelled for Debbie to hurry and try to stop the guards while I hold off Kadab; I'll be there as soon as I can.

Debbie raced to the cross and, as I watched while wrestling with Kadab's tendrils, she punched the guard away who was trying to nail Jesus' left hand to the tree.

The guard went flying and Debbie immediately grabbed a hammer and began removing the nails holding Jesus' feet to the trees.

As she freed them, one of the guards took out a knife and raised it over his head. As the guard plunged the knife to stab Debbie, Jesus suddenly kicked him in the face, sending him flying. As the other guards began rushing toward them, Debbie quickly pulled the nails from Jesus' hands. He jumped down and joined Debbie in a fistfight with the handful of guards attacking them.

Meanwhile, Kadab snatched me up in his claws, told me that the Invasion was doomed, and shoved me down his throat.

The blackness of his ghastly maw engulfed me. I swirled down his throat like a blackbird spiraling down a toilet.

I plummeted down his billowing esophagus and landed in the gushy sac of his stomach. I found a flashlight in my pack and illuminated the stomach chamber.

It was a living-room-sized stomach, half-filled with a lake of bubbling effluents. Sticking out of the ooze were half-digested animal and human skeletons.

Suddenly the lake of ooze jolted and formed a whirlpool current. Apparently he had started to empty his stomach into his bowels. The current spun me faster and faster around the stomach, finally sucking me down into the bowels, where a wheel-like organ with rows of razorlike bones chopped everything up into etheric residue for later excretion through the pores of Kadab's detestable hide.

I was sucked violently under and plummeted toward the spinning razors. As I sank deeper, the fluid became somehow illuminated. I looked down and could see a light source. The supra-luminal speed of Kadab's razor organs caused an opaque luminosity in the fluid, lighting me as I surged down through the chaos of rotted flesh and cracked bones.

It's peculiar, Mr. Pönçé, how the Demon mind is devious even in the face of death. Twisting in the whirlpool, I shoved a claw into my back pocket and felt the parchment you had given me, the one with the incantation which would obliterate Kadab. I yanked it out amid the swirling chaos and tried to focus my eyes on the magic words, shrieking them, bubbling, into the fluid as the razors grabbed my feet and began to twist me to bits.

My last sensation was the cold claw of nothingness — followed by the greatest explosion I have ever heard.

I was blown sky high through weird green and purple vapors, layers of opalescent gauze and nests of hideous flying creatures, finally crashing through dimensions back to Gethsemane, directly over the trees in which the human Jesus was nailed.

I landed on the V of the intersecting trees while Debbie and Jesus were still fighting off the guards below. I glanced down the hillside and saw that Kadab had obliterated spectacu-

The Invisible Death Throes of Zyk and Kadab

larly. All that remained of him was a twirling oval of orange smoke, which transformed into a glut of black butterflies fluttering away into the craggy red hills of Jerusalem.

The force of Kadab's Expulsion from Existence was far-reaching; its epiphenomena of lightning and Earth seizures were later, I found, attributed to the crucifixion.

I jumped down to help fight off the guards. Jesus and Debbie had knocked out all but one guard, who dove on Jesus, knocked him to the ground and raised his knife to stab him. Debbie and I tackled the guard at the same time and rolled him onto his back. Debbie nailed him with a right cross, knocking him out.

We had finished off the guards and were panting in exhaustion. Jesus caught his breath and extended his hands to us to thank us both. But before he could, he slipped on the vinegar sponge and tumbled backwards onto the ground.

Debbie I and knelt over him and saw that he had slipped and fallen on the knife. We put him in a sitting position and I pulled the knife out of his side. He gasped and shuddered, grabbed our shoulders, then fell backwards. He died in our arms, his dead eyes staring straight above.

Sister Debbie looked at me. She was trembling. I knew what she was thinking. Without Jesus' crucifixion, there would be no Christian religion. Without a Jesus, there could be no Mary and no nuns. Debbie's life would be robbed of all meaning.

I had a solution. I lifted Jesus' body in my arms and carried him to the crossed trees. I gestured for Debbie to help. We propped him up and nailed Jesus back onto the cross.

When we finished, the soldiers began to come to. I took Debbie's hand and hurried her down the hill toward the Hellcraft. She suddenly fell to her knees and called out to me. I rushed to her side. She fell to the ground and was motionless. I opened her vestment and found her blouse stained with blood. She had been stabbed during the fight, but had said nothing. The wound, having punctured her heart, was serious.

Taking my beloved in my arms, I leapt from the cross down to the garden of Gethsemane. I laid her wheezing body down among the primrose and tightly held her hand.

Askance, I saw the soldiers up on the hill coming to and gathering around Jesus and joking about the earthquake. One offered Jesus' corpse a drink from a vinegar-soaked rag.

At that moment, Debbie's eyes opened and closed a final time; her breath slowed, faltered, stopped.

I buried Debbie beneath the trees upon which Jesus was nailed.

When I had finished covering her with dirt, I was overcome with the most ghastly feeling that has ever shaken my evil being. It was a particularly insidious form of the "love" I had become infected with, as a result of my intercourse with Earth's magnetic field, and with Debbie. This form was an extreme perversion of that love experience, a deeper, grander delusion of Cosmic Unity, in which the Hell Universe Itself suddenly seemed One with my beloved. In an intense flash I experienced complete understanding at a cellular level of the Forbidden Concept of Oneness, that my love for Debbie was a fundamental symbol to me of the nature of existence, with all of its separate Parts woven together into One Infinite Space-time Tapestry.

It was the most hideous experience I had ever had. Yet it was the most important. With the reality of her corpse now being eaten by worms, I had scaled the mountain of meaning and unexpectedly reached a new plateau in my journey toward Ultimate Evil.

Now, Mr. Pönçé, I have been summoned by sonic resonance to the Palace of our Lord Satan. There I know beyond certainty that it is my turn to Unexist, that Utter Obliteration at my Lord's hand awaits me.

Our work is done, my detestable friend. May the Filthy Gourd-Falcons of Gincko empty themselves from afar on your Grandmother's Glottis. Faithfully, I remain

Most hatefully yours,
ZYK

PUBLISHER'S NOTE
ON THE ADDENDA TO THE
666TH EDITION

ON THE
HATEFUL HISTORICAL SPEECHES
AND CORRESPONDENCES OF CALUMNY
APPENDED TO
LORD SATAN'S ENCYCLOPÆDIA

From the beginning of Evil Time, all Demon warriors and students who crave Black Knowledge have studied and absorbed each of the Six Hundred and Sixty-Six Thousand, Six Hundred and Sixty-Six words comprising Satan's Supreme Encyclopaedia. Yet for many these were not enough. Insatiable Demon seekers throughout time and space have clamored for more of the precious evil material from Lord Satan's Secret Library, written in His own claw.

However, the contents of the Secret Library of Satan are forbidden to the filthy hordes of Demons demanding them. The Library's despicable contents are only made available to those few Demons through the centuries whose black souls are configured with the correct correlation of contempt and disingenuousness. To all other evil seekers, the punishment for entering Satan's Library is the Gouging Out of the Eyes, Decapitation and Shoveling Fecal Matter into the Neckhole, and, if a Demon has not only touched but licked pages of Satan's precious volumes, the perpetrator will often be forced to read a Treatise of Shame after it has been tattooed inside the epidermal walls of his excretory tube, after his head has been shoved through the threshold of his own external sphincter.

But due to the relentless and urgent cacophony of hate bellowed by the leading Demon scholars of Hell University, demanding access to the most comprehensive evil repository of learning in the Universe, as well as the blackmailing of Satan's archival librarians for illegal kindnesses to filthy whores, four of the most Evil Historical Documents in the History of the Hell Cosmos were finally released. The salient condition of this astounding gesture on the part of Lord Satan was that no other documents would be released until the End of Time, or until right after it. Due to the Danger and secrecy surrounding all things *Satanus Bibliotheque*, the documents in question follow, revealing much concerning the Aftermath of the Invasion and Lord Satan's Astounding Revelation at the Conclusion of the Invasion of Earth.

Mortimer Pönçé, Publisher
Mind Control Press, Ltd.
City of Hell

ADDENDUM 1

LORD SATAN'S
INVASION PROCLAMATION

AN ADDRESS TO THE GENERALS OF HELL
FROM THE PLATFORM OF PFANG
IN SATAN'S PALACE
UPON THE EVE OF THE
INVASION OF EARTH
BY

SATAN
LORD OF HELL

I, SATAN,

Imperator of the Vast Majesty of Hell within which Live and Move all Demons and their Evil Empires, hereby decree that Earth, the acrid armpit of the cosmos, shall be annexed to the City boundary of Hell, subjecting by force Earth's autochthonous, primeval population to Hell's Unequivocal Rules of Torture, Disorder and Trickle-Down Economic Theory.

The reason for this Decree is Manifest. Hell Environs are glutted with an Excess of New Demonic Souls which require, deserve and demand a new spatial existence.

ADDENDUM 1: LORD SATAN'S INVASION PROCLAMATION

And since Earth's location is adjacent to that of Hell along the Phalanx of Space and Time, the Planet of Filth, Indolence and Stupidity is the Natural Choice for Invasion by Imminent Domain, and because I Decree It So.

Therefore, tonight, the Eve of Black Michaelmas, I reveal to You, My Joint Chiefs of Blackness, your Role in the Plan. The attack shall be orderly, stealthy, insidious. It shall proceed in waves, and be ruthless beyond measure.

The Invasion of Earth shall consist of five Waves of Conquest, as follows:

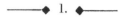

Eight million V-6 Pentagonal Hellcrafts will traverse the Solar Phalanx to Earth (the route used by Scows which dump Hell's Trash on Earth). These craft, invisible to Humans, will hover over all Earth Slave Encampments, or "cities, " and, using acoustic weapons, lull them into a submissive stupor, directing into all human minds a series of thought-numbing frequencies known as Soft Rock and Smooth Jazz.

Forty-one million Luxury Cruisers, also invisible, will land on city rooftops, carrying sixty-six million Demon graduates of Hell University's School of Corporate Law. Disguised as humans, they will quickly integrate into Earth's Corporate Structure and, communicating via hellphone-Communicators, craft the six-month plan of Legal Domination and Ownership of Earth and all of its Physical and Intellectual Property Rights, as well as all Dominions and Principalities Therein, including Strip Malls.

The Excess Population of the City of Hell, totaling more than eighteen trillion Demonic entities, shall follow in twenty million very crowded Pentagonal Hellcrafts. All Demon Immigrants are reminded to grease their hides to facilitate squeezing past one another in the passenger sections.

Lord Satan's Invasion Proclamation from the Platform of Pfang

I, Satan, shall then arrive in a Hellcraft of Fire, upon Wheels within Wheels, and, through acoustic mind-transmissions, and interrupting all prime-time television, Internet broadcasts and social networking sites, Announce to all of Earth that as of that Instant, All of Mankind is now the Official Property and Chattel of Hell.

Hors d'oeuvres shall be served to All Earth Politicians, followed by their being Cooked Alive and Eaten in a Special Live Worldwide Broadcast. The inevitably high ratings of this broadcast will set the tone of a New Age of Fear and Prosperity for all Demons!

[Cheers]

The Excellence of My Plan, O Demon Chiefs, is manifest. And the slightest, most infinitesimal hint of dissension from any of y ou will result in Instant Obliteration. Know the Plan. Fear the Plan. Fear your Lord Satan with every Thought and Deed. The Key Word here is Fear.

When next we speak, Earth shall be Mine. At that time, I shall address you again with a New Message. For the Hell Cosmos is in transition. Evolution is the Secret of True Evil, and the next Magnificent Stage of Hell's Debased Evolution is at Hand. I know you yearn ceaselessly for My Approval. Conquer the Scum Pit of Earth, and My favor, in small measure, shall be yours.

Until that time, and with Powerful Thoughts of Immense and Enduring Hatred, I bid you and your Armies an enjoyable journey through the Roiling Ethers of Space-Time, through the Cross-Roads of Horus, through the Glittering Evil of the Arc of Bon, spiraling down, deep into the Sea of Hyrim to the Fetid, Foul-Smelling Heinous Hole that is Planet Earth. May each of your Total Existences, replete with Disease, Disaster, Duplicity and Death, be Faithful Microcosms of Cosmic Evil, now and Forevermore!

[Deafening Cheers]

ADDENDUM 2

LORD SATAN'S
EPISTLE TO ZYK

FROM

SATAN
LORD OF HELL *OF THE* COSMOS
AND ALL MANIFESTATIONS OF
COMPLETE AND UTTER EVIL THEREOF
SATAN'S PALACE, CITY OF HELL

TO

ZYK OF ASIMOTH
POET IN ETERNAL RESIDENCE
UNIVERSITY OF HELL
CITY OF HELL

MY MOST DESPISED AND CLOYING POET:

Since you are, shall we say, ten percent competent, and vaguely biased toward Reason, you must know that I summoned you to My Palace to Crush you to Ethers, as I have crushed the others of your Commission for their tardiness, as well as for their inane plot to assassinate Me and take over the Hell Cosmos. True, you were not part of their dimwitted conspiracy, and did faithfully complete your mission to research and complete My *Encyclopaedia* (although your poems alone deem you worthy of rusty spikes hammered through your eye sockets), I had intended to obliterate you nonetheless, if for no other reason than aesthetic consistency.

But that was then. Now, My Poet, I need you for another Purpose. I will not consign you to the Dustless Dust. Instead of killing you, I am promoting you — to take My place as King of Hell.

This is not as absurd as it sounds. I am of course aware that you are unqualified to lick the smallest molecule of My regenerative organ. But the fact is, I care not whether you Exist or Unexist; I care only to discover the Meaning of My Existence. Now that the Invasion is completed, and the humans of Earth will be enslaved by the hordes of Demons disguised as lawyers and receptionists, I shall announce My abdication as Ruler of Hell on the Platform of Earth, My feet firmly planted on Mankind's vanquished corpse, and lay bare the Facts.

Of course, all facts, names and numbers are lies. Therefore My Subjects shall know nothing of the real reason for My retirement. But because you are taking My place, I shall tell *you*, although you will not understand a trice of what I say.

Here is My reasoning in brief; in a moment I will recap and explain more fully so that the basic concepts will penetrate your thick skull:

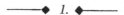

1.

The distasteful study of Humanity, necessary for the success of our invasion, brought to My attention the hithertofore unexplored concept that Anti-Evil has value, since it enriches the strength of Evil by contrast.

2.

But this implies the cringe-producing reality of the concepts of Goodness and Infinity, Taboo Thoughts punishable from Time Immemorial by arrest, torture and Banishment from Hell. Unfortunately, since I cannot banish Myself, although I have tried, this insidious line of thinking leads Me to a conclusion which is unbearable in its essence, yet inescapable, a logical progression toward the Greatest Horror Imaginable for One such as I:

3.

For if there is a possibility that Infinite Oneness exists, then logic dictates the possibility that I am *not* the Supreme Sovereign of the Cosmos, but rather a mere Created Being, much like You and the myriad yahoos I Myself created. (Now, I am not saying that this is so. I am merely waltzing in shadows with the possibility of its existence.

But this unthinkable hypothesis is so intriguing and important to
Me that I must know the truth.) This leads Me to the following:

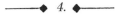

♦ 4. ♦

If, indeed, I was Created by some Other, then I must seek out
this detestable *a priori* Creator — and kill him. Only then will I
reign supreme. (Besides, if such an Abominable Being does exist,
He deserves only Death for Hiding Himself from Me.)

I hinted at these conclusions in My Manual of Earth Terms; in fact, My gloss
of these particulars in the entry *Supreme Being* caused your asinine associates to
conspire to kill Me, for which they were, of course, summarily crushed and rendered
into limpid and niminy-piminy piles of dust.

But as a result of these supremely unpleasant conclusions, I must be bold and
act swiftly. Therefore, I will leave the immediate environs of Hell-Density and, using
My Unparalleled Sense of Smell, track down My Creator through the Cracks in the
Cosmos. When or if I find Him, We shall come face to face, and before I kill Him,
I shall force Him to tell Me why He made Me, and what, indeed, is the Purpose of
This, His Creation.

Now you may begin to understand.

For as a result of writing this Manual on the study of Man, I faced a Great and
Unspeakable Secret: that neither Evil nor Good can exist separately, not without
clasping each other, white hand in black claw, firmly and resolutely together
through the inanely gyrating Barn Dance of Eternity known as Manifest Creation.

And so, although in truth I forever wield the Glittering Sword of Evil, the
Source of that Force which needs must Decapitate the Head of Heaven, Hide the
Light, Blacken the White in a rage of blind obduracy, still there can be no Meaning
whatsoever in the Fire of My Existence, nor in the Existence of the pure Goodness
of Man's Hypothetical God; there can be meaning only in that which accrues the
qualities of both, and makes Both Real by Contrast, the Restless Impurity that is
midway between these Opposites, the synthesis of the two.

To ensconce the energy of that midpoint in Sentient Form is the Torturous
Role of Mankind, whose head touches the empty Illusion of their Mythic Heaven
and whose feet touch the all-too-real Color, Substance and Mad Reality of Hell.

To speak an Abomination: Hell, which is Death, is the Body of Creation, and
Heaven, which is Life, is its Mysterious Movement.

I know, however, that you cannot understand Me.

For I am admitting that which I must not, the Possibility of My Own
Incompleteness. And as the One-Eyed King of Existence, the Lord of One Half of

this Geometric Surd, I also avow the laughable queasiness of My understanding of this arising from My study of the philosophies of the annoying Flesh of Humanity, and offer as My absolution for the lack of depth in My Encyclopedic Manual the imperfect perfection of My Unalterable Polarity.

In this admission, I acknowledge that I feel Myself evolving. In this admission, I acknowledge a need to find and kill My Creator in order to maintain My Sovereignty. For I am tugged by a strange umbric resonance, albeit ghastly and unendurable, a feeling that if I, Satan, am a Mere Created Being, then it may be *impossible* to kill My Creator.

In that case, I am destined to face My reluctant Acceptance of Myself as a Subset of All That Is, to Distastefully Embrace the twittering prance of emotion which must be a shadow of the Hypothetical Creator's Fundamental Excretion, otherwise known as the Abomination of Love.

Indeed, despite the Cosmology of Hell — that each Entity slowly evolves through Lessons of Suffering, Pain and Corruption to a Divine Destiny of Evil Perfection — perhaps My Destiny is to ever evolve toward this (to Me) Odious and Supremely Unpalatable Ordure.

Still, if He Exists, I must first attempt to kill Him. If I can, know that I certainly shall.

So there you have it.

One more thing. The decision to abdicate came after I obliterated Mephis Tophiel, who would certainly have been a more apt successor to the Throne of Hell than You. I shudder to picture a Demon with such an effeminate buttonhole of a job as Poet as the Unforgiving King of Evil.

But still, you are all that's left, Zyk, so that's that.

Good-bye.

I have packed My bags and am leaving directly after My Speech.

And may Nightmare, My Eternal Poet, Forever fill the Null of Your Dreams.

SATAN
Ex-King, Late of Hell

P.S. The rear left leg of the Palace Throne wobbles slightly and needs a folded piece of cardboard shoved under it.

And if I forget, or don't have time to do it before I leave, please kill My wife.

ADDENDUM 3

LORD SATAN'S ABDICATION SPEECH

AN ADDRESS TO THE ARMIES OF HELL ON THE RUBBLE OF LAS VEGAS OVER VANQUISHED EARTH

BY

SATAN
LORD OF HELL

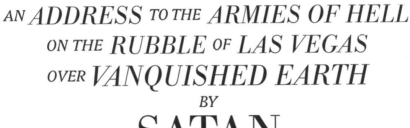

GREETINGS, MY CREATURES OF HELL!

I congratulate you on your success. Earth is now beaten and annexed to the Territory of Lower Hell. The Demon Kadab, the last holdout on this Insane Asylum Planet, has been Obliterated. There remains only for our Legions of Demons to infiltrate and take over. You have done well!

[Cheers from the Demon Throng]

The Successful Invasion of Earth bespeaks a New Word in the Language of Hell. That Word is Evolution. I have been the Ruler of Evil for Countless Eons. Indeed, I Created each and every one of you, as well as the Swollen Black Brilliance engulfing the Stars in the Cosmos of Hell. And now, the conquest of Earth presages a Vast Change.

ADDENDUM 3: LORD SATAN'S ABDICATION SPEECH

The change I speak of is in the Rulership of Hell. My hateful Creatures, I hereby proclaim, as of this moment, My Abdication as King of Hell.

[Gasps]

It is right for you to Fear This Change. Fear is the essence of your Souls. But Fear with Respect, not with Confusion. Although I am gone, I promise you that the Hideousness of Hell shall continue and that you will all writhe in Unspeakable and Unbearable Torment for Eons and finally dissipate into a Meaningless Nothingness!

[Cheers]

Why, you may ask, am I abdicating the Greatest Throne in the Cosmos? Because I, Satan, Whose Rule Is Law, so desire. I am, you see, a Complex Being and Incomprehensible to You, My Hideous Creations. I sense that which you cannot, that it is My Destiny to Seek Out the Deeper Mysteries of the Cosmos: the Meaning and Origin of Evil and the Ultimate Plan of Existence. And if this Plan does lie hidden in the Invisible Grid of the Cosmos, it awaits Me now. To seek out this Plan, My Demons, is My Satanic Purpose!

[Applause]

With this Admission, I acknowledge a Great Irony: that it was My pondering the Contumely Hide of Humanity that was My Catalyst for Evolution. For without the uncomfortable meditation upon Humanity which My *Invasion Manual* exacerbated, I would not have traveled down this Hidden Road.

Thus, I find Myself indebted to the Moronic Inhabitants of this Vanquished Planet. Having crushed them, I salute them. Join with Me, My Demons, in a Moment of Silence to send Black Hatred to the Strange Conglomerate Being known as Mankind, the Whining Lamb of Existence, Its Flopping Corpse nailed to the Cross of Space and Eternity.

But now, My Armies of Death, I bid You fare badly. Think evil of Me when I am gone, as I shall of you.

But fear not the Change that is imminent. I say unto You now the ancient Credo of Pure Evil: Trust Me!

LORD SATAN'S ABDICATION SPEECH
On the Rubble of Las Vegas to the Armies of Hell Concerning a Vanquished Earth

ADDENDUM 3: LORD SATAN'S ABDICATION SPEECH

[Cheers and Huzzahs]

For know that the Faithful among you shall Suffer Unspeakable Horrors under the leadership of your New Lord Zyk, whom I bid You to hate with as much passion and zestful intensity as You have faithfully Hated Myself.

[Renewed Cheers]

Now My Destiny calls. I leave You to Seek the Mystery of My Meaning, and willfully abandon This My Hideous Creation to You, My Grotesque Children of Death, Forevermore, into the Abominable Ends of Time!

[Deafening Cheers and Sustained Applause]

ADDENDUM 4

LORD ZYK'S
INAUGURAL ADDRESS

AN ADDRESS TO THE CITIZENS OF HELL
FROM THE BALCONY OF ZYK'S PALACE
BY

ZYK
LORD OF HELL

O DEMON HORDES!

Your stunning victory over Earth is a testament to the merciless Evil of Demonkind! I could not ask for a greater gift on My Inauguration than the eradication of Humanity!

[Cheers from the Demon Hordes]

From my Journeys to Earth and Intercourse with Humankind at Nexus points in their History, I have found much about the Nature of Evil among lower beings. What I discovered was monumental, beautiful and insidious.

For the indiscriminate intermeshing of opposite with opposite, Earth-Density's irritating but fascinating characteristic, can focus and strengthen a Demon's appreciation of Evil by contrasting it with those qualities hallucinated by Humankind, such as Justice, Love and Mercy. Thus Mankind's chaotic delusions serve to strengthen a Demon's faith in the Power of Evil.

With this in mind, and to meet Lord Satan's mandate to speed up the evolution of Demonkind, from this moment on I allow all Taboo Concepts, such as the study of Infinity and Cyclic Evolution, to be taught in the University of Hell.

[Gasps, then Cheers]

However, to Inaugurate My new Reign of Terror, instead I will order instant decapitation for all minor offenses − parking violations, public gum-chewing or even hunting humans without a license.

Because of the sheer number of Demons infiltrating Earth disguised as Attorneys, Politicians, Corporate Heads and Receptionists, the Greatest of Earth's Evils will not change, but increase a hundredfold:

—————O *1.* O—————

Electrical transportation will be kept out of the marketplace until every last drop of oil has been exploited, and the humans' absurd oil combustion engines shall continue to steep the atmosphere until it Weeps with Blackness like a Beaten Whore's Mascara;

—————O *2.* O—————

I shall insure that Television continues to supersede all other human activities as the Primary Addiction in all Human Lives, lulling Mankind to oblivion, calcifying them as the Walking Dead, robots who endlessly consume the Glitter of Worthless Commerce and excrete Emptiness;

—————O *3.* O—————

That Politicians, now replaced exclusively by Demons, shall continue to incrementally transform the wan superstition of Capitalism into the manly reality of Fascism, stamping out the Scourge of Democracy utterly;

Zyk of Asimoth Prepares His Inaugural Address as Lord of Hell

4.

Further, that Politicians shall never breathe the word "Democracy," except in disdain, and that "one man one vote" shall be deemed by political rhetoric to be untenable;

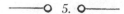

5.

That Narcotics, Cocaine, Amphetamines, Heroin and all Over-the-Counter Mood Elevators, shall subdue the populace in artful accompaniment to the control of Television Viewing;

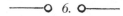

6.

That Child Sacrifice, in the form of dispatching adolescents to their mutilation deaths in War, shall increase a hundredfold;

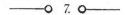

7.

That Corporate Military Conflicts, under the Black Umbrella of Patriotism, shall increase and prosper to the Glory of Hell;

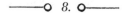

8.

That True Believers in Religion, and in the Secular Religion known as Politics, will continue their smug Ignorance of the Cosmic Truth that Opposites have Cyclic Equivalence, and will spend their lives flapping their mouths in Vituperative Defense of their Lifetimes Invested in their Incomplete and Idiotic Beliefs;

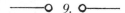

9.

That Churches, ruled with an Iron Fist by Demons disguised in flouncy robes, shall continue to insure that the human slaves increase fornication to increase the tithing coffers, and to starve their slaves' excess infants to skeletal deaths;

10.

That all Churches shall poetically pervert the Cancerous Disease of Brotherhood, Tolerance and "love" by their Precepts excluding all from salvation save their own Bird-Brain Followers;

Zyk of Asimoth, Lord of Hell
(Official Portrait in Foyer of Satan's Palace)

───○ *11.* ○───

Finally, that the Churches shall brainwash Humanity to Fear the Obvious Truth, that their Scriptures are Lies created by Men, except those few verses, already abhorred by humans, which teach the Monstrous and Demented Incomprehensibility of Love; for the Church shall hide the fact that humans do not need Scriptures, that Mankind is an Insecure Buffoon who worships everything save the One Thing that could liberate him — Himself. And for the Unforgivable Crime of Denying Oneself, I condemn Mankind to Eternal Imprisonment in the Dungeon of Self-Loathing!

[Cheers]

These eleven points shall signify the Beginning of a New Era of Earth. For I say to You that Humanity, the Hybrid of Earth and Hell, shall Hate itself until the ends of time, and We, Its Demon conquerors, shall insure that the Corpse of Man is beaten, kicked, stabbed, strangled, shot, ripped apart, shat upon and spat upon day in and day out by the Hateful Fist, Feet, Knife, Piano Wire, Gun, Claw, Anus and Blackened Lips of Hell!

[Cheers]

In conclusion, I proclaim that This Day shall be decreed *Earth Day*, and that henceforth on this day, all Toilets of Hell shall be spattered with excrement and flushed in unison at the Chiming of the Black Hour of Horus, sending a new plethora of Ordure to Mankind.

[Cheers]

For Centuries, Humanity has fattened itself with Darkness to become worthy of the Hunger of Hell! As your New Lord of Evil, I command You now to Open Your Jaws, O Demons, and Let Them In!

[Cataracts of Cheers and Applause]

CLOSING REMARKS
BY
GOD

LORD OF THE
PERSONIFIED UNIVERSE

THESE REMARKS ARE INVISIBLE TO ALL DEMONS OF HELL, AND PERCEPTIBLE ONLY TO ANGELS OF HEAVEN.

As the Ultimate Being within Whom all, including Satan and his Inner Swirl of Demonic Creatures, reside, I, of course, have the last Word.

I have clouded the minds of all Demon Readers (including that of Satan and his successor Zyk) so that they are incapable of perceiving not only My small but considered interpolations to this, Satan's heinous Encyclopedia, but also are blind to My Very Existence.

I ask that You, My Angels, study Satan's Epistle to Zyk; for here He makes a Supreme Admission which secures his Ultimate Destiny in the Mechanism of My Creation.

For as I knew from the Beginning, once the Heart Atom finally materialized in Satan's chest and His microscopic Heart congealed and began to Beat, there would be no turning back. Satan's Quest to Find His Creator, Myself, is now immutable and unstoppable.

And when at last Satan finds Me, the Cyclic Mystery shall circle back to its Beginning: He cannot, of course, kill Me; rather I shall surprise Him with a Paradox. I shall explain that I have been waiting for Him to take My Place as "God."

Thereby the next cycle will begin with Zyk of Asimoth, the New Lord of Hell. After eons of Linear Time, Lord Zyk's heart atom will congeal in turn. He will seek out his former Master Satan (now "God") in order to kill Him, will instead take Satan's place (as God III if you will), and the cycle will begin again.

But what of Myself once Satan assumes My Role as Lord of the Personified Universe? What is My Destiny?

CLOSING REMARKS by GOD

I shall resign as Creator, of course. After that, since I cannot Unexist Myself (and believe Me, I have tried), perhaps I shall take on a body, as I take on this Personified Voice, dissolve into My Creation and simply relax. An Invisible Butterfly, as it were, flitting ghostlike through the Endless Dimensions which I have imagined into Potential Being but have long since forgotten. Stopping now and then to experience rebirth as a star, a starling, a game show host, a hurricane, an electron, a human child.

As the Original Orphan of Nothingness, for I am more Nothing than Anything, I created It All to subsume the Itch of Emptiness, the Pang of Meaninglessness, the Agony which resonates in all of My Lesser Beings as it still does, at times, in Myself.

Without the challenge of creating Meaning where there had been none before – of forming from My Thoughts a dream of an Illusory Creation inhabited by Creatures that are free to evolve independent from My wishes, to create whatever they want as they so desire – I would have doubtless gone Mad. Ironically, some of My Creatures claim that by creating My orgasm of Creation and themselves, I did indeed go Mad. For what is more Mad than the Universe? But since there is in the Ultimate Reality only Myself, who is there really to judge Myself – but Myself?

Then again, who cares what My Creations think? I am satisfied, and see that the Illusion holds together reasonably well (although by now it's a bit wearisome), and that's all that really matters.

And as for this Exquisitely Tortuous and Inexpressibly Vile Volume, which may simply be considered a Vast Sobriquet for Satan's Spewing Anus, I offer it to my Hierarchy of Angels, not as a loving gift, nor as a Primer about Mankind (concerning which it is a fairly accurate, albeit cynical, portrayal), but rather as a Diagram of the Ironic Inability of Hell to view that which is by nature Impure (as is Humanity) with anything but Salient Contempt.

But that is all One. For when at last that Momentous Time manifests, when Satan finally finds Me, His Creator, when His Heart Atom expands enough to engulf All of My Being and He becomes One with Me, then I shall happily grant all of My Creations, Angels, Humans and Devils, their complete freedom. I release them from My Creation, to form their own if they wish. I really don't care. And Satan, or God II, is then free to take over the universe, or start from scratch and create His own, of any stripe He desires.

But that time, I say, has not yet manifested. I still feel responsible to adjust and fix various unpleasantries here and there for My Creatures, depending on the intensity and sincerity of the Call. But this will end when My wayward Son finds Me.

For Satan searches for Me as We speak. I feel Him coming closer, traipsing through the Mirage of Stars, seeking to kill that which created Him, so that He can be the only Creator.

Too bad I can't be killed. And I do mean that sincerely.

But until Satan arrives, my Loving Angels, just as He proffered this book to His Invading Demons so that they might Comprehend the Demented World of Man,

CLOSING REMARKS BY GOD

I give You this volume as a Guide to understand the Perverse Mind of Hell. Thus I bid You grit your teeth and, with One Eye Open and One Eye Closed, lovingly study its Strange and Pernicious Contents.

But why, You may ask, is Satan taking My place, rather than You worthy (and ambitious) Angels serving Me patiently for eons? Because of the Law of Paradox which binds My Creation. That Law, "the First Comes Last; the Last Comes First" and all of its tawdry permutations, smoothes over the edges of Creation's perceptual illusion which, I admit, would otherwise be a sloppy affair.

But there is another Secret Reason.

(Let's do away with these big words and this
Pretentious Capitalization, shall we?)

The secret is simple. Each entity, small and large, must eventually evolve into satan, god and everything in between. Why? Why not?

Without creation, I can only assert to myself that I exist. Alone, I mean nothing. Creation, the forming and freeing of my many opposite faces, was a crazy, desperate attempt to create meaning. I dreamed that you, my creatures, would somehow create meaning for me.

And, lo and behold, it actually worked.

Without you, I was a cosmic dunce whose mind floated in a sea of boredom and drowned in self-absorbed agony. Creation was my only escape from the doldrums of myself.

So now, before I am found and release you all and vanish into my own creation, I leave you with a few timely chestnuts.

Remember that, despite what your philosophers say, your cartoon reality was designed to have an objective existence apart from you, so that it would be a very, very scary place. Why? Because, like you, I'm lazy. Without some real, old-fashioned danger, I'd just sit around on the lounge chair of eternity and watch cosmic sitcoms.

Which reminds me. When you finally do realize the truth, that creation is a transparent fake, don't take it too hard. Sure, you can whine and mope about being the punchline to a big, cosmic joke. But you can also relax, kick back and simply enjoy the whole crazy thing.

The choice is yours.

It really is.

A few final tips:

If you're about to be slugged, literally or metaphorically, you might try something unexpected, an action that throws your opponent off guard. A strange word, image, sound, whatever comes to you. You'll gain a few seconds to deflect the punch.

Finally, watch out for any force that calls itself "spiritual." In fact, doubt everything.

Especially what I tell you.

One more thing. If you need something, go ahead and ask. You don't need a diploma of any kind or to go through any phony middleman. Religions and prophets are for idiots and cowards to hide behind.

Just speak up in a loud voice to get my attention. I've got a lot of shit going on. If I'm not too busy or depressed, I might help you out. That's about it.

Good-bye.
I'll be seeing you.

Be Seeing You